"*B.S., Incorporated* exposes th<
tution and skewers the heck o
more!"

—*Jayne J. Jones, Author of* Capitol Hell,
a 2013 USA Best Book of the Year

"Funny as hell, with sharp observations and cunning insights. It reads like the best happy-hour story you've ever heard."

—*Matt Kramer, CEO,*
Saint Paul Area Chamber of Commerce

"Rock and Voss have smartly mined their experiences to deliver a story focusing on the unsung heroes of corporate America: business communicators. Their spot-on dialogue and keen observations— about antiseptic jargon, kooky consultants, and well-meaning companies that lose their way—ring funny and true."

—*Susan Busch Nehring, Retired Vice President,*
Communications, UnitedHealthcare

"I enjoyed the hell out of this book. It harpoons the bloated, mindlessly self-destructive tendencies of American corporations. But it's also a human story. Which is why—despite the absurdity and arrogance and plain ol' stupidity on display at BSI—I'd kind of like to work there. Are they hiring?"

—*Bill Anderson, President,*
One Voice Creative Media

"Entertaining, eerily familiar, and full of compelling characters who are witty and smart, yet flawed in all the right ways. I loved this story for the same reason I love great companies: at their core, they represent ordinary people who accomplish extraordinary things (demonstrating my deeply held belief that there are no such thing as ordinary people)."

—*Brian J. Dunn, Chairman of Upsie, Ltd.*
and Founder and Principal of the Dunn Group

INCREMENTAL
GROWTH

SYNERPOINT

B.S.

INCORPORATED

COPIER
BUSINESS

OPTELLIGENCE
"△"

JENNIFER ROCK
and
MICHAEL VOSS

a novel

HELP

B S I

MARKET
LEADER

GAME
CHANGER

WISE
CREATIVE + PUBLISHING
Ink

ISBN 978-1-63489-905-5
eISBN 978-1-63489-904-8

Library of Congress Catalog Number: 2016934263
Printed in the United States of America
First Printing: 2016
20   19   18   17   16   5   4   3   2   1

Cover design by Jessie Sayward Bright

Wise Ink Creative Publishing
837 Glenwood Ave.
Minneapolis, MN 55405
www.wiseinkpub.com

To order, visit www.SeattleBookCompany.com or call
(734)426-6248. Wholesaler and reseller discounts available.

For the overworked and underappreciated. The dedicated employees who arrive early to turn on the lights and who drive the last car out of the lot at night. The selfless utility players who manage the minutiae, juggle impossible workloads, and save their companies in countless ways every day.

This story is for you.

Minneapolis Star Tribune: 100 Best Companies to Work For

#4: Business Solutions, Inc. (BSI)

It's no surprise that Business Solutions, Inc., is near the top of our list. This local powerhouse continues to gain national accolades for its savvy leadership and the innovative ways it values and rewards employees.

BSI offers employees a host of benefits—among them a new headquarters building with an award-winning cafeteria, on-site daycare, meditation rooms, a well-appointed company store and plenty of collaboration spaces. Comprehensive career path options for each employee—at every level —keeps turnover low. And executives have tossed out timecards and stringent dress codes in favor of "treating employees like the adults they are."

Jerry Pruitt, co-CEO of BSI, says he's proud of how his company empowers and nurtures employees. "We have the utmost respect for every individual who works here. Employees are our secret sauce."

CHAPTER 1

"So did he actually make visual contact with the, um . . . southern region?" The middle-aged lawyer fidgeted in his conference room chair.

"Nah." The HR guy sipped from his steaming coffee mug. "He just said she was dressed more like a call girl than a call center rep."

The Employee Relations woman rolled her eyes. "Well, female employees aren't the only ones in noncompliance. Have you seen the guys from the cycling club wearing those Lycra outfits? Clearly they're falling short of the policy."

HR Guy chuckled. "Oh, yeah. With those painted-on shorts, everyone can see who doesn't measure up."

Other attendees stifled laughter as a phone vibrated on the table—a welcome distraction.

"Not it." Pete Coffee glanced at his phone. He wore a yellow shirt that gave his skin the jaundiced glow of liver failure—not a good look for a guy who favored single-malt scotch.

"Not it."

"Not it."

"Not it," others repeated, examining their devices.

"Damn." Will Evans looked at his caller ID. Lois Emery summoned. As the co-CEOs' primary executive assistant, she took particular pleasure in being a pain in the ass to everyone outside the C-suite.

"Sorry, I need to take this." Will stepped into the hall.

"William," Lois said in her patented, condescending tone. "Mr. Blankenship and Mr. Pruitt need to see you."

"Yes, absolutely. When?"

"Right now, please."

"Um, sure. I just need to—"

"Right now, please, William." Her tenor offered less politeness than her words.

"Yes, of course. I'll be right up." Will poked his head back into the conference room. "Sorry, that was the CEOs' office. I need to go."

Taking a quick bite of the microwave breakfast burrito he'd now be unable to finish, he tossed the rest in the trash. He couldn't remember the last time he'd had a decent meal—breakfast, lunch or otherwise. Probably since his ex moved out and took the cookware with her.

He snatched his laptop from the table and headed toward the door.

"Godspeed, my good man." Coffee gave him a crooked grin. "Better you than me."

"What about the dress code policy?" HR Guy called. Will hadn't caught his name. Human Resources, a huge department, often threw fresh faces at old problems. "We need to talk about gym-wear in the office, too! Yoga pants, muscle shirts, and such."

"Ping me the details," Will said over his shoulder. "I'll dust off the old message and update it."

He strode toward the eighteenth-floor elevators only to see a crowd waiting. He kept moving to the stairwell and hiked toward the executive suite on the twenty-second floor, marveling how, three years into this corporate job, an unscheduled meeting with BSI's cofounders still filled him with exhilaration and dread. He loved the rush of working directly with the CEOs, intense and unpredictable as they were. Two hard-driving alpha males at the wheel of a twenty-billion-dollar copier and office supply distributor.

His pace slowed as he cleared the next landing. Lungs and calves burning from the climb, Will laughed at himself for becoming such a weak-legged desk jockey. He'd grown soft since leaving the warehouse.

Realizing he had passed the twenty-second floor, he turned around at the rooftop entrance landing . . . and stepped over a dress sock and hoop earring. Not shocking, seeing stray clothing in odd places at BSI. The rumor mill churned with stories of employees jumping each other's bones in the tower's various nooks and crannies. But a stairwell landing? With the cold tile floor and iron railing? Will shook his head as he headed back down. Hard to imagine doing your best work there.

He pushed hard on the heavy steel door and stepped into the empty CEO reception area, accented with familiar scents of cherrywood and fear. He sat in a puffy guest chair, glad he didn't have to fake any small talk with Lois and Ambrosia, the executive assistants.

Will had learned that being an effective corporate shill meant charming the overworked and underappreciated admins who controlled access to senior leaders. He took pride in winning over some of the most hardened assistants, showing them the respect and warmth their bosses didn't.

But Lois proved to be too hard a nut to crack. And Ambrosia? Too damn beautiful. She made Will nervous, even though her shyness verged on painful. In her two years at BSI, he had never heard her utter one word. She had joined the company after Lois lobbied the CEOs for a new title—chief of staff—and a young assistant of her own to mistreat. But in Will's imagination, Ambrosia played a silent ninja assassin hired to protect the company's inner sanctum.

Muffled voices drifted in from the boardroom, mingling with the stale, piped-in jazz music. Will studied the reception area's oversized map dotted with hundreds of purple pins—representing BSI's nationwide network of warehouses. He still felt like an outsider in the confines of the corporate tower, an offhanded notion that Big Al had imparted during Will's going-away party. Al, his former boss, joked he'd sent Will to infiltrate headquarters and represent his brothers staying behind in the field. "You can take the man out of the warehouse," Al liked to say, "but you can't take the warehouse out of the man."

Even so, Will wondered if he'd someday be exposed as an imposter amid the tailored suits and pencil skirts at corporate—an infiltrator who needed to be taken out.

Will propped his head against the recently painted wall, closing his eyes as he pondered what the CEOs wanted. A shadowy movement in the corner of the room caught his eye—Ambrosia, crouching in a skintight bodysuit, ready to attack. Will stood as the tiny killer performed a backflip worthy of an Olympic gymnast, launching herself toward him with a series of kicks and punches. Holding her fist just short of his nose, she pulled off her mask and tossed her shimmering black hair over her shoulders. Will leaned forward, slipped his hand behind her neck and drew her close. She pressed her palms against his chest as if to push him away. He paused, looked deep into her eyes, and then began to kiss her until her resistance faded into submission. His concentration absorbed by the sensation of her soft lips, Will didn't notice the boardroom door swing open.

"Will Evans, communications extraordinaire!" A booming voice snapped Will out of his fantasy. Jerry, one of the co-CEOs, slapped a hand on Will's shoulder. "Thinking about my chamber speech?"

"Yeah, um . . . your speech." Will blinked a few times and mentally scolded himself for allowing his subconscious to distract him again. Teachers used to call Will's daydreaming harmless; "it shows creativity," they told his mom. But for Will as an adult, his Walter Mitty moments came at the worst possible times, like right before an important meeting or looming deadline.

Will followed Jerry into the boardroom adjoining the two CEO offices, taking in the sweeping views of downtown Minneapolis, Loring Park, and the Twins' ballpark. On a clear day, the execs could look toward the Mississippi, beyond the historic Grain Belt sign, and see FB-One—their first warehouse and modest birthplace of the company they founded.

They rarely did.

Distinguished, charming, and always impeccably dressed, Jerry paced near the windows. Women around the office called him "the silver fox." Ron sat at the table, presenting a stark contrast to his polished partner. The older, heavier man slouched in a wrinkled blue shirt, his off-the-rack suit coat draped haphazardly on a chair. He grunted a greeting at Will.

Nice to see you, too, Ron.

A man's voice, hampered by static, came from the speakerphone in the center of the table. Jerry cut him off midsentence. "Hold on. Will Evans is here. Let's take it from the top."

Will slid into a chair and opened his laptop.

"First things first." Jerry stroked his striped tie with a glance at Will. "On the phone is Salvador Chan, our new Chief Marketing Officer in Palo Alto."

Will raised an eyebrow. The founders rarely allowed other execs to reach C-level status. Will Googled the new hire. Silicon Valley entrepreneur, thirty-nine years old. Cofounded a software company, sold it for millions. Most recently at a venture capital firm.

"We need to announce he's been hired." Jerry took a seat at the head of the table.

"Got it." Will looked at Ron, who mashed his hands together—eyes closed—shoeless left foot pressed against the bottom of his right thigh, his wool-blend slacks straining in protest. The sitting tree pose. A yoga move the CEO had picked up after reading yet another New Agey business bestseller—*Downward Dog for the Upwardly Mobile: 52 Office-Friendly Yoga Poses for Busy Executives.*

Jerry smiled. "Mr. Chan is coming aboard to help us launch this new, three-pronged strategy to fast-track our growth. And we're calling it"—he held his hands up, slowly moving them apart as if unveiling an invisible theater marquis—"Optelligence."

Damn, Jerry loved the show. The CEO could get employees fired up about anything, from an updated mission statement to crunchier croutons at the cafeteria salad bar.

"Optelligence." Will tried not to smirk. Word-mergers had become unmistakable calling cards of consulting firms—process-oriented third parties hired to oversee massive internal projects. And butcher the English language. In this case, Synerpoint, the CEOs soulless consultancy of choice, had likely coined the ridiculous catchword.

Will knew where this was going: a request for another hokey internal marketing campaign. *Please don't tell me you want to stamp Optelligence on coffee cups, shoelaces, and lip balm.*

"Let me tell you where this is going." Jerry clapped his hands together and raised a single eyebrow. "We need another dynamic internal marketing campaign. I want you to stamp Optelligence on everything: posters, T-shirts, stress balls. Get the troops fired up!"

"Of course." Will suppressed a sigh. *But don't forget the lip balm. Nothing says "incremental earnings growth" like a branded tube of carnauba wax.*

Will made a mental note to check with the company store to see if they certified their lip balm as gluten-free . . . and, shit, was it vegan? He couldn't remember. He made a second mental note.

Jerry uncapped a purple marker. "And it should look like this." The room filled with the smell of dry-erase ink as he wrote OPTEL-LIGENCE on the board. He framed the dark letters with a triangle.

"Jerry," Ron interrupted. "Leave that stuff to the kid. Let's talk details."

"That'd be great." Will ignored the slight.

Jerry tapped his onyx ring on each corner of the triangle as he spoke. "Well, Optelligence comprises three interconnected strategies—Talent, Technology, and Innovation. And it all begins with Talent. New skills for a new era."

Will nodded with a furrowed brow. Every company relied on talent, touting their employees as the secret sauce that sets them apart from other faceless, bureaucratic businesses. But BSI's people rocked. Like Will's former warehouse colleagues—some of the most amazing, dedicated people he'd ever met. And plenty of good people worked in the tower, too—the ones who didn't seem too starchy and formal, anyway. Yet the CEOs had isolated themselves from employees over the years, which made their "people power" statements ring hollow. This time, Will hoped it wasn't empty rhetoric.

Before Will could ask a question, Ron banged a fist on the table. "No, no, no. The story starts with Technology. A new platform offering highly integrated management of operational and compliance systems."

Will didn't know what that meant, but a technology upgrade certainly made sense. BSI had patched together its IT infrastructure with a jumble of homebuilt systems, off-the-shelf software, and leftover ColecoVision circuit boards.

"Wrong! We start with people." Jerry spun away from the whiteboard. "And the technology fol—"

Ron held up a hand. "I don't want to hear it."

Will eyed the two men with suspicion. The co-CEO's often butted heads, but they seemed more abrupt than usual. Testy, almost.

"Ron, Jerry," Chan's voice pleaded from the phone. Will had forgotten about the CMO. "Let's talk Innovation."

"Fine." Ron waved a hand and grumbled.

Chan cleared his throat. "Innovation will yield additional strategies and initiatives, continually allowing us to curve-jump. We'll create an internal, pro-innovation bias . . ."

Will stopped typing. No need to capture this nonsense. Another example of corporate America's love affair with the idea of innovation: an ill-defined but ever-present topic in ad campaigns, conference keynotes, and nonfiction bestsellers. Executives at plateauing companies chased innovation the way aging Hollywood actresses scrambled for facelifts and tummy tucks. Desperate bids for relevance in a world passing them by.

The phone fell silent as Will tried to connect the dots of Optelligence—nonsensical umbrella term, with three murky, marginally connected projects underneath. *Perfect.* "So Optelligence is the strategy, and the other three are . . . tactics?"

"Pillars!" Jerry declared, jutting a finger into the air.

Ron crossed his arms. "No, Talent, Technology, and Innovation are strategies. In support of our primary objective."

Will scratched his head. "Optelligence is the objective."

"Optelligence is our strategic imperative," Chan offered. "Supported by three strategically aligned, tactical pillars."

"Um, let's not get hung up on labels." Will motioned with his arm, hoping to distract them from the rabbit hole he'd inadvertently led them down. "What does Optelligence mean, exactly?"

"Exponential growth." Jerry leaned back in his chair.

"It's about being the market leader." Chan's voice crackled over the speakerphone. "In Optelligence."

Will resisted the urge to bang his forehead on the table.

"It's operational intelligence." Ron shook his head. "Over the years we've developed world-class operations as a purveyor of other companies' goods. But the new knowledge economy creates an opportunity to monetize that expertise vis-à-vis a new business model."

"New business model," Will repeated, typing as he spoke. "How does that fit with our current business model? The copier business and the warehouses?"

"We're not here to talk about copiers," Ron shot back. "We've pushed that model as far as we can. It's old news. We're transforming around Optelligence, and that's the story we're taking to the Street and to employees. New growth—to get our share price moving again."

Will felt his stomach turn. He'd never seen the CEOs so dismissive of the copier business, the sole source of their immense wealth and outsized reputations. Something about Optelligence didn't add up. "Okay, I understand." He decided to tread lightly. "But, um . . . I'm going to need more details to help craft the story."

Ron's face reddened. Apparently, the conference-room yoga didn't help his blood pressure much. "Fine. Synerpoint is holding an overview meeting later today. Ask your questions there." He pecked at his phone. "Lois will send you the invite."

Will hung his head. *Aaaaaand . . . more Synerpoint. Perfect.*

"Let's move on." Ron nodded at Jerry, who stepped to the board-room door and threw it open. He motioned for someone to enter. Anita Roswell, Will's manager and head of HR, waddled in, nodded toward Will and Ron, and took a seat.

Will's stomach flipped again. *Why would they call her in?* He began toggling through potential worst-case scenarios. She wouldn't fire him, not after Ron and Jerry tapped him to help launch Optelligence. Some kind of disciplinary action? Not something the CEOs would dirty their hands with. Besides, most people considered Will a model employee, save for the time he expensed a bottle of tequila to see if anyone would notice.

Will pressed his palms against the table and scanned the three blank faces, wondering how long they planned to leave him hanging.

Jerry broke the uncomfortable silence. "Optelligence is going to bring significant changes to how we operate, Will. And how we're organized."

"What we're doing today," Roswell added, "is the first of many organizational shifts."

As bland as they come, Roswell had a soft voice, nondescript features, and a penchant for wearing beige jackets and cream tur-tlenecks. Company gossips said she wore colorless, full-coverage outfits to conceal a canvas of body art—from full-sleeve tattoos to private piercings. But Will didn't buy it.

"I'll cut to the chase—we're centralizing the Internal Communi-cations function," Jerry announced. "All communicators are being placed on a single team. And we want you to lead it."

"Wha—me?" Will wished he'd said something smarter. Or at least coherent. *Real smooth, Evans.*

"Yes, you!" Jerry burst into laughter. "We're punching your ticket, Sport. You're being promoted." He reached over and shook Will's shoulder.

The faux affection—classic Jerry. Once, while traveling to an industry event, Will had let it slip that, at the tender age of eleven, he'd lost his dad. Jerry had busted out the same superficial shoulder shake.

Will scanned the expectant faces around the table, realizing he owed them a response.

"Wow, that's great. Thank you . . . I accept." He closed his eyes, wishing he could take back the last two words. *You accept? You're being promoted, dumbass, not nominated for the presidency.*

"You accept." Jerry smiled. "Terrific. We thought you might." He laughed again.

"As part of this change," Roswell added, "you now report to Salvador Chan."

Will's eyes darted to the speakerphone. Once again, he'd forgotten the new CMO existed.

Jerry leaned forward. "Salvador. You still there?"

The speaker remained silent as the execs exchanged puzzled glances. "Salvador!" Ron barked.

"I'm here." Chan's voice, a soft echo, grew louder as he spoke. "I was, ah . . . looking for my org chart." The unmistakable sound of a toilet flushing in the background made Will cringe.

Ron stifled a laugh. "We informed Will of his promotion and transfer."

"Welcome to the team, Will," Chan bellowed. "I'll send you a copy of my book. To prepare you for the scope and tenor of the innovative paradigm shift coming down the pike."

"Great." Will hoped his response didn't sound sarcastic. The scope and tenor of the last twenty minutes already had his head swimming.

Roswell slid a manila folder toward Will. "This is your new team. Please reach out and get them activated."

"Activated?"

"Around Optelligence." Jerry tapped the table with his ring.

"I want the comm plan by close of business tomorrow and then a launch event ASAP. Got it?"

A launch event. Of course.

Jerry loved presenting to the masses, though he had little patience for rehearsals. When announcing a new partnership with Storm Canyon Paper a few months earlier, he spent all of two minutes reviewing the speech Will had written but a full hour selecting the perfect thunderclap sound effect for Will to play every time Jerry said "Storm Canyon."

Will swallowed and nodded. "Got it," he said with more conviction than he felt. His stomach roiled—maybe from the half-eaten burrito. More likely from the mountain of unsolicited responsibility the CEOs had just heaped onto his plate. An undefined new role with a poorly defined manager. A directive to roll out a hazy strategy—one that appeared at odds with BSI's touchstone copier business. And a requirement to work with Synerpoint, the evil empire of business consulting.

Awesome. I should come to meetings up here more often.

Will gathered his laptop and folder and then paused before turning toward the door. "Thank you for your confidence in me."

"You're welcome." Ron nodded at him. "Don't let us down, now."

Exiting through the reception area, Will spotted Lois near the file cabinets. "Thank you, Lois. Have a good day."

"William." She cocked her head toward him, a scowl clouding her face. "Please remember to close the door when you exit the boardroom."

"Of course," he said over his shoulder. "Sorry."

19

CHAPTER 2

"Great shoes!" the coffee barista called to Anna as he balanced a tray of mocha samples. The morning skyway crowd surfed around him.

Anna smiled as she glided toward LaSalle Plaza in her red leather heels. They looked ridiculously flashy and stood too high to be practical, especially on this long walk from the car. But they served an important purpose. Anna's first boss always talked about his "Superman Suit"—his most expensive, tailored three-piece he wore when he needed to feel invincible. These shoes did the same for Anna. They also boosted her to a shade under six feet—tall enough to loom over most female colleagues and stand eye-to-eye with the men.

She sped up to keep pace with the other professionals teeming in the second-story skyway. The eight-mile network of glass walkways connected Minneapolis's office buildings, restaurants, and theaters, shielding pedestrians from extreme summers and brutal winters. Anna appreciated the protection on this chilly February morning.

She slipped past a line of people at the muffin shop and then slowed to admire her destination. Straight ahead, the twenty-two-story tower with blue-tinted windows acted like a divining rod. She nodded at the shoeshine guy in the doorway and stepped into the BSI lobby. Morning light poured through the floor-to-ceiling windows as Anna's authoritative heels echoed on the marble floor. She took a deep breath to calm her exuberance. *First day on the job.*

Rumored to receive 5,000 résumés per month, BSI had its pick of prospective employees. Landing an interview was tough—getting a job, damn near impossible. But Anna didn't base her professional plan on impossibilities. She built her goals on determination, persistence, and Alissa—Anna's freshman-year roommate and one of the metro's top headhunters. Alissa called Anna a dear friend. Anna called Alissa when she needed to move on. According to the carefully mapped, patent-pending Anna Reed Career Trajectory, this occurred every 3.2 years.

Approximately.

"May I help you?" the receptionist asked.

The lobby looked fresh and well funded. Anna could smell the lilies in the enormous vase on the table nearby. A far cry from her previous employer, a once-promising tech startup that lacked an actual business model, BSI had called her up to the majors.

"I'm Anna Reed. For Kari Fisher, please."

The receptionist smiled, despite juggling a headset call, three flashing phone lines, and an open laptop. "One moment, please."

Anna strolled to the windows, feeling the caffeine from her latte kicking in. *This job is going to rock. Carole can go to hell.*

Carole—a hot mess with a chronic antacid habit—had hired Anna at the tech startup. When Anna submitted her two weeks' notice, Carole shook a few Rolaids straight from the bottle into her mouth. "Why become a small fish in a big pond?" she asked while crunching the chalky tablets. "There's so much opportunity here."

But Anna saw through the underhanded tactic to get her to stay. The company had just agreed to an ill-advised buyout, and layoffs would surely follow. Anna prided herself on reading the chessboard and staying one step ahead of the fray. Any time things got complicated—bad bosses, restructures, layoffs—she found a way to make a clean exit.

Kari Fisher—who did double-duty in HR and as a change manager for the senior VP of Operations—burst through the glass double doors and tripped as she crossed the lobby.

"Great to see you again. So great." She tugged on her crooked hair barrette, attempting to right her falling brown curls.

Hard to fathom how someone so disheveled and distracted could be the direct line to Lyle Kirkland, Anna's new boss. Still, if he could put up with her, so could Anna.

"Thanks for skipping orientation and jumping in. It's been crazy," Kari panted.

Anna grinned, noting Kari had missed a button on her blouse, causing a gap that revealed her gray sports bra.

"Your parking pass worked okay?"

Anna started to respond, but Kari had already spun around and trekked back toward the employee entrance. Anna clicked after her, taking care to land every step. Her kick-ass heels functioned well on modular carpet or hardwood but created one hell of a risk on marble tile. She didn't want to pull another Bambi. Last month, her stilettos had disagreed with a restaurant's slick floor, turning Anna into a flailing baby deer on ice—limbs splayed, skirt up, Spanx exposed.

"You'll get your workspace and laptop later." Kari nudged Anna to turn left at a hallway intersection. "Our schedule today is packed! So packed. We're already late for PMO."

Anna weaved around employees, trying to stay alongside this tiny sandstorm.

"Oh, and don't forget to TEPIL your time today."

"TEPIL?" Anna asked. "I'm not familiar with—"

"Silly me. It's our Technology-Enabled Productivity Increment Log. Great system Synerpoint built for us. You know them? One of the 'big six' consultancies." Kari's short legs continued churning, and she tapped Anna's shoulder to turn left again. "Anyhoo, we got rid of timecards—thank God! Now we use TEPIL to bucketize our work and track productivity in fifteen-minute increments. Just choose one of the fifty-six sanctioned workplace activities from the drop-down menu."

Anna couldn't help but smirk. "Sanctioned workplace activities?"

"So great, right? For today, you can TEPIL your time under code 249: Training, Learning, and Self-Advocacy."

Kari stepped onto a waiting elevator and punched the button. "Cafeteria is on the fifth floor. Company store, too. Great place to pick up a BSI T-shirt or umbrella." She put a hand on Anna's arm, her eyes wide. "Ooh, and be sure to check out the store's new spa services. Today is Massage Monday. TEPIL that as 298: Employee Wellness. Last week was Wax-It Wednesday! Got a Brazilian. Not gonna lie: I'm still tender. So tender."

Anna wrinkled her nose at the unusual employee perks. *What ever happened to gym passes and free pizza?* "So how did you TEPIL that, if you don't mind me asking." She chuckled. "Landscaping and Grounds Maintenance?"

Kari continued ticking off today's to-do list. "Gotta get your security badge, too. Can't get back in the tower without it." She tugged on the laminated card clipped to her waist, flashing the image at Anna. The ID photo featured the same striped shirt, the same I-just-woke-up hair. The plastic card snapped back on a retractable cord.

"The most important meeting you have today is in Loni Anderson."

Anna chuckled. "With Loni Anderson?"

"In," Kari corrected, lowering her voice to a raspy whisper as they stepped onto their destination floor. "It's a conference room. For a meeting about Optelligence."

"Optelligence?"

Kari nodded. "Top-secret strategy. Total game changer. It's why you were hired. Kirkland's the exec sponsor, and he needed a comm pro."

Anna straightened her shoulders and smiled. She wanted to inquire further, but Kari threw open the door to a room full of people, mid-discussion.

They found seats near the back as the meeting organizer introduced himself. Anna listened as the group reviewed an arcane budget proposal, and she jotted a few acronyms to ask about later. But she kept thinking about the Optelligence meeting. If this strategy was a game changer like Kari said, Anna needed to be sharp and useful to Kirkland right off the bat.

"Off to nineteen!" Kari chirped after the budget review, guiding Anna onto the elevator again. "Next is our biweekly status with HR and Change Management. TEPIL it as 721: Human Performance."

Anna didn't need to jot down the code. She could still rattle off the digits of her favorite Thai delivery joint that closed six years ago. And the routing number from her first checking account. But the name of the guy leading the last meeting? Gone. Like rainwater through a sewer grate. She'd tried all the usual tricks to improve her name-recall skills, but nothing worked. Eventually she realized—cold as it sounded—that not everyone could, or should, be remembered.

Instead, she'd developed a system for categorizing new colleagues. "Usefuls"—people who had access to information, executives, and other essentials. She'd write their names down and commit them to memory, no matter how long it took. And "Work-Arounds"—low-rung employees, chairwarmers, and assorted speed bumps to progress. They'd remain anonymous outliers. Nothing personal. Anna simply didn't have the file space in her brain for everyone.

Kari led them into a corner conference room where a woman in casual attire highlighted by a skull-adorned scarf greeted them. She introduced herself as a change management specialist. An entry-level role with minimal influence. Anna caught the woman's first name, and then promptly forgot it.

"You must be Kirkland's new speechwriter," the woman said.

"Anna Reed, Executive Communications." Anna extended a hand.

"Oh yes, we've heard."

The woman's fingers felt fragile, so Anna eased off her usual handshake. A thin guy in a plaid shirt sat across the table. He smiled, waiting to introduce himself as Kari jabbered about BSI's change management program. Anna considered sitting down but could feel Skull Scarf eyeballing her, head to toe. Anna stayed on her feet, stole a backward glance and caught "The Look"—the self-righteous, pursed-lipped judgment of a corporate mean-girl.

Anna had seen this look before. Every workplace had at least one Skull Scarf. A peculiarly insecure woman who treated other female colleagues as threats to be disarmed. She had likely branded Anna with one of two eye-rolling stereotypes: "Hell on Heels" or "Office Sexpot."

Anna would never allow herself to be stuck with the Sexpot label—though the flashy, red fuck-me pumps didn't help. But Hell on Heels? Not entirely off base. Anna enjoyed wielding her natural forcefulness and pragmatism. She'd inherited her logical focus from her father's side of the family. The Lovejoys descended from uncomplicated, working-class Minnesotans. People who didn't believe in anything they couldn't touch. Faith. Hope. The Vince Lombardi trophy.

Yet Anna also possessed a hearty scoop of her mother's DNA. The Willums hailed from a long line of poets, dreamers, and tarot card readers. But their artsy, sensitive influence proved pretty damn useless to Anna's career.

Executives surrounded themselves with logical, analytical types. The C-suite had little room for people who led with intuition and compassion. So Anna made a choice: lean on her Lovejoy practicality and minimize the softheartedness of the Willums.

If that made her a ball-busting archetype, so be it. Anna enjoyed showing strength and decisiveness, and she loved getting shit done. It's why she couldn't wait to get her head and hands wrapped around Optelligence.

"Wow. Those shoes." Skull Scarf raised her eyebrows as she reclaimed her seat.

"I'm sorry?"

"Your shoes. They're terrific." Skull Scarf broke into a phony smile. "Probably not real practical for a place like this, though. Your feet must be killing you."

Anna felt a flash of irritation, and she considered putting the catty colleague in her place. She could've pointed out that the woman's desperate attempt at biker-chick-cool represented a shallow stereotype all its own: Apprehensive Suburban Mom Trying to Resurrect Career after Kids Enter School.

But Anna thought better of it. *I get it. We all put up fronts to get by.* She settled into a chair and pulled a notebook from her bag. "I'm fine." She infused her voice with a dose of nonthreatening warmth. "I've developed a thick skin over the years. Even on my feet."

Plaid-Shirt Guy stood and leaned over the table. "Hey, I'm Judd from Org Dev."

Anna studied him as they shook hands. Genuine smile, friendly eye contact, expensive watch. Probably a director or VP. Likely plugged into critical people and projects. *Useful.* She jotted down his name and repeated it three times in her mind.

"Glad you're here." Judd handed out a stack of reports. "A lot of change coming our way. Kari's probably told you about Optelligence."

"She has." Anna smiled, accepting one of the reports. "Can't wait to learn more."

"It's too early to know all the implications, but I do know this . . ." Judd bobbed his head to a beat only he could hear, a wry smile on his face. "When it's time to change, you've got to rearrange. Don't fight the tide; come along for the ride."

Kari perked up. "Wait! I know that song from somewhere. Was it in the Synerpoint Curvature of Change training module?"

"Nah. It's from *The Brady Bunch*." Judd croaked the *sha-na-na* chorus, motioning for the others to join in.

No one did, but Anna laughed at the unexpected and off-key musical interlude. She loved *The Brady Bunch*, and Judd seemed like a good guy. But what she really wanted? To get the skinny on this Optelligence strategy.

CHAPTER 3

Will closed the door to Roswell's office and broke into a corporate hallway sprint to the elevators, his laptop clutched to his chest and ID badge fluttering at his waist. The Optelligence meeting had started twenty minutes ago, and he hated being late. But catching up with Roswell had reached DEFCON 1.

His list of new team members held deep flaws, with three people who didn't belong: two marketing designers and a former corporate trainer who'd died years earlier in a freak snowshoeing accident. If Will hadn't acted, his team would've featured a handful of communicators, two wannabe Picassos, and a dead guy. He pulled some strings with Roswell behind the scenes to make things right.

Will had also challenged a handwritten name at the bottom of the list—Anna Reed. But Roswell assured him the late addition belonged.

Will arrived at the Loni Anderson room and crept into the Optelligence meeting. The lights had been dimmed, but the room's $2,000, state-of-the-art projector's failing bulb washed out the detailed slides. Will picked his way past the crowded table, angling for one of the chairs lining the back wall—near the framed poster of Jennifer Marlowe, Venus Flytrap, and Dr. Johnny Fever.

Lyle Kirkland spoke from the head of the horseshoe-shaped table. He wore a crisp, white shirt, amethyst cufflinks, and a silver Rolex. The small, square-jawed exec spoke about Innovation as Will skimmed the other attendees. The usual menagerie of BSI project managers lined one side of the table. Hair-Plug Guy, the woman with the weird tooth, that guy who looked like a turtle, plus other random BSIers.

Across from them sat a row of mostly unfamiliar faces in formal business attire. Synerpoint drones.

Peyton Rayburn—a bone-thin, platinum-haired waif who took great pains to appear much younger—had assumed her usual perch of power, stuck like a half-licked lollipop to Kirkland's side.

Peyton served as managing partner at Synerpoint, a monolithic East Coast consultancy with bloated practices in strategy, technology, animal husbandry, and call centers. The general public didn't understand what Synerpoint did, aside from running artistically cryptic ads during televised golf tournaments. But business types knew all about the firm's dazzle-and-dash model. They sent in the polished, well-traveled partners first—hypnotizing company execs with PowerPoint promises of world-class efficiencies and unbridled growth. Once the multiyear, multimillion-dollar contract had been signed, they unleashed swarms of young MBAs hopped up on triple espressos and blinding ambition to create reams of additional charts while shifting the people and pieces of the host company like a three-card monte street hustle.

Will hated everything about them.

"In summary," Peyton motioned to a colorless slide on the screen, "Innovation is paramount to our growth." She nodded toward a blue-suited underling.

The Synerminion stood and introduced the Technology strategy, rattling off much of the same vague lingo Will had heard from the CEOs. The content sounded even less compelling coming from an overdressed kid who didn't appear old enough to earn a driver's license, much less a college degree. But the mention of "portability and scalability" caught Will's attention.

Are we developing technology to sell to other companies?

That hardly made sense, given BSI's legendary IT ineptitude. Ask any employee who fell victim to the forced, network-password resets every fourteen days. After ten years with the company, Will had run out of family, friend, and childhood pet names to use as passwords. Recently, out of desperation, he'd turned to vegetables.

"I should also mention," Peyton interrupted her junior staffer, "in the interest of decision-rights accountability, all BSI project managers will report to a Synerpoint integration lead."

Will bristled. Same kind of crap Synerpoint had pulled with TEPIL, the painful, time-wasting workplace equivalent of a toenail infection. In hindsight, TEPIL had been Synerpoint's Trojan horse. A sleazy foot in the door, giving them a path to exert more and more influence on company execs. And now Synerpoint had flipped the script entirely, forcing BSIers to report to their people, while they managed all aspects of Optelligence. Like a virus overtaking the host.

Will shifted his focus to the slide, smirking at the footer declaring BSI as "The Market Leader in Optelligence."

A stylish blonde woman on Kirkland's left cleared her throat, drawing Will's attention. He studied her tailored shirt, intense blue eyes, and perfect teeth in the dim glow of the Managing Risk & Volatility slide. She looked thirty-something, about his age. Red-hot heels. No badge, no laptop, constantly scribbling notes.

The blue-suited minion concluded his presentation by describing the Synerpoint-BSI relationship as an unbeatable partnership.

"Excuse me." The blonde looked first toward the junior consultant and then at Kirkland. "Can you provide more context on the 'unbeatable partnership'? Just a turn of phrase, I assume?"

Peyton jumped in. "The contract between BSI and Synerpoint isn't material to this discussion." She raised a clear, plastic tumbler to her mouth, sucking some kind of green goop through the straw. Few people had ever seen Peyton consume solid foods. Hallway whispers said she sustained herself solely on protein shakes, kale chips, and the souls of Synerpoint interns.

"I'm not prying." The stylish woman smiled with a hint of conde-scension. "'Partnership' has a very specific legal connotation. I want to ensure it doesn't get used in the wrong context."

Kirkland raised one eyebrow. "Interesting. Say one more sentence about that."

Will rolled his eyes at Kirkland's favorite catchphrase. A smooth, phony line intended to convey his deep interest or curiosity. *From a guy whose only true interest is getting paid more and laid more.*

"Establishing the right terminology on a project is like making a dessert." The blonde's eyes shone with a hint of mischief. "If you're not clear on the recipe, your soufflé is going to suck."

Laughter filled the room, and Peyton's face reddened.

Kirkland offered an amused half-smile. He leaned over and said something to the unnamed woman, who sat up a little straighter and nodded. Kirkland had a reputation for dipping into BSI's pool of office hotties, but this one didn't show the usual flirty receptive-ness. No extended eye contact. No sexy hair toss.

Peyton made a rolling motion with her bony hand, and the next slide advanced. "Talent. New skills for a new era."

"Talent" struck a chord, and Will's mind began to drift. People had always called him a talented writer. One day he'd complete his unfinished novel, a surefire best seller. There'd be book signings and movie deals . . .

He shook his head and forced himself back into the moment. He needed to create the CEOs' comm plan—fast—and he needed spe-cifics. Especially about "Talent," which would likely affect BSIers the most.

"Um, can you clarify what kind of talent and skills we're talking about?" Will loathed the attention as heads pivoted toward him.

"The simplest way to describe this," Kirkland didn't even look in Will's direction, "is that we are developing the expertise we need for Optelligence."

"Yes, Optelligence is the end state," Peyton added, as if Kirkland had said something of substance. "It would help if we continued."

"It would help if someone described this end state." The blonde crossed her arms and frowned.

Peyton's pained attempt at a smile had all the warmth of a viper baring fangs.

"The two of you can take this offline." Kirkland nodded for Peyton to continue with the Talent presentation.

Will leaned back, disgusted with the lack of information but intrigued with the woman who kept infuriating Peyton. The heeled firecracker didn't fall in with Synerpoint. Consultants made bank as political animals, and even the cubs knew not to challenge a managing partner. But she wasn't a BSIer, either. *Too formal, too bold.*

The blonde shifted in her chair and recrossed her legs, banging her knee on the underside of the table. Coffee cups shuddered around the horseshoe. The collision must have hurt like hell, but she didn't even blink.

And tough.

Will's phone lit up with a text from TK.

"Hey, boss. Company store can order Optelligence chip clips for the kickoff."

Will thumbed him a thanks.

Holding a companywide Optelligence event made no sense, given the lack of substance available. But Will had his orders, and he'd have to do his best to get BSIers on board.

After all, nothing says "market leader" like a chip clip.

CHAPTER 4

Kirkland adjourned the Optelligence meeting, and Anna followed the other attendees into the hallway.

Kari Fisher waited for her. "Hey there. I have some news for you."

"I've got a desk?" Anna didn't need anything fancy—just a home base where she could drop her purse every day.

"Um . . . in due time."

Kari stepped into the empty Bronko Nagurski room. Anna joined her and selected a chair.

"So." Kari clasped her hands in her lap. "Remember how I said Optelligence was going to bring big changes to BSI?"

"I do remember. You said it about five hours ago."

Kari smiled. "Well, it will create many changes to our org structure. The first change came today. We're forming a centralized Internal Communications team."

A prickle of excitement ran up Anna's spine as her mind leapt to the opportunities this could create. "That's great!"

"So great. Starting tomorrow, you'll report to Will Evans, communications director." Kari held up a hand. "Don't worry, there's no change in your salary."

Anna's mouth fell open. Kirkland had hired her as a director, and now she reported to one instead of a senior VP? *Demoted on day one. Son of a bitch.*

She kept her voice steady but felt her left eye twitch. "Kirkland approved this?"

Kari nodded. "We all agree this gives you better career-pathing opportunities."

Anna leaned forward, pressing her lips together for a moment as she tried to calm herself. "You can understand my concern, right? Until ninety seconds ago, my career path was to become Kirkland's chief of staff."

Kari kept nodding. "We're not saying that's not still a possibility."

Anna could feel her carefully orchestrated Career Trajectory disintegrating in her hands. She started grasping at the fragments of her plan. "I expect I'll still work on Optelligence and support Kirkland in this new role? My involvement in the strategy won't change?"

"You'll have to work that out with Will Evans. He'll be reaching out tomorrow. It'll be great, Anna. So great."

Anna watched Kari traipse from the room. People like her were the worst kind of corporate lackeys. They served up difficult news leaders were too busy or unwilling to deliver themselves—with a stale side of company cheerleader bullshit. With a tightening in her chest, Anna plucked Kari from the Useful category—as if mentally controlling an arcade claw machine—and dropped her into the growing pile of BSI Work-Arounds.

Anna took the elevator to the lobby and melded into the river of commuters flowing out of the tower. Her mind scrambled to rationalize the day.

She'd adapt to BSI's dense forest of jargon and bureaucracy. She could also handle the judgment from the Skull Scarves of the world—it wasn't the first, and it wouldn't be the last. The demotion felt like a blow, but most companies made rash decisions. Anna could deal with unanticipated changes. And she could prove herself to this new boss, Will Evans, while still impressing Kirkland.

Still . . .

On a normal day, Anna could slay any one of these challenges and bounce back for more. But bombard her with all of them on her first day?

She continued hobbling through the skyway, becoming acutely aware of the table-inflicted knee bruise and every excruciating spot where the red heels had rubbed her feet raw. A lump began to rise in her throat, and she swallowed hard to stave it off.

Anna checked her phone and felt the familiar urge to call Erik. She slowed her pace and tried to convince herself not to dial. *He doesn't want to hear about my problems.*

She impulsively pressed the speed-dial button for his number. A half-ring, and then straight to voicemail. "You've reached Erik Reed. Please leave a—"

In a panic, Anna jabbed the end-call button. She slumped, dropped the phone in her purse, and limped into the parking garage. Standing next to her Prius, she took off her shoes and stood for a moment, letting the cold pavement soothe her throbbing feet.

"Get it together, Reed. Game plan, game plan . . ."

She threw the killer shoes into the backseat and climbed behind the wheel. Backing out into the swell of departing cars, she jammed on the brakes.

"Shit! My badge."

The lump pushed its way back into her throat, and her vision began to blur with tears.

"Stop it. You're stronger than this."

A car behind her honked twice. She wiped her eyes with the edge of her hand and shifted into drive.

Throughout the course of her career, Anna had never been broken by a situation and had never cried about work. She eased the Prius down the spiral garage exit.

"Like hell I'll start now."

FROM WAREHOUSE TO PENTHOUSE: THE RISE OF A MIDWESTERN GIANT

American Company Magazine

███ Business Solutions, Incorporated, started as a heated argument over runny eggs. Two competing copier salesmen—Ron Blankenship and Jerry Pruitt—met at Key's Café to metaphorically arm wrestle for the local sales territory. When they realized they could triple their respective commissions by working together, the two men formed an uneasy alliance.

Within six months of their initial, yolk-fueled quarrel, they quit their jobs and launched J&R Office Supply, a business-to-business venture selling everything from office machines to paper clips. J&R was the humble precursor to BSI, an eventual nationwide powerhouse.

They launched the company in a nondescript Northeast Minneapolis warehouse, built in the late 1800s by one of the city's giant flour mills. Pruitt dubbed their home "the Flourbox"—and it stuck as the facility became the model for the multitude of distribution centers they built across the U.S.

"It's an important part of our history," Pruitt said. "That first Flourbox was the launchpad for the market leader we've become today."

Continued, page 16

CHAPTER 5

"Hello, Lunch Buddy!!"

Anna, sitting at a two-person table in the cafeteria, grimaced at the email's subject line. Kari had scrounged up a laptop on day two, and Anna already struggled to organize her new email box—a tsunami of TEPIL reminders, weather alerts, and meeting invitations. And now this. Some kind of forced corporate socialization.

"Welcome!!!" the missive read. *"Every new employee gets a Lunch Buddy to help them learn about BSI!! Let's meet this week and chat! ☺"*

The email featured all the telltale signs of a company culture-keeper—those well-meaning, passionate employees who trafficked in exclamation points and emoticons the way prison inmates peddled cigarettes. Self-appointed culture-keepers organized potlucks and baby showers, headed up charitable activities and staffed job fairs—all to showcase their employer as the greatest company in the entire, caramel-coated universe.

Anna sighed. There's a fine line between company culture and company cult.

Spending time with these types of employees exhausted her, and Anna needed to meet Will Evans in thirty minutes. But considering a cafeteria booth served as Anna's makeshift cube, she decided to play along. *Maybe Lunch Buddy can introduce me to Desk Getter.*

Anna typed back to the sender, Holly Porter. *"Sounds great. Can I stop by now?"*

Holly answered in nine seconds flat. *"Yes! HR area, floor 5, cube 292!!"*

Anna arrived on the fifth floor and strolled past cubes adorned with the usual HR-softie indicators: silk flowers, stuffed animals, and posters declaring "Every Forest Begins with One Seedling." She found Holly waiting in her cube by the window.

"Anna?" The fifty-something, curly-haired woman sprang from her seat.

"Yes, it's nice to meet you." Anna shook Holly's hand. "Thanks for making time for me this morning."

"No problem! Take a seat! I do have a hard stop at 9:30."

"And I have a meeting at 9:00."

"Well, then let's get to it," Holly chirped. "Welcome to BSI! I'm sure you'll love it here. I sure do. I've been here six years in HR Communications. I work on things like benefits and training information." She smiled and ignored her ringing desk phone. "And you were hired to lead Lyle Kirkland's communications. I got your info from the NEO team."

Anna raised her eyebrows at yet another unfamiliar term.

"New Employee Orientation. I'm sorry. We have too many acronyms around here." Holly scooted to the edge of her chair. "So did you grow up around here?"

"Superior, actually. North End." Anna smiled, bracing for the obligatory small talk. True to form—culture-keepers love the personal stuff.

"Cool! And what do you do for fun?"

Anna made a point to keep a smile on her face. "A lot of things, but I love baseball. I'm a big Twins fan."

"Then you must be thrilled that spring training is starting." Holly scrutinized the chunky diamond band on Anna's finger. "And you're married. What does your spouse do?"

Anna looked down at the ring. For the first three months after Erik proposed, she couldn't take her eyes off it—studying every diamond, admiring the sparkle under different lights. But after so many years, she rarely noticed it anymore. The thought gave her a twinge of guilt, and she squirmed in her chair.

"He's an international business consultant."

"Neat! How did you meet? College?"

"No, at a previous job. He studied overseas. But it's—"

"Ooh, what college did you go to?"

Anna exhaled, glad the questions were getting less private—but still wishing they would altogether cease. "Here at the U."

"Fellow Golden Gopher!" Holly squeaked. "But you probably graduated YEARS after me. I'm ancient. Did you—"

Jesus Christ. If she asks for my high school locker combination, I'm bolting.

"—major in Communications? Me, I have an English degree. With a concentration in classic literature. But I ended up in HR Comm. Funny, huh?"

Anna nodded. Actually, Human Resources intersected rather nicely with classic literature. HR departments operated like the ninth circle of hell from Dante's *Inferno*: a frozen lake of blood and guilt. The staffers tended to either be barbarians—slashing headcount with impunity—or bleeding-heart softies with no guts or authority to add any value. And employees needing help skated circles on that frozen pond, twirling between continuously changing generalists who listened with great empathy, before routing the hapless skaters to a call center in Mumbai.

"Funny." Anna stole a glance at her watch. "Hey, we've both got other meetings, but I have some quick questions—"

"Sure! First, let me give you this." Holly opened a folder on her desk, licked her finger, and started leafing through papers. "I've gathered some stuff for you—contact lists, TEPIL tips, my silly hand-drawn map of common meeting rooms."

Anna's eyes widened. "Wow. Terrific. Thanks much." *Okay, Holly*

Porter. You are officially Useful.

Holly closed the folder and handed it to Anna. "What else can I—"

"Holy Mabel, Mother of Cheeses!" Out of nowhere, a wild-eyed little woman rushed toward Holly's cube, shrieking as she ran. "You didn't pick up your phone. Got a reporter from the *Post* up my ass—Dirty Business After Dark. Shit!"

Anna spun to get a look and tried to decipher the squawking. *After dock? No, after DARK.* The thick Boston accent sure didn't help.

The cursing munchkin skidded to a stop and bent forward, gulping for breath, hands on her knees. "Holy shit-copter . . ."

"What on earth are you talking about so loudly?" Holly shushed the woman.

"Sorry, took the stairs." The woman panted. "Some guy's shooting fuck films with his phone . . . above twenty-second floor . . . posting 'em . . ." She took a final gulping breath and stood up straight.

Holly shook her head. "He—what? A BSI employee's using our tower stairwell as a porn studio? Goodness, what is wrong with people?"

"Gotta kill this story, fast. Find me that ethics policy gobbledygurdle you people write. We gotta fire this little Larry Flynt before the reporter connects us to him. Cuz if BSI shows up as the backdrop on BoobTube, some amateur porn princess won't be the only one grabbing her ankles and taking it straight up the—"

"Okay! Okay!" Holly clapped her hands over her ears for a moment. "This is a place of business, Bennie, not an Amsterdam saloon! Good heavens. Let me find our ethics policy." She turned to her computer.

"Christ, I can't even—" The Bostonian stopped, looked at Anna, and placed her hand on her heart. "Well, fuck me sideways. Where are my manners?" She extended a hand. "Sue Benedetti, Public Relations. Call me Bennie. You must be new. Love your boots, hon."

Anna shook Bennie's hand, trying not to let the woman's brazen personality prevent her from making a strong first impression. PR directors worked directly with execs and had access to all kinds of insider information—anything companies wanted to keep out of the press. *Useful.*

"Anna Reed, Executive Communications. I'm working with Lyle Kirkland and—"

"Listen, if you see that cocksucker today, tell him I still need a quote for the American Company follow-up. Maybe if he wasn't so busy screwing Peyton Rayburn six ways from Tallahassee, he'd have time to help me promote this goddamn company."

Anna gasped. "Kirkland and Peyton?"

"Oh, yeah." Bennie scratched her head, causing some of her hair to spill out of her messy bun. "That horny hedgehog screws any golden-haired girlie with a nice rack and an expense account. Except his wife. Ya know how execs get to upgrade to the latest smartphone every quarter? Kirkland's contract guarantees him fresh tail every three months."

Anna tapped her fingers on the desk as a few mental tumblers clicked into place. If Kirkland had a reputation for bagging blondes, of course Peyton would treat Anna as a threat. And "The Look" from Skull Scarf now made more sense, too. *People are assuming why Kirkland wanted me on his staff. So to speak.* She stifled a giggle.

"Oh, shit!" Bennie placed one hand on Anna's shoulder and one across her heart again. "I didn't even think . . . you're not his latest model, are you?"

Anna laughed. Bennie's brash style trumped the usual hallway whispers and assumptive glances. Anna held up a protesting hand. "Oh, no. His plan doesn't include this much of an upgrade." She gestured to herself. "He wouldn't even know how to turn this on."

Bennie laughed, too. "You, I like."

"Okay, one ethics policy, coming up." Holly retrieved the document from the tiny printer in her cube.

Bennie snatched the paper from Holly's hand, wheeled around, and sped away. "Adios, chicas. It's time to go play cream police."

Will walked into the cafeteria hoping to nab the good booth, but someone had already claimed the spot. He settled for a small table near the windows.

The BSI tower had hundreds of meeting rooms, but they were a pain in the ass to find—haphazardly placed and randomly named for quasi-famous Minnesotans. Many employees bypassed these dim and drab meeting spaces and instead chose to meet in the bright, airy cafeteria—with its walls of two-story windows and live greenery.

Will settled in and opened his laptop, staring at the ceiling until he could recall his latest password: "favaBean89." A woman clutching a stack of folders approached the empty chair across from him. "Kevin Olmsted?"

Will smiled and shook his head. "No, sorry. But good luck." One problem with meeting in the cafeteria—finding unfamiliar colleagues among the crowd always proved tricky.

His phone vibrated with a text from Les, his friend from Investor Relations.

"Code Crocker on 17. Operation marble, gold watch edition. Eyes on target?"

Will paused to decode the message. Crocker referred to baked goods, with marble as the type. Gold watch represented the situation. He laughed as it came into focus. Les—a sucker for free food—wanted someone to sneak him a piece of marble cake from a retirement celebration on the seventeenth floor.

"Negative," Will responded. He had a new team member to meet. *"Diplomacy mission commencing at 0900 hours."*

A tall man in a black shirt ambled over to the table. "Mitch? Mitch Ludwig?"

"Sorry."

Will scanned the cafeteria for any sign of this mysterious Anna

Reed person and then opened his Facebook feed to kill time.

He chuckled at a picture posted by Dee Dee Ruggles, Kirkland's assistant—a group of bundled-up BSIers on an ice rink the previous evening. *"Holy Hat-Trick of Happiness: boot hockey with my BFFs and the bazillion-watt brightness of the Lord's Love!!!!! :)"*

Dee Dee's updates contained a disturbing, syrupy blend of kitty-cat pics, religious zealotry, and sports analogies—each post peppered with a near-lethal dose of exclamation points and smiley faces. She revealed herself to be a human Splenda packet. Kind of sweet and benign enough—in small doses.

He continued scrolling, stumbling onto an update from his sister: a picture of two monster Bloody Marys. *"Liquid brunch! #bloodybuddies #sistafromanothamotha—with Beth Hokensen."*

Will's stomach dropped at the sight of his ex-fiancé's name. *Why the hell are those two hanging out?*

He hovered his cursor over Beth's name, tempted to peek in on her life. One click would bring up her profile, chock-full of recent pictures, updates, and messages from the latest sucker wrapped around her little finger. A virtual scrapbook of old wounds waiting to be reopened.

He slammed the laptop shut. *Move on, Evans.*

Will took a long, slow breath to regain focus. He slid Anna Reed's résumé from a folder and reviewed the details—impressive credentials, actionable verbs, and measurable examples. She came across as formal, corporatey, and traditional—maybe fifty years old.

A portly woman wearing a black pantsuit and no makeup passed his table, and Will leaned forward in his chair. "Anna Reed?"

"No, sorry."

He frowned and perused the crowd, noticing the tall blonde in knee-high boots strolling through the main entrance—the woman from the Optelligence meeting. Will did a double take and then turned toward the side entry and cashier lanes. No sign of a woman searching for a meeting partner. He looked toward the windows—*nothing*—then turned back and saw the knee-high boots standing beside his table.

"Will Evans?"

He nodded.

"I'm Anna. Nice to meet you." She pulled up a chair.

"You, too." Will's heart picked up pace. He cleared his throat and processed this unexpected turn of events. "Um, I saw you in the Optelligence meeting yesterday."

"Likewise." She smiled and focused on hanging her laptop bag on the back of her chair.

Will snuck a peek at her snug sweater—and the sizable, sparkling wedding ring on her left hand. He waited until she turned to face him again.

"So." She folded her hands in her lap. "I report to you now."

Will nodded again. "I know this was a surprise. I didn't know about it, either. Until yesterday. Sorry this got sprung on you during your first week."

Anna tucked a section of hair behind her ear. "I've been here two days, and I've already had two bosses. Can't wait to see what happens tomorrow."

Her voice sounded calm and a little sarcastic. Maybe tinged with irritation. Not that he could blame her.

Will sat forward in his chair, careful to look only at her eyes. "I get it. This is pretty awkward for both of us. Maybe we should start by just getting to know each other."

"Sure. I'd love to hear more about my new manager."

"Well . . . I'm Will Evans." He blushed a little. "I'm responsible for CEO communications, all-company messages, and now the Internal Comm team. The new team didn't come together in the best way—obviously—but it's a great group of people. And I'm really excited about the work we'll do together."

Anna nodded with a slight smile.

"So, been here about ten years," Will continued. "Started out part-time at FB-One while I was going to college."

"FB-One?"

"Oh, sorry. That's BSI's first warehouse. The place where the company started."

Anna's eyebrows lowered. "Wow, that's quite a jump—from warehouse grunt to CEO support."

Did she just call me a grunt? Will studied her face for a moment and then chalked it up to a poor choice of words.

"It might seem funny now, but it wasn't a huge leap at the time. The CEOs were more connected to the Promisekeeper crews back then. We were growing like mad, and FB-One was at the heart of it all—it's where we tested new things before rolling them to other locations." Will smiled at the memory. "Man, it was a great place to be."

Anna tilted her head. "I'm sorry—what are 'Promisekeepers'?"

"Oh, those are the Flourbox teams. Anyone who works in a warehouse role. Delivery, shipping, copier techs, that kind of thing. Then there are the Rainmakers—when it all started, they were the Sales teams. But now everyone at corporate is considered a Rainmaker."

A tiny crease formed between Anna's eyebrows. Will waited while she processed the information.

"Interesting. So you went from being a Promisekeeper to a Rainmaker?"

"Never." Will laughed. "I'm a Promisekeeper. I just happen to work at Rainmaker Central." *As an undercover operative.* He smiled to himself.

She gave him a quizzical look.

"It's hard to explain. There's a sort of . . . internal competition around here. Dates back to the J&R Office Supply days." He laid his left palm at the edge of the table. "On this side, Jerry, who was the CEO in charge of sales, gave his reps unlimited expense accounts and huge commissions. They'd promise customers the world but never follow up on details. They were paid to close deals. Rainmakers."

He placed his right hand on the other side of the tabletop. "And over here, Ron was building the Flourboxes into a model of customer-focused efficiency. We took great care of our customers and mopped up Rainmaker messes—on-time and on-budget. Hence, the Promisekeepers."

A group of chatty employees walked past, and Will waited until their voices faded into the dull murmur of the cafeteria crowd. "So it created a bit of a rift that still exists today."

"A rift?" Anna drummed her fingers on the tabletop. "That can't be good for the culture. Or teamwork between corporate and the field. Sounds like a productivity-killer."

"Rift is too strong a word." He didn't want her to get the wrong idea. "It's just people bonding with one group or the other. A team pride thing."

Anna nodded. "And a jealousy thing, I'd imagine. A lot of companies have that between their more educated, white-collar employees and the workers in menial jobs." She leaned back and folded her arms. "Classic case of haves versus have-nots."

Will scowled at the generalization. She had painted his warehouse brethren as uneducated, bitter box-movers. *Sounds like something Peyton Rayburn would say.*

He shifted the conversation in a more neutral direction. "So, tell me a little about yourself."

Anna ticked through some of the accomplishments Will had seen on her LinkedIn profile. He smiled and nodded, noting her professional, polished delivery.

"And what were you hired to do at BSI? Before getting summarily transferred to my team?"

"Executive Communications for Lyle Kirkland."

Will's smile faded. Kirkland hired his own communicator? *That son of a . . .*

"I think my experience from my last job—working with a chief executive—was appealing to him."

Will's rising anger prevented him from listening.

Kirkland had asked for Will's help months earlier with a keynote address at a prestigious business school. Will had bent over backwards writing and rewriting that speech, incorporating all the jargon and doublespeak Kirkland—the Little Dictator—insisted on using. But when Kirkland took to the podium, he didn't use a word. Instead, he told the crowd that BSI's spin doctors always tried to put words in his mouth. But he preferred to speak from the heart. *As if he had one.*

Afterward, he told Will the speech failed to live up to his standards, and he wouldn't be asking for Will's assistance again.

Kirkland didn't trust me, so he smuggled Anna through the back door.

"I assume I'll continue to support Kirkland going forward." Anna folded her hands on her lap. "Despite the change in reporting relationships."

"Of course." *He's all yours.*

"That's great. And my role supporting Optelligence won't change either? I started working on the comm plan, and Kirkland wants a draft right away."

"The Optelligence plan? Jerry and Ron asked me for a draft by end of day today."

"Oh, sorry. Must be a miscommunication among the execs."

"Wires get crossed." Will rubbed the back of his neck. "Not your fault." No, the fault rested with Kirkland. He had bypassed Will, deciding his new communicator could better handle the task.

"Well." She sat up straighter. "It shouldn't be too difficult to merge the two plans. I can you send you what I have. I framed it up as a transformation story."

Will tried not to wince. Transformation. Another hackneyed corporate buzzword, trotted out whenever companies wanted to divert attention from their failures. By hyping paper-thin promises of a better future.

"Yeah, um . . ." Will shifted in his chair. "We'll have to be careful with that. Can't make Optelligence sound like an indictment of our existing copier business. But yes, I'll combine the plans and put it in the format the CEOs expect to see."

"Sure. And I can free my calendar to help you present. When is the meeting?"

Will hesitated. He had a tough enough time handling Ron and Jerry without a wild card in the room. Someone trying to make an impression for herself rather than letting the plan take center stage.

"We don't have anything scheduled. Lois said she'd call me when they're ready, so I'll handle it. And I wouldn't want to put you in an awkward position with the CEOs your first week on the job. Getting questions you can't answer. That kind of thing."

Anna seemed to sulk for a microsecond and then recovered with a polite smile. "Sure. Can you send me the plan when it's approved today? I'll still need to run it past Kirkland. He'll have input."

"Sure." Will squeezed the back of his neck again. He didn't need Kirkland mucking up his comm plan, with Anna serving as the persistent, opinionated go-between.

Anna's phone lit up with a calendar alert. "That's my next meeting." She glanced at her cell. "I should go. I'll send you the plan. Nice to meet you."

"You, too," Will said, unsure if he meant it. He had the feeling his life wouldn't get any easier with Anna Reed on his new team.

Anna gathered her things and slipped from the table in one fluid motion. Will watched her walk through the cafeteria with long strides and her chin up, the picture of confidence. He chuckled as her toe caught the carpet and she stumbled ever so slightly before disappearing into the crowd.

"Carl?" A woman stopped beside him.

"Huh?"

"Carl Lockner?"

"Oh, no, sorry. But good luck."

CHAPTER 6

Anna sat in Kirkland's crowded staff meeting, watching the conference room's clock edge past the top of the hour. Day three threatened to career off the rails, much like her first two. She already found herself late for Will Evans's first staff meeting but didn't dare slip out now. Peyton had just suggested Anna be removed from all Optelligence activities, given her transfer to the new Internal Comm team. Fortunately, Kirkland vetoed Peyton's self-serving scheme. For now, at least.

As an extra-special treat—for some godforsaken reason—Kirkland decided to adjourn the meeting by quoting Machiavelli the way other execs might cite a line from Patton, Churchill, or Drucker. *As your comm expert, Lyle, I'd recommend avoiding the handbook of immoral tyrants when searching for inspirational material. But, you know, baby steps.*

The meeting dismissed, Anna snatched up her things, followed Kirkland into the hall, and inserted herself between him and some suck-up finance guy.

"Sorry to interrupt, Lyle," she said as they walked, "but do you have a few minutes? I'd like to talk about my continued support of Optelligence and what that means for my career path."

Kirkland stopped, eyes glued to his smartphone. "Booked solid this week. Check with Dee Dee to find something further out."

Anna stopped, too, as the other staff meeting attendees swerved around them on both sides. A school of corporate mackerel migrating to their next pool of meetings.

"I will, thanks. I want to reiterate that I'm fully committed to you and the success of Optelligence. And I'm still very interested in your chief of staff role."

He raised his eyes to Anna's face several inches above him. Kirkland, a Napoleonic leader, needed to feel like he loomed larger than his subordinates, despite his pocket-size stature. Anna took a barely perceptible step backward and relaxed her posture to level their perspectives.

"And I am still very interested in seeing an Optelligence communication plan—which is overdue."

The verbal hand-slap stung. Anna nodded and played the only trump card she had. "The CEOs asked to see it first. You'll have a draft shortly."

Kirkland juggled his phone and a folder as he pulled a PowerPoint presentation from the materials. "In the meantime, you can summarize this for me by end of day."

Anna felt the heft of the 115-page PowerPoint deck in her hands. She didn't expect the exec would read an entire Synerpoint manifesto, but writing a book report fell far below her pay grade, too. *He's punishing me with busywork.* "Happy to help. I look forward to talking with you later."

"To be clear, my time is a precious resource, and I reserve it for those making the greatest impact." He turned and marched away.

Anna watched him merge into the crowded corridor and then settled her gaze on a man and a woman standing several feet away. They spoke in hushed tones, their eyes toggling between Anna and Kirkland. Realizing they'd been spotted, the woman nudged her friend, who averted his eyes. The BSI grapevine had forged an official link between Kirkland's blonde-banging tendencies and his new communicator.

Anna took a deep breath. *Head in the game, Reed. Game plan.* She looked down at the deck in her hand. *First things first: find Will Evans's meeting.* Everything else could wait.

She tucked the stack of papers under her arm and headed toward the elevators, brushing past the schoolyard gossips without a second look.

"Ugh, this goddamn Laura Ingalls Wilder room!" Bennie tossed her Blackberry onto the unfinished, pioneer-style table as she walked in. "These wooden chairs give me ass-splinters."

"Ah, I see our Mistress of Propaganda has arrived to class up the joint." Coffee chuckled, arms folded across his barrel chest. He lounged at the far end of the table, next to Holly. TK sat across from her, nose in his laptop.

"Bennie's our special guest." Will stood near the whiteboard, reviewing his agenda. "Think of her as an extended member of our new team."

He looked at his watch, not surprised that Bennie had arrived a full twelve minutes late—as a decade-long BSI vet, she had earned the right to wander in and out of meetings as needed. But Anna had no such excuse and hadn't shown up yet. Not a great impression for a newbie. And not helpful, given Will's nervousness for his first staff meeting.

"When are you going to ditch that first-gen Crackberry and get a touch screen?" Coffee pointed at Bennie's dented device.

"Try never! I love my little bomb-proof Blackberry with the clickety-clack keyboard." She picked up the phone, smooched the screen, and then turned to Will. "Chop-chop, Evans. Daylight's wastin'."

"Hold tight a minute. We're waiting on Anna Reed."

TK nodded. "Oh yeah, Kirkland's new comm person." He wore a new sport coat, a size too big for his bony shoulders

The kid reminded Will of his younger self—nice, eager, and naïve, but plenty smart. Will had been trying to mentor TK and help him develop more confidence and professionalism. The jacket offered one of a few signs of progress to date, but Will held out hope. *Baby steps.*

The door flew open, and Anna rushed through, hair and laptop bag swinging. "Sorry, Kirkland's meeting ran long." She fell into an empty chair next to TK.

"It's fine." Will stretched the truth. The late start put a crimp in his agenda. He skimmed his prep notes to steady his nerves. He reminded himself that he'd learned a ton about leadership working for Big Al. Now he'd use that knowledge to run his own crew.

"Thanks for coming, everyone." He smiled and motioned toward the group. "I'm really excited about this new team. We're going to do great things for BSIers." Will took his chair at the head of the table. "We have a few items to cover, but we'll start with some intros and team-building. Most of us know each other, but Anna's new."

He scanned the faces at the table. "We'll start with the fun little icebreaker HR recommended."

Coffee grimaced. "Dear God. What is it this time? Share a traumatic childhood experience? Strangest medical procedure? Ooh, favorite sea mammal?" He banged his fist on the table and held a finger in the air. "Dibs on manatee!"

Will chuckled and shifted in his seat. HR had suggested employees articulate what cartoon character they'd be and why. No way he'd use that now.

"No offense, huffnaggle." Bennie scratched her nose with the back of her hand. "But fuck the foreplay. Let's get to the real work."

"Like talent assessments." Coffee leaned forward.

Anna nodded. "And an update on the Optelligence comm plan, if you have one."

"And the Chan announcement," Bennie prodded.

"All right, listen." Will held up a hand. He could be flexible, but he wouldn't abandon the team-building without a fight. His Flourbox days had taught him the importance of being part of something bigger than yourself. "We can jump ahead to that stuff. But at least introduce yourselves when you speak up—what you do at BSI and your cocktail of choice. Not too much to ask, right?"

"Right." Coffee jumped in. "So, these talent assessments—"

Will gave him a patient smile. "Your intro, Pete?"

"Ah, dammit. Pete Coffee, long-time listener, first-time caller."

Will stole a look at Anna, who seemed intently focused on Pete. Maybe the sound of his elongated vowels—the obvious sign of a northern Minnesotan—hypnotized her. Or maybe she found Coffee's overall stout appearance fascinating: thick neck, arms, fingers, and graying eyebrows.

"I manage communications between Sales teams and Flourboxes," Coffee said. "Before BSI, I worked for a bunch of different companies in a bunch of different industries—most of which you've never heard of." He twirled a pen through his stubby fingers. "Favorite drink? Scotch. Whenever I get laid off somewhere, I try a new label."

"How many times have you been laid off?" Holly piped up.

"Well, there are about a hundred domestic brands. Let's just say I'm approaching the imports."

Will smiled at Holly. "You spoke, so please introduce yourself, too."

"Oh, Anna and I met already." Holly adjusted the beaded necklace resting on her chest. "I'm the HR communications manager. And my drink . . . well, I used to love boilermakers, but the '92 Super Bowl ruined that. Along with pork nachos. And C+C Music Factory."

Will tried to picture sweet, matronly Holly knocking back whiskey shots at a tailgate party. Wearing a horned helmet. Or maybe puking into one.

"So, these sales assessments . . ." Coffee ran his topic up the flagpole again. "Feels like another shortsighted Synerpoint special with a humungo price tag. Like TEPIL."

"Speaking of TEPIL," TK interrupted. "How should we code this meeting?"

"Good question." Holly pointed a finger at him from across the table. "Could be 438—Status Reporting and Knowledge Transfer. Or maybe 922—Team Building and Staff Development."

Will shook his head to bypass the TEPIL talk. "Wait, go back; what's Synerpoint doing?"

"Forcing the Sales teams to take surveys about their adaptability and motivation," Coffee answered. "There's no explanation behind it, and it's scaring the shit out of the reps. Is it part of this top-secret Optelligence thing?"

Anna spoke up. "Yes, it's part of Optelligence—someone mentioned it in Kirkland's meeting today. The surveys are called ITIs: Internal Talent Inventories."

Will turned his head to hide the look of disgust on his face. ITIs. Another example of Synerpoint's mold-like blanketing of BSI.

"Your intro, dear," Holly whispered to Anna.

"Oh, yes. Anna Reed. Executive Communications for Lyle Kirkand. And I won't turn down a vodka martini."

"Ah, the 'elixir of quietude.'" Coffee leaned forward in his chair. "Now, back to these talent assessments. I hear Sales completes them in March. Then what?"

"Not sure." Anna hefted Kirkland's thick PowerPoint deck onto her lap, "but I saw a timeline in here earlier . . ." She thumbed through the presentation and then stopped and tapped her finger on a specific page. "Here it is. After Sales, the corporate teams start the survey process."

"Which corporate teams?" Will asked.

"Not sure," Anna repeated, flipping a few more pages, cocking her head as she read. She shrugged and tossed the presentation back on the table. "It doesn't say."

Will leaned forward to get a look at the deck's title page: Confidential Executive Sponsor Update—Talent Strategy. *How did she get her hands on that? And what other Optelligence info is she sitting on?*

"Hey, I have another Synerpoint thing." TK's voice sounded tentative. "My buddy at FB-022 says they're also leading a project to get all the Flourboxes painted and cleaned."

"TK, can you intro—"

"Are you kidding me?" Coffee tossed his hands in the air. "Now we're paying those Madison Avenue extortionists to show FB crews how to push brooms and hold paintbrushes?"

"Well, I think it's a great idea." Holly pursed her lips. "Sprucing up those drab warehouses could really help the Promisekeepers feel a sense of pride about their workplace."

Will rubbed his palm against his forehead. He shared Coffee's indignation. *Is there any part of this company Synerpoint isn't trying to wrap their bony fingers around?*

"Maybe. But spring cleaning doesn't strike me as a 'game changer.'" Coffee carved out air quotes with his stout fingers.

"We almost done here?" Bennie checked her phone and then spun the Blackberry on the tabletop. "I gotta see a man about a horse's ass."

Will shook his head. "I thought you wanted to talk about Chan. And you haven't introduced yourself yet."

"Oh, for Chrissake, Evans. Fine. Sue Benedetti, resident spin doctor. Been here eleven years. And I'll take a swig of whatever you jerk-wagons have in your boot flasks." She pulled the elastic band out of the back of her hair, twirled the unruly black strands into a knot, and reattached them to the back of her head. "Good enough? Good. Because the Chan announcement is in two hours, and I've got to prep him for press calls."

"Bah." Coffee waved off her concern. "Just give the reporters the ol' Synerpoint special. Tell 'em Chan's going to make us the market leader in Optelligence."

"Oh, he's gonna make us a market leader, all right," Bennie shot back. "In boardroom circle jerks."

Everyone laughed. Even Anna. Until she turned serious again.

"Speaking of Optelligence." She turned to Will. "Did the CEOs approve the communication plan?"

"We were supposed to review it yesterday, but the meeting got bumped."

Anna pressed her lips together. "Well, when can I expect it? Kirkland is asking."

Her abruptness took Will by surprise, and his face warmed. "I'll get it to you when the CEOs approve it—but I don't control their schedules." He kept his voice firm and steady.

"But you'll get it approved soon, correct?" Anna looked at him, eyebrows high, head cocked. Waiting for an answer.

His shoulders stiffened. He didn't appreciate her condescending tone or her body language, especially during his first staff meeting. *So much for the friendly, team-building atmosphere I was trying to create.* "Yes, Anna, I wi—"

"Oh shit, kiddos. I gotta bounce!" Bennie squinted at the clock. "Hit me in a couple hours, Evans. We'll blast the Chan news through our blowholes and call it a wrap."

Bennie grabbed her phone, threw open the door, and shot into the hallway. The sudden exit drew everyone's attention and released a rush of stale meeting room air—sucking some of the tension along with it. Will looked back toward Anna, who held his gaze for a second, then gathered her own things. Coffee did the same.

"Well, I guess that's it for today." Will conceded his loss.

"Will." Holly's voice barely rose above a whisper. She motioned toward TK with her head.

Crap. Will had tried earlier to include his protégé in the icebreaker exercise and then completely forgot about it.

"Oh, sure, of course. TK, could you introduce yourself?"

The young man hunched over his laptop. Holly reached over and patted his arm.

TK looked up. "Sorry. I was tracking a snowstorm from the Dakotas. It's a big boy."

TK's fascination with meteorological conditions bordered on obsession. He even had developed a weather blog, one of the tower's most popular communications vehicles, much to Will's bewilderment. Maybe employees disillusioned by BSI's stagnant share price needed a diversion. At least barometric pressure rose periodically.

"Um, I'm Will Kohler, but everyone calls me TK—Tall Kid. That way they don't confuse me with Will Evans."

Will nodded, encouraging him to continue.

"Oh, yeah, I like Pabst Tall Boys." TK shrugged.

Will looked around the table. Most of the team members held their notebooks and devices, waiting to be dismissed. "Thanks, everyone. Good first meeting. We'll, ah, do it again soon." He wished he'd come up with a stronger closing line.

The meeting hadn't gone as planned, but Will would get his team whipped into shape. Once he got his sea legs.

And more of a handle on Optelligence.

Coffee and Holly wandered out, with Anna a few steps behind. Will leaned forward to get TK's attention again. "Hey, I'm meeting with Les from Investor Relations tonight. Going to get more of the scoop on Optelligence. You should come. Great opportunity to learn more about the business."

TK clicked his tongue several times. "Hm. Better not. This storm will make for icy roads. I should send an employee weather alert."

"I'll come along." Anna stood in the doorway. "I'd like to hear more about Optelligence."

Will hesitated. He wasn't wild about the prospect of spending more time with pushy Anna. But no good manager would freeze her out, either. *And who knows—maybe she'll lighten up after a drink or two?*

Anna took a small step forward. "Unless you don't want me there."

"No, no, not at all." Will stepped backward. *Jesus, she has the personality of eighty-grit sandpaper.* "You're welcome to join. The Drunken Monk. Around five thirty."

"I'll be there."

CHAPTER 7

Will dashed across Hennepin Avenue shortly after five thirty p.m., hunching his shoulders against the freezing rain. He hung a right at the Third Street bus stop, avoiding the puddles as he headed to the North Loop's Walker-Patterson building.

A Minneapolis landmark of sorts, the six-story structure opened as an opera house in the 1890s and became a flophouse during the Depression and a shady massage parlor in the 1980s. Like many abandoned warehouses in the area, the city converted the old bones to upscale housing and trendy storefronts. The building's four central floors contained high-rent lofts, while the street level housed a cupcake bakery and a cigar shop. The refurbished top floor became the Drunken Monk.

Will stepped into the lobby, cursing the city for not extending the skyway system to his favorite watering hole. He ran a hand through his thick, dark hair, removing some ice crystals. Tapping the unlabeled elevator button, he wondered if Anna would find the place. The Monk had no signs on the street level, no Facebook fan page, and no Twitter flash-mob invitations featuring the Bud Light Girls or second-rate local athletes. The place operated as if the owners didn't care whether patrons found it, which ultimately made it a word-of-mouth hot spot among thirsty, young professionals.

Arriving on the sixth floor, Will paused outside the bar's glass doors and thought about texting Anna directions. *Screw it. She invited herself—she can find it herself.*

He stepped inside, absorbing the rush of warm air and loud music. A heavily tattooed waitress met him at the hostess stand. Her blackened hair jutted out from a zebra-print hairband as she sized him up. "Been here before?"

"Too many times to be healthy." Though he'd never seen this particular barmaid. "There'll be two of us. Possibly three."

Will followed as she weaved her way between high-top tables to a booth near one of three garage doors. On summer nights, the staff cranked open the overhead doors, providing access to the rooftop patio where patrons consumed overcooked burgers beneath starry skies—and the neon sign advertising the topless club next door.

The waitress tossed a few menus on the table. Will checked out her ink as she walked away. Her white, lollipop-stick legs revealed a tattooed garter peeking out of her extraordinarily short skirt. Her left calf featured a full-length portrait of a woman in a bikini, snow boots, and ski hat.

With Les nowhere to be seen, Will perused the drink specials. He contemplated a Geezer Three-Way, MILF & Cookies, or a rum concoction called Scrawny Joe in the Corner. But when the waitress returned, he ordered his usual: vodka and Sprite, no fruit.

"Three mixologists behind the bar, and you go with a rail drink? Way to branch out, slugger." She stalked away.

Feeling his phone vibrate every minute or two, Will scrolled through a series of new meeting invitations from random colleagues—typical when new projects like Optelligence were afoot. Middle managers lacking access to the CEOs tried to get the inside scoop from Will. He accepted their overtures when he needed favors or information in return.

Inky came back with his drink in a hearty lowball glass. "The pours are generous," she said over heavy guitar riffs. "Make sure your tip is, too."

"Hüsker Dü." Les appeared at the edge of the table. "Great tune." Will reached for his drink. "Not a big punk fan."

Leslie Dansby-Mullholland III had the name of a British viceroy, though he didn't look or act the part. Opinionated and always disheveled, he also happened to be whip-smart and well connected, which made him Will's go-to guy for the inside scoop on financial matters. As BSI's liaison to Wall Street, Les always ponied up good intel as long as free food and drinks were involved.

He slumped into the booth and ran a large hand over his thinning, uneven hair. Will smiled. Les, forever the miser, trimmed his own wispy mane with kitchen shears—even though the BSI company store offered nine-dollar haircuts on "Trim-It-Up Tuesdays."

"Good to see ya, Evans. Can't wait to talk about this Optelligence debacle. But first, a bourbon." He raised one hand to signal Inky and used the other to take off his frameless glasses, fogging from the transition into the warm bar.

"Did you read that CMO release today?" Les grinned as he slipped his glasses back on and squinted at Will. "Of course you did. You probably wrote the damn thing. Always love when the CEOs are quoted together, like 'we couldn't be more thrilled,' said Jerry Pruitt and Ron Blankenship. How many takes did that require for them to say it in unison like that?"

"You know how these things come together." Will smirked and removed the straw from his drink. "Mostly an exercise in ego-stroking."

Inky returned, and Les ordered a bourbon, neat.

"Too bad you're not what you drink." She eyed his wrinkled, rain-soaked shirt.

"Ooh, I like this one. Fiery." Les raised his eyebrows at Will before turning toward the waitress. "Hey, I think Bob Mould and the boys are a bit much for my suburban friend here." He pointed to the overhead speakers. "Do you have anything lighter? Michael Bublé, perhaps?"

Inky rolled her eyes so hard that Will wondered if they would return to their sockets.

"Listen, Rumply Stilskin. This is a rock bar. Local rock, real rock, garage rock, all forms of punk," she said in monotone. "We might spin some pre-'69 psychedelic rock, early metal minus the power ballads, alternative rock that doesn't suck, and indie rock that isn't pseudointellectual bullshit. But we do *not* play country rock, soft rock, emo, electronica, nu-metal, post-metal, Christian rock, or glam. And we sure as hell don't have any Michael Bublé."

She paused and eyeballed Will. "If that's what you're into, No Fruit, I suggest you shuffle your Hush Puppies to the Applebee's down the street."

"Thanks." Will jabbed at Les after the waitress sauntered away. "I was hoping she'd despise me, and you clinched it."

"Better you than me. I think she finds me fascinating."

"You're fascinating, all right."

"Even more so now that I'm on the open market." Les smoothed the back of his hair as if preening for a photo op.

"Women of the world take flight," Will joked. "Les is on the prowl."

"Speaking of flights, how long until Chan touches down in the Mini-Apple?"

"Who knows? I suppose it'd be nice to meet him eventually. What with him being my boss and all."

"For now, anyway." Les leaned forward. "Check this out. Chan negotiated a massive signing bonus, mostly in cash, fully vested on day one. This cat isn't on board for the long haul."

"Really." Will let the news roll around in his brain. "Not surprising, right? This is his first stint at a public company. He probably won't like being accountable to shareholders."

"And we *all* need to be accountable to shareholders. Malcontents that they are."

Will smiled. Les may be a cynic and a social misfit, but he wanted the best for BSI. And he always shot straight with Will, a trait not easy to find around the tower. "I don't how you do it, dealing with cranky investors all day."

"The key is to not take things personally." Les raised his glass. "And to end each day with an IV drip of Kentucky Fire."

Anna studied Kirkland's Optelligence Talent deck, then looked at her computer screen, and then looked at the deck again. Most of the presentation, ripped straight out of the Synerpoint playbook, featured data-dense charts and graphs, ten-dollar adjectives, and the firm's signature contributions to the verbing of America. But this section on job descriptions seemed out of place, possibly even imported from another strategy by mistake.

She removed her earbuds and laid them on the Monk's table. The silvery jazz of Ella Fitzgerald immediately dissipated in the clamor of the bar. She downed the last of her Stoli Doli and signaled a waitress to bring the tab.

She'd been worried about locating the Monk, so she left the tower early in case she got lost. Once inside, she procured a table near the back, set up shop, and plugged away on Kirkland's inconsequential assignment.

With Will and Les now on-site, Anna emailed the completed book report to Kirkland, packed up her things, and signed the bill. She felt productive, and the strong pineapple martini had helped her decompress. With a satisfied smile, she made a path toward her new colleagues.

"Not surprising, the aggressive timeline," Les said. "The natives on the Street are getting restless."

"Hey, hi." Anna nodded at the men, making eye contact.

"Hi." Will glanced up from the discussion, a few strands of unruly brown hair falling across his forehead—obvious collateral damage from the icy rain. He looked surprised to see her. Maybe he assumed she lacked the courage to actually show up after inviting herself. But he didn't know Anna—and her incessant need to make a strong impression.

Will introduced Les as BSI's Investor Relations director and then slid over to make room for her.

"Hey to you, Anna." Les's voice lowered as his eyebrows arched. He offered her room on his bench seat as well.

Anna weighed her options. Noting Les's too-eager half-smile, she set her bag on the floor next to Will's side of the table and slipped in next to him. Les reached over for a handshake, his massive paw swallowing Anna's hand as if she had plunged her fingers into a bowl of rising bread dough.

"Welcome to BSI—the Purple Palace, as we say. Though our brand color is more akin to eggplant," Les crooned. An obvious attempt to show intelligence.

A tattooed waitress appeared with a complimentary basket of orange popcorn. "Another round for the corporate commoners." She noted the near-empty glasses on the table, then Anna. "And you?"

"Stoli Doli." A second martini might be a risky move, but the first one went down well, and she'd already had a hell of a week.

"So, Anna." Les swirled the bourbon in his glass. "Tell me all about your fine self."

"You'll have to excuse my friend." Will motioned across the table. "He's recently divorced, and it's made him more of a cad than usual."

"Jesus, Evans. I'm paying her a compliment. Let the woman speak for herself."

Anna smiled, giving Les a once-over. She knew the type. Flirty but harmless. Like a big, obnoxious puppy who wanted to play. He might nip at your fingers but would never bite. *Okay, let's play.* She gave her hair an exaggerated flip off her shoulder. "Well, I enjoy long walks on the beach, whimsical French films, and men with a keen understanding of U.S. financial markets. But"—she held up her left hand, wiggling the wedding ring on her finger—"you're a little late to the party. Now I get my kicks by working on three-pronged growth strategies nobody can explain."

Les laughed and slapped his hand on the table. "Well played, Ms. Reed. Let's talk about Optelligence, shall we?"

"We shall." Anna took a handful of popcorn.

"I'm not getting many straight answers." Will laced his fingers behind his head. "I'm hoping you can provide the financial angle."

"To hell with financials." Les shook his head. "Ron and Jerry completely threw their own CAPEX process out the window for Optelligence. Held a top-of-the-house meeting and allocated the cash by fiat. I can't figure out what the endgame is. But I'll share what I know. You prefer a CliffsNotes version?"

"Everything you've got." Their drinks arrived as Will silenced his buzzing phone. "Full-frontal stupidity."

"'Full-Frontal Stupidity' would be a great band name," Anna said and then wordlessly chided herself. Martinis tended to throw open the gate between her inner thoughts and her mouth.

Les grinned and tossed a kernel of popcorn into his mouth. "Here's the way I think about Optelligence. Let's say BSI is the average Joe, your typical American male with a decent job at the popcorn-topping factory, cheddar cheese division. Joe's job is like our copier business. Honest, steady work."

Anna studied the orange popcorn residue on her fingers. "Joe's got quality control issues."

"I'm happy to wait while you lick those off." Les's voice dripped with hope.

"How about continuing your riveting analogy instead?" Anna teased.

She had the sense Will was watching her, but she couldn't see him without an obvious turn of her head. In every meeting they'd had, he stiffened his posture whenever she spoke—as if each word grated on him. Maybe strong women threatened him. Or strong people in general. Or maybe he just didn't like outsiders. Whatever the case, she needed to work with him. She'd try to be less intrusive this time.

Les flashed a half-smile and took a gulp of bourbon. "So all is good for Average Joe until he starts getting jealous about how the other half lives. And he starts making plans. Big plans."

"Planning is good," Anna countered. "That's how people get ahead in the world."

"Sure." Les licked his thumb and smudged a fingerprint off the side of his lowball. "But Average Joe isn't realistic. His kids are community college material, probably bound for a factory job like the old man. But Joe wants to give them Ivy League educations, even though he can't afford it. And where does that leave him? With a massive pile of debt and two college dropouts living in the basement."

Will leaned forward. "You lost me."

"It's like BSI's Talent strategy. Sounds like a great plan: recruit and develop a bunch of really smart people to do really smart things. But what are these smart people going to do? What exactly does this plan deliver?"

Will chuckled. "A hundred MBAs living in the tower basement?"

"More than that." Anna examined the pineapple pulp floating in her cocktail. "Kirkland said we'll hire up to a thousand people."

"To do what?" Les's puffy, pouting face reminded Anna of a Cabbage Patch Doll.

"I don't know yet." She sipped her martini. "There's a section in Kirkland's deck on job descriptions, but it looks like it's just a placeholder."

"A thousand new heads with no new revenue in sight?" Les rubbed his temples. "We're screwed."

"Oh, don't be so melodramatic." Will sighed, leaning back against the wooden booth.

Les raised his eyebrows. "You expected optimism?"

"I'm just saying, you Finance types are born pessimists. There's a reason your mother didn't name you More."

Anna suppressed a laugh, not wanting to look like an ass-kisser who giggled every time the boss uttered a funny line.

"But it's not just Talent. Technology is also in over their heads." Les gestured with his glass. "This is like Average Joe deciding to remodel his house. He could keep costs down if he got multiple bids to find a reasonable contractor, did some of the work himself, and so on. But Joe hires the remodeler all the rich neighbors use. He's paying to keep up appearances."

Will reached for the popcorn. "I get it. Synerpoint is the expensive contractor. Hired to build custom systems instead of using our own IT department. But here's what I don't get: they keep saying the technology will be scalable. Like we're building it for someone else."

"I caught that, too." Anna clicked her ring against the side of her glass. "I didn't think Synerpoint was a leading expert in prepackaged tech solutions."

Will showing some business savvy pleased her. With his talk about the good ol' days in the company and the good ol' boys in the warehouse, she'd pegged him as a culture-keeper type. A Work-Around.

"Oh, Ron and Jerry think Synerpoint is the cat's ass." Les threw his hands up. "But their rates are astronomical, and their projects lag and nag like bureaucratic hangnails. I mean, look at TEPIL. Jesus."

"Tell me about it." Will groaned. "When it first came out, I spent more time TEPIL-ing than working and drinking combined. Now I just log everything as 999: Other Strategic Activities."

Anna smiled. Could her new boss also be capable of a little mischievous rebellion? *Nice.*

"Good for you!" Les raised his glass. "Screw Synerpoint. We've given them enough. We didn't even bid out the Optelligence work."

Will frowned. "Happenstance approved a no-bid contract?"

"Happenstance isn't paid to produce independent thought."

"'Happenstance'?" Another name Anna didn't recognize.

"Clifford Hampelranz," Will explained. "CFO."

"He made CFO by being the right mild-mannered ass-kisser in the right place at the right time." Les drained the rest of his brown booze. "Ergo, he is Happenstance."

Will shook his head. "The way he's allowing the company to blow cash? We ought to call him 'Fiscal Cliff.'"

Inky returned with a fresh bourbon for Les. He swished it around in his glass. "Put it on his tab." He nodded at Will. "So, where are we?"

"Mr. Changorium's Wonder Emporium." Will pointed at the IR director. "Innovation."

"Right. Poor Joe. His income hasn't changed, and the Yale tuition and remodeling projects have him tilting over his skis. He heads down to the local watering hole, hoping a few barley pops will clear his head. And then, in walks strategy number three: Inna Vation."

Anna smiled. Les appeared to be kind of a rake, but he could spin bone-dry financial updates into one hell of a good story. *Useful.*

"Oh, Inna. This smokin' hot temptress hooks Joe like a walleye, and he knows she's going to rock his world. But not yet, of course. Because Inna Vation is a high-maintenance tease. No matter how much attention and money Joe lavishes on her, she never puts out. Joe doesn't realize he's throwing good money after bad until it's too late. Like Chan's boondoggle strategy." Les rolled his hands in a dramatic flourish. "And that, my friends, is what I know about Optelligence. A big financial suck-hole with no discernable end-state."

The din of the bar filled the air around them. Les stopped talking and turned his attention to his bourbon. Anna took another drink of her martini, resisting the urge to jump in with a comment.

Will stared at the ceiling. "Jerry and Ron need to show the Street our next stage of growth, right?"

Les nodded.

"And Innovation is a stand-alone strategy. Outside work, led by an outside exec." Will reached for his discarded straw, bouncing the plastic against the rough-hewn tabletop.

Anna wanted to correct him. Chan an outsider? No, just an external hire, like her. But she thought better of it.

"Talent and Technology are being managed inside BSI. It all has to add up to something . . ."

"Yeah, a death spiral," Les retorted.

Will ignored him. "If we're hiring a thousand new people and building systems that could be licensed to other companies, maybe the new people are—"

"Selling!" Anna bolted upright in the booth. A rush of adrenaline spiked as the last piece of the puzzle clicked into place. *Of course!* She turned to Will. "In Kirkland's deck—those job descriptions weren't placeholders. They're Synerpoint roles. Consulting jobs. From entry-level to managing partner."

"Holy shit." Les sputtered a little. "Are you—"

"Optelligence is consulting. BSI is going to build its own consulting practice." Anna looked out across the darkened bar, ruminating on this exciting development. *Damn, Optelligence is a game changer after all.*

"Only one problem with that theory." Les poked his glasses farther up the bridge of his nose. "Conflict of interest. Why would Synerpoint help us build a business that competes with them?"

"They wouldn't. And they aren't." Will turned toward Anna, scowling. "Synerpoint is a strategy firm, right? Optelligence is the flip side—operational expertise. That's the unbeatable partnership you asked about in the Loni Anderson room. Jerry and Ron get a growth initiative to take to the Street, and Synerpoint gets paid to build a complementary consulting practice for a valued client."

Anna nodded. "And I bet they've agreed to share customer data and referrals. It's brilliant." In her excitement, she nearly knocked over her half-empty martini. Will slid the stemware toward the center of the table, out of harm's way. She caught a whiff of his cologne as he leaned in—an alluring blend of cedar, business savvy, and C-suite access.

She turned away and chided herself again. *Head in the game, Reed.* She couldn't let one martini-fueled conversation tarnish her professional image. She took a few calming breaths and mentally nudged Will in the direction of a more appropriate category—from Work-Around toward Useful.

"It might be most brilliant for Synerpoint." Les wiped his cheesy hand on the thigh of his Dockers. "I'd imagine they get a cut of every deal we sign. Maybe they haven't worked out the details yet, which is why the CEOs are being so secretive."

Will shook his head. "They can't roll it out until they explain how the copier business fits into Optelligence."

Anna raised one shoulder in a half-shrug. "Maybe they're reluctant to admit it doesn't fit. And they need to run the copier business quietly in the background until Optelligence proves itself."

"You're talking about a twenty-billion-dollar business. Hardly something that runs in the background." Will took another drink.

"Maybe 'background' isn't quite right." Anna bit her cheek, thinking through her words. Long-term employees like Will always defended their turfs—even legacy business models near the end of their runways. But companies bucking progress crashed and burned, taking families down with them. Will needed to understand that. "Companies need to evolve, and this feels like a fresh—"

Shaking his head, Will cut her off. "Bait and switch. That's what it'll feel like to customers. They don't want another cookie-cutter, consultant-driven—"

"Will, you don't seem to—"

"Whoa, whoa, whoa." Les held up his orange-streaked hands. "I didn't come down here to watch the beautiful people argue. It's like the *Real Housewives of Minneapolis* in here all of a sudden. Let's get back to the bottom line."

Will set down his near-empty glass. "Bottom line is, I owe the CEOs a comm plan on Optelligence tomorrow."

"And you'll send it to me, right? For Kirkland?" Anna didn't want to piss off Will, but she couldn't risk showing up to another Kirkland meeting empty-handed, either.

Will glanced sideways at her. "Yes. Like I said earlier."

"Do you think there are tactics we can fast-track after it's approved? I know Kirkland will expect to see immediate action." Execs always pushed for immediate action—surely Will understood that.

"The kickoff event will be the first activity. We have to control the story until we know exactly what the story is."

Anna saw a muscle in Will's jaw twitch. She'd irritated him again. She scooped up her martini. *Maybe he's a Work-Around after all.*

"Wow, I don't envy you two." Les slumped into the back of the booth. "How do you talk about Optelligence without talking about what it is?"

"Not sure." Will shrugged. "Try to steer the CEOs toward more transparency, I guess. Hopefully they see the logic in being straight with employees."

An eerie guitar riff kicked in overhead, and Les pointed to the ceiling. "The Clash. Straight to Hell."

JENNIFER ROCK AND MICHAEL VOSS

Fund Analysis > **Analyst Report Archive**

Business Solutions, Inc. (NYSE: BSI): Is the Bloom off the Rose?

Goldman Sachs

Discuss
See what other
investors are saying
about BSI

SUMMARY: BSI is slated to release year-end earnings late next week, and we are forecasting flat to slightly negative comps and EPS. While the company has an impressive history of steady growth, we believe BSI likely has reached the end of its domestic runway. It's clear the office supply giant is over-reliant on the core copier business and needs to find new avenues to deliver shareholder returns. Until management can articulate such a strategy, we suggest investors exercise caution. We currently rate the stock a HOLD.

CHAPTER 8

Will undocked his laptop and rushed down the cube aisle, stopping near the printer at the end. Four copies of the Optelligence communication strategy rolled off the Rayzor 5732G—single-sided, full-color, on a BSI template. The CEOs insisted on such details, and a trivial oversight such as missing page numbers could derail an entire conversation. They also demanded their visitors show up on time—something now at risk for Will.

He grabbed his printouts, hustled down the hall, and squeezed between the closing doors of an elevator half-full of BSIers, workout bags slung over their shoulders.

"Sounds like some trendy, intraprenurial training program Synerpoint would develop." The guy's Lycra bike shorts left little to the imagination. "I'm sure we'll all be tossing fish or cleansing chakras before the quarter's up."

"Or trust falls." A woman laughed as she and the others exited on the eighteenth.

Will checked out the source of their conversation: a poster, now visible on the back wall of the empty elevator, featuring a large purple triangle with Optelligence in exploding, Superman-style lettering and Talent, Technology, and Innovation named along the bottom. Will's head filled with a rush of obscenities, blood, and anger.

What. The. Hell.

The elevator arrived on the top floor, and Will stalked out, making a beeline for the restrooms. He threw his shoulder into the men's room door and then paced in front of the imported marble sinks.

Had to be Anna.

In her rush to please master Kirkland, she somehow fast-tracked this ridiculous, isolated tactic—maybe after she left the bar last night. Kirkland probably loved the abominable artwork and in-your-face elevator placement. All flash and no context, like the man himself.

Focus, Evans. Deal with this later. Will tilted his head from side to side, attempting to loosen his taut neck muscles. He forced a natural-looking smile onto his face, checked his expression in the mirror, and then made his way to the reception area.

"Afternoon, Lois." He sidled up to the cantankerous assistant. "Our fearless leaders ready for me?"

"Good afternoon, William," Lois responded with robotic pleasantry. "Take a seat. I have to bring this file down to seventeen. When Mr. Kirkland leaves, you may join Mr. Blankenship and Mr. Pruitt."

"Great, thank you very much." He plastered a fake smile on his face. "I appreciate it."

Will settled into a guest chair, wondering how the CEOs would react to his Optelligence comm strategy. They might finally applaud his good work—his unique ability to connect the dots between the CEOs' soul-crushing business-speak and what BSIers needed to hear. Jerry would slap him on the back, while Ron reached across the table to shake his hand. "This is exactly why we promoted you," they would say in unison, laughing at the unintended verbal jinx. Jerry would insist on giving Will a spot bonus from a roll of hundreds he fished out of his pocket while Ron offered the use of his lake home for the weekend.

Lyle Kirkland opened the boardroom door and marched into the reception area, bringing Will back to reality.

"Hello," Will said as he passed the exec. Kirkland pretended not to notice. Will pretended not to care.

Ron and Jerry looked up as Will tapped on the frame of the open door. "Good afternoon, gentlemen. Is this still a good time to go over the Optelligence comm strategy?"

Jerry checked his thick Movado watch and then glanced at Ron. "Is this on our schedule?"

"Lois rescheduled us from Tuesday." Will held the presentations tighter in his hand.

Ron sighed, leaned back, and dropped his glasses on the table, mumbling an obscenity about Goldman Sachs.

"I can see you're busy." Will dared a step inside the door. He valued time with the CEOs more than two-for-one night at the Monk, and he wanted to cut off any talk of rescheduling again. "Lois scheduled an hour, but I can cover it in twenty minutes. We need a coordinated launch, and the earlier we agree on—"

"All right," Ron snapped. "What do you have?"

Will closed the door and placed a copy of the small deck in front of each founder. He hated contributing to the company's PowerPoint addiction, but decks served as the primary communication currency for BSI execs. Unlike most people, Will kept text to a minimum and used imagery to help convey the message. "It's what you say that matters, not what's on the slide," he had often counseled company leaders. Few of them followed the advice.

"Lois said Salvador Chan would join." Will pulled up a chair between the co-CEOs. "Should we dial him in?"

"No." Ron picked up the deck and replaced the glasses on his face.

Will nodded. "What you see in front of you is a holistic internal and external communication strategy."

The execs thumbed ahead through the presentation.

"I'd like to call your attention to—"

"I saw the poster in the elevator this morning." Ron flipped his presentation upside-down on the table. "It looks like you already have things rolling."

"Well, actually—"

"The triangle on the poster is all wrong, though." Jerry leaned back in his chair, now ignoring the deck in front of him. "It should be equilateral, demonstrating how Talent, Technology, and Innovation are of equal importance." He drew the ideal triangle in the air with his index fingers. "Your triangle has two long sides and a shorter one along the bottom. It's an isosceles."

"Isosceles?" Will searched his brain for a way to keep this conversation from unraveling further.

"You know," Jerry used his patronizing mentor tone, "I appreciate how quickly you took action on this, Will. But in the future, run these things past us before you go to print."

"The posters are just one small tactic." Will abhorred the idea of assuming responsibility for the purple elevator placards, but the most expedient way to shift the conversation to real work required he take one for the team. "Our strategy is centered on leaders carrying the message with employees, and—"

"Makes sense." Ron peered over his reading glasses at Will. "We done here?"

"Wait." Jerry grabbed the deck and held it in the air. "I assume there's a kickoff party in here somewhere?"

"An all-employee event in the cafeteria, yes. We need time to plan and create the content, so it's three weeks from—"

"Why that late? The posters are already out there. Let's move it up." Jerry looked past Will, at Ron. "We're both in town next week for earnings. Chan will be here, too. How about Wednesday at eight thirty?"

Ron checked the calendar on his phone and nodded.

Will hesitated. Today was Thursday. *Goddamn posters.* "Um, yeah, sure. That means we need to start talking content. We'll need prep time with the two of you—"

Ron waved his hand in Will's direction. "Fine. Set it up with Lois."

"How's my marketing campaign coming?" Jerry boomed with a grin. "Like we talked about last time. Paperweights, poker chips, fedoras." He shook Will's shoulder. "But let's get that logo straightened out, okay, buddy?"

Will responded with all the diplomacy he could muster. "We'll correct the triangle going forward, but—"

"Atta boy." Jerry patted his arm. "And make sure you dress the place up a bit. We need a fun, upbeat event so that employees know we're excited and confident. Streamers and cookies, that kind of thing."

Will realized he'd begun to shake his head. He feigned a cough, cleared his throat, and tightened his fingers around his favorite J&R Office Supply pen. "I'd like to talk more about the messaging—"

"Oh, and balloons. Maybe we should . . ." Jerry stroked his chin.

If he asks for triangle-shaped balloons, one of us is leaving this room with a ballpoint tracheotomy. Will mulled over if he should unleash the pen on himself or the silver-haired huckster.

"Wait a minute. Where the hell did this come from?" Ron examined the back page of the deck—the risks associated with the Optelligence rollout.

Will's minimal use of text now threatened to bite him in the ass. He had intended to relay the importance of transparency by showing them the worst-case scenario—what employees might say if BSI didn't articulate the Optelligence story well. But Ron had no context for the provocative statements on the page.

"Optelligence feels hollow." Ron read the slide aloud. "What about the copier biz? I'm scared for my job. Are leaders telling the truth?" He tossed the deck in Will's direction, the bundle slapping the wood. "What the hell do you think you're doing, Evans?"

"We didn't get a chance to talk this through." Will cleared his throat. "But any effective comm plan identifies potential risks. These are worst-case examples—"

"Listen." The veins in Ron's neck bulged. "I don't need a speechwriter trying to poke holes in business strategies. Your job is to get people on board. Period."

"Ron, that's exactly what I—"

"I don't *care* what you think the risks are. We tell *you* what to communicate and how to do it, not the other way around."

Ron stood, wheeled around, and threw open the side door leading to his office. Jerry gave Will a wink and then headed for his own office. Will stood for a moment, alone in the boardroom, his anger rising with every breath. His hands trembled as he stacked his laptop and presentations into the crook of his arm.

"I need to set up for an evening meeting." Lois poked her head through the main boardroom door. "You'll need to leave."

"Of course. I'm going."

Will walked to the elevator bank, his pace growing faster with each step. With his free hand, he thumbed through his phone's contact list and called Anna.

She started talking the moment she picked up. "Hi, Will. How'd it go with the CEOs?"

"Not good. The elevator posters set off the plan prematurely, and the CEOs want everything moved up. We talked about the kickoff being the first activity! What happened?"

The line fell silent, and Will wondered for a second if Anna had hung up in defiance.

"I don't know what happened, Will. I'm not sure what you think I did."

Will paced in the hallway. "Those god-awful elevator posters! For Kirkland."

This pause grew longer. When Anna spoke again, her voice sounded measured but firm. "I had nothing to do with those posters. I don't know why you'd assume I did. They're unprofessional, off-brand, and against the plan. That's not the kind of work I do."

Will stopped in his tracks, trying to process her response. *She didn't do it?* He dropped his chin to his chest. *Real smooth, Evans.*

"Oh, uh, sorry . . ." The elevator opened. He stepped inside, trying to backtrack from his accusation as the doors closed behind him. "I was—" His phone beeped three times to indicate a lost signal. *Dammit!*

He slipped the phone into his pocket and stared at the floor, his mind spinning. *You just attacked Anna for no reason and then hung up on her. Worst boss ever.* He banged his head against the side wall—hard enough to hurt, without leaving a mark. The elevator stopped at twenty, and three people stepped on, wearing lightweight jackets and gloves, probably headed for the light-rail station. Will's mind shifted from Anna to the kickoff event. More commuters boarded on the nineteenth and sixteenth floors, their loaded backpacks and oversized purses pressing Will against the back wall, next to the stupid Optelligence poster. A dull ache crept into his chest as he pondered the logistics of an event he had only five days to produce. To unveil a strategy some idiot had already unveiled.

The doors opened on Will's floor. "Excuse me," he said through gritted teeth.

The crowd parted, and someone held the door open so he could make his way out. He wedged himself to the front of the car, but paused before stepping off, Ron's words pinballing in his head. *We tell you what to communicate and how to do it.*

He let out a low growl, then spun around and lashed out with his free arm—past the North Face jackets and puzzled faces—ripping the poster down, leaving only two small remnants where tape had held the corners.

Will bolted out, past the hushed riders, flinging the offensive tag board aside like a Frisbee. The poster whipsawed in the air a few times and then dived onto the floor into his path. He stomped on the piece of trash with his right foot, which slid out sideways, taking him down to one knee, his laptop and comm plans spilling onto the floor.

Son of a . . .

He scrambled to gather his scattered materials as the doors slid shut behind him, laughter echoing from the elevator shaft.

CHAPTER 9

Anna raced around the corner and darted into her cubicle. The Optelligence kickoff started in less than an hour, and the team needed an extra laptop cord to keep the Q&A site up and running.

Her new cube hid deep in the bowels of Marketing, a location both random and inconvenient. She'd visited only once before, to drop off a box she never planned to unpack, given that she'd eventually move nearer to the rest of the Comm team.

Anna fished the cord from under the desk and then froze, catching a movement out of the corner of her eye. She sprang up on her leopard-print heels and wheeled around, ready to fend off whoever threatened to invade her personal space.

But no creepy colleague or dawdling duster from the early morning cleaning crew skulked nearby. Her gaze locked onto the item that had drawn her attention: a huge carnation-pink penis swaying atop a neighboring file cabinet.

What in God's name . . . ?

She glanced at her watch—*got to get back*—but couldn't keep from taking one step forward to inspect the dancing dong swaying in the breeze of an overhead air vent. Eighteen inches high and made of construction paper, it sported a bulbous head and cylindrical base held with tape.

What kind of perverted shit is going on around here?

She took another step forward and spied the cube nameplate: Richard Witkowski. From this angle, she could see the penis had two googly eyes and five paper tentacles.

"Oh my God." She gasped out loud. "It's a *squid.*" The pink sea creature—obviously a child's work—nodded as she roared in laughter. This Witkowski character didn't realize his kid's art looked like a beacon for an adult toy store.

Anna poked through the guy's cube as the rational side of her brain scolded her to get back to the kickoff. Album artwork from obscure bands. Two Dalí prints. A stack of *Esquire* magazines. *Clearly the insufferable hipster type.* She studied his hanging folders. Project Parker, The Phoenix Protocol, and other meaningless project code names. She peeked down the hall and then turned her head to read an upside-down stack of papers fanned out on his desk. An invoice on top showed the cost of a dozen full-color posters.

"Son of a bitch." Anna took a closer look.

Will had blamed her for those goddamn Optelligence posters five days ago and then blew it off. She'd found the real culprit. Right here under her nose—and the googly-eyed schlong. *Catch the poster bandit and score some points with my erratic new boss. Win-win.*

She picked up the invoice, kicked off her heels, and sprinted to the Rayzor copier down the hall.

Will leaned over his computer, fingers flying across the keyboard as the pre-event chaos swirled around him. He sat at one end of a production table in the cafeteria balcony, tucked behind a row of potted plants. Workers below unfolded hundreds of chairs—setup that should have been completed last night. One guy from the freelance A/V crew unrolled cables while another adhered them to the floor with gaffer tape. Coffee waited to test the video switcher as Will checked the font size on the teleprompter.

He scanned his to-do list, realizing he needed to start the walk-in music. Lois, sticking her nose where it didn't belong, had asked Will to play something snappy and respectful. In a perfect world, he'd have created a playlist to telegraph what BSIers should expect from the shrouded-in-secrecy story of Optelligence: "Lying Eyes," "Runnin' with the Devil," and "The Wreck of the Edmund Fitzgerald."

Will sighed and called up his most benign default music: Big Band Hits from the '40s.

TK walked up, steaming mug in hand. "The A/V crew is ready to test the webcast."

Will burst out laughing at the wet circle staining the front of his colleague's khakis. "Problem?"

TK glanced down at his crotch. "Some nice lady spilled a latte on me in the skyway. Not her fault. Think it'll stain?"

"Nah." Will looked at the clock, wishing the minute hand would slow the hell down. "Are we ready to test the webcast?"

TK tilted his head. "That's what I just said. You okay?"

"Sorry. A little distracted."

Anna slipped behind Will and handed the laptop cord to TK. "Problem?" She nodded at his trousers.

"Lap latte. Think it'll stain?"

"Without a doubt." She slapped a document onto the table next to Will. "Check this out."

Will frowned and peered around his laptop. He didn't have time for anything unrelated to this kickoff. "What is it?"

"An invoice for those Optelligence posters." Anna crossed her arms with a satisfied smile. "I found the perpetrator."

He picked up the page and squinted. "How do you know it's for the posters? This could be any print job."

Anna leaned in, brushing against Will's shoulder as she pointed to the page. "Look at the cost-center number—it's Optelligence."

"You recognize the fourteen-digit number?" Will couldn't remember his four-numeral desk phone extension. "What are you, some kind of savant?"

ed more interest in showcasing his token knowledge of production terms than worrying about the giant crater now residing in the center of their agenda. *If we had a greenroom, I'd take you there right now and kick your pompous ass.*

He snuck a peek at the cafeteria below as Chan's video loaded on the laptop. Employees wandered in, and Holly scrambled to the entrance to hand out Optelligence chip clips. Dee Dee, Kirkland's assistant, clomped in, her red head bobbing through the cafeteria like one of the balloons fastened to the doorframe. Peyton took a front-row seat, talking with a Synerminion but quite obviously watching Kirkland ascend the balcony stairs. The dance of the illicit affair. A guy in faded jeans and a Schlitz Beer T-shirt plopped down next to Peyton.

Will sighed. *Dammit, still have to communicate those dress code policy changes.*

Coffee stared at the subtitled video over Will's shoulder. A young woman on the screen guided a blind man through the streets of Paris, explaining everything he "saw."

Anna stood to join the movie screening.

"What the hell is this?" Will asked.

"*Amelie.*" Anna nodded. "It's French."

The record player needle in Will's brain skipped. "What the hell *is* this?"

"Who's making my changes?" Ron marched to the front of the table. He held a disheveled pile of marked-up slides and what looked like sketches of a few new charts.

"Changes?" Will croaked.

"The Technology story is too soft." Ron rapped on the table with his knuckles. "We need solid projections and more financials. People need to see the math—revenue, margin, NOPAT."

Anna extended her hand. "Hello, Ron. I'm Anna. I'll be helping you out this morning."

She steered him away from the table, and Will sprang back into action. He finished editing Jerry's speaking notes and then spun through the movie clip with Coffee one more time. Okay, I have an angle." His fingers attacked the keyboard.

TK came bounding up the steps. "Camera's in one piece; the webcast is back up."

Will didn't respond. "Pete—notes are ready. I need live monitors."

"Roger that."

"Where's Ron?" Will twisted in his seat to search the balcony.

"Getting mic'ed up." Coffee pointed to the A/V guy threading battery pack cords through the CEOs' suit jackets.

Will wheeled around and saw Anna talking to Kirkland near the railing. She caught his eye and walked over.

"Where are Ron's edits?" Will spoke over the swelling crowd noise and increasingly annoying clarinet solo blaring from the speakers.

"No changes required." Anna settled into her chair.

Will's mouth dropped open, but as the seconds ticked down, he decided to accept the death-row pardon and stay focused.

He stood, held the headset to his ear and addressed everyone at the production table. "Heads up, people. We're on in five. I'll introduce Jerry, and off we go."

Will snatched mic number two from the table. "Ladies and gentlemen." His voice boomed through the sound system as Jerry marched to the balcony's edge, arms raised, Evita-style. "Please give a warm BSI welcome to your co-CEO and cofounder, Jerry Pruitt!"

"Good morning." The co-CEO's voice crackled through the speakers. "Nice to see you all here despite the weather. It was so darn cold today, I saw one of our corporate lawyers with his hands in his *own* pockets!"

A smattering of laughter and groans followed as Jerry transitioned into Optelligence—work that would "catapult BSI to new heights."

Will used his mouse and a steady hand to ensure the prompter notes kept pace with the CEO's delivery. Jerry appeared to be on his game, smooth and natural. He went off-script to accentuate key points where appropriate, seamlessly merging back into the prepared remarks at just the right juncture. Unfortunately, the message floated at a nebulous and high level, prompting Will to carry on a running a translation in his head.

We're flipping this company on its head, folks—a helluva transformation that lands us squarely on that elusive bandwagon known as the "knowledge economy." We're calling it Optelligence, but that's a word we made up to mask what we're really talking about: consulting. And, hey, some of you might fare all right in the new world order. So there's that.

"I'm grateful for everything you do to keep the core business humming along, and I'm excited to talk about what's next." Jerry paced in front of the teleprompter. "Optelligence is a game changer."

He finished his speech with an overview of the Talent strategy before turning the podium over to Ron, who outlined Technology in twenty minutes of lifeless generalities and exhaustive detail.

"Salvador Chan is the newest member of our executive team." Ron used the fresh speaking notes Will had crafted. "Unfortunately, he is unable to join us today. You will have a chance to meet him soon. In the meantime, let's take a look at the video he sent."

Will held his breath as the clip played on screens below. Jerry took one look, marched over to the table, and—shielding his lapel mic—leaned into Will's face. "What the hell is this?"

"It's Chan's video. I assumed you'd seen—"

"Screening the video is your job."

"I watched it, Jerry." Will locked eyes with the CEO. "And I took a shot at some comments you can use to put it context."

He pointed to his screen. Jerry scanned the scripted paragraph, nodded, and returned to the podium as the video ended and the lights came up.

"Ah . . . Paris in the springtime," Jerry ad-libbed before picking up his remarks on the prompter. "This video is a metaphor for our Innovation strategy. Innovation is represented by the young woman, leading our shareholders, colleagues, and partners through the streets of our industry, and opening their eyes to the possibilities all around them."

Will couldn't help but beam as BSIers nodded at the fabricated explanation. He looked down the table to see if anyone else had noticed the near-crisis, but they focused on other tasks. Everyone except Anna, who had slipped away and whispered to Kirkland just offstage.

"Of course, Talent, Technology, and Innovation require a massive, well-coordinated program." Jerry smoothed his tie with a rub of his hand. "Lyle Kirkland is leading this effort, and he's here to tell you more about it. Lyle?"

Kirkland crossed the balcony to shake Jerry's hand and then stepped to the podium to applause from below.

"Good morning, everyone." Kirkland looked over the audience and then nodded to the co-CEOs standing in the wings. "And thank you, Jerry and Ron. As always, you've set the bar. You can count on us to get this company growing again as we build a future worthy of our incredible past."

The crowd responded with spontaneous, sustained applause. Kirkland tapped his fist on his chest, as if his heart, too, burst with company pride. *As if he wasn't the only human born with a Power-Point deck where his heart was supposed to be.*

No longer needing to run the prompter—Kirkland preferred the age-old, monotonous method of reading slides aloud—Will studied Anna from his perch behind the shrubbery. She didn't look at Kirkland the way Peyton did: ready to rip off her Synerpoint-issued pantsuit and beg for his meaty consulting contract. No, Anna scrutinized Kirkland like a coach would study game film, with intense eyes and a creased brow. All business.

"If you'd turn your attention to the next graph—" Kirkland stopped and squinted at the prompter monitors displaying his slides. "Wow, I'm sorry that's difficult to read. I told the Communications team to create a *pie* chart, not an *eye* chart."

The audience laughed as Anna rolled her eyes.

"We tried," Coffee mouthed in response.

Kirkland droned about charts as Will queued up Jerry's final comments. The SVP's remarks ran long, but Chan's unplanned movie premiere had been brief and had bumped the event ahead of schedule.

Kirkland wrapped up his presentation with an intricate analogy from *The Art of War* as Jerry moved into position to reclaim the stage. He shot Will a wink, pumped Kirkland's hand, and addressed the crowd again. This time, though, he showed no interest in the agreed-upon remarks scrolling on the monitors; instead, he trotted out the most overused, shopworn cliché in the western hemisphere—comparing Optelligence to the Apollo 13 space mission.

Will hung his head as Jerry likened himself and his co-CEO to Neil Armstrong and Buzz Aldrin, the heroic astronauts from Apollo 11, not 13. No matter. Jerry never let facts get in the way of a good story. He built toward a crescendo, whipping the crowd into a frenzy with his compelling and marginally accurate recollection of Hollywood's version of the mission—capping it with the inevitable mantra: "Failure is not an option!"

The audience sent him off with a spirited ovation.

Employees filed out as the execs reconvened at the production table. Jerry patted Will on the shoulder. "Great job on the Chan video, buddy. That came out of left field, but I knew we'd come through in the clutch."

"Thanks." Will steadied himself with one hand on the table.

"We got their attention." Kirkland placed the mic and battery pack in Anna's outstretched hand. "That felt like the right amount of detail at this point."

"It wasn't specific enough." Ron shook his head. "In the future, this Communications team needs to understand fundamental business metrics and make sure they're woven into our remarks."

"Trust me, Ron, we understand the metrics." Anna showed him a sweet-but-steely smile.

Will raised his eyebrows at her tone of voice—outwardly polite, but laced with an underlying "fuck you." The same tone he'd heard on the phone when he accused her of the elevator posters. Probably honed to perfection after years of derisive remarks from execs.

"Remember that we're here to support you *and* protect you." Anna wrapped the cord around the battery pack. "Citing those numbers to an audience of this size would qualify as a material financial disclosure. Given that we release earnings tomorrow, it was best to keep it high-level."

"Maybe." Ron harrumphed. "But we need to strike a balance going forward."

"Gentlemen, we have the Synerpoint call in ten minutes." Lois shepherded the three execs toward the staircase.

"Nice job with Ron," Coffee said to Anna. "He can be kind of a bear."

"We know what we're doing." She smiled. "Sometimes people need to be reminded of that." She and Holly headed for the stairs.

"Hey, before you all take off," Will called out to his team. "I just want to say great job pulling this thing together on such short notice. Let's knock off early tomorrow and head to the Monk. First round's on me."

Coffee voiced approval on behalf of the team as Will stepped to the balcony railing and watched the last of the crowd dissipate. *A standing "O."* Despite the lack of prep time, employees seemed to buy the flimsy story, and the execs appeared satisfied.

Wonder how the Street will react tomorrow.

BSI Hits the Skids

Shares plummet on tepid results, lackluster strategies

by WALTER LUCIA

Investors dove for cover today when Business Solutions, Inc., reported a second consecutive quarter of sluggish performance, sending its stock plummeting more than 11% at the close of trading. In a conference call with analysts, company executives attempted a boardroom bait and switch, diverting attention from their flagging core business by touting their new three-pronged growth strategy dubbed "Optelligence." Wall Street reacted with a punishing sell-off amid a flurry of skeptical research notes.
Full Story, C1

CHAPTER 10

The Monk had grown thick with happy hour revelers as Will waded through the bar. Hoping to avoid any BSI shareholders drowning their sorrows or the sarcastic waitress from his previous visit, he tried to blend into a pack of out-of-town pharma reps still sporting their stick-on name tags. But Inky spotted him when he strayed from the herd.

"You look depressed. What's wrong? Corporate hair salon run out of mousse?"

Bennie cackled, walking up beside him. "She got you good, Evans."

"Table for seven," Will told Inky before turning to Bennie. "Can't believe you're on time today after the media blitz."

"What? I'm always on time."

They followed Inky to a round table toward the back of the bar.

"Actually, you're always on Benedetti Time, which is about sixteen minutes behind what the rest of the world considers 'on time.'"

Inky eyed them as they sat down. "A fruitless usual for the boy, I assume. And you, goth girl?"

"Sam Adams, kinky."

The waitress bit the inside of her cheek. "You want I should deliver it in furry handcuffs?"

Bennie laughed. "Sorry, hon—that's back-home, harbor-style. Sink a shot of Jack and a skewer of olives." She turned to Will and offered up a weary smile. Strands of hair were breaking loose from her bun, her eyes were red, and mascara ran down her cheek.

"How'd it go today?" Will winced. "The papers are all over us."

"It's a shit storm. But here's the thing: the articles aren't completely awful. Reporters know to get their facts straight, or I'll swoop down like the angel of death. It's the editors I can't control, writing wild-ass headlines and teaser copy and making it look like we're going under."

Will nodded. "Financial blogs are worse."

"Bloggers," Bennie spat. "Remember when reporters were actually journalists? Trusted sources of unbiased information and all that? Now any fuckwad with an abacus and a Wi-Fi signal can post half-assed speculation about our balance sheet. The Twitterazzi can burn in hell."

"Most of the coverage seems pretty skeptical about Optelligence." Inky set their drinks onto the table.

"Well, fuck, Evans." Bennie took a gulp of beer. "Do ya blame them? The Street's looking for a game changer, and what do Ron and Jerry tell them? 'We're gonna be the market leaders in Optelligence?' Shit. 'Market leaders in verbal masturbation' is more like it."

"I know it's not a perfect story, but you think they'd give us a little credit for trying something new." Will stirred his glass a few times and took a long drink. The hearty mixture of vodka and carbonation gave his stomach an immediate, warm tingle.

"Yeah, you'd think they'd give us some benefit of the goddamn doubt. I'm mean, sure, we're kind of a mess. Always have been. But we're a beautiful mess, you know?"

"I know." Will tilted his glass toward her. "Everything will work out. It always does."

"Fuckin' A!" Bennie gestured with her mug, tilting the shot glass in the bottom and sloshing some beer onto the table. "And we're good people! Jerry and Ron gave a million dollars *each* to the Boys and Girls Club. We give a ton of money to the National Literacy Council and the local arts scene. We have armies of employee volunteers! And what's that Flourbox gig—the one hiring disabled vets?"

"Purple Patriots." Will raised his glass in salute. "Great program. We had a guy at FB-One. Edison. Lost a leg in Afghanistan. Dude was a genius programmer, revamped our entire scheduling system."

"Ya think Walter Lucia writes about any of that? He wouldn't know a good story if it crawled outta his shorts and made him pancakes." Bennie dug in her purse for a mirror and flipped open the compact. "Holy hand job, I look like a back-alley hooker."

Will smiled. "Screw Walter Lucia. We'll get through this."

"Yeah, probably." Bennie moistened her napkin with the condensation from her beer mug and used the sogginess to wipe off her smeared mascara. "I've pitched stories for a lot of companies—saw some crazy stuff—before my hubby dragged me to this frozen outpost. Yeah, I thought this place was pretty jacked up at first—two CEOs, Rainmakers and Promisekeepers, projects named after comic books 'n' shit. But I love my job and this big, stupid company. I do."

"I do too. We bleed purple. Not many do anymore. Not at corporate, anyway."

"The last of a dying breed." Bennie lifted her mug.

"Yep." Will clinked his glass to hers. "The elusive, beaten-down balloon buyers who get drunk in the middle of the day."

Bennie took a gulp of her drink. "We're old timers from the J&R days. Pre-tower orphans." She winced. "Ah shit. Sorry, Evans. Shouldn't use that word."

Will laughed. "I'm not an orphan, Ben."

"You said that after your dad died, your mom abandoned you."

"Metaphorically. Remember? I've told you the story, like, fifteen times. When she remarried, she didn't need to worry about me—the good kid. They had their hands full with my crazy sister and Ken's three teenage demons."

Bennie nodded and took another swig from her mug. "Oh yeah.

Sure. The bully, the compulsive gambler, and the annoying pacifist."
Will rolled his eyes. "Narcissist. Annoying narcissist."

He had never blamed his mom for spending so much time and effort on her new stepchildren. She helped him out when he needed her, which wasn't often. But Ken turned out to be a dolt of a stepfather. A far cry from Will's real dad—a guy who lit up every room he entered. A guy who taught Will how to roll with the punches. Like the time young Will got cut from the baseball team, and his dad encouraged him to spend the summer learning guitar instead.

A whoop went up from a group playing darts near the stage. Will nodded in their direction, more than ready to change the subject. "What do you call a cluster of annoying, young, ad agency types? You know, like a murder of crows or gaggle of geese?"

"I dunno." Bennie reached for the menu of drink specials. "A swagger? A menace?"

Coffee arrived from out of nowhere and dropped his keys on the table. "A collection of adholes. And obnoxious little pitches."

Inky reappeared with a second round they didn't order. Coffee wrinkled his nose at the underwhelming scotch selection, opting for a Fat Tire Amber Ale instead.

"Sorry about the coverage today." Coffee nudged Bennie's shoulder. "From a standing 'O' one day to hitting the skids the next. You holdin' up?"

"Peachy. Spent the day trying to get reporters excited about a Technology strategy that makes no money and a Talent initiative that makes no sense. Might as well be hawking ghost whispers and angel farts." She took a swig of beer and exhaled as she replaced the glass on the table. "Give me a good product story to push—copier, staple gun, a goddamn pencil for all I care—and I'll get you coverage from Framingham to Frisco. But this ethereal, knowledge economy crap? I'd rather shoot my face off."

Will gulped down the last of his drink and pushed his glass to the table edge. Building this stupid consultancy practice could impact more people in more ways than he had imagined. Friends like Bennie might jump ship—a possibility he didn't want to entertain. And what about people like Big Al—far enough from corporate to steer clear of the bullshit, but smart enough to see through it?

"Makes me wonder what the Promisekeepers think of all this." Will stared across the room. "They watch a grainy webcast with our execs claiming Optelligence is the land of milk and honey and then see BSI get body-slammed by every media outlet in the country."

TK arrived and ordered a strawberry daiquiri as Inky returned with the drink orders.

"We don't usually let dudes order off the Ladies' Night menu." She placed a hand on her hip. "But I'll make an exception."

"Thanks!" TK either missed the insult or didn't care.

Les arrived as the server spun away.

"You again." She took in the full glory of Les's wrinkled linen pants—and the mustard stain splashed across his breast pocket. "Bottom-shelf bourbon, I presume?"

"You got it, babe." Les clicked his tongue twice and formed his thumb and forefinger into a gun.

"Holster that '70s finger pistol, Dirty Harry." Inky patted his shoulder. "And I mean Dirty in the traditional, unhygienic sense. And Hairy with an 'I.'"

Les shrugged as she walked away. "She wants me." He pulled up a chair next to Coffee and scanned the other faces at the table. "Good we could get together to celebrate today's earnings calamity."

"We were just talking about Bennie getting her ass handed to her." Will tipped his head in the PR director's direction. "You probably got the same from the Street."

Les raised an eyebrow toward Bennie. "At least reporters were kind enough to hand your lovely ass back . . . analysts chewed mine off and spit it out." He glanced around the table and smoothed the front of his dirty dress shirt with his big hands. "No Anna?"

"She and Holly left a few minutes after me," TK piped up.

Bennie pointed her finger at Les. "Cool your jets, Mr. Slutwaffle. Anna's married, ya know."

Les drummed his hands on the table. "Marriage is but an unfortunate, transitory state."

"So . . . down double digits at market close." Coffee grunted toward the IR director. "Shareholders must be skittish."

Les adjusted his glasses. "It'll get worse, my friends. OfficeWorld releases earnings Tuesday—and the whisper number is *not* good. If they miss, we'll take another hit."

"How's that fair?" TK asked.

"It's the way it works. The Street looks at BSI and OFW as bellwethers for our sector. If they release a big pile of dog shit on Tuesday, analysts will see it as further evidence of a contracting industry." Les tried to rub the yellow mark from his shirt with his knuckles. "And our share-price depreciation will continue."

"Well, we *are* the market leader in share-price depreciation." Coffee offered a deadpan look.

"We'll be fine." Will studied the growing assembly at the door who waited for tables.

Anna stepped through the door and, standing tall on her high heels, searched the crowd. She pointed to the table and tugged Holly's arm. The pair made their way through the busy pub. Several men eyeballed Anna as she passed. A guy in a bowtie elbowed his buddy and cocked his head in her direction. Another stopped her and whispered something in her ear. She shook her head and pointed again to the table near the back.

As they got closer, Holly said something to Anna that made her eyes light up and her mouth widen with a smile. She let out an unexpectedly uninhibited laugh.

"What's with the getup?" Anna nodded to Bennie as she sat. "Job interview?"

"I wish." Bennie grinned. "Anybody hiring in this town? Tarzhay? Medtronic? Hot Babes R Us?"

Holly pulled out a chair. "Oh, you're a lifer, and you know it."

"Hey, I love this company. I said that a second ago. But after two straight days as town crier for Optelligence, I'd rather—"

"Shovel shit from here to Shinola?" Holly offered with a sheepish squint.

"Blow Kirkland while looking at Dee Dee's Facebook cat pictures?" Anna suggested.

Bennie laughed and then coughed and sputtered a mouthful of beer. "Jiminy Crackpipe, that's fucking disgusting. And I love you for it."

"Jiminy Crackpipe would be a nice band name." Holly handed a napkin to Bennie. "An Irish Celtic group, maybe."

The two latecomers ordered drinks as TK leaned over to Will. "Hey, we were busy with the kickoff and earnings, but I wanted to tell you something. Because I'm going to need some time off."

Will searched his protégé's face for any hint of the nature of this news. He hoped TK hadn't planned some weird meteorological sabbatical. "What is it?"

TK grinned. "Kelsey and I are getting married!"

Will slapped him on the back. "That's great news, big guy." He'd met Kelsey a few times—a sweet girl who worked as a teacher in a needy south-metro school. TK took a few days off every fall to help with the annual coat drive for her students' families.

"Really?" TK lowered his voice. "I didn't know if a wedding would bring up, you know . . . bad memories for you."

Will's smile faded. "Beth? That was a long time ago."

Two years, to be exact, from the time his calculating ex-fiancé had dumped him. Her personal ambition hadn't ruined things. Rather, she'd directed her relentless aspirations onto Will. The breaking point came when he'd been reluctant to pursue a comm director opening at American Federal Life—the type of stale, fastidious company where young, innovative communicators go to die. But Beth kept pushing. She wanted a husband with more money and a better title. "You're holding back," she said as she placed the ring in his palm and folded his fingers around it. "And it's hurting both of us."

That was a long time ago. But hearing her name out loud brought it all back. He could feel the sharp edge of the diamond pressing into the center of his hand. Along with a gnawing in the pit in his stomach. As if she'd walked out that morning.

"Wedding?" Holly heard the word like a dog whistle— somehow picking it up over the bar noise. "What wedding?" Her gaze zeroed in on one person to the next.

TK's face reddened when the attention turned to him. "Kels and I are tying the knot."

Holly screamed, bolted from her chair, and ran to hug TK, burying his face awkwardly in her bosom.

Coffee raised his mug in salute. "Congrats! When's the big date?"

"Next winter, probably."

TK watched the group exchange furtive smiles. "What?"

Anna patted the table in his direction. "Sweetie, I haven't known you that long. But winter doesn't strike me as your strong season."

"Hell, if you see as much as a flurry," Bennie guffawed. "You'll have to send one of your fucking weather bulletins and end up missing the ceremony."

"Hell hath no flurry . . ." Les smirked while others joined in the laughter.

Will rattled the ice in his empty glass, noticing a small lime slice he'd failed to see in the full drink. *I told her no fruit.* He studied his growing pile of cocktail straws. Inky had been sneaky with his refills tonight, and he'd lost track of how many he'd consumed. *Not enough to get Beth out of my head.*

A group near the garage doors started cheering about something, and Will turned to see people fist-bumping each other. "Hey, Anna." He gestured with his glass. Was he slurring his words? He couldn't tell. "There's your poster boy. The one who made the Optelligence posters."

Anna spun around. "Which one?"

"Ponytail, red sweater."

"European pencil pants?"

"That's him."

Coffee turned to look. "Who's the D-bag in the man clogs?"

"Richard Witkowski." Will sucked up an ice cube and then spit it back into his glass. "Sommersby."

Bennie shook her head. "Summer-who?"

"That was his Flourbox nickname. Remember the old Richard Gere movie? He returns from war and assumes a different identity." Will nodded toward the hipster by the doors. "That's Sommersby—all blue-collar and work boots when he worked at FB-One. Became a Rainmaker and turned into a leather-blazer-and-Italian-loafers guy. Big Al named him Sommersby. Total poseur. Not even a trained designer."

Thank God he didn't end up on my team. Will had bumped Sommersby from his original team list, along with the other designer. And the dead snowshoer.

"I've been looking into this." Anna leaned across the table toward Will. "Apparently, Synerpoint green-lit the posters without talking to any of us." She looked back at Sommersby and then started to rise from her seat.

"Whoa, what're you doing?" Will sat up straight and held up a hand.

She flipped her hair back from her shoulder. "I'm going to introduce myself and tell him we own all Optelligence communication."

"You can't just accost him in the bar." Will clicked through the potential ramifications of Anna's planned confrontation. *If she cold-cocks him, I'll be up to my ass in HR inquiries and paperwork.* "Just sit tight. Everything will work out."

Anna hesitated for a moment and then sat down. Her look? Somewhere between obstinate and completely pissed off—a narrow range. "It seemed pretty important to you when you called me after meeting with the CEOs. If you don't put an end to rogue activities like this, he'll continue to be a problem."

Will lacked the energy to respond. He considered ordering another drink, before thinking better of it. He watched as his colleagues laughed and joked about TK's wedding, Optelligence, and

'80s hair-metal bands. Everyone except Anna, who sat stone-faced until Bennie lured her into the conversation with a playful insult.

He picked up his phone and scrolled through yet another pile of meaningless meeting invitations. Plans for a TEPIL software update. A proposal to add pet-grooming services at the company store. A discussion of Synerpoint's stupid Flourbox spring-cleaning project. He shook his head, imagining what Big Al would have to say about that. Not to mention Optelligence.

He drummed his fingers on the table. Al had been on his mind for weeks—a sign Will had allowed too much time and distance to get between them.

No more.

It's time to go back to the 'Box.

To:	*BSI Corporate
From:	*BSI Newsdesk
Subject:	Re: Stairwell Safety and Security

Please be advised of BSI's Safety and Security policy as it relates to stairwells in the company's office tower. The changes outlined below are necessary to ensure BSI's corporate office remains a safe, secure, and respectful work environment.

Effective immediately, the stairwell doors on every floor will remain unlocked from 6:00 to 9:00 a.m., and 4:00 to 6:00 p.m. for employee use when arriving or departing from work. The stairwell doors will remain locked, and elevators should be used, during all other business and nonbusiness hours. In the case of emergency, the Security department will ensure the stairwells are unlocked and available for usage.

CHAPTER 11

Will parked his car near the FB-One loading docks, checking emails on his phone before going inside to meet with Big Al.

"VP of Security needed memo ASAP," TK's note said. *"Anna took care of it."*

Will wished TK had the confidence to handle company leaders, especially on something like this—a simple, two-paragraph stairwell memo. An easy assignment, even for a junior team member.

Will read the announcement again. He considered himself an expert at spotting code words communicators used to broach sensitive topics. These cryptic references were a necessary part of the trade, and over the years, he'd mastered the art of communicating perfectly vague but important information about a variety of delicate subjects. He even joked about writing a manual on the topic: *The Professional Communicator's Handbook—How to Artfully Communicate Something When You Can't Reveal What's Really Going On.*

A communiqué about "efficiency" indicated department budgets were about to be slashed. "Aligning leadership roles with the company's priorities" meant senior execs had granted themselves new titles and stock options. A memo wishing a departing employee "the best of luck in his future endeavors" was a sure sign the guy had gotten his sorry ass fired.

He smiled at the stairwell memo, marveling how the word "respectful" leapt off his tiny screen. Any form of the word in official company communication masked a reference to sex. Copulating colleagues ran rampant in corporate America, and communications teams often got the task of reminding employees—in perfectly professional, wonderfully vague language—to keep it in their pants.

This particular memo confirmed employees had been humping in the stairwells—a new phenomenon. Most amorous offenders tried to find more discreet locales. The basement storeroom. Unoccupied offices. The meditation rooms. According to the grapevine, one enterprising couple had a standing rendezvous in the back of a pickup truck in the parking garage. The problem—neither of them owned the truck. And the guy who did found the situation less than respectful.

Will leaned his head against the driver's seat headrest and smiled. *I wonder how you TEPIL sex in the workplace . . . Horizontal Integration? Back-End Collaboration?*

He stepped out of the car and approached FB-One's side door, near the shipping desk. Will's former warehouse colleague—nicknamed DEVO—stood inside, his dyed blond-on-black hair partially covered by a pair of professional-grade headphones. He had a tape gun in his hand and bobbed his head to some inaudible beat as he packed boxes.

"Hey . . ." Will waved, trying to get DEVO's attention. "Hey!"

"Oh, hey, man." DEVO pulled his headphones off. The sound blared into his neck. "You here to pick up that case of toner?"

"No, dude, it's me. Will Evans."

The aging punk rocker squinted in Will's direction. He said nothing. Maybe he had finally blown out his eardrums. "Will Evans. From corporate."

DEVO straightened up and pushed the button on his iPod to stop the throbbing headphones. "Oh. How can I help you, sir?"

"DEVO! For Chrissake, we worked together for years."

DEVO squinted again and cocked his head.

"Jesus Christ," Will muttered to himself. Then louder: "It's me. Frodo."

Will had received his Flourbox nickname during his first week on the job, after Big Al suggested Will might be too pretty for warehouse work. He despised being named after an ugly hobbit, but Al had clear rules on the subject: accept your Flourbox nickname without question or complaint. It's a badge of honor.

DEVO's face lit up, and he offered a handshake and then pulled Will in for a bro-hug. "Frodo! Hell, yeah, I remember you. I was just messin' with ya. What's up? You seem a little uptight."

"Never mind. Listen, I'll catch up with you and the guys in a little bit. But I should find Big Al. You know if he's around?"

"Yeah, dude, I'm sure he is." DEVO re-covered his ears with the headphones. "Big Al's always around."

Will left the shipping desk and headed to the copier staging area. He smiled as he remembered the hours he spent moving machines around the 'Box, checking them into the inventory system, and moving them into storage. Later, he'd prep a copier for delivery, load it onto a truck, and take it to a customer's office. Something about that work felt achingly simple and honest. He missed it.

"Excuse me. Vendors need a badge to be in this area."

Will turned to find one of the twin brothers from the Delivery crew.

"Hey, Thing Two! What's up?"

The tall, thin man stepped back, studying Will.

"It's me. Will Evans."

Thing Two gave him a blank look.

"Will Evans. From a few years ago."

Faint recognition flickered in the beanpole's eyes. "Oh, yeah. Pretty sure I remember you. Who are you with now? Rayzor? Clarion? Either way, you're still going to need a badge."

Will blinked hard a few times and shook his head. "No, dude, I'm not a vendor. I took a job at corporate, remember? Communications? Speechwriter for the CEOs?"

"Sure, yeah. Good for you. Here to check inventory counts or something?"

"No, I'm here to see Big Al." Will waited for a response that never came. "Um, is his office still up front, near the bathrooms?"

"Yup." Thing Two walked away.

Will headed toward the front of the building. *What the hell is wrong with everyone around here?* He took a right and walked between two massive racks of office supplies, toward the back of the countertop where the warehouse crew filled orders for the Sales staff.

A young worker leaned over the counter, completing some kind of paperwork. He had a Justin Bieber haircut, acne scars on his cheeks, and an earring in one ear. It relieved Will to see someone he didn't recognize, versus the other way around.

"Hi, I'm Will Evans from corporate. Here to see Big Al. Would you mind opening the gate for me?"

"You're from corporate?"

"Yep, here to see Big Al."

"I wonder if you can help me with something."

"Uh, I'm not sure, I guess. What do you need help with?"

"I've been trying to get reimbursed for a medical procedure I had a few weeks ago and not having any luck."

Will felt an urge to be a good corporate soldier and help the kid navigate BSI's bureaucracy, but he had no expertise in this area. "Um, sure. I think there's an 800-number you can call—"

"Yeah, I tried that." The kid tossed his pen onto the counter. "I keep getting connected to someone who doesn't even speak English. Last time I called, they signed me up for the 401(k) plan. Which is fine, I guess, but it's not gonna help me pay for this."

The young man lifted his standard-issue warehouse shirt to reveal a large gauze bandage near the bottom of his rib cage. Will winced at the moist, red splotch darkening the center of the bandage.

"Oh, Jesus," Will blurted. "I think you should have that looked at. Today. Like, immediately."

"Yeah, the doctor said the bleeding should stop in a few hours, but it's been three days." He didn't seem particularly concerned.

"You need to go back and see him."

"Her."

"What?"

"My doctor. It's a her. I mean she's a her. A woman. My doctor is a woman."

"Whatever. Listen, you need to go see someone."

"Someone. You mean like a doctor?"

"Yes. *Yes. Go. See. A doctor.*"

"Okay, thanks. That's good advice." The young man let go of his shirt. "You want me to open the gate and let you through?"

Will could only nod. He hurried through the chain-link gate and heard it closing behind him. He desperately wanted to leave Bieber the Bleeder in his rearview mirror. *If the kid collapses and dies, I'll tell the authorities I went for help.*

He slowed his pace as he approached the office. Will had been gone three years, which might explain why the culture felt different. But Big Al wouldn't change. The guy never changed. Will knocked three times on the doorframe with a single knuckle. "Wake up, old man. Nap time is over!"

Al looked up from his computer screen. "Hey, Frodo. How are you?" He paused, looked back at his computer, clicked his mouse a few times, and frowned. "Is our meeting today? Oh, looks like it is. My mistake."

"Is this still a good time?" He smiled to mask his disappointment. *Al forgot I was coming back?*

"Sure, this works. Come in; sit down. What's on your mind?"

Will plopped into the only guest chair in the tiny, windowless office. "I was hoping to talk about a couple things. But I won't take much of your time. I know you have important things to do: surf the internet for porn, reserve a table at Jarro's for happy hour—that kind of thing."

Big Al gave him a phony smile. "Funny."

Will cleared his throat. "So, um, I was hoping to get your perspective on a few things. Optelligence. The copier business. Whether the story we're trying to land resonates with the Promisekeepers."

"Sure, what do you—"

Someone knocked at the open door. Will swiveled in his chair to see Joe Hamlin, a tad grayer and heavier than before.

"Joe the Hammer!" Will got up to shake the man's hand. "Looks like you're not getting any younger." He added a smile and a wink.

"Frodo." Hammer chewed on the end of a broken zip tie. "Looks like you're not getting any smarter. Is that your silver Volkswagen parked near the docks?"

"Yeah."

"Well, it's being towed."

"Son of a bitch!"

Will bolted past Hammer, toward the warehouse. With nobody available to open the gate, he vaulted over the counter and kept running. He darted down the office supply aisle and then cut left, toward the shipping area where he'd entered. Will dodged a stack of boxes, threw the back door open, and headed for his parking spot in a dead run. He rounded the outside corner of the building and stopped dead in his tracks.

His car sat there, right where he'd left it. He spun around and looked toward the street. No tow truck. He took a few steps forward to peer down the alley—still nothing. *What the . . .*

Then it hit him. Nobody leaves FB-One and returns in a parade of glory. Big Al would make sure of that. He'd made it number one on his list of unwritten-but-omnipresent rules: Don't take yourself too seriously—or you'll get taken down.

Will started to chuckle, quietly at first, before laughing out loud. He walked back toward the shipping entrance, ready to take his medicine. He pulled the heavy steel door open and stepped inside. The chant began immediately.

"Frodo! Frodo!"

The voices came from every corner of the building. They grew louder as the entire crew moved out of the shadows to converge on the shipping area. Zombies zeroing in on the planet's last living human.

"Frodo! Frodo!" They pumped their fists amid smiles and laughter.

They were all in on it. DEVO, Thing Two, Joe the Hammer, even the new kid, apparently. Will recognized other friendly faces as the group advanced. The Pink Pantser and Spud. Big Sexy. Hench and Cobra. The Hinkster.

The chanting continued as the crew moved in, enveloping him in a giant group hug. Will worked hard to swallow the football-sized lump materializing in his throat.

Now this *is my Flourbox.*

Big Al shouted above the commotion. "What happened to you, Frodo? Working at the Magic Castle dull your senses? You should have spotted the old towing ploy from the other side of University Avenue!"

"Even Tito got you." Hammer pushed the teenager with the bleeding torso to the center of the human circle. Tito lifted his shirt again, and Hammer ripped the bandage off, holding it up for all to see. He poked his finger into the red, moist center, popped the digit into his mouth, and grinned.

"Mm . . . Mama Hammer's homemade hot sauce!" He cackled as his colleagues shrieked with laughter.

Big Al stood at the back of the loosely assembled group, ample arms crossed over his expansive chest, smiling as Will accepted handshakes and back slaps. For a few minutes, all the bullshit and stress of the last few weeks disappeared. A palpable sense of comfort and belonging washed over him.

He was home.

After a few minutes, Big Al dispersed the group. "All right, Promisekeepers, this ain't no bingo parlor. Let's break it down and bring it home," he said, invoking his daily mantra. "Frodo, to the office."

Will followed Al, trying to keep pace with his long strides. "Hey, is Edison still around?"

"Nope. He went to that new 3D printing company. Got promoted, I hear. And do you remember Dottie P? She graduated from St. Olaf and is going for her MBA. She's a smart one."

Will walked back into the musty office.

"How's life at Rainmaker Central?" Al settled back into his seat. "Getting your fill of three-hour status meetings and four-martini lunches?"

Will closed the door behind him and sat down. "Hey, life at corporate isn't the gravy train you think it is. They're cracking down. Get this—we're no longer allowed to fornicate in the stairwells. For real. Got the memo today."

"What? That's a travesty. I mean, Kirkland can afford hotel rooms, but what're the rest of you poor bastards supposed to do?"

"I don't know." Will laughed. "Listen, things are a little crazy right now, and that's why I'm here. To get a reality check. On Optelligence."

"Oh, yeah. We watched the kickoff." Al fidgeted in his rusty office chair. "Listen, we need new ways to grow, that's for sure. And I'm all for exploring options. But I've got fifty-three crew members here, and when we gather 'round to hear our founders lay out the company vision, they don't say a single mother-trucking word about what we do?"

Will nodded. "Yeah, I—"

"I'm sure you can't put words in their mouths. But I gotta tell ya: after that meeting I had a steady stream of people coming into my office, asking whether anyone at corporate even cares about the copier business anymore."

"I get that." Will studied his thumbnail for a second, trying not to react to Al's disappointment. "Sorry we didn't tell a more complete story."

Al patted his hand on the desk a few times. "Not your fault. But you know what I worry about? That this whole Optelligence thing is just another mountain to climb for Ron and Jerry. It's like a game to see if they can make BSI even more of a Wall Street highflier." He shook his head. "But it's not a game to the people here, Will. Our livelihoods depend on this company. For us, it's personal. Lately, it's felt intensely personal—and a little scary."

Will thought about the smiling faces he had just reconnected with. "I get it."

Al leaned back in his squeaky chair and sighed. "Sure, they're patting us on the head—throwing some money our way to paint the common areas and reorganize the inventory. As if that's going to drive business. What we need is for someone at corporate to pick up the goddamn phone."

"What do you mean?"

"We can generate more revenue, Will. It's right there on the table, and my guys know it. Take 3M for example. They're our largest client in this region. I roll ten vans a week to their various locations. Ten a week! That means my Promisekeepers spend twenty hours a week with people at our largest, most profitable client. The Rainmaker on the account? He gets commission for landing new clients—not supporting the ones we already have."

Something on the computer screen captured Big Al's attention. He clicked the mouse and typed a few words with his index fingers. "That's why I'm glad you called. I need your help."

"Help. With what?"

"Rattling cages. Getting some attention back on the copier business. I need more support for my guys—especially from Sonny's reps. I need Sales to listen to us. I need a hotline. A bat phone."

Will nodded, pursing his lips.

"What is it?"

"I'm just thinking . . . there's a lot of focus on Optelligence right now. I'm not sure—"

"C'mon. You saw how investors responded to Optelligence. Like a fart in church. I've seen this a hundred times. Jerry and Ron fall in love with a new idea, throw some money at it . . . maybe it works, maybe it doesn't. Either way, they always come back to their bread and butter—the copier business." Big Al rocked forward in his chair and locked eyes with Will. "But, now, with the state of our business and share price, we can't wait for them to come back around. We need action."

"I get it." A knot formed in Will's stomach. A burgeoning, consultancy-sized knot. His sense of responsibility and level of concern for the company's direction were rising at equal rates. "Would it help if I talked with Sonny? Maybe we can figure out a connection point between your guys and the Sales team."

Al leaned back again, and his chair groaned. "It would be a start, Frodo. I'm just asking you to do what you can. You're one of us. You know what it's like out here, working in a 'Box. You know what we can do and what we need. That's why I sent you to the tower in the first place." Al grinned and offered a wink.

Will returned the smile. *The infiltrator is on the case.* "Got it." He picked up his phone and scrolled for Sonny's number.

CHAPTER 12

"Thanks for taking a mobile lunch meeting." Sonny reached for his steaming lunch bowl from the food truck window. A stiff wind howled down 10th Street, sending leaves and a few stray newspaper pages to swirl around his feet. Sonny hunched his shoulders against the cold air.

"No problem. I love Tot Boss." Will nodded to the van. "Thanks for making time on such short notice."

Will stared at his tater-tot burrito, trying to determine how to keep the creation either in the bowl or his mouth rather than the front of his shirt. He also wished he'd have grabbed his jacket before they braved having lunch outside the tower.

"Mind if we hit the skyway?" Sonny patted his ample belly with his free hand. "My extra layer of spring bulk still isn't enough to keep me from shivering my butt off."

"Let's do it." Will nodded toward the department store entry. He glanced over his shoulder to make sure Sonny could handle the stairs. The Sales exec was one big dude—a former football player whose constant travel and fast food habit had taken a toll on his middle-aged body.

Will nibbled the edge of his burrito and held open the skyway door with his foot. He had seen Sonny only in passing the last few years, but the guy hadn't changed much. Same wispy blond hair, wire-frame glasses, and bulbous nose.

"I like the idea of exercising." Sonny puffed as they entered the busy walkway. "I'm just not into, you know, all the running and lifting and stretching."

Will smiled. "Hard to keep a workout schedule when you're on the road so much."

"Well, I should have more time at HQ now." The exec turned toward Will as they walked. "Not sure if you've heard. Jerry and Ron are consolidating key functions—from Sales through the Flourboxes—into a single business line called Copiers and Office Supplies. They've asked me to run it."

"Wow. That's huge." Will tried to visualize the org chart while thinking through the implications for the Flourbox teams. "Congrats."

Sonny dipped his head and snatched a tater tot with his mouth. "Thanks, pal." The exec swallowed the morsel and shook his head. "Being tapped to run the core business this company was founded on? That Jerry and Ron built from scratch? It's an honor—it really is."

"Well, they picked the right guy. How long have you been slinging duplexes and document feeders, anyway?"

"Twenty-nine years." Sonny articulated every syllable. Will let out a whistle.

"Started as a sales associate, shadowing Jerry on his calls. I wish you could have seen him then, Will. The guy was such a natural. We always joked he could sell a Rayzor to Xerox—he was that good. Never in my wildest dreams did I think I could sell like him, much less end up with a job like this."

Will smiled. Typical Sonny. Promoted to run a multibillion-dollar business line, but still humble to the core. "And now you're the guy behind the wheel. Rainmakers and Promisekeepers all on the same bus."

"Not exactly. The top sales reps are being tapped for Optelligence.

There's only a skeleton staff coming with me." Sonny took another bite and continued talking through a mouthful of deep-fried potato. "But at least the reps I kept respect the core business. Veteran road dogs with toner running through their veins. The way I look at it, I'm taking over a business line of Promisekeepers—top to bottom."

Will nodded, happy Sonny could hang onto reps who appreciated BSI's roots. Not many of those around anymore. But it had to sting to lose dozens of top performers. "So, Optelligence raided your cupboard, huh?"

Sonny laughed. "Yeah. No idea what the hell those reps will be selling, mind you, but off they go. I'm also kissing half the budget good-bye—another Optelligence redirect."

They passed a bookstore Will had ducked into a few summers ago to buy some inane management manifesto Ron had been quoting. By the time Will finished the book, the speed-reading CEO had moved onto a new tome du jour—*Shear Brilliance*, leadership lessons gleaned from Peruvian sheep herders.

Sonny held the next door open for Will and a few other passersby. "So, we're going to have to be damn creative if we're going to grow Copiers this year."

"Funny." Will waited for the exec to catch up. "That's why I wanted to talk with you. Met with Big Al a few days ago. He wants to strengthen the communication between his team and Sales. He mentioned some customer ideas they'd like to kick around. Could be some growth opportunities there."

"Interesting. Might be helpful to me, too. I've got a learning curve when it comes to the Flourboxes." Sonny smiled. "After all, I grew up as a Rainmaker, Frodo."

Will winced at his Flourbox handle, glad no corporate types walked within earshot. "Sure, you started out as a Rainmaker. But you've always been an honorary Promisekeeper. Hell, Tenz, I think you're the only Sales guy with an official nickname. That's why you're the perfect guy to run the new business line."

Sonny laughed. "Nobody has called me Tenz in a long time."

Big Al had named the unassuming exec after Tenzig Norgay, the Sherpa who guided Sir Edmund Hillary's first summit of Mount Everest. A nod to Sonny's selfless leadership style. He had been the rarest of Rainmakers—a guy who never sought the spotlight for himself.

"Seriously, Will, I'm going to need visibility to all aspects of the business." Sonny sidestepped two women power walking the skyway, arms pumping. "Copiers get us in the door, but we make all our margin in paper and ink and the like. We're probably leaving money on the table. If you can get us all connected, that'd be great." He sucked another tater tot into his mouth.

Will nodded and stopped at the BSI lobby doors. "Great—appreciate your support. I'll let you know when I've got a plan laid out."

"Good. Let's talk soon. I want to put some early points on the board."

Sonny's phone—in the back pocket of his faded Wranglers—erupted with an old-fashioned rotary ringtone. He tossed his half-finished lunch into a nearby garbage can, checked the phone, and slid it back into his pocket.

"Sorry, I have to jump on a call." Sonny extended his right hand and then cupped his left on top of Will's to shake it. The charming habit of a seasoned salesman. "Thanks for your time, Will. Great seeing you."

"Good to see you, too."

"Oh, one more thing." Sonny turned back toward Will. "From a communications standpoint, Copiers has been left in the dust. The Optelligence kickoff made that clear. Anything you can do to give us equal billing, that'd be terrific."

Will grimaced. "I'll do what I can, but the three Optelligence strategies clearly have favored-nation status right now." Sonny gave a resigned nod of his head, as Will walked toward the BSI lobby. The CEOs would never agree to equal billing.

God forbid Jerry's beloved triangle turns into a square.

"You're late, too?" Holly sounded relieved when she bumped into Anna outside the tenth-floor elevators.

"My meeting with Kirkland ran late. But it was worth it—I got him to agree to team town halls."

"Great work! How did you get him on board?"

"Well, Kirkland doesn't really care about what employees want." Anna looked back to make sure her colleague kept up. "So I played to his ego. Described how he'd have his own bully pulpit every month. He loved it." And she loved to run a good corporate hustle. Identify an exec's motivations, use them to sway his thinking—make a difference for employees.

"Hey, Bob Dylan is this way," Holly called out as Anna overshot their left turn.

"You know, companies typically map out their meeting rooms."

"The times may be a-changing, my dear, but BSI will never be typical."

Holly's voice echoed in the deserted hallway, a sure sign that meetings starting on the hour had captured their prey. Anna's nerves jangled, reminding her of rushing to junior-high social studies class to beat the second bell. She quickened her step.

"I hope you don't mind me tagging along." Holly hurried to stay even with her colleague and almost dropped the stack of papers she had in her hand. "When you said this was related to the Talent strategy . . ."

"You should be there." Anna read the nameplates on the rooms. "This is a huge undertaking—talent assessments, HR training programs, recruitment positioning. It all has to fit with our comm strategy."

Anna envisioned a number of smaller, interconnected comm plans feeding into the master strategy. A series of carefully orchestrated activities linked to business outcomes, all laddering up to

Optelligence and ultimately demonstrating how Communications could drive the transformation of a multibillion-dollar business. Thinking about it nearly made her drool.

Holly and Anna waded into the packed room and found seats across from each other, squeezing their laptops and folders onto the already crowded tabletop. More attendees stood in the back, some dragging in chairs from other rooms. Anna didn't recognize most of the faces, except for Peyton, Judd—the guy who sang *The Brady Bunch* tune—and the ever-present Synerpoint gofers whose names Anna never bothered to remember.

"We're tasked with a significant shift in human capital to align with the company's strategy and future state." The woman at the whiteboard spoke with professional boredom. Her average height, medium build, and mousy hair made her an entirely unmemorable human being. "Peyton Rayburn, Synerpoint partner, is going to give us the overview of Talent and what's expected of us."

Anna noted Peyton's crisp white shirt. Kirkland's? Perhaps she accidentally grabbed it while scrambling to dress in the hotel room this morning. And maybe Kirkland strutted into the office wearing her fuzzy pink sweater with the crystal-beaded lace flowers across the shoulder.

Anna opened Instant Message on her laptop and connected to Holly while Peyton took a sip from her protein shake and mechanically described her excitement for this journey to empowerment.

@AReed: *"Who is that bland woman who introduced Peyton?"*

Anna caught Holly's eye from across the table.

@HPorter: *"I'd call her brunette."*

@AReed: *"Not blond. BLAND."*

Holly raised her reading glasses from the cord around her neck and rested them on her nose.

@HPorter: *"Oh. Anita Roswell, HR exec."*

@AReed: *"Roswell? Like UFO landing, Area 51?"*

@HPorter: *"Yep. Both Roswells are sources of shady events we disavow. I don't believe it, but some people say she's covered in tattoos under that beige polyester.*"

Anna gave Roswell a discreet once-over, scanning for a stray rose petal or the tip of a butterfly wing peeking from under her sleeve or turtleneck. No ink in sight. But it could've been true.

Leave it to an HR exec—someone who encourages others to "bring their whole selves to work"—to be the one who masks her true nature.

Peyton handed out a tower of PowerPoint decks and paused while the participants passed them around.

@AReed: *"67 pages. Somewhere a forest is screaming in anguish."*

@HPorter: *"Synerpoint is occuponomous . . . their sins are PowerPoint-based."*

"Talent is the anchor strategy in the three-pronged Optelligence approach," Peyton explained. For possibly the forty-second time— Anna had lost count. "We need to build our bench to build our business. Talent is not only foundational but also transformational and reputational."

@AReed: *"She forgot sensational and space-stational."*

@HPorter: *"I need a vacational."*

@AReed: *"I believe she said 'a comprehensive and comprehensible dynamic.'"*

@HPorter: *"Ooh, non-world-class operational disconnects. That sounds painful."*

@HPorter: *"Leadership guidepost. Double-loop learning."*

@AReed: *"Wrap the double-loop around that guidepost, & I'll be first to hang myself from it."*

Consultants like Peyton always spoke in ambiguous, academic-sounding terminology. They lifted their fabricated jargon from proprietary templates and then repackaged and arranged it on slides. All designed to appear as if they'd created the business-ese specifically for the current client. Petyon and her underlings had probably constructed this particular deck with reusable modules from the Synerpoint Consultancy Playbook, Vol. 3.4. The perfect talent solution for a plateauing Fortune 100 company struggling to outperform its stagnant industry. Call now, and receive fifty bonus pages of indiscernible jargon! All for the low, low price of $9.6 million.

@AReed: *"Seriously? 'Intimacy at Scale'?"*

@HPorter: *"Where I come from, we call that 'Being a Slut.'"*

@AReed: *"Haha! Know why BSI meeting rooms don't have exterior windows? So we don't jump."*

@HPorter: *"There's a window down the hall. Tell my husband I loved him."*

@AReed: *"Whatev. You'd never go through with it—you'd feel bad for the janitors assigned to clean up the mess."*

Anna grew impatient with Peyton's protracted Talent overview—taken right from the huge deck Kirkland had made Anna summarize. A familiar story. No plot and, apparently, no ending.

@HPorter: *"All that $ we're paying Synerpoint, you think they'd send Peyton to a presentation skills class."*

@AReed: *"Can't she say 'completed by this time' instead of 'pressing up against a hard date'?"*

@HPorter: *"Honey, I haven't pressed up against a hard date since my college homecoming dance."*

Anna suppressed a laugh as a minion flicked the presentation to the next slide.

"As you're aware, this is a multistep roadmap. We start by aligning the role requirements." Peyton swirled the green goop in her plastic tumbler and took another drag from the straw. "We've also established a comprehensive perspective for decision rights and hierarchical leadership accountabilities."

@HPorter: *"Go to 39. I don't get it."*

Anna placed the deck on her lap and covertly flipped to slide thirty-nine. Tiny, stacked boxes—strung together by solid and dotted lines—displayed BSI's new organizational structure. The support functions stayed put. HR still reported to Roswell, Legal reported to Legal Bob, while Marketing and Innovation tucked under Chan. The IT department stayed with Larabee, and Happenstance kept Finance. Each of the named execs still reported to the CEOs. A shared-services model supporting the rest of the company. *Makes sense.*

The left side of the chart stopped the presses. The remainder of the company filtered into one of two business lines, with a senior executive assigned to run each.

Kirkland's new organization sported an Optelligence label. The Boy Wonder's vast empire included his current corporate departments—Merchandising, Procurement, and Supply Chain—and a sizable Sales team. In addition, BSI transitioned two of the Optelligence strategies—Talent and Technology—into official, fully staffed corporate functions under Kirkland's leadership.

Anna frowned. These teams seemed redundant with HR and IT. Maybe Kirkland intended to take responsibilities away from them. *Roswell and Larabee can't be thrilled with that.*

She shifted attention to the other half of the chart: Copiers and Office Supplies. All the Flourboxes and a piece of Sales had been combined under the leadership of someone named Sonny Larsson.

@AReed: *"Who's Larsson?"*

@HPorter: *"Head of copier sales."*

Anna tuned Peyton out and skimmed over the next few pages. She drummed her fingers on the table. With Kirkland taking over a large chunk of corporate, and the consolidated field organization moving under this Sonny character, BSI made its informal rift official.

@AReed: *"They're splitting the company down the middle. Rainmakers on one side, Promisekeepers on the other."*

"We are looking at the least disruptive approach to migration in the short-term," Peyton announced over the sound of turning pages. Many attendees skipped ahead to get to specifics. "If your team hasn't completed its ITIs, do so by EOD so we can leverage the results for the TSDs."

A BSI-badged woman interrupted. "Who's making the decisions on which employees move where? Several layers of leadership will want to weigh in."

"Synerpoint is directing the overarching process and gathering both TEPIL and ITI data. BSI executives will finalize all decisions. Some corporate teams—HR, Marketing, Legal—will support both business lines, requiring team structure changes as well. Net-net, we estimate eighty-five percent of the employee base will be at least partially affected."

A murmur rolled through the room, and other hands went up.

"Widespread impact, yes." Peyton raised her voice. "But we've accomplished similar re-orgs at larger, more complex corporations. I assure you it's feasible if we stick to our structured program plan."

Anna thumbed to the back of the deck, looking for any sign of a comm plan to support this massive game of musical chairs. Seeing nothing, she spoke up. "We need a robust communication plan. With tactics, timing, and audiences laid out in exacting detail. Starting with leaders getting meaningfully involved and keeping panic from setting in with their teams."

"We have a plan." With her plastic tumbler, Peyton motioned to a man in the back of the room, partially obscured by the Synerpoint herd. Too cool for the table, he lounged atop the built-in countertop, next to the coffee and pastries.

Sommersby.

"Richard Witkowski is here. Many of you are familiar with his previous work on Optelligence. I've asked him to help us to be more proactive and tangible with our communications." Peyton shot a sideways glare at Anna as she emphasized the last few words.

Son of a bitch—Peyton's shutting me out.

Anna glanced at Holly, who shrugged.

Sommersby hopped off the cabinet and grunted when his artificially weathered boots hit the floor. "Thanks, Peyton. Yes, proactivity and tangibility will be very important." He nodded to the Synerminion running the slides. "Can you toggle over to the site?"

The projected slide disappeared, replaced with a website home page. As the site blipped into view, a bouncy tune filled the room and an animated presentation overtook the screen—using the same

Superman-style lettering from the elevator posters: *"BSI—The Market Leader in Optelligence."* Talent, Technology, and Innovation appeared amid blooming, purple flowers.

"Here's the scoop," Sommersby explained over the music. "We're going to launch this destination where people can get information. Employees simply enter a hashtag and their name, and it'll show exactly where they fit in the new structure and whom they report to. It's pretty sweet."

Anna opened her mouth to ask a question, but a woman next to her spoke first. "Why a hashtag with their name?"

"You know, like Twitter uses for trending topics." Sommersby's upper lip curved into a half-smile. "Hashtags are swag. Employees will love it."

"I don't see the search box." Judd poked up his hand.

"It appears after the presentation, which is only about seven minutes long."

Judd frowned. "If I'm an employee who wants to skip to the part where I find out what's happening with my job . . . can I opt out of this movie?"

"No." Sommersby leaned back against the wall. "It's important for all employees to be level-set on the strategy."

"Seven minutes. Is it at least interactive in some way?"

Sommersby raised and lowered his hands, wiggling his fingers to mimic rainfall. "We want this to wash over them. It's a PVLE—Passive Virtual Learning Experience."

A steampunk machine labeled "Technology" chugged off-screen and then reappeared pushing a massive light bulb called "Innovation."

"That's super cool." A man's voice piped up from the back of the room.

When the big light bulb shattered and created a hundred tiny, fluttering birds, the attendees oohed as if watching Fourth of July fireworks.

Sommersby held up a humble hand, silencing the nonexistent

applause. "This was a team effort. A lot of folks behind the scenes pulled it off."

Anna could no longer hold back. "I'm sure a lot of work went into the site, but employees' jobs are on the line. They want honest conversations with their managers. Asking them to plug their names into a search engine to find out their roles creates an enormous risk to productivity and mora—"

"Excuse me." Peyton banged her cup on the table. "We are moving forward with a bias for action. This communication plan is bleeding-edge."

"This isn't a plan." Anna pointed at the screen. "It's one incredibly myopic tactic that raises more questions than it answers. Like the elevator posters." She shot Sommersby a nasty look. "If you alienate employees now, you may never get them back."

No one responded for a moment. Holly stared down at her laptop screen, her cheeks flushed.

Peyton pursed her lips. "If you wish to discuss your opinion on communications, you can speak to Richard offline."

Anna held her ground. "This company's Communications team will create a plan and get approval from executives—that's our role."

"We simply don't have headspace or cycle-time to change the communication strategy at this late date. All job decisions and announcements will be made in four days."

The room erupted with questions and commentary from around the table.

"Four days? That's ludicrous."

"How is that even logistically possible?"

Judd closed his eyes and tipped his head back. "Oh my God. We're going to be like Lucy and Ethel—desperately trying to wrap all the little candies as the conveyor belt keeps speeding up."

Peyton raised a hand to regain control. "It's aggressive, yes. But I've been assured this team is up to the task. We must move fast to ensure minimal disruption to the business."

Anna's screen lit up with another message from Holly.

@HPorter: *"Anna, thank God you were here. Someone needed to stand up to them."*

@AReed: *"Didn't do much good. Yet."*

@HPorter: *"What do we do now?"*

@AReed: *"We fight for what's right."*

Anna grabbed her phone and texted Will. *"Where r u? Optelligence = Armageddon."*

CHAPTER 13

Will dashed off the elevator on the eleventh floor and turned left. He dodged two men standing near the restrooms while checking his growing list of missed texts: a request from TK to send his latest weather report, another Code Crocker from Les, and an accidental "luv u" message from Coffee, intended for his wife—Will hoped.

He played the worst-case scenario game in his head as he continued down the hall. Whenever he received an urgent text or call, he tried to imagine the most dreadful situation he might possibly encounter. That way, whatever actually happened wouldn't seem as bad.

Still considering situations, he stepped inside the tiny Herb Brooks room. A round table and four chairs filled the space. Unlike many BSI meeting rooms, this one appeared well stocked with a full complement of whiteboard markers and a functioning wall clock.

He chuckled to himself. *Do you believe in miracles?*

Anna had filled the whiteboard with action items and a timeline. "Thanks for meeting." Her cheeks were pinker than usual, and she tapped a marker against the palm of her hand. "This is messed up."

She took a deep breath.

"They're splitting the company in half. A giant re-org is coming, where they're moving employees from the core business to Optelligence. Copiers gets strafed, and the secret consultant practice gets a huge influx of internal talent. And then we hire a thousand new bodies on top of it."

"Hang on. I just—"

"Synerpoint estimates eighty-five percent of employees will get new managers or new roles." Anna pointed the marker at Will. "It's corporate Jenga. Pull out as many pieces as you can, hoping the tower doesn't come crashing down."

Will leaned away from Anna's felt-tipped weapon, trying to reconcile her deluge with the organizational changes Sonny had outlined during their skyway lunch conversation.

"And it gets worse." Anna stepped to the blue timeline and drew a hard, hasty circle on a specific date. "It's all happening by Friday."

Will fell against the back of his chair. "Damn. That's so much worse than my worst-case scenario."

Anna fidgeted with the marker, grinding the cap against her palm. "This is complete craziness, Will. There's no way to do something like this in four days without something—possibly many things—going wrong."

Will nodded, still struggling to get his thoughts together. "Sonny told me about the new Copier and Office Supplies business line. And that he was losing some of his Sales staff."

"Remember the ITIs? Those assessments determined which salespeople were capable of selling consultant services. Reps scoring the highest get transferred to Optelligence."

"Wow." Will sketched out the new org chart in his mind. "Sonny's got the core business. Who's leading the whole consultancy practice?"

"Kirkland."

"Fuck." The knee-jerk reaction slipped out before Will could stop himself. "Sorry."

He looked again at the whiteboard timeline, focusing on the four-day gap before this massive re-org.

Anna placed a hand on her hip. "Kirkland is bowing to Synerpoint's so-called expertise on the timeline. I think there's only one play we can make."

Will nodded. "I agree. Cobble together an abbreviated comm strategy to minimize the fallout."

"Damage control? Come on, Will. We can do better than that." She placed the marker on the whiteboard and leveled her gaze on him. "We have a chance to control how this whole thing plays out."

Will frowned. "No, you come on, Anna. The two of us are not going to control a companywide re-org."

She plunked into a chair and leaned forward. "Listen. At my last job, the CEO announced he was reducing paid vacation time to save twenty million dollars. Employees were livid. I gathered their feedback, did a little math, and convinced him that morale and turnover issues would cost him more in the long run. And he reversed his decision."

"So . . ."

"So, you have pull with the CEOs—let's talk to them. Outline the risks. A huge productivity decline and negative PR, for starters."

Will's stomach rebelled—he could still hear Ron yelling at him about the Optelligence comm plan. "Jerry and Ron aren't very receptive to talking about risks. We're not going to fight city hall on this."

"We have to try." Anna looked at him. "It's the right thing to do."

Will couldn't decode her assertiveness. Did she want to do the right thing for BSI—or her career? Did she actually think the CEOs would applaud her spirit and bravery?

He shook his head. "BSI doesn't work like that. I can't run to Jerry and Ron with every question or complaint. They delegate those decisions."

Since his first days in the tower, Will had viewed every piece of good work he delivered as an earned poker chip in a high-stakes game with the company's two highest rollers. Mostly he chose to bank those chips for a genuine crisis. This re-org might be a mess, but it didn't rise to the catastrophic level necessary to insist on an emergency meeting with the CEOs. "We need to realize our place in all of this and do what we can with what we've got."

Anna gave him a skeptical squint. "What about the employees, then? You're just going sit back and watch them get tossed around like socks in a dryer?"

Will sat upright in his seat. "Who said anything about sitting back and watching? We're going to help them through it." He leaned across the table and met her stare head on. "And I need you to get on board with that approach."

Anna leaned backward and crossed her arms. "Well . . . either way, you're going to have to wrestle the comm plan away from Sommersby. He's been working with Peyton, and he built a reprehensible website to announce all the individual role changes. If that thing launches, nothing we do is going to help. Morale will go straight into the toilet."

"Then we need to outflank him." Will stood and paced in the cramped corner near the whiteboard. "There's no way that site has gone through QA testing in this short timeframe. And our IT network administrator is a fussy, paranoid little man. If I tell him that come Friday morning, four thousand corporate employees will be simultaneously trying to hit an untested, unsecured site, he'll stroke out. Then he'll insist on six months of scoping and testing before it comes anywhere near his network." He stopped moving and focused on Anna. "Problem solved, and we take the comm plan back."

She held her gaze on him for a moment, then looked down at the table. "Fine, but that's just one of the issues. I don't understand why you want to muck around with middle managers when we could fix this faster by going to the top of the house."

"You're going to have to trust me." Will reached for his phone and thumbed through its contacts to find the IT guy. "Everything will work out."

CHAPTER 14

Will leaned against the doorframe of the Artist Formerly Known as Prince room, straining to hear the muffled conversation inside. For the last two days, BSI execs had sequestered themselves there, haggling and bartering over employees up for grabs as part of the re-org.

Two men approached, and Will straightened up, pretending to read something on his phone as they passed. He needed to extract Judd, who might have been inside, documenting the employee transfers. Dark paper covered the hallway windows—an obvious sign of confidential conversations—so Will couldn't see. He could have texted Judd, but decided instead he'd satisfy his curiosity and steal a peek at the secretive, contentious process playing out behind the closed door.

He looked down the hallway in each direction—for what, he wasn't sure—then slipped inside, closing the door behind him. Org charts and hundreds of employee ID photos plastered the walls; some were in orderly rows, while others had been removed then restuck, clinging only by a corner. Job descriptions and talent assessments littered the guitar-shaped table—interspersed with an assortment of staplers, highlighters, and tape dispensers. The execs paced the room's perimeter, debating the merits of various individuals and lobbying for favorites. They plucked pictures off the wall, waved them about with passion, or scanned them with disinterest, photos slipping between their greedy hands like children swapping collectible cards.

A black-market trading post had sprung to life, and employee pelts were on BOGO.

Kirkland stood near the front of the room, holding a mug shot in the air. "Mohit Phakdar is critical to building out our Technology infrastructure."

"Bullshit, Lyle!" Sonny, red-faced, belted from a few feet away. "You already cannibalized most of the development teams." He pointed at BSI's head of IT, cowering near the whiteboard. "Larabee needs to maintain some expertise to keep my business running."

"If you insist." Kirkland shrugged. He stepped around the neck of the guitar to deliver the snapshot and nearly slipped to the floor before regaining his balance. He lifted his right foot and removed an employee photo from the bottom of his tasseled loafer. "Randy Martin. Slippery little devil, aren't you?"

Judd nodded and whispered something to a Synerpoint notetaker in the next seat before following Will out the door.

"Looks pretty messy in there," Will said as they walked. He'd never seen that much executive dysfunction on full display. "Something tells me that's not how you drew it up."

Judd ran a hand through his hair and sighed. "Yeah, it's turned into the 'Red Wedding' from *Game of Thrones*."

Will slowed his pace and grabbed Judd's arm. "Wait. That's a recent entertainment reference. Not exactly consistent with your personal brand."

"When in Dorne . . ."

"So what happened?"

"We had a decent process in place. Given the timeframe, anyway. Then the CEOs pulled the rug out, insisting Kirkland and Optelligence got first pick."

Will pressed the elevator button. "He got to choose first, then other execs got to go next? Like a draft?"

"No, Kirkland got dibs on *everybody* he wanted." Judd stepped into an empty car. "The other execs had to fight over the poor souls who were leftover."

"Then why was Kirkland still in there, lobbying for more people?"

Judd smirked. "If you're building a kingdom, you can never have enough peasants, I suppose. Or maybe he just enjoys the jousting."

"Wow. Career-pathing at its finest."

They stepped off the elevator and headed for the Jessica Lange room. "So, we're ready to review the leader's guide and other materials?" Judd asked.

"Yep. Anna has copies."

"And that disgraceful Witkowski website?"

"Roadkill. IT squashed it."

Judd pushed open the door as Kari paged through the leader's guide. "We have a particular voice we use for materials like this. Comforting. Contextual. The tone in this guide is—well—aggressive. So aggressive."

Will took a chair at the end of the table.

"Aggressive." Anna gave a sweet smile, holding the guide in the air. "Interesting. Can you please point out the words you see as aggressive?"

Will suppressed a laugh. Something in Anna's response made him picture her as a police psychiatrist, extending a rag doll and asking Kari to show where she'd been inappropriately touched. He thought about the BSIers who would soon be told they were getting transferred from their teams to support strategies they didn't understand. Maybe BSI should provide them with therapy to help with the transition. "I know this is difficult," the counselor would say, "but can you show me on this doll exactly where the company screwed you?"

"As change agents, we must gently persuade." Kari held out her hands, palms up. "After all, employees tomorrow will only be in stage one of Synerpoint's Curvature of Change." She swooshed out of her chair and drew a large semicircle on the whiteboard with a waning green marker.

Kari had clearly downshifted from her day job as an HR generalist into full-on change-manager mode. Will stole a glance at Anna, whose chest rose and fell with intentional breaths. Time ticked away. Will could hear it. Anna likely could, too.

Kari kept talking. "Employees are in stage one." She scrawled a circle under the arc. "They're frozen snowballs who need context on *why* the change is occurring."

"Snowballs," Will repeated, trying to be polite for the greater good. Maybe if Kari felt they took her point of view seriously, she'd be more agreeable to the content in the guide. "Okay, what's stage two?"

"That's when we help them thaw—they begin to see, feel, and embrace the change. Then in stage three, we refreeze the liquefied employees into a newly desired shape. It's a deliberate, comforting process. So comforting."

Anna glanced at Will and patted the table. "You know, it would be great if we had time to sit our little snowballs down and coach them through a comforting, contextual meltdown, but we only have about twenty minutes for each conversation."

Will understood her frustration. Once Anna had relinquished the fantasy of storming the CEOs' office and conceded to the four-day plan, she had worked hard as hell. They both had. Now, at this late hour, Kari kept throwing up roadblocks, and Will needed to keep things from falling apart.

"What Anna's saying," he chimed in, "is that we barely have enough time to discuss the basic changes to each individual's role."

"What I'm saying," Anna clarified, "is that we're going to have to roll the little buggers into the fire. They'll melt just fine."

Kari's cheeks went from pink to bright red. "That's just wrong. So wrong." Her gesturing hands shook. "BSI has invested heavily in the Curvature of Change methodology, and this is exactly the time we should be putting it in motion. If we helicopter up and rewrite the guide—"

Anna opened her mouth, but Will inserted a response before she pushed Kari too far. "I don't think we need to rewrite the whole guide, Kari. Maybe we can just soften some language. Let's work on minimal but impactful edits at this point. Deal?"

"Agreed." Judd reached for the neat pile of papers in front of Kari. "We'll dive into it as soon as we get through our other agenda items. Next, let's talk schedule." He fanned out a stack of spreadsheets and passed them around. "You're looking at this tower's two hundred meeting rooms, nooks, closets, and otherwise available spaces not locked down due to amorous activities. Alphabetically listed by room name."

"There's a Jessica Biel room?" Anna skimmed the list.

"She was born in Ely." Kari didn't look up. Will hoped he hadn't hurt her feelings, but he didn't have time to backtrack.

"I've never been in that room," Judd admitted. "Though I've heard it's much like its namesake: beautiful but empty."

Will managed a tired chuckle. "You've got the rooms. How does the rest of it work?"

"Each room has a schedule broken into twenty-four-minute slots." Judd pointed to his spreadsheet. "Managers stay in the rooms. Employees rotate through. We'll have twenty conversations per room during the day, four thousand total. Every employee gets a meeting, whether or not their role is changing."

"There's no map." Anna flipped through the document. "And no room assignments. It's going to be tough for 3,987 people to find their right place at the right time."

"We'll merge all that data once we get the final org charts." Judd checked his watch. "It's already late. We're ordering pizza if you'll be around."

"I'm sure we will be." Will reached for his vibrating phone as the others reviewed the schedules. "Hello, Lois."

"Mr. Blankenship and Mr. Pruitt would like to see you immediately, William."

"Sure. Do you—" Of course she wouldn't know the topic. Jerry and Ron never told her these things, and she never asked. "Be right there."

Will stood. "Sorry, guys, got to run. You think we'll get all the materials across the finish line within the hour? The CEOs should see it."

"We'll push it," Anna confirmed. "Snowballs to the wall."

Will saw Lois's stern visage the moment he stepped onto the twenty-second floor. She peered out from the next elevator, Ambrosia at her side.

"They're finishing up in Mr. Pruitt's office," Lois said as the door closed. "Wait in the boardroom."

Will paused at the edge of the reception area, allowing his eyes to adjust to the darkened suite. He wandered past the sliver of light under Jerry's office door, toward the empty, unlit boardroom. Once inside, he hesitated at the light switch and then walked to the window.

The nighttime view of the city was spectacular.

He sank into a high-back leather chair, looking down at the neon club lights and theater marquees. The light towers over the Twins' ballpark glowed in the distance. He imagined a line of people gathered outside the new Argentinean steakhouse on Hennepin. A crowd of twenty-somethings with new money soaking up craft cocktails at Prohibition. Couples holding hands on their way to see Jerry Seinfeld at the Orpheum.

People with balanced lives, having fun.

Will envisioned himself twenty-two floors below, throwing open the door to the swanky tapas bar across the street. Hipsters of all ages raised their cocktails in salute. "Will!" Someone handed him a chilled vodka Sprite—no fruit. "Play for us!" a beautiful woman begged, holding out a black Fender. Will nodded, shot the redhead a wink and grabbed the guitar neck. The crowd roared and parted as he—

"Will Evans! Communications guru to the stars," Jerry boomed and clicked on the lights. "Why in the world are you sitting in the dark?"

Will squinted against the sudden brightness. "Just, um, enjoying the view."

"Of the lobby?"

Will realized he'd spun in his chair as he'd grabbed the guitar and now faced away from the windows. "I was . . . ah . . ." Lacking a plausible explanation, he shut up.

Jerry rubbed his eyes as he sat. "I trust everything is ready for tomorrow."

Ron had left Jerry's office and paced the lobby, cell phone to his ear.

"Yes, we're ready. Anna Reed should be emailing you the leader's guide within the hour."

"Who?"

"Anna Reed. On my team."

Jerry gave him a blank look. He had met Anna several times. But Jerry had a knack for remembering faces, not names. He relied on familiar terms like "buddy" and "my friend" along with hearty handshakes and pats on the shoulder. All part of his skilled and grand façade.

"Good, good," Jerry mumbled.

"They can't send someone until Tuesday." Ron ambled in. "Can you believe that?"

"Tuesday," Jerry said. "That's bullshit."

Ron nodded in Will's direction. "The baize on my snooker table."

The three sat in silence for an awkward moment. Ron closed his eyes and twisted his arms together, raising them toward the ceiling. Will hated to interrupt the CEO's textbook Eagle Arms pose—*God knows he needs to center himself, what with his heartrending billiards debacle*—but time and pizza waited for no one.

"I'm sure you're busy with tomorrow's activities." Will resisted the urge to point out, unlike the others in this room, he had real re-org work left to do. "Should we get started?"

Ron's eyes popped open, his gaze locking on Jerry. "This was your call. Go."

Jerry folded his hands in front of him and tapped his onyx pinky ring on the tabletop. "We called you here for a reason, Will. It's time to accelerate Optelligence."

Will raised his eyebrows. *Accelerate it? We haven't even staffed the damn thing yet.* "Can you say one more sentence about that?" Kirkland's catch phrase tumbled out of his mouth, but the CEOs didn't react.

"We need to accelerate this transformation," Jerry clarified. "The Street needs to see fast, substantive action."

"Investments and divestitures." Ron untangled his arms and dropped them on the table with a thud.

Jerry smiled. "Let me tell you a story I think will provide some context and clarity."

"Sure." Will leaned back in the extravagant chair and prepared to be mentored. He hoped this late-night meeting had a point. And that someone downstairs would save him a slice of pepperoni.

"You may not know this, but IBM started as a small company called CTR, selling coffee grinders and meat slicers." Jerry swept a hand across the table. "They eventually changed their name and spent a half-century developing and perfecting mainframe comput-ers before moving into desktops and laptops in the '80s and '90s. That led them into the next wave of innovation: software, services, and solutions. Today, they are essentially a technology and consult-ing company."

Will nodded. BSI had some parallels with IBM, to be sure. But IBM evolved over the course of about 130 years. BSI wanted to flip its business model within a few fiscal quarters.

"So, IBM added consulting to their existing business lines." Will cut to the chase of Jerry's little parable. "I assume you're telling me this because BSI is doing the same?"

Jerry beamed, first at Ron—then Will. "Can't put anything past you, Mr. Evans!"

Ron harrumphed and slid his glasses onto the table. "IBM didn't 'add' to their business lines. Think about it. They don't sell meat slicers anymore. Or mainframes. Or ThinkPads. They shed product lines and the associated overhead and focused on where their industry was headed."

Will's brow furrowed as he glanced between the co-CEOs. "I understand. But IBM had a lot of product lines over the years. We have a pretty lean set of offerings—our core business, Copiers and Office Supplies. And now a consultancy practice."

Jerry raised his eyebrows. "You've got it backwards, sport. The consultancy is our core business now. We're divesting from the copier business and everything that goes along with it."

Will replayed the words in his head. "We're . . . what?"

"We're selling the Copier and Office Supplies business—Flourboxes, land, trucks, systems, existing contracts. It's all on the block." Jerry tapped his ring on the table once more. "This is top secret, of course."

Will's mind blurred. "Of course," he heard himself say.

"Rayzor is the most likely buyer at this point." Ron fumbled into his breast pocket for his reading glasses so that he could better see the screen of his vibrating phone. "We're renegotiating our exclusive distribution deal with them, and they're looking to expand. The acquisition would provide them with an established distribution network and every customer contract we have, across all brands. We gain a significant infusion of cash to invest in Optelligence while showing the Street we're serious about our transformation."

Will closed his eyes for a second, forcing his brain to focus on retrofitting this new, dastardly piece of information into the strategic puzzle he thought he'd understood.

"And serious we are." Jerry raised an eyebrow. "We've got an existing client—a big retailer from St. Louis—already signed up for Optelligence. They love our Technology strategy. No prototype in place yet, and they're clamoring for it! Lyle closed the deal last week."

"So . . . Rayzor will buy our copier business." Will's hands trembled.

Jerry leaned back in his chair. "OfficeWorld is another possibility. But that's a long shot. The only thing we have that OFW might want is Rayzor's distribution rights. On everything else, we're direct competitors. It doesn't make sense for them to buy the whole business line. They'd be more likely to try to beat us head-to-head—spark a price war to batter our margins and drive us out of the business."

"Let them." Ron chuckled. "That'll soon be Rayzor's problem."

Will placed his thumb and forefinger on his pulsating temples. "What happens to the Promisek—" he caught himself. "The Flourbox employees?"

"This will be best for them in the long run," Jerry said. "Sure, the buyer may trim a few layers of leadership. But most employees will end up with a company that's committed to the copier and office supply industry. That's no longer true of BSI."

Ron shook his head. "Let's not get ahead of ourselves, Jerry. Decisions about staffing will be up to the buyer. No promises."

Will looked down at the table. Trimming leadership layers placed guys like Big Al directly in the crosshairs of the new organization. "I have a clarifying question." He steadied his voice. "In less than twenty-four hours, you'll announce the creation of this Copiers and Office Supplies business line, with Sonny Larsson promoted to lead it. Why bother, if you're planning to jettison that part of the company?"

"Simple," Jerry said. "It's easier—and more lucrative—to sell it as an end-to-end business. That way it can operate independently while the buyer works on post-acquisition integration."

Integration. A perfect entry for Will's Communicator's Handbook—in the chapter on smokescreen phrases. On paper, integration signaled a seamless meshing of organizational components, where complementary pieces aligned to create a more effective whole. In reality, it represented a ruthless activity where forensic accountants hunted down perceived redundancies. Followed by a brutal assessment process, pitting employees against one another for a sharply reduced number of roles. See also, Workplace Darwinism.

"And Sonny?" Will asked.

"He'll probably run the thing for a few months." Jerry stifled a yawn. "But the buyer usually likes to put one of their own in charge. Instill the culture and all that. But don't worry; he'll get a soft landing. Hell, I bet he's ready for some extra fairway time anyway."

Will turned his head toward the windows. He blinked hard a few times. "How does this affect the re-org activities tomorrow?"

"It doesn't," Jerry answered. "We had to decide which employees to keep for BSI's future, people who are potential assets for the consulting practice. For those who fall on the copier side—it'll be that much cleaner to make the split when a sale is finalized."

Will's wooziness turned to nausea.

"Listen." Jerry patted the table. "I know what you're thinking, Will."

Will gave him a blank look.

"You're wondering how this affects you. But don't worry. We need people like you to help tell the Optelligence story. You're going to end up on the right side of history, my friend."

The right side of history? These guys had no appreciation for the history of their own damn company. Much less the people who built it.

"No promises, Jerry," Ron repeated, checking his watch against the time on his phone. "Let's move on."

"Right." Jerry turned to Will. "Here's the upshot. We need to make this business as attractive as possible, to get top-dollar for the sale. And that requires more than a fresh coat of paint on the Flourboxes. We need to maintain productivity while also keeping rumors out of the press. Any hint of a sale to Rayzor would scare the other manufacturers like Clarion, PointStart, and Hone. We can't jeopardize existing contracts—or Optelligence—before we reach a principle agreement."

Will felt himself nod as though someone else completed the action. "What would you like me to do?"

"Keep an ear to the ground. Alert us to anything that might hinder productivity." Jerry smoothed down his Monet-print tie. "Or any whiff of a sale rumor."

"I can do that."

"Then we're done here. Remember, keep this confidential." Ron narrowed his eyes. "There's a very small number of people under the tent right now. If there's a leak, we'll know where it came from."

"Of course."

Will left the room and forgot to close the door, but with Lois gone, no one slapped his hand. Feeling numb, he moved slowly through the dark suite, following the illuminated, rectangular path extending from the boardroom doorway. The corridor of light stretched across the carpet and up the opposite wall, highlighting the US map dotted with purple Flourbox pins.

Will blinked hard as he examined the network of warehouses and crews, once a shining example of BSI's ingenuity and prosperity. Now nothing more than a depreciating, saleable asset that had outlived the interest of its owners. Like a rich kid's dollhouse collection.

He shook his head and walked away as the boardroom lights clicked off behind him.

To:	*BSI Corporate
From:	Anita Roswell
Subject:	ALERT: Significant Company Event Today

Team,

As we discussed in our last all-company meeting, we are launching an exciting growth strategy called Optelligence. The success of this ambitious plan centers on our ability to deploy the right resources, in the right places, at the right time. And that time is now.

Today we are reorganizing our corporate teams to build an Optelligence capability. Every employee will have a meeting with his/her manager to discuss this reorganization and, in some cases, changes in roles and reporting relationships. The meeting schedule will be posted in the lobby at six a.m.

Please arrive early to review the schedule and determine your meeting time and location. TEPIL this meeting as 398: Manager-Employee Dialog and/or Goal-Setting.

Thank you for your flexibility and cooperation. Change is always difficult, but I have every faith our employees will rise to the challenge.

Anita

CHAPTER 15

"You're here early." Coffee caught up to Anna in the skyway. "Or didn't you bother going home last night?"

"I grabbed a few hours of sleep." Anna sidestepped a woman in yoga pants.

"You know, my dog barks at me now when I come home. My wife says Butters thinks I'm a burglar because I'm always working late. I think it's the Jesus beard."

His usual, lazy face-shadow had grown into something bushier, giving him the uncanny appearance of a corporate lumberjack.

"Barking at Jesus would be a good band name." Anna suppressed a yawn.

"You see the memo from Roswell this mor—?" Coffee stopped himself. "Of course you did. You probably wrote the damn thing."

Anna indeed had pinch-hit for Will and drafted the executive memo. She tried to inject a subtle dose of poise and empathy into the predawn message—two attributes Roswell, a human manila folder, lacked in real life. Still, Anna loathed the cattle-call approach to the meetings.

Coffee opened the lobby door, and the dull murmur they heard from the skyway became a roar. Hundreds of BSIers crammed the space from the entrance to the reception desk, coffee tumblers and computer bags in tow, vying to get to the meeting lists.

"So much for avoiding the rush," Coffee shouted over the racket. He weaved past Anna and angled for the elevators.

"Aren't you going to check the schedule?"

"Bah," he called over his shoulder. "Someone'll tell me where I need to go."

He disappeared into the mob as people continued to enter from the skyway, jostling toward the spreadsheets. Someone bumped Anna from behind, and her coffee splashed through her travel mug lid onto her white blouse.

Fantastic. Welcome to life's most ridiculous re-org.

Will hurried into the cafeteria and slid into the only booth directly across from the entrance—the most coveted meeting spot in the BSI cafeteria. This seat offered all the critical sight lines an employee needed to flag down a colleague—while also providing cover. Four bushy trees stood in sunken pots a few feet away, making it easy to avoid the leering guard at the security desk, or the back-slapping Albanian maintenance man who considered himself everyone's best friend.

Laptop pushed to the edge of the table, Will dug into his double order of bacon in an attempt to sop up his low-level hangover. He'd spent his precious few hours between workdays with vodka in hand, trying to vanquish his qualms about the impending Flourbox sale and its impact on his friends in the field.

The same sick feeling returned when he woke up, of course. But he couldn't worry about the Promisekeepers today. Not when he had to play maestro to a companywide game of musical chairs while also tending to his own team. *One family at a time, Evans.*

"Jimmy Banker?" A man had sidled up to Will's table.

Will stood to leave. "No, sorry. But good luck."

According to the master spreadsheet, he needed to meet TK in twenty minutes. Will decided to hit the restroom first to get the bacon grease off his fingers and was surprised to find his young employee near the sinks.

"Busy day, huh?" TK moved out of his way.

"Crazy." Will turned on the faucet.

TK leaned over and rubbed his hands from the top of his khaki-covered thighs to his knees, then made the motion again. And again. Will grabbed for a paper towel, realizing TK wasn't drying his hands—the kid appeared nervous as hell. Will scanned the empty restroom and decided to hold his manager-employee meeting right then and there, between the urinals and the sink.

"Hey, your job isn't changing. We got our re-org out of the way a few weeks ago—when Holly, Anna, and Coffee joined our team. There's nothing to worry about."

TK's shoulders fell with a loud exhale. "Wow, okay. Cool."

"I've got some things to take care of today." Will decided the other leader's guide points could wait. "We'll talk more after things settle down."

He patted TK on the shoulder and headed for the elevator bank. The brief restroom discussion had gone so well, Will almost considered ditching the HR-assigned room for his subsequent meetings in favor of urinal-side conversations, awkward as it might be for Holly. Anna, however, would probably kick open the men's room door without batting an eye. He smiled at the thought as he rounded the corner. The scene at the elevators stopped him in his tracks.

An impenetrable mass of employees filled the cramped space, waiting for the next available ride. The bell chimed, and the crowd surged forward. A lucky few made it aboard the packed car; the rest groaned in frustration as the doors slid shut.

Dammit! Apparently nobody on the re-org planning team remembered the 9:00 a.m. antifornication stairwell lockdown, leaving the elevators as the only mode of tower transportation. He shuddered at the realization that, on every floor, waves of BSIers—two hundred more every twenty-four minutes—were trying to get to meetings to learn what the hell would happen to their jobs.

Will pulled out his phone and tapped a hasty email to the VP of Security, urging him to unlock the stairwells. An immediate autoreply informed him the exec would be buttonholed in meetings all day and unlikely to respond. He cursed again and scrolled through his contacts, trying to recall the name of that security desk guy. *Kramer. Kroeger. Creeper.*

Will bolted from the crowd and slipped around the corner and into the maintenance area on the back side of the elevator bank. As he'd hoped, the freight elevator sat unused, overlooked by the hordes. He pressed the down button, hoping Security Guy could free the stairwell without VP approval.

Anna leaned over the sink and scrubbed at her shirt with a sodden paper towel laden with pump-soap.

"Is that you, Marlene?" A voice piped up from the middle stall.

"Mm-hmm," someone murmured from the stall next door.

"I thought I saw you coming in ahead of me. It's me—Anita. We're scheduled to meet later today, but being we're both here . . . I wonder if you wouldn't mind having a little chat now instead."

"Um, I guess."

Anna looked in the mirror, then around the otherwise empty latrine, wondering if this could possibly be true.

"Terrific." Papers rustled in the middle stall. "With the changes taking place in our business, BSI is making adjustments to how we're structured . . ."

Anna's jaw dropped. Anita Roswell, head of HR, held a manager-employee meeting right then and there, between two occupied stalls.

Poor Marlene—whoever you are. Talk about getting caught with your pants down.

Having spent nearly two hours looking for someone with the authority to unlock the emergency exits, Will gave up. Out of options, he headed to his midday debrief with the re-org working team. An opportunity to review the day's progress and hopefully rectify a few things for the afternoon.

He gathered his thoughts on the silent freight elevator ride to eleven. The stairwell lockdown topped his list of things that should've gone better. Also, Security had apparently busted up a potential fistfight between two employees—one guy threatening to pull the fire alarm to release the emergency doors, with another dead-set on stopping him. And that fray in the lobby—the meeting spreadsheets should have been posted throughout the tower.

Arriving on his target floor, Will took a sharp right and opened the door to the Verne Gagne room, squinting into what appeared to be an empty space. His eyes adjusted to the low light. A half-dozen people sat in the dark, their chairs pulled into a haphazard ring. Tibetan meditation music emanated from an iPod speaker. A kaleidoscope of colors and shapes rotated on the projection screen.

"Welcome to the Zen Den. Please join us," Kari cooed. Apparently, she'd forgiven him for riding roughshod over her Change Management principles the night before.

Will froze, blinking as his eyes detected more shapes and forms in the darkness. Another HR underling sat nearby, humming softly. A man in a red shirt wept to himself.

Across the room sat a massage station, flanking a wall adorned with framed photos of '70s-era AWA wrestlers. A woman draped herself over one chair, a male masseuse kneading her shoulders as Mean Gene Okerlund looked on. Mad Dog Vachon and Baron von Raschke—brandishing his trademark claw—stood sentry over the second, unoccupied chair.

"Take a moment for self-reflection." Kari waved for Will to join the circle. "We're spending a lot of time today taking care of employees—right now it's important we take care of the caretakers. So important."

"Um, excuse me," Will stammered. "I just stopped by to tell someone about the stairwell issue." He shuffled back a few wary steps. "But, ah, I'm going to see if I can find someone . . . else."

He snatched a granola bar from the heaping basket of snacks on the side table, wheeled, and dashed out the door. He'd grapple with his feelings another time.

Anna paced outside the meeting room, waiting for Kirkland to finish up his conversation. She checked her texts. Then email. Then Facebook, to kill time.

The door opened a crack as Anna closed the app, trying to stay unseen while peeking inside. She spotted one of Kirkland's elbows on the table.

Anna chewed on her thumbnail. Kirkland likely saw this re-org as an opportunity to plot his Optelligence empire. If so, his org chart would include a chief of staff role. Surely, he wanted Anna to fill it. Why else did Dee Dee set up this meeting? Today of all days?

The door opened wide, and a finance director walked out. He raised his chin to acknowledge Anna. She returned the nod.

"Hello, Lyle." Anna slipped into the small room. "Are you ready for our meeting?"

They had only ten minutes left of their appointment time, but his smartphone had his full attention. "Give me a moment."

Anna sat in the warm chair Finance Guy had occupied and set her phone on the table. Kirkland wore the starched, tailored white shirt he favored. He probably had one for every day of the month. Disposable, executive couture.

"You've seen the new Optelligence org chart?" He darted his eyes from his phone to Anna's face, pausing on the faint coffee mark on her chest. She bristled at the attention.

"At a high level."

He thumbed at his phone while he spoke. "My organization is growing by fifty percent. My new teams need to be brought up to speed immediately, before we start the next hiring phase. You need to be thinking about that."

Anna nodded. "Of course. I've asked Dee Dee to update the email distribution lists, and I've drafted a welcome email you can send. I've also checked with the webcast vendor to make sure we can handle the additional employees logging into your town halls."

Kirkland raised his eyebrows. Anna smiled. She loved surprising him with smart, preemptive strikes.

He checked his watch. "And touch base with NEO. Orientation sessions should be updated with Optelligence information."

"Got it. Is that . . . all?"

"For the time being." He looked down at his phone again.

Anna kept her eyes on him and cleared her throat. "I was thinking, with the re-org, this would be an opportunity to discuss your chief of staff role."

"I've always felt these types of promotions reveal themselves when they're ready."

Anna frowned. *What the hell does that mean?*

"You should also know that I don't appreciate you consistently bringing up this aspirational position." He raised his beady peepers to her. "It would be best if you minimized your distractions and focused performing well in the job you currently hold."

Anna steadied herself with a long, quiet breath. "Is there something I should be doing better or differently?"

Kirkland tipped his head and took on a contemplative expression. Anna had seen it before. He loved imparting his wisdom to her. "You can improve your attitude. I can often tell by the look on your face that you don't agree with me. You need to work on not making that face."

Anna concentrated on showing any other expression than "that face," whatever the hell that might be. She settled on a phony half-smile.

"I need everyone fully on board to make Optelligence a success." Kirkland tapped a manicured finger on the table. "Once the Copier and Office Supplies business line is sold, there will be no fallback position."

Anna tried to mask her surprise, not wanting to get called out for making a "holy-shit-they're-selling-the-core-business" face.

Kirkland's attention, however, had returned to his phone. "Close the door on your way out."

Will thanked Holly, stepped into the hallway and headed toward the cafeteria. He'd made a quick call to Anna an hour earlier, leaving him with one team member yet to contact—Pete Coffee, who had no slot on the schedule. With four thousand BSIers to corral, not shocking someone had fallen through the cracks. He ducked back into the good booth to make the call.

"Talk to me," Pete answered.

"Hey. It's Will. Where are you?"

"I'm at Haskell's, looking for a peaty Aberfeldy."

"Petey who?"

"Aberfeldy. It's a scotch."

Will paused, not sure what to say next. "You're at a liquor store?"

"Yep."

"Why?"

"Like I said, every time I get downsized, I find a good single-malt and toast what I've learned before thinking about next steps."

"Um, Pete. Hate to break it to you, but you didn't get laid off."

The line fell quiet. "Say one more sentence about that."

Will chuckled. "You still have a job. And it's not changing."

"I wasn't on the meeting list. Figured that meant I got the ax again. So I headed home."

"You're still a BSIer, so buy something good. And have a good weekend."

"Sure. Will do, boss." He hung up.

Boss.

Nothing about the last several weeks made Will feel like a boss, much less a good one. He hadn't even scheduled a series of regular team meetings yet. Too much work to do.

Will stared out one of the cafeteria's two-story windows, pondering what to do next. A woman balancing two large stacks of paper passed by, heading toward the exit. Barely in control of her cargo, she tilted to the right and accelerated her pace, trying to keep one of the leaning piles from toppling out of her arms. Despite her efforts, hundreds of loose-leaf pages fell and slithered across the walkway.

Will sprang out of the booth and helped gather the materials.

"Thank you!" the woman gushed. "That was clumsy."

Dozens of Rainmakers streamed past, sidestepping the mess. A type of self-absorption that'd never happen in a Flourbox.

Big Al made sure of it. He had a cardinal rule: "Don't come through the front if you ain't got my back." Will had learned that law his second week on the job, when he ducked under a forklift raising an unsteady pallet of parts. Thing One knocked him clear with a forearm to the chest, sending Will sprawling onto his ass. And saving it at the same time.

Will handed the last few papers to the grateful woman and returned to the booth. Maybe setting up regular team meetings—a task mandated by the corporate handbook—shouldn't be his first priority. Maybe he should run his team more like a Flourbox crew. *Like Big Al would.*

Anna's mind roiled with the sale of the Copier business as she walked to the twelfth-floor Cabin. The BSI tower contained these small kitchenettes on every floor—outfitted with microwaves, refrigerators, and vending machines—and decked out in Northwoods décor. Bennie stood just outside, gnawing on half a Snickers bar.

"I've had this piece of crap stuck to my ear all afternoon." Bennie shook her Blackberry at Anna. The more tired and irritated Bennie got, the more her East Coast accent intensified—a broken dam of harsh vowels and clipped consonants. "Every fucking reporter and their cousin has been calling to find out why we're locking employees in the tower like Rapunzel. But there's no story."

Oh, there's a story all right. But nobody knows it yet.

Bennie put a hand on Anna's shoulder. "It's six thirty, and I never even ate lunch. I'm so wiped I could pass out. You'll catch me if I do, right?"

Anna smiled and had started to respond when Bennie started yelling and pointing at the TV hanging in the corner.

"Judas Priest! They're showing our logo. What the—turn it up, Reed."

Anna rocked up onto her toes and stretched to reach the volume. The scene moved from the news anchor desk to a live shot on the street in front of the BSI tower. The TV volume increased as a reporter interviewed a BSI employee. Anna and Bennie gasped as his face filled the screen.

Sommersby.

"You were inside BSI's headquarters all day," the correspondent noted. "Can you tell us about the chaos that transpired?"

"Well, Nietzsche believed that chaos gave birth to the stars." Sommersby waved his hand. "And BSI is giving birth to a new growth strategy. We're striving to be the market leader in Optelligence."

Bennie let loose a primitive scream that Anna half-expected to shatter the windows.

The reporter continued talking as Sommersby walked away. "Minneapolis police report two 911 calls were made by employees inside the building claiming to be trapped in an elevator without basic necessities . . ."

The camera began a slow pan up the tower as he spoke, the fluorescent interior of each floor becoming visible on the screen. Fourth floor, fifth floor . . .

Bennie scrambled to the window looking to the street below. "Yeah? Oh yeah, fucking Channel 3?" Her breath fogged the glass. "You run a story after we agreed there was nothing to it?"

Her eyes wild, Bennie hoisted herself up to kneel on the narrow windowsill. She lifted her shirt, exposing her black bra. Face and breasts mashed against the window, she thrust both middle fingers high over her head. "You want a shot of the action? B-roll this, bitches!"

Anna took another look at the screen as the camera ascended the tower floor by floor. She dove forward, hooking an arm around her friend's neck, yanking her off the ledge. They hit the floor together and slid across the tile, stopping in a heap against the cupboard. Bennie's ancient Blackberry bounced off the windowsill and rained down on them in tiny pieces of circuitry, plastic, and glass.

"Holy shit," Bennie groaned, staring up at the ceiling.

Anna rolled off to the side, grabbing her elbow. She hoped she hadn't broken her limb, though it seemed to have lost some skin. She looked at Bennie, lying on her back, feet in the air, the tiny keyboard letter "L" resting perfectly on the center of her forehead.

Anna began to laugh, a little at first, then freely and loudly until tears streamed from her eyes.

Bennie howled as well, curling into a fetal position and holding her stomach as the keyboard digit slid off her face. "I told you to *catch* me, bitch—not *kill* me!"

The reporter's voice boomed from the TV overhead. "A BSI spokesperson tells us no jobs were eliminated, describing the activities here today as a fairly typical corporate reorganization."

Making Change: Why Can't Companies Get It Right?

Posted by: Harvey Fredrickson
BUSINESS EDITOR—PIONEER PRESS

The current spate of news generated by local Fortune 500 companies reflects fundamental challenges each faces in maintaining their market position. As pressure builds, they start talking transformation. Or turnaround. Or transition. Call it what you will, it's all about change—and most organizations are not particularly good at it.

"Companies often fall victim to Shiny Object Syndrome," says Ken Adams, University of Minnesota business professor. "They focus on the magical end-state a change is intended to deliver rather than the less-sexy building blocks required along the way."

He cites the recent missteps at Business Solutions, Inc. Sources close to BSI suggest the B2B powerhouse reorganized its corporate staff by plunking thousands of employees into new jobs with little explanation or support.

"This is a classic case of support function failure," Adams explains. "BSI's senior executives articulated a vision, but the HR, communications and training functions fell down in the execution. And it's the employees who pay the price."

What should companies do to avoid the same mistakes? "If you don't have the expertise internally, you need to import it. Hire a firm with a strong change management practice and let them guide you through," Adams said. He cited Synerpoint as a benchmark firm, highly regarded for their ability to help clients implement significant change in a thoughtful, controlled manner.

CHAPTER 16

Moving day followed re-org day, as BSIers scrambled to migrate—cubicle contents in tow—to their new tower locations. It made for a messy Monday, but thankfully lacking the chaos and drama of the previous week—a mild aftershock compared to Friday's quake.

Will dodged a few boxes in the aisle as he made his way toward his new desk. Most of his team's cubicles were in disarray this early in the morning, with one notable exception. Holly's new workspace looked perfectly lived-in.

"What's with the old-school display?" Will pointed to her huge tube-style monitor. "I think my grandparents watched the moon landing on that thing."

Holly tapped a fingernail on the glass screen. "I got it from my friend in Facilities. I hate the way my cube faces the aisle. No privacy. They wouldn't give me another wall. This was the next best thing."

"Smart," Anna added from across the aisle. Her cube held two bulging moving boxes. "And functional. Throw some rabbit ears on that sucker and maybe we can pull in the *Ed Sullivan Show.*"

Will smiled and stepped over the stack of three-ring binders in front of his bare desk. TK stood nearby, repeatedly poking the thermostat button.

"You know that doesn't work." Anna walked into the aisle.

"It's hotter than an Ecuadorian cooking class in here. I turned it down to sixty-three."

Anna reached past him and plucked the box from the wall, revealing no wires curled inside, just a battery for the digital readout on the front.

"What? It's not even connected to anything," TK gasped.

"Of course not." Anna snapped the box back into place. "It's the illusion of environmental control. Employees complain less and work more when they think they can adjust the temp. I learned it at an architecture firm I worked for. It's a productivity ploy."

"Like those stupid collaboration pods the Optelligence teams are using?" Coffee strolled up the aisle and into the conversation. "Typical executive groupthink—let's blow up their jobs and take what little personal space they had. Nothing boosts productivity like anxious employees sitting around an overpriced banquet table."

"I hope we're not getting those," TK said. "I'm kind of a packrat."

"We're sticking with cubes." Will docked his laptop. "We don't need communal furniture to be collaborative."

"Smart man." Coffee tossed his laptop bag onto his chair. "When I worked at Eventall, a guy in our pod ate tuna fish out of a can. With his fingers. He got a collaborative punch in the neck."

"Holly's definitely not a pod-dweller." TK nodded in her direction. "I mean, look at her cube. Did she hire an interior designer or something?"

"A team of Disney forest animals." Anna chuckled.

"I heard that!" Holly called from behind her Zenith console.

"Speaking of chirpy little birds, I hear Sommersby got his ass chewed for talking to the media without approval." Coffee twirled a pen between his fingers. "And he got transferred to HR. So get ready for an influx of die-cut benefits brochures. And fancy websites that don't work. Hashtag: douchebag."

"Fantastic." Anna shot Will a look he couldn't decipher. Hard to believe she'd still be irked about the Sommersby nonconfrontation at the Monk. But that didn't matter now—Sommersby had become Roswell's problem.

"How about all the crazy stuff that went down on Friday?" TK's eyes widened. "I heard a copier client was here for a contract negotiation when our sales rep ducked out to run to his manager meeting. Then a different guy came back to the room and said *he* was now the sales contact."

"That's true," Coffee confirmed. "The first guy was Damien Cavello. He got moved to the Optelligence Sales team. A sales guy with nothing to sell."

Holly stood up to whisper like she had CIA covert op plans to share. "A handful of employees got stuck on the stairs. They got in before lockdown, and by the time they made it to their floors, the doors were locked. And Security is still trying to identify some mystery man who rode the freight elevator all day without authorization."

Will's face got warm. *Thank God that elevator doesn't have a security camera.*

"And some employees left, assuming they'd been let go. One guy from Accounts Payable dropped off the grid and hasn't been heard from since."

Will made eye contact with Coffee, who shrugged.

"It's all part of the legend of Lemur," Anna said.

"Lemur?" Holly asked.

"It's an acronym. L-M-R-R. Life's Most Ridiculous Re-org. Lemur."

"Is that, like, an actual thing?" TK wondered.

Anna smiled. "Listen, this lingo around here . . . 'Take the CER to the BGMs and the NEO for the USOG.' It's like being trapped in an alphabet soup convention. I figured no one would notice if I made up some of my own."

"I'll add Lemur to the glossary!" Holly giggled.

Will waited for the conversation to die down before he walked into the aisle and addressed the troops. "Since we're all here, can we huddle for a few minutes? I have a couple things I'd like to discuss."

Nobody moved. Will nodded and waved them forward. "C'mon. Just stand in the aisle with me. I'm not going to bite."

They meandered from their cubes and gathered around him. Uncomfortably.

"First things first. Rather than a staff meeting, I'd like us to huddle for a few minutes each morning. Check in, see what's on our plates, and get on with our days."

"Oh." Holly scowled. "That's different than the weekly status meeting that HR suggests."

Will expected some resistance. Meetings were a form of legal tender around the tower. More meetings on more topics with more attendees made people feel like their jobs were somehow more important—even if nothing got accomplished. All part of the corporate manual Will intended to burn.

Instead, he called an audible straight from his mentor's playbook. Big Al abhorred meetings—considering them a vestige of the Rainmaker culture. He held huddles every day before the delivery guys scattered for their various routes. And if it worked for BSI's top Flourbox, it'd work for Will's crew.

"Do we still TEPIL this 922?" TK asked. "Because that's the code for team meetings."

"Yes, 922 is fine." Will didn't really care.

"Do we need to prepare materials for these huddles?" Coffee wondered.

"Nope. It's a conversation."

"I could book us a room," Holly offered.

"Not necessary."

"How 'bout the cafeteria?" Coffee suggested. "They have bagels."

"Right here is fine."

"Why don't we s—"

"Why don't we let Will conduct this huddle and see how it goes?" Anna suggested.

Will nodded. "Yeah, let's give it a shot. Today I want to share an idea I've been thinking about. Mull it over, and we'll discuss it more tomorrow."

He paused before continuing. The weekend had finally given him time to wrap his head around the imminent sale of the copier business, the CEOs' need to monitor the Flourbox grapevine, and Big Al's and Sonny's request for help. Fiddling on a guitar always helped clear his head, and he'd spent most of Sunday with a hollow-bodied acoustic in his hands. By midafternoon, he'd landed on a way to accomplish all objectives.

His plan provided a shared project to bond his new crew together. And with a little luck, it might even put the Flourboxes on stronger footing with a buyer, showing the Promisekeepers' value and intelligence.

But with competing interests on all sides and a cloak of confidentiality hanging overhead, he needed to tread lightly.

"It's about Copiers and Office Supplies. We all know Optelligence is getting a lot of people, money, and attention right now. But the CEOs and Sonny Larsson have asked that we ramp up our support of the copier business, too."

"Interesting," Coffee said. "All we've been hearing from Jerry and Ron is Talent, Technology, and Innovation."

"Maybe the re-org has something to do with it." Holly shifted her notebook from one hand to the other. "Now that we have two business lines, they should be getting equal support."

Will tried not to wince. "I wouldn't go that far. Optelligence needs more resources to get going. The CEOs want to make sure the Flourboxes aren't entirely overlooked. And Sonny needs more active support."

"Like what?" TK asked.

"He's lost budget and people, but he still wants to grow the Copier business." Will leaned back against his file cabinet. "He's a sales guy and doesn't know Flourbox ops very well. He wants help connecting with the Promisekeepers. To find opportunities and ideas."

"Won't be easy." Coffee slurped a steaming liquid from a stainless steel tumbler. "Not a lot of trust between Promisekeepers and Rainmakers."

"I get that." Will nodded. "Warehouses and corporate have been battling since the old days. When I started at FB-One—before we expanded across the US—we had a company picnic every summer, with a supposedly friendly game of softball. Jerry's Rainmakers against Ron's Promisekeepers. And every year a fistfight broke out. Every. Year."

Coffee chuckled, and Holly gasped. Will could see Anna's shoulders rise and fall with a sigh. She didn't seem to enjoy interruptions to her workday. Or colorful company folklore.

"That's outta control." TK's eyes widened again.

"It's the way it's always been." Will shrugged. "But after the game, they'd gather around the keg, drinking beer and slapping backs like nothing happened."

Coffee shook his head. "Like a big group of Irish brothers." He shook a fist in the air and adopted an Irish brogue. "If there's nobody outside the house to fight, by golly, we'll fight each other!"

"Exactly." Will pointed at his burly colleague. "But pit them against a common enemy and watch out."

Holly raised her free hand. "Maybe our middling performance can be the common enemy."

"Nice way to put it." Will smiled. "There's history between these teams, but with the right tool, we can help the Promisekeepers get their voices heard. And Sonny will get his corporate teams to listen. We can be the bridge."

Coffee nodded. "If it's simple and easy for everyone, it could work."

"Sounds cool," TK agreed.

Anna didn't shower her praise as quickly. "I'm wondering . . . could you help me understand exactly what we're trying to solve? I'm not sure I get it. Is it a lack of information? Or a lack of places for employees to submit ideas?"

"Both." Will stood up straight again. "Sonny wants insights and information. And Big Al told me his crews need someone at corporate to pick up the phone."

"Like a hotline?" Holly wondered.

"Not that literal," Will clarified. "They want a place or a person to bring their customer issues and ideas."

Anna twisted her bracelet around her wrist. "I hate to play devil's advocate, but I've worked on employee forums in the past, and they're tricky. Let's say we build it. The warehouse employees stick their necks out and trust someone will respond. What happens when nobody answers?"

"Fair point." Coffee took another sip from his tumbler. "That could create a bigger rift between the Promisekeepers and Rainmakers."

Will shook his head. "It's not really a r—"

"And the re-org already widened that rift by formalizing the gap between the haves and have-nots," Anna pointed out. "If Rainmakers don't listen, the new tool is doomed from the start."

"But we're not dependent on only the Sales team—we have corporate teams like us, Legal, and HR." Will narrowed his gaze on Anna. "Promisekeeper input will be valuable for everyone."

Anna raised her eyebrows. "Are you sure? I mean, these are warehouse teams. How much business knowledge can they offer?"

Holly and TK looked at the floor, perhaps sensing a bell had just rung—and they had accidentally found themselves in ringside seats.

"Listen." Will's eyes met Anna's. "The warehouse crews may not have MBAs, but they're smart. They spend more time with customers than anyone, and they know how this business works. At minimum, giving them a forum will get them more engaged because we're finally not treating them like order-takers."

"But isn't that their job?" Anna countered. "Literally. To take sales orders from corporate?"

Will mashed his teeth together. *Spoken like a true Rainmaker.* "I don't think you've been around a warehouse enough to understand what those crews bring to the big picture. I know you're very focused on Optelligence, but we have a responsibility to support our front-line employees, too."

"A lot of people are focused on Optelligence. It's the company's future." Anna placed a hand on her hip. "I appreciate your passion for helping warehouse types, Will, but discussion forums—even if they're simple to build—take extraordinary time and effort to manage. You have to create buy-in, trust, and a comfort level to participate. You have to seed and monitor the conversations . . ."

Will studied his team members as they considered Anna's points, concern registering on their faces. *For fuck's sake, Anna, they were excited a minute ago.* "I get your point, Anna. We can figure that stuff out on the fly—as we build. We'll divvy things up."

"Great," Anna said. "I'm happy to take on some of your CEO work. If it helps with your capacity to work on this new tool."

Will clenched his jaw. "Thanks, but I can manage." He turned to the rest of the team. "We need to get cranking on this. I've got a meeting with Big Al late next week to talk it through—let's get as far as we can by then, okay?"

Heads nodded, and the team started to disperse. Will made mental notes on how to make tomorrow's huddle go more smoothly. *Maybe I should encourage Anna not to show up. Hell, maybe I shouldn't show up.*

He checked the calendar alert on his phone—signaling his regular Mid-Quarter Update with PR and IR at the Monk tonight. A strong cocktail sounded good right now.

"Solid huddle, team." Coffee blocked the others from leaving while stretching his hand into the middle of the aisle. "Internal Comm on three!"

Holly gave him a bemused look, ducking under his arm on the way to her desk. Anna backpedaled and spun into her neighboring cube. Only TK offered to join the cheer—clasping his bony hand on top of Coffee's thick fist—but the moment had passed, and the team's first huddle ended just as it began: awkwardly.

CHAPTER 17

Bennie and Will wandered into the Monk, and Les waved them over from a booth near the open garage doors. They were intercepted by Inky, sporting a black midriff shirt, weathered leather skirt, and dominatrix-style boots.

"We'll have the usuals," Bennie told her over the bar music and clamor. "And I love the outfit! Cute."

Inky dropped her chin. "I don't do cute. I was going for hot."

"Well, I think it's hot," Will blurted without thinking. "It's kind of post-punk urban chic."

Inky looked him up and down, one corner of her top lip raised. He instantly wished he had on something more fashion-forward than Dockers and a purple golf polo—a summer closeout special from the company store.

"So Opie Taylor likes my style. And what's your style, exactly? Upscale hobo-sexual?"

Bennie cackled and led Will to the booth as Inky stalked back toward the bar.

"Giving my paramour a hard time?" Les teased.

"Paramour!" Bennie snorted, sliding into the open seat. "Kitten, she'd chew you up and spit you out like bad tilapia."

"And I'd enjoy every sadistic second of it."

Will rolled his eyes and motioned for Bennie to scoot over. "You've always been a glutton for punishment, Les."

"I work at BSI, don't I?" He patted his hands on the table and looked around the room. "Alrighty, then. Let us commence the official Mid-Quarter PR, IR, and Internal Comm Update. All in favor?"

"Aye." Bennie and Will voted.

Les grinned. "Let's start with PR. What's new with you, my fine Spin Mistress?"

"Caught the porn peddler." Bennie shook a victorious fist in the air. "I mean, we always knew who the little fuck-toad was—finally got the proof and compiled enough paperwork to fire him. He films a bunch of fifth-rate, late-night pornos in our goddamn stairwell, and we worry *he* might sue *us*."

"Was it that Accounts Payable guy with the comb-over?" Will wondered. "That's what I heard."

Bennie shook her head. "Overnight security dude. Richard Danger. Know him?"

"No," Les said, "but with a name like Dick Danger one would suppose he's predestined for porn."

"Or international intrigue," Will added.

Inky returned with the drinks and waters and then sauntered away.

"Damn!" Les marveled. "Those gams, in those boots . . . only a matter of time 'til they're wrapped around my head like a scarf."

Bennie turned her head and held an open hand toward him. "That's the last sick-ass visual my brain needs right now. Good God. I haven't even had dinner."

"Order some cheese curds and charge 'em to BSI." Les reached for his lowball. "Hell, order a round for everyone. No one would notice given the way this company throws money around."

"Crap, now what are we doing?" Bennie raised her eyebrows.

"Let's just say our CAPEX process has turned into a soup kitchen. There's a line around the corner, and nobody's getting turned away."

"Well, we allocated more capital than usual this year, right?" Will asked between gulps of his drink. "You told us all about it—the secret meeting, the CEOs forcing Optelligence down the other execs' throats."

"Yeah, but we didn't plan on people coming back for seconds."

"What do you mean?"

Les swirled the bourbon in his glass. "Take Innovation, for example. It had a total CAPEX budget of thirteen mil this year. Chan immediately sank 9.5 into seed money with a dozen consultants, throwing cash at them to brainstorm growth ideas. Stupid, sure, but it's his budget. Now he's telling our goofball CFO Happenstance we need to establish a Silicon Valley presence with a hybrid think tank/software startup to the tune of thirty-three mil."

He stopped to sample his drink before continuing.

"And Talent tore through two-thirds of their budget already. What isn't earmarked for new-hire salaries is getting spent on an overhaul of recruiting and training. Based on that run rate, they're back at the trough for another ten. And Technology? Whoo-boy."

Les paused for a moment to check—and then ignore—his vibrating phone.

"Technology's an epic freak show. All the warring tribes within IT are trying to outmaneuver each other for funding. Shoring up the antiquated systems to run the business? That's an incremental forty mil, easy. Building the new Optelligence infrastructure—a convoluted web of platforms, applications, and databases that all need to talk to each other? Seventy-five million over the next couple years, thank you very much."

Bennie grimaced. "Holy shit on a popsicle stick."

"Speaking of popsicles, you catch Dee Dee's selfie on Facebook this morning?" Les's shoulders shook with a laugh. "She and one of her meowing multitude, licking the same damn Eskimo Pie."

"Yes!" Bennie shrieked with laughter. "Jesus Sneezus, I'll never be able to unsee that unholy trinity: ice cream, cat spit, and Dee Dee's tongue." She shuddered.

"I found it oddly erotic," Les admitted.

Will halted them with a raised hand. He didn't want a digression to ruin this debrief. Or his dinner. "Back to the soup kitchen. How much does the double-dipping hurt us?"

"Plenty." Les pointed a meaty finger at his colleague. "We're taking cash off our balance sheet for things that should have been part of our operating budget. The analysts are going to blow a gasket when we disclose that juicy little nugget." He ran a hand over his stringy hair. "Thank God for Copiers and Office Supplies. It's not exactly kicking ass. But it's the only part of the company generating a profit right now."

Will sighed while swallowing some of his drink, causing him to cough and grab for a napkin. *Hell of a strategy this company's got going.*

"All right, enough of this wicked-depressing financial bullshit." Bennie smacked a hand on Will's back to help with his choking episode. "Let's talk Internal Comm. Tell us a story, Evans. How goes the new team?"

Will cleared his throat. "Not bad. Still adjusting to managing all these people."

Les pushed his glasses farther up the bridge of his nose. "Adjusting to what? We're glorified babysitters. Wipe the spittle off their faces and sprinkle some Cheerios on their highchair trays. If no one shoves a fork in a socket, it's a good day."

"You're an ass." Bennie glared at Les. "Don't listen to him, Evans."

Les snapped his fingers in the air to call for the waitress. Will could see Inky's eyes narrow with irritation from across the crowded room.

"Seriously." Bennie patted Will's arm. "Anything I can do to help?"

He turned to face her. "Not unless you can get Anna to go with the program once in a while. To stop questioning every damn thing I say or do."

"I see," Les murmured. "Get her to talk less and put those perfect lips to better use."

Bennie jabbed a finger at him. "That's sexist as hell. Don't talk about her like that. Anna doesn't need some pumpkin-headed perv talking smack about her. She's got more brains than most guys at BSI. More balls, too."

Les raised his eyebrows. "Oh, she's ballsy, all right. And smart. Less than a year in this company, and she's gotten herself a golden ticket—if she can stay on Kirkland's good side. And more power to her if she can do *that* without doing *him*."

"What do you mean 'golden ticket'?" Will noticed a stray lemon wedge in his vodka. He fished the offending yellow crescent out and dropped it on the table. *How hard can it be to serve a drink without fruit?*

"Well, Ron and Jerry aren't going to be around forever." Les looked up at the overhead speakers, waiting for Neal Peart's drum solo to finish. "They're both pushing up against a sensible retirement age. And they just gave Kirkland keys to half the kingdom. Don't you think the CEOs are testing him? Seeing if he's capable of taking the throne someday? I'm just saying, good for Anna. She's hitching her wagon to the odds-on favorite horse in the ring."

"Think you can squeeze one more mixed fuckin' metaphor in there, Shakespeare?" Bennie snickered.

Will frowned, picturing Kirkland at BSI's helm, wreaking his own special brand of selfish havoc. Ron and Jerry weren't much better, but . . .

I'd rather stick with the devils I know.

"Back to Anna." Bennie punched Will in the shoulder. "She's questioning . . . what? The meaning of life? Your manhood? What?"

Will shot her a look. "Everything. She questions everything. I'm walking a damn tightrope between the CEOs, Sonny, and Big Al. I came up with a plan to pilot a new tool at FB-One—something that'll make them all happy and do some good for this company. But when I pitched it to my team, Anna tried to shoot it down."

"Why?"

"She said trying to build a bridge between Promisekeepers and

Rainmakers doesn't solve a real problem—and corporate won't participate anyway. Oh, and we should focus on Optelligence instead of warehouse workers." Will flicked the lemon wedge off the table.

Les glanced at Bennie, then Will. "Sorry, my man. But score one for Reed. BSI's doubling down on Optelligence. The Copier business runs itself. Seems like you should prioritize your work accordingly."

Will blanched at the uninvited commentary. But Les didn't know about the Copier business being on the block or the specifics of what the CEOs had requested. And that wasn't the point, anyway. Anna was.

"You're oversimplifying." Will scowled. "This comm forum will help corporate, the warehouses—everyone. It's a great idea. But Anna cared less about helping out than finagling her way in with the CEOs."

Bennie eyed Will's empty glass as she refashioned her hair-bun. "Slow down, Stoli McParanoid. What makes you think that?"

"She said she'd take on some CEO work to—" Will made exaggerated air quotes, "—'help with my capacity.'"

"Oh my God!" Bennie gasped in exaggerated horror. "Anna offered to help with your ungodly workload by doing something she's good at? So you can dick around with your pet project and maybe get a few hours of sleep at night?" She squeezed Will's arm and narrowed her eyes. "That fucking bitch."

Les chuckled at Bennie's performance. Will found her less amusing. For his covert mission to help the Promisekeepers look good for a prospective buyer, he needed every team member's help. Even Anna's. But no useful managerial tips could come from these two. Bennie's friendship with Anna clouded her objectivity, and Les had the interpersonal skills of a picnic ham.

Bennie nudged Will with her elbow. "Listen, mister sister-kisser. Think about it from Anna's perspective. She wants to make her mark, and right now she's trying like hell to hold her own. This company sucks for newbies. And a woman? Under Kirkland of all pompous-ass pricks? Forget about it. You didn't join from the outside like

Anna and me. You came up through the—" Bennie slammed her fist on the table, and bourbon slopped from Les's lowball. "That's it!"

Will and Les lifted all the full glasses within reach—in case she decided to continue pounding on the table.

"You said you're piloting a project at FB-One, right? Bring Anna! Show her what it's all about. She'd appreciate you making an effort."

Will groaned and sipped from his water glass. He double-checked the location of Bennie's fists before setting it back down. "I don't know, Ben. She made it clear she has no interest in that side of the business. I can't have her seeding doubt about this project with Big Al like she did with the team."

"Come on. This is a great idea, Evans. Have I ever steered you wrong before?"

"Actually, yes. You told me I could win Kirkland's respect by being nice to Dee Dee. Now she keeps asking me to join her church—a congregation of seven, worshipping Dixie cups in an abandoned meth lab."

Les guffawed as Bennie clapped a hand to her chest. "Wha—? Me?"

"Or the time I asked you to replace the word 'dialogue' with 'discourse' on Jerry's teleprompter. But you typed in 'dysentery.' And a thousand business leaders left that conference thinking he had diarrhea. So, yes, you've steered me wrong once or twice."

Bennie laughed and dug through her purse. "So I screwed the pooch a few times. Big deal."

Will turned his attention to Les, who worked Inky with every ounce of charm he could muster.

"Let's cut to the chase, my dear. You. Me. Drinks. Aruba. Let me take you away from all this." Les made a grand, sweeping motion with his arm.

Inky cocked her head. "Hate to break it to you, Rip Van Wrinkle . . . but I like girls."

"Perfect! So do I!"

"The difference is . . ." A wry smile creased Inky's face. "I actually take one home occasionally."

The cat-and-mouse exchange captivated Will—Les serving up one clichéd come-on after another, Inky batting each of them away with ease. He became so engrossed that he barely noticed when Bennie set her phone on the table and tapped his arm.

"She's in."

"Uh, I don't think so." Will watched Les plead his case. "She's a lesbian."

"What the hell are you talking about? She's married. To a man. And even if she was gay, she can visit a Flourbox like anybody else."

Will turned back to Bennie. "Why would she go to the Flourbox?"

"To help you with that thing you were talking about!"

"Her?" Will nodded in Inky's direction.

"No, Anna!"

Will couldn't hide his smile now. "Anna's a lesbian?"

"Son of a snitch!" She hit him in the shoulder. Twice. "I just texted her to go with you to the Flourbox. What the fuck is wrong with you?"

Will burst into laughter.

"For the love of meatloaf, Evans," she sighed. "No wonder Anna thinks you're an asshole."

Will turned toward Bennie, his laughter gone. True or not, the comment stung. He had been doing his best with Anna—at least he thought he had. It's not like she made it easy on him, either.

But maybe Bennie had a point. Maybe it was hard being new— getting thrown into the BSI machine with no context and no clue. Forced to sink or swim from the start.

And maybe it made sense to bring Anna to FB-One. Maybe she'd actually get something out of the visit. Learn about the copier business. Meet some Promisekeepers. Cool her jets a little.

Maybe.

CHAPTER 18

Anna found FB-One amid the aging factories and industrial sites lining the northeastern bank of the Mississippi. Will waited on the steps as she eased her car into a parking space and stepped into the morning light.

She noticed his eyes flicking over her outfit as she approached. Male colleagues often gave their female counterparts the micro up-down. Too often, though, these men paired the subtle examination with a salacious half-smile—the look a backyard cook might give a saucy rack of ribs. But Will's version appeared to be innocuous, mixed with a touch of concern.

"Hey." Will nodded at the spike-heeled, sky-blue masterpieces on her feet. "I hope you'll be okay in those. We'll be on our feet a good part of the morning."

Anna smiled. *Confidence over comfort.* "I'll be fine. Should we go in?"

"Let's wait a few, until the huddle kicks off. I don't want to be a distraction."

Anna nodded, determined to be a good team player today. She had a sense she still had to climb out of a hole with Will—after her logical points about the rift between Promisekeepers and Rainmakers seemed to strike a nerve.

But today's Flourbox tour offered a trifecta of new opportunities. A chance to learn more about Copiers and Office Supplies, to see it the way a prospective buyer might view the business. To be a cheerleader for Will's new communication forum—despite the fact that it seemed to be a boondoggle. And to score some runs with Will by showing interest in a place that obviously meant a lot to him—even though he had moved on years ago.

She studied the squat, brick building as they waited. People like Will talked about BSI's original headquarters in almost reverential tones, describing it as hallowed ground. But it didn't look like much.

Will broke the silence. "Thanks for coming."

"Happy to. I've heard a lot about it."

"Les had to come here for an analyst tour one time, and he said he's never recovered." Will chuckled. "He's more of a country club guy. I think this side of the river is too gritty for him."

Anna heard a series of reverberating bangs from inside FB-One. She decided to continue with the chitchat. Try to build a little rapport. "What's the story with Les, anyway? You said he was recently divorced?"

"Yeah, I met his ex at a charity event once—a free-spirited, Renaissance fair type. Reminded me of Stevie Nicks. She was deep into vortex healing crystals."

"That doesn't sound like Les's type." Anna smiled and then cocked her head. "Then again, I guess everything is his type."

Will's eyes lit up. "At one point, she became convinced she was allergic to her own teeth and blew Les's entire annual bonus by having them all pulled."

Anna burst out laughing. "Shut. Up." She reached over and prodded Will's shoulder. "You made that up!"

"God's honest truth." He held up his hand. "I'm nowhere near that creative."

Will grinned, the corners of his chocolate eyes crinkling. He held her gaze briefly and then looked down at his boots, a few strands of wavy hair tumbling across his forehead. His bashfulness made

Anna smile. When he didn't block her Career Trajectory or languish with the other Work-Arounds, Will Evans was completely adorable.

Will cleared his throat. "After the huddle, Al will give us a tour, then we'll see if he has any questions for us about the forum."

Anna nodded, in part to agree, but also to clear her stupid brain. Adorable or not, she reported to him. And they had work to do. "You lead. I'll chime in when it makes sense."

"Sounds good. And I want to prepare you for a few things in there. The FB-One culture is different. It's not"—he glanced again at her pressed blouse and smart slacks—"corporate."

She eyeballed Will's untucked plaid shirt and jeans. He seemed to be afraid she would embarrass him outside the cosmopolitan confines of the downtown tower.

"What do I need to know?"

"Everyone's on a tight schedule. We can't take up too much time. We've got to be brief and to the point," Will paused while she nodded. "And Big Al might not look it, but he's revered like a C-level exec here—so treat him like the CEOs or Kirkland."

Anna stiffened at the implication that she would be disrespectful, but nodded again.

"Also, Big Al gives everyone who works here a nickname—it's a badge of honor. They don't use their real names—ever. So don't bother asking." Will stuffed his hands into the front pockets of his jeans. "It's one of the ways Al instills his team-first philosophy. He says to be part of a great crew, you have to give up part of yourself."

"Got it."

"Let's go."

Anna followed Will through the door, taking mental notes on the cloudy windows, cracked floor, and duct-taped pipes overhead. FB-One hadn't put their paltry "refresh and repaint" budget to good use yet.

The hallway walls held framed posters of the BSI logo, ethics policy, and Optelligence triangle—freshly printed propaganda. "Top Dock" banners, too many to count, ringed the warehouse ceiling—a sign FB-One regularly posted the best results in its region. Quarter after quarter, year after year.

The crew gathered in the center of the massive space. A tall, dark-haired man commanded the attention of forty to fifty people forming a semicircle in front of him. Will and Anna found a place near the back.

"All right, who knows where we're at in on-time delivery percentage?" The man pointed to a flip chart with a hand-drawn grid. Anna spotted the name patch embroidered on his purple shirt. Big Al.

A handful of attendees began shouting numbers until one of them delivered the correct answer: 98.2.

"Ninety-eight point two!" Al jotted the percentage in one of the grid's empty squares. "And what's our goal?"

"Ninety-seven!" the group shouted in unison.

"Why so shy? What's our goal?"

"NINETY-SEVEN!" they roared.

"That's right. We're ahead of the game for the month. How 'bout return trips? Where we at?"

Not hearing the answer he wanted, Al bailed them out. "Three point three percent." He filled in the number. "And our goal?"

"Two point five," the team grumbled.

"*Ooooh* . . . two point five. That's not gonna earn us any extra cheese. And you know that that means: We're going to DEFCON 1. From now until quarter, I want every manifest verified by a supervisor . . . and every load buddy-checked before a single truck pulls away from that dock."

The crew released a good-natured groan. Will leaned toward Anna as Al outlined FB-One's variable expenses—fuel costs, utilities, facility maintenance.

"First day of the month," Will whispered. "He's updating them on their bonus metrics. It's all about efficiency."

Anna nodded and listened to Al break down FB-One's operating budget and which levers would help them obtain their coveted quarterly checks.

"Do you know what the annual turnover is for Flourbox employees?" she whispered near Will's ear.

He shook his head. "Not sure. But well below the national average for similar warehouse-type jobs. Full-timers tend to stick around. A lot of these people have been here twenty years or more."

"All right, shifting gears," Al said. "Time for Big Al's Super Quiz." He waited as a cheer erupted. "First up, a fifty-dollar gift card to Gasthof's. Who can tell me what SG&A stands for and whether BSI's went up or down last quarter?"

Several hands shot up, and Al called on a burly guy with a gray handlebar mustache. "Uncle Silas. What say you?"

"Sales, general, and administrative expenses," Silas recited. "And they were up about fifteen percent due to increased investments in Optelligence."

"Someone's been reading BSI news releases in the shotgun seat." Al handed over the gift card and squeezed his employee's shoulder. "Enjoy das boot of beer, but steer clear of the snuff lady."

Al turned back to the group. "Next, fifty bones in the form of a Visa gift card. Who knows what a comp is, and what BSI's comps have been for the last two quarters?"

Only a few hands went up, and Al pointed to a man a few feet from Anna. "Young Skyhawk, what's a comp?"

"Um, it's related to sales." The young worker looked toward the ceiling as if searching for the answer. "Like, how much we had in sales one quarter compared to the last quarter?"

"Compared to the same quarter the previous year." Al set his jaw and nodded. "But close enough. And what were our comps the last two quarters?"

"Um, flat and minus . . . two?"

"Correct!" Al waded through the crowd to deliver the prize. "You said it's your fiancée's birthday this weekend, right?" Skyhawk nodded as Al draped a weighty forearm across the kid's shoulders. "Well, you take her somewhere nice. And tell her we appreciate her understanding with all the overtime you've been putting in lately."

Goosebumps prickled up Anna's arms as Skyhawk held up his prize. The guys around him hooted and slapped him on the back.

Al noted he chose these quiz questions to explain why BSI's share price hovered near its fifty-two-week low. "Declining sales and higher expenses eat into our profits. And Wall Street hasn't seen enough progress on Optelligence to know if it's going to offset that trend."

Al paused.

"But they don't know what's in here." He pounded once on his chest. "We're gonna show 'em, like we always do." The crew applauded in agreement. They enveloped him in a circle, and Al led them in a group cheer.

"Who's the country's Top Dock?"

"FB-One!"

"Who's always on the clock?"

"FB-One!"

"Who goes beyond and above?"

"FB-One!"

"Who does yo momma love?"

"FB-One! FB-One! FB-ONE!!"

"All right, Promisekeepers, let's break it down and bring it home!" Al shouted above the clamor. A man standing behind a lopsided table pushed a few buttons on a rigged-up speaker box, and AC/DC began thumping throughout the warehouse.

The crew dispersed as Anna tried to quell the emotion rising in her chest. She pretended to adjust a strap on her shoe so Will wouldn't see the moisture in her eyes. *Jesus, Reed, what the hell is wrong with you? Hold it together.*

"Good huddle, huh?" Will said as the music faded out.

"Good." She tried to shake the inexplicable urge to climb into the cab of a truck and go deliver . . . something . . . somewhere.

She and Will stepped back to let people move past them. A stout man in a faded J&R Office Supply jacket grabbed Will's hand to shake it. "Hey there, Frodo!"

Anna raised her eyebrows at the nickname but kept her comments to herself—as instructed.

"Good to see you, Huck. This is Anna."

Huck nodded her way. "Good to meet ya. Big Al said you guys are getting us a Bat Phone—so we can bark orders to the twenty-second floor."

"Actually," Anna clarified. "It's not quite like that. It's an online discussion forum where employees can share customer service information and improvements with their corporate counterparts. We're hoping to implement a pilot with—"

Will winced and cut her off. "I think Huck gets the general idea."

The delivery man nodded and glanced down at Anna's shoes. "Yep, we're a pretty informal bunch."

Shit. Keep it brief. Anna started to apologize but jumped as a deafening, mechanical noise erupted from deep inside the walls—gears grinding, metal pipes clanging—as though a wrench-wielding army was trying to break through the plaster. Anna's eyes darted from Huck to Will. "What the hell is that?"

Huck shook his head and waited—nearly two full minutes—for the ear-splitting ruckus to end. "Trudy. Biggest, ugliest heating and cooling system you've ever seen. Kicks in at 9:08 every morning."

"You barely notice it after a while," Will added.

"She still works—so they won't replace her," Huck said. "Wouldn't want to deprive you corporate types of your free parking and company-store massages."

A warmth crept into Anna's cheeks as another Flourboxer approached, a lean man with ghost-white hair.

"Amadeus." He introduced himself to Anna and nodded at Will. "Big Al said you're creating an idea hotline?"

"Actually, it's a forum—"

"Sure." Will cut Anna off. "Got something to share?"

Amadeus scratched the side of his head, above his ear. "Been asking for this for like a year. I think I should meet with my regional Sales rep monthly to talk about client service and upsell opportunities."

Anna made a mental note of the suggestion. *Simple, smart.*

"Would you mind submitting that once we get this tool up and running?" Will asked.

"You got it. Thanks." Amadeus headed for the doorway, where Big Al signed a clipboard document for some guy with a craggy face and huge headphones around his neck.

Will touched Anna's arm to slow their approach. "Give him a minute with DEVO." The two men chatted for a while, and then Al sent DEVO back to the dock and turned to his guests.

"Hey, old man." Will shook his former boss's hand. "When does the tour start?"

Anna extended her hand as well. "Anna Reed. Nice to meet you."

"Al Jansen." He zeroed in on Anna's shoes as he released her fingers. "You know I can't let you back here wearing those strappy death traps. This floor is crooked as a congressman. You twist an ankle, and I'll spend the rest of the week filling out OSHA forms."

Will started to speak, but Anna responded faster. "I'll watch my step."

"A pallet falls on your foot and my insurance goes through the damn roof," Big Al grumbled.

Anna smiled. "If a pallet falls on my foot, you've got an issue with your block stacking. Even so, I'll sign a waiver that puts all legal and fiscal accountability on me."

Al studied her with narrowed eyes and then turned and gestured for them to follow. Anna sensed Will eyeing her as they walked. He might have been unhappy with the way she addressed Big Al. Or shocked she knew about block stacking. She flicked her hair back on her shoulders. *I'm no warehouse virgin, Evans.*

Big Al led them through the product processing area and loading dock, explaining how things worked as they went. "Trucks are coming today . . . that's why you're not seeing stacks to the roof."

They wound through storage. Rows of metal and wooden shelves lined the floors and walls, many of them empty.

"How much inventory do you keep on site?" Anna wondered.

"In dollars or square footage?"

"Space."

"Thirty-five thousand square feet."

"Why all the Clearys? You're out of most of the other copier brands," Anna prodded.

Big Al strode up to the copier space and patted a hand on the shrink-wrapped machine in front of Anna.

"Cleary used to be our top-seller, but they've slipped in share. Good machines, but they had some issues a while back and never fully recovered."

"They had a big parts recall a few years ago, right?" Anna had done her research on the copier industry. "Something about wire harnesses causing a fire hazard?"

Al nodded. "That's right. Big problem for a company whose tagline was 'First in Quality.'"

"They're one of the few American manufacturers left." Will picked up a wadded ball of plastic wrap and tossed it in the trash.

"The industrial printers traditionally came from the US or Japan," Al explained. "And some still do—Cleary, Hone, and Pointstart. They still sell. Especially to the niches, like small print shops. Can't beat Hone for that. Cleary still has its loyalists, especially for businesses that want the 'made in the USA' label."

He pointed to two rows of empty shelves. "But Rayzor is number one. They led the rise of the Korean manufacturers. Like in cars and CE, these guys established themselves overseas and then stormed the US with quality hardware at unmatched prices. Course, it didn't hurt that Cleary's machines were bursting into flames in offices all over the US."

Anna studied the empty area where Rayzors were usually stored. "Number one in terms of units? Or margin?"

"Both," Will and Big Al said simultaneously.

"There are a couple new European and Japanese outfits now." Al hiked up his Carhartt pants using the oversized belt loops. "Some of them are getting pretty good with the new digital technologies. If one of them comes stateside with good price points, they could give Rayzor a run for its money."

He began a slow stroll up the hallway and motioned for his visitors to follow. Will fell into step beside his former boss.

"What do you think about Synerpoint's spring cleaning initiative for the 'Boxes?" Will chuckled.

Big Al's booming laugh filled the narrow corridor. He told Will exactly what he thought—in a thoughtful, reasoned, and obscenity-threaded stump speech about consultants interfering with his crew.

Anna, a few steps behind, smiled as she listened to the easygoing rapport between the two men. Until her heel caught in a floor crack—"Uh!"—causing her ankle to buckle and sending her reeling sideways into the opposite wall.

Al and Will glanced backward at the sound of her grunt and stumble, but she faked a cough and pretended to be inspecting the wall for peeling paint. *If I break an ankle in these heels, Will would probably beat me to death with one of them.*

They continued on to FB-One's lone conference room, the only closed-door space that held more than two chairs. A tall, plastic plant stood in a dusty basket in the corner, leaning miserably to one side.

"Coffee?" Al offered Anna. "Strong as a farmhand's pit stain— and tastes about the same."

"I'm fine, thanks." Anna nudged her chair up, trying not to cringe at the crusty, white substance adhered to the table's edge.

Will turned to Big Al. "Last time I was here, you told me how we've got a dozen trucks going to 3M every week. How many upsell opportunities and customer requests do you think they're getting each week? Three? Four, maybe?"

"Each week? Try every day," Big Al stood up, stuck his head out the opened door and called for someone named Atticus at full volume. Anna smiled—*To Kill a Mockingbird* was her favorite book. But she kept the commentary to herself. A wiry man walked in the door and stood, fidgeting, until Al gestured for him to sit.

"You were at 3M yesterday." Big Al sipped coffee from a faded, red Gas N Go travel mug. "Tell these good people what you told me about the billing."

The man looked at Anna and then turned to Al. "Is this a legal thing or something?

"You're not in trouble," Al said with a supportive undertone. "Just tell the story, ya lug nut."

Atticus shrugged. "We've got a forty-five-day billing cycle, but their purchase order cycle is thirty days. Their purchasing guy tells me they're better off buying office supplies off-the-shelf than going through us and trying to get their accounting department to cut special checks."

Will nodded. "Did you ask corporate to change the billing cycle?"

"I don't know who to call."

Big Al offered Atticus a cup of coffee from the communal pot before he walked out.

"Like I explained in the overview I sent, the new forum would provide a place to discuss things like this." Will leaned forward. "It's an online version of the hotline you talked about."

Big Al crossed his arms. "What's our assurance from Sonny's team that they'll take my crew seriously? You know we've tried things like this before. Remember that big meeting where my guys brainstormed with Rainmakers? What did they call that?"

"The Melting Pot."

"Right. Shoulda called it the Meeting-Go-Round. Talk in circles 'til we puke on our tennies and then run back to our separate neighborhoods and pretend it never happened."

"That was a one-time event," Will said. "And this is an ongoing forum. Sonny's supportive of this, too."

Big Al turned to Anna, who listened from across the table. "You got awfully quiet. What do you think?"

Anna folded her hands on the table, careful not to brush against the white crustiness, which she'd identified as prehistoric clam chowder. "Many companies are experimenting with internal social channels right now. Piloting with a few geographies is a great way to determine volume and intensity before a full-scale implementation."

Al listened, took a sip from his mug, and then allowed silence to hang in the air for a few moments.

"Will probably should have told you about some of my rules." He dabbed a drop of spilled coffee from the front of his shirt. "When you're in my 'Box, you speak to what you believe—not what you think you should say." He paused a second time. "So. With all due respect, kindly remove the corporate fuck-stick from your ass, and let's try this again. What do you think?"

Anna appreciated the straightforward request, but she hesitated. *If Will blanched at my harmless questions during his huddle...*

"Well..."

Big Al kept his eyes on her. "Spill it."

Anna took a healthy breath. "I think it will fail."

She heard Will sigh, but she forged ahead. "There are several reasons not to do this—including the labor and time involved. The big one, though: there isn't an ounce of trust between Rainmakers and Promisekeepers. You can't build an online tool and expect people will magically embrace it."

She let that sink in for a second. "I also think I'm uniquely qualified to speak for all of the heartless, humorless, corporate trolls when I say most of us don't think Promisekeepers know enough about the business to offer any substantive ideas."

Will cupped his face in his hands. "Anna, you—"

Big Al halted him with a firm look and encouraged Anna to continue.

"But I still think we should try. Because I've seen more engaged, business-savvy employees in the last hour than I've ever seen at corporate. If we can keep this pilot focused on simple suggestions for Copiers, rather than trying to solve decades of hostility, we might win over a few corporate types." *Whether at BSI or whatever company owns this business next.*

She waited while Al considered her comments, hoping he would green-light the project. His approval might help Will overlook her comments about the tool failing. And keep him from strangling her in the parking lot on the way out.

"First off . . ." Al rested his forearms on the tabletop. "Thank you for your honesty. Most corporate trolls aren't that frank—or self-aware enough to call themselves heartless and humorless, much less admit when they're wrong about people. That tells me you've got a good soul underneath the doublespeak and ridiculous heels."

Anna smiled and shot a look at Will.

"Second: I'll agree to this thing for my crew. As long as you commit to getting the Rainmakers out there."

Will patted his hand on the table. "Great. You have my word. And I'll be bringing regular reports to Jerry and Ron about what we're hearing. I'll get you an update on the launch by the end of next week . . . and we can get out of your hair for today."

Amadeus appeared in the doorway with a bakery box. "Sorry. It's Yosemite Pam's B-day . . ."

"Come on in." Big Al sprung up from his seat. "Frodo and Pearl were just leaving."

"Pearl?" Anna tilted her head.

"You may hail from the land of Rainmakers," Al proclaimed. "But there's hope for you. So I'm giving you a Flourbox nickname. Provisional, of course." He turned to Will. "I'll look for that update—thanks for swinging by."

Anna tried to gauge the look on Will's face as the two of them rose to leave. Surprise? Confusion? He shook his head as they started down the hall.

"Pearl?" she whispered, not sure if Al could still hear them. "I don't get—"

"Like I said earlier . . ." Will hushed her. "Don't question it. It's a badge of honor."

They finished the walk in silence, stepping outside and pausing in the parking lot. Anna studied Will, trying to gauge his reaction to the meeting. Did she need to apologize for being so candid? She rolled a few mea culpas around in her head, but nothing sounded right.

"So, um, thanks for coming." Will sounded less than sincere.

"Listen, Will, don't know if I—"

"Don't worry about it. Not quite how I expected it to go, but we got what I came for." He shrugged. "And you got a little something, too."

Say one more sentence about that.

Will started walking toward his car. "See you back at the tower."

Anna watched him drive away, feeling more baffled than usual about BSI. This company had a unique ability to throw her for a loop. She had always tightly managed her professional image and behavior, but BSI had her constantly fighting to control both.

She nudged a piece of broken stair with her toe, taking care not to scuff the suede on her heels. A passing train blew its horn, drowning out her thoughts. Anna turned toward the sound.

She stood, drawn in by the tempo of the rail cars—the familiar, rhythmic clacking that had lulled her to sleep as a kid every summer. The sound of the train and the nearby rumbling trucks put her right back in that tiny house—in the shadow of the Great Lakes grain elevators and the Burlington Northern building where her father served as a supervisor. Until the layoffs. When he lost his job, his pension, and every shred of his self-worth.

After high school, Anna couldn't put enough distance—physically and emotionally—between herself and her blue-collar hometown. A place where careers were measured through the endless succession of eight-hour shifts.

She wanted more. So she left for college. And never looked back.

But as she stood in her two-hundred-dollar, confidence-boosting heels on the crumbling steps of FB-One, she grew more aware how the sounds and smells of this timeworn, industrial neighborhood made her feel. She felt . . . uneasy.

This feels like home.

CHAPTER 19

Will weaved through the Thursday Farmer's Market, looking for TK. They had decided to walk and talk for this week's one-on-one meeting, and Will planned to use the time to refocus on mentoring his young employee—which had again fallen onto his back burner.

Yet as he ventured through the various fruit and vegetable stands, Will couldn't get Anna off his mind. He kept sifting through their FB-One visit from the previous week, trying to decide how he felt about that weird day. And her.

She came across as corporatey on the tour—*nothing too outrageous*—trying to be all smart about the copier business. But got downright erratic when they talked about the pilot. First she's on board. Then she torpedoes the whole thing, saying it'll fail. Then she backtracks again, saying do it anyway. And what does Al do? Green-lights the project and gives her a nickname. To someone who wouldn't know a warehouse from a frat house.

Still . . . she practically flirted with him in the parking lot beforehand, with that playful shoulder nudge. A strange move for someone so formal. But he couldn't shake the memory of that effusive laugh and those bright blue eyes. When she didn't insist on being proper and pushy, Anna Reed was attractive as hell.

Will found TK tasting a sample from a Stillwater honey mead

booth.

"Good stuff?"

"She's a beekeeper, too." TK pointed at the winemaker. "That'd be a killer gig for me. Like, literally. With the whole anaphylactic shock thing."

"Yeah, stick to communications." Will followed him back onto the sidewalk. "Keyboards rarely kill."

"Can't believe I got you outside." TK grinned as they walked. "It's good for you to see daylight sometimes."

Will felt guilty for not working through lunch as usual but happy to be stretching his legs and feeling the sun. TK had a point. *Daylight is good.*

TK frowned. "Should I TEPIL this as a Work Off-Site or a Manager-Employee Dialog? It's kind of both."

"Either is fine." Will sighed. "A walking meeting was a great idea. Let's take care of business first, then we can talk about some developmental stuff." He patted TK on the shoulder. "I promised Big Al an update on the Chatterbox tomorrow—can you give me an update?" Hearing the forum's name out loud, Will still didn't love it, but there wasn't time to get fancy with the branding.

"It's totally up and running on the dev site. You can send him and Sonny the link if you want."

They stepped into the shadow of a high-rise, where TK paused to browse a table heaped with bread. "IT's doing the security check—fast, like you told them. I think they're kind of pissed we didn't have them build it." He smelled a loaf of rye and put it back on the pile.

Will smirked. "We didn't want to get caught up in their Perpetual Scoping Cyclone."

"What's that?" TK laughed.

"IT's standard operating procedure—basically, a circular flurry of useless activity. Phase one is always scoping—collecting requirements, setting a timeline, and getting the plan approved. Then they bring on more resources, people whose way of adding value is to revisit the plan and recommend a more detailed scoping phase."

Will nodded at a BSI employee who passed them—a face he recognized from the hallways. "When that's done, you think you're finally ready to start building. But—oh, wait—the second scoping phase ate up most of the budget. Then half the project team rolls off until the next fiscal year when more money can be allocated. Now it's been a year since the original project was approved, and what do you think happens during the budget process? Start all over by scoping it again."

"A year—that's crazy," TK said. "Our freelance guys built the Chatterbox in, like, twelve days."

"That's great, because we need it operational in two weeks. I want to get ahead of the upcoming earnings release."

TK nodded. "How do you think results will be this quarter?"

Will hesitated. He wanted to be honest with TK but stop short of scaring the kid. "Well, the Optelligence strategies seem to be taking the scenic route, so we don't have much of a story to tell. And the Street wants a nice, clean transformation story with lots of new dollar signs attached. So there's a good chance the news will be disappointing. But if we have the Chatterbox up and running, we can get a read on what employees are thinking and provide some additional information if necessary."

TK slowed to accept a sample of almond milk from a girl holding a tray of cups. "Funny, I never knew business was like dominos." He tipped his head back and downed the dairy shot. "All the strategies have to line up and fall into place before a company gets any credit."

Will shrugged. "Dominos is too linear for BSI. Remember that game Mousetrap? It's more like that. You flip the lever to roll the ball, which turns the crank, which spins the wheel . . . and eventually the cage drops down on the cheese. Well, we don't get any cheese from the Street until we start generating revenue by selling the new Optelligence services. And we need more new people to sell these services, but we can't hire the people until we have something in place to sell . . ."

He left out the part about divesting Copiers and the Flourboxes—

which would be the first lever flipped. The thought still cramped his gut like a kick to the torso.

"Mm, cheese. I wonder if there's a cheddar vendor around here." TK stepped off the curb.

"Will Evans!" Hearing his name being called from a distance, Will stopped in the middle of Sixth Street and turned in a circle, but he didn't see anyone he recognized.

"Will! Over here!" A man inside a white food truck waved to get his attention. The side of the rig was adorned with red lettering: *Kilanowski's Sausage and Meats, A Minneapolis Tradition Since 1964.* Will took a few steps closer, TK close behind.

"Hey, it's Jasper." The freckled man removed a white hat, revealing a shock of strawberry-blond hair. He pointed to the name on the truck.

The name finally clicked—a former college classmate.

"Hey, Jasper," Will called. "How are you? Been a long time!"

"Yeah, long time." Jasper replaced the hat and extended a hand. "What are you up to these days? Working at the Strib?"

"No, I'm at BSI. Business Solutions." Will nodded in the direction of the office tower. "Never followed through on the journalism career."

"Yeah, well, I'm not at ESPN either." Kilanowski laughed. "Hey, check this out. You guys gotta try this."

He pulled a large sausage off the smoky grill, grabbed a knife, and sliced medallions onto the shelf in front of him. He stabbed one of the pieces and extended it toward Will.

"It's our new apple chicken brat," Jasper gushed. "Made with real chicken and ground crab apples from the Riggleton farm up in Osseo. You've never tasted anything like it."

Will looked at the circular meat dangling from the end of the massive butcher knife and didn't know what to do. *Do I take it off with my fingers? Wait 'til it drops into my hand? Lean in and eat it off the blade?*

He shrugged and plucked the hot bratwurst off the knife before popping it into his mouth.

"Damn, that's good." He chuckled as he chewed. "The apple is amazing. TK, you need to try one."

Jasper speared another piece of sausage and held it out. The sample dropped off the knife, but TK reached down and snatched the chunk out of the air, inches above the sidewalk.

"Nice grab!" Jasper laughed.

TK shrugged, tilted his head back, and tossed the meat into the air, catching it in his mouth. "I'm pretty good with flying food."

Will stepped aside, allowing a waiting customer to claim an order. Jasper handed the man two steaming brats and a bag of Cheetos.

"I remember you talking about your family business. But you said you'd rather put a skewer in your eye than sell sausages on the street like your dad." Will winced at his poor choice of words. "Sorry. I mean, you said you wanted to go in a different direction."

"Yeah, I thought I did." Jasper leaned out the window. "Thanks," he called to double-sausage guy. "I was young. Full of piss and vinegar. And I was gonna show my old man and everyone else. But I couldn't see what was right in front of me—this good, honorable business. People love our stuff."

"I can see why," TK said with a toothy grin. "That brat is fan-freakin'-tastic."

Jasper stabbed another meat sample and held it toward TK as he spoke. "Yeah, there was a time I thought slinging sausages was beneath me. But there's something to be said for sticking to what you know and being damn good at it. And you ask anybody . . . the Kilanowski family knows sausage."

"You'll get no argument from me." Will reached into his pocket to retrieve his vibrating phone.

A text from Bennie: *"Call me ASAP, need ur help fast."*

"I've got to make a quick call." Will stepped away from the truck. "Jasper, this is TK. TK, Jasper."

He hit Bennie's number, hoping for another typical overreaction to something dumb. Like the time she called to vent about Dee Dee doing a full-on breast self-exam in front of the women's locker room mirrors. Classic Bennie story, full of vulgarities and disturbing imagery, with a damn funny payoff—she canceled her company gym membership on the spot. But hardly a code-red emergency.

She picked up after half a ring. "Evans! Holy hell—where have you been?"

"Hey, I got your text fifteen sec—"

"No time. We're taking a red-hot poker up the ass, and I need you."

"Bennie, slow down. What the hell are you talking about?"

"Rayzor. They're dropping us, Evans. Holy fuck."

"Dropping us?" Will steadied himself against a light pole.

"Dropping us! Effective immediately, we no longer sell, represent, service, or look at their fucking products. We're dead to them—they're going to jump in bed with OfficeWorld. Exclusive contract. They're announcing it in twenty minutes. This is bad, Evans. Real, fucking bad."

Will looked back at the food truck, where Jasper used a spatula to launch brat medallions into the air, with TK catching them in his mouth like a trained seal. A few onlookers clapped appreciatively.

"Jesus," Will mumbled as Bennie hung up. He shouted over to the Kilanowski truck. "TK, we gotta go. Sorry."

Jasper waved with his spatula. "Swing by again sometime!"

Will weaved back through the market, trusting TK to keep up. Maybe TK had a point about this, too. BSI's business strategies might as well be dominos. Lined up precisely—until a trusted partner pulls a fast one and all the pieces fall in the wrong direction.

"Everything okay?" TK shouted.

"No," Will called back. "Everything is definitely not okay."

BSI: Watching the Wheels Come Off

By Rodrick Timmers
Forbes Contributor

BSI's quarterly earnings release delivered a waterfall of bad news today. The most devastating news had been announced two weeks ago. Rayzor, the company's top copier supplier — in terms of revenue and margin — ended the relationship between the two companies. BSI's co-CEOs Ron Blankenship and Jerry Pruitt called the loss "a natural transition as we pursue a more diversified business model."

Rayzor attributes the split to its inability to negotiate an extension of its exclusive distribution deal with BSI. Talks broke down when BSI missed a payment for goods Rayzor had already delivered. Whether driven by a cash crunch or wielded as a negotiating ploy, the snafu spooked Rayzor into ending its relationship with the embattled Minneapolis company.

Ultimately, Rayzor landed a lucrative deal with OfficeWorld (OFW) — a New Jersey dealer with a flair for the less dramatic — to exclusively handle its product line.

Making matters worse, BSI reported a loss of ($.03) per share in the quarter, compared to a Street consensus of $.01 to $.04 per share of earnings. In addition, the company reported taking cash off its balance sheet to fund and accelerate Optelligence. Insiders suggest much of that capital was directed to Synerpoint, as BSI has become increasingly reliant on the consulting firm to guide and direct the Optelligence transformation.

Finally, BSI noted its copier business line — when broken out from total performance — turned a smaller-than-expected profit of $.01 per share. Astute investors will note these results reflect a quarter with nine weeks of Rayzor-backed performance. With Rayzor now out of the picture, BSI's path to profitability is unclear.

BSI's share price plummeted 23% today — the second consecutive quarter the company has experienced a double-digit decline.

CHAPTER 20

"Evans, you hear about this MX bullshit?" Bennie's voice blasted from the phone the instant Will picked up.

He shifted the phone to his left hand and continued scrolling through Chatterbox comments with the right. "MX? Say one more sentence about that."

"Some Japanese manufacturer. Supposedly 'the new Rayzor.' Some idiot trade blogger is poking around—last thing we need during earnings week. Pretty sure he's only fishing. You hearing anything inside?"

Will continued scanning the Chatterbox. "Nothing of substance. People know we need to replace Rayzor, but nobody's naming names."

Calls like this had become a near-daily occurrence in the weeks following Rayzor's dumping of BSI. Will and Bennie compared notes on rumors, brainstormed reactive messaging, and in general tried to keep the company story from unraveling like a cheap sweater.

"Well, shields up, Sulu." Bennie talked over the sound of another ringing phone. "If this asshat runs something, the mainstream media will jump all over it."

"Damn, that'd stir things up." Will leaned back in his chair. "Not only for us, but it could hurt talks with potential partners, too. Can you kill it?"

"Fuckin' A. That's all I do these days. Kill stories. I'm a tabloid button-man. A goddamn publicity sniper." She gasped. "Ooh, Publicity Sniper would be a great band name . . . I have to text Anna. Hang on."

Will turned his attention back to the Chatterbox, grimacing at what he saw. He knew the FB-One crew would have concerns about the earnings report but didn't expect such blunt and biting comments. They ripped BSI on a number of fronts, contrasting every internal message with conjecture in the media. They mocked the CEOs for calling Rayzor's departure a "natural transition." Lamented the ballooning price of Optelligence. Bitched about Synerpoint pulling strings and lining their own pockets.

Normally, Will would've dived in to defend BSI. But the complaints had merit.

Bennie's voice came back on the line. "You there?"

"Yep."

"You hear about Fred Kathan going to OfficeWorld? They bought out his noncompete."

"Yeah." Will lowered his voice. "Not surprising, right? He was the account manager on Rayzor for years. But going straight to a competitor. I suppose he got the victory parade, huh?"

"Kirkland made sure of it. Waited 'til next morning and then had two security goons perp-walk the dude out. Right through the main lobby as the huddled masses were showing up for work."

Will shook his head. "Wow. You getting calls about that?"

"Nah. But if the talent poaching ramps up, sure as shit, some jack-wagon will file a story. So now I've got to jump on that—start calling all the hacks on our beat, remind 'em that people leave companies all the damn time."

Bennie's voice had an irritated, determined edge. Will imagined her as the knight at BSI's front gate, wielding her sword against the marauding media horde. While he'd been safely hiding out atop the tower with the other milksop nobles. He looked again at the cynical comments on the Chatterbox. *Maybe it's time to strap on some armor and go save the villagers from themselves.*

"Hey, Ben, how do you steer reporters away from negative story ang—"

"Got to go," Bennie interrupted. "My phone's hoppin' like a one-legged hooker at a televangelist convention."

Anna stepped into the Dino Ciccarelli room and surveyed the space. The table resembled a giant hockey puck emblazoned with the venerable North Stars logo and ringed by a set of replica arena seats. She selected one facing the doorway—13C—and folded down the plastic seat before settling in.

Will stepped through the doorway and plopped into a seat, out of breath. "Sorry I'm late. Got caught up with Bennie." He dropped his phone onto the hard rubber table. "I need your help."

Anna raised her eyebrows. She had assumed Will called her here for a reprimand. Peyton had blown a gasket over a Kirkland email Anna had ghostwritten—providing his team context and steadying the waters after the awful earnings news. But Anna hadn't routed it to Peyton for approval. And why would she? *I don't need Synerpoint's approval to communicate to our own damn employees.*

"What's up?"

Will laced his fingers behind his head. "Not sure if you've been on the Chatterbox, but we need to turn it around. Show some positive progress."

Anna nodded, making sure to think through a potential response. *Turn it around. How the hell do we do that?* Will had launched it at a terrible time—right after Rayzor's defection. Although she hadn't been deeply involved with its development, Anna had been poking around on the site. Ugly stuff.

Will must have detected her hesitancy. "I know you have a lot on your plate with Kirkland and Optelligence. But we made a promise to Big Al, Sonny, and the CEOs."

"Oh, the issue isn't my capacity." Anna sat up a little straighter. "And I know we made a commitment. But . . . have you been out there? Some of Sonny's guys are getting trolled pretty hard. His Sales reps started calling it the Bitch Box. I think most of them dropped off. I doubt they'll be back."

Will's phone buzzed on the tabletop—a text from Coffee. He ignored it. "I know. That's why we need people around here who can tolerate the bitching and encourage Promisekeepers to submit ideas like we heard at FB-One. I can't be the only one. We should both do it."

"We?" Anna pointed at herself and then Will. "But we're not the people they need. They need Sales reps or execs—people who know the issues and have the authority to help."

"To them, we're all Rainmakers. Corporate. That's what matters." Will rubbed the back of his neck with both hands, his toned arms exposed by his short-sleeved shirt.

Anna shifted her gaze to the logo on the table. For the second time, Will's looks distracted her, and she didn't like it. *Focus, Reed.*

"This won't be easy. We've got to be thick-skinned but also sensitive around certain topics. We'll have to be . . . careful." Will looked at Anna, stressing the word "careful."

She wondered if he'd ever forgive her bluntness with Big Al. But she nodded in agreement.

"Good." Will fidgeted in his chair. "I also have some confidential information I need to share. It's the sensitive topic I just mentioned. And it can't go past this room."

Anna nodded again and held her breath. *Now what is this company doing?*

Will leaned forward, steadying his hands on the edge of the puck table. "There's a bigger reason the CEOs split the company into two business units. We're selling one of them off. The Copier and Office Supplies business—the Flourboxes, the Promisekeepers, everything." He frowned.

Anna relaxed her shoulders. Thank God this wasn't a new bombshell.

"I know. Kirkland told me on Lemur Day." She furrowed her brow, reviewing the timeline in her brain. "Wait. When did you learn they were selling off the Promisekeepers?"

Will flinched a little, and she chided herself for her insensitive word choice.

"The night before Lemur."

"But you still went ahead with the Chatterbox?" Why on earth would he put this much effort into this forum when he knew the Promisekeepers were all but gone? *You're smarter than that, Will.*

"Of course. The CEOs asked for it. They want to monitor employee chatter. Make sure no rumors get out and ruin the deal. Besides, the Promisekeepers deserve to have their voices heard, regardless of the state of the—"

Will's phone buzzed again, and they both looked down at the screen. Someone named Beth—no last name. The color drained from Will's face. He grabbed the phone, ran his thumb over the answer button as if unsure what to do, and then clicked to silence it.

"Do you need to get that?" Anna watched as he set the device on the table, eyes glued to the screen until the name disappeared. His natural color washed back into his cheeks.

Who's Beth? Someone important. A colleague or casual friend would have a last name attached. *Sister? Girlfriend?* Anna realized with some embarrassment she knew nothing about Will's personal life. But it's not like he'd bent over backwards to learn about hers, either.

She prodded them back to business. Where they belonged. "I still don't understand. Why not push back on the execs or come up with something simpler—like a phone hotline? Something we could set up and walk away from. Especially now."

Will looked up from his phone and narrowed his eyes. "Walk away? Especially now?"

Anna tilted her head back. *Why does everything I say to him seem to come out wrong?* She leveled her gaze on him. "What I'm trying to say is, with Rayzor gone and the stock slipping, BSI is looking to cut costs everywhere. You've seen all the notices coming out of HR, right?"

"Yep, cuts to travel and corporate perks. And Sommersby wrote that shitty email about no more fresh flowers in the lobby." His tone became more abrupt. "What's your point?"

Anna paused. Her honesty about BSI's troubles always seemed to shatter his rosy view of the company. She needed to be downright delicate.

"I've seen this happen at other companies, Will. It'll be death by a thousand cuts for employees. Expense accounts, lunch budgets, all the little things that make corporate life more tolerable." Anna kept her tone soft but steady. "But at the top of the house, they need to find material savings—big buckets of money—fast. So they're sure to jettison Copiers as soon as possible. Find any buyer they can."

Will appeared to be considering what she said. His eyes locked on hers, his expression neutral. Anna tucked her hair behind her ear and continued.

"Let's think it through. The copier contracts and the Flourboxes would go for sure. But anyone whose job is to support the Promise-keepers could be cut, too. Like people working on the Chatterbox instead of Optelligence."

Will leaned back in his faux arena seat. "I get it. You think we should be looking out for ourselves, making sure we land in a good spot."

"Exactly."

"From a team perspective, I agree. I'll do everything I can to look out for my crew. But I'm not going to abandon the Promisekeepers just to save my own ass. At BSI, we take care of our own."

"It's not about abandoning anyone, Will. It's about making smart decisions based on facts. And the fact is, the Promisekeepers aren't going to be part of this company much longer."

Anna thought about Big Al and his crew—earnest, hard workers who cared about the company and each other. No matter what Will believed, Anna did want to help. Hell, she was practically the daughter of a Promisekeeper. Her dad and his guys broke their backs for every dollar they earned, giving most of their lives to the railroad. And when they got laid off, it shattered them. She'd wanted to help her father, too. But she couldn't wish away or stop the inevitable and couldn't help a man who didn't want it. That's when she knew—*sometimes you have to save yourself.*

Anna reached over and patted the table in front of him. "It's really admirable what you're trying to do—build a bridge between the Promisekeepers and Rainmakers. But it's no small gap. It's a continental divide, and it's getting wider every day. You've got to make sure you're standing on the right side when the break becomes permanent."

Will exhaled, a twitch in his jaw. "Listen, everything will work out. It always does. So I'm going to keep working the Chatterbox and ride this thing out."

Anna sat back in her chair, dumbfounded by his passive approach. Leaving his future to chance. Hoping for the best. Hammering away on that damn bridge until the tectonic plates under the company shifted so hard he fell into the abyss.

"You don't have to prove anything to anybody, Will. You're not the captain of this ship—you don't have to go down with it." Anna heard the emotion in her voice but didn't care. Will needed a wake-up call. "And you know what?" Her heart beat faster than normal. "When a captain goes down with a ship, it's because he makes a *choice.* He's not just lounging on the deck, 'riding this thing out,' and then—oops—he accidentally drowns."

Will looked down at the table, moving his head side to side. Like a pitcher shaking off signs from his catcher. He appeared to be searching for what to say—and censoring himself at every turn.

"I approach things differently than you do, Anna. No amount of pushing is going to change that."

Anna stared at the floor. She began to wonder if she had driven the wedge further between them. Again.

"I'm only trying to help." She tried to sound persuasive, but she worried she came across as soft. Weak.

Will fixed his eyes on her, his voice low but firm. "I know. But that's not the help I need. I need you on the Chatterbox. Like I said before." His teeth clenched again.

Anna studied his face. *I guess we're done here.* "Fine."

"Just pop out there once or twice a day, and be visible, okay?" Will gathered his things and stood to leave. "You don't need to be the face of it. And I promise to do everything possible to help you land with Optelligence when everything shakes out." He paused. "Deal?"

"Deal."

Will swiveled and headed toward the door. Without thinking, Anna called his name. He took his hand off the knob and turned back to her.

She hesitated. *Don't make it worse, Reed. Just let him know . . .* "There's no shame in saving yourself, you know."

Will's face didn't show any emotion. "I know. And I know you don't understand it. But that's exactly what I'm doing."

CHAPTER 21

"What a bunch of garbage." Anna clicked to close her web browser. The week-after media coverage of BSI's quarterly earnings made her sick. She popped open the Chatterbox to see what the Promisekeepers had to say today.

She had been visiting the forum, just as Will had asked. Tentative at first—holding back her opinions and personality—Anna had found a groove with the warehouse guys, surprising even herself. Scrolling through the comments, she noticed an FB-One Delivery driver had just posted a link to a particularly ruthless article about the company.

Anna typed a response. *"Not criticizing you for sharing an opinion, big guy. But the blogger you cite is a paid shill—his firm holds a boatload of OFW. Journalistic equivalent of a baboon flinging poo. Here's a more balanced view."* She attached a link to a reputable financial analyst's report—not exactly a glowing review, but at least grounded in facts—and clicked to publish her comment.

Almost immediately, her post earned a response by Lee Miller from FB-061: *"Right on, a-reed . . . glad your listenin and givin some strait talk . . . but aren't rainmakers supposed to filter out bad words like poo? or isn't that your doody?"*

Anna laughed at his silly response and rated up his comment.

The Chatterbox had been gaining steam with Promisekeepers from across the country as Big Al and his crew forwarded the site to far-flung colleagues.

"Hey! You have some things on your desk."

Anna looked up to find TK's lanky arms hanging over her cube wall. A white tee—frayed around the neck—peeked from under his black dress shirt. Anna smiled. *Tall Kid would rather spend nine bucks on a microbrew than a Hanes three-pack.*

"I finally had some time." She sipped from her coffee mug—her third refill that morning.

TK studied the reference books on her shelf, her Chia-Head-turned-penholder and the framed photos of major league ballparks—Fenway, Wrigley, and Target Field.

"No pictures of Erik?"

Anna forced a smile and kicked one of the cartons under her desk. "Haven't unpacked that box yet."

TK pointed to her postcard of the Minnesota Twins' spring training facility. "Hey, is that Fort Myers?"

"Yeah. Good eye."

"My dad and I have been there three times. He's always had season tickets, too. I grew up at the Dome."

She opened her mouth to denounce the concept of indoor baseball, but he reached over and picked up a small crystal bus from her desk.

"What's this?"

Anna turned in her chair and smiled as he ran his fingers over the detailed replica.

"I got that from the president of Federated Financial. I started there in college—as a communications intern."

"Why a double-decker bus?"

"Long story."

TK didn't appear anxious to go back to his cube.

"Federated was establishing a presence in the UK," Anna explained. "Expanding globally was a big deal for them. They were planning to spend millions on TV commercials, newspaper ads—a marketing blitz. I was invited to the New York meeting where they were choosing the final campaign creative."

"That sounds great."

"I was told to sit quietly and observe." Anna watched TK turn the bus over in his hands. "The discussion came down to which image they should use to represent the company: the Concorde jet or a double-decker bus. Everybody, of course, chose the cool, powerful, supersonic jet."

"Sure. The bus is slow and old-school, right?" TK bobbled the crystal figurine for a second but recovered and gripped his long fingers around it more tightly.

"True." Anna nodded. "But I had this overwhelming feeling the jet was a bad idea. I spoke up and described how the bus was the right choice. It's stable, timeless, and iconic . . . and accessible to everyone, not only millionaires. The bus *was* Federated. The president liked what I said, and he changed his mind and went with the bus."

TK's eyes widened. "So the president made a million-dollar decision based on input from an intern."

"Multimillion," Anna corrected. "I was pretty convincing. A few weeks later, the ads began to run. And then the Concorde crashed in real life, killing everyone on board."

TK's jaw fell open. "Shut. Up. I got chills."

"The accident happened two days after our bus ad hit the *Wall Street Journal*. Mechanical failures grounded the entire fleet. The Concorde reappeared a few years later, but the business never got over the damage to its reputation."

TK carefully returned the Waterford Crystal bus to her desk. "Without you, they would've used the Concorde and been totally screwed."

"Yes, they were grateful."

TK rested his chin on top of Anna's wall as he stared at the knick-knack. She considered returning to the Chatterbox, but he appeared to be formulating a thought.

Anna took another sip of coffee, wrapping her chilly hands around the warm cup. BSI's Facilities engineers must have overestimated the power of the gentle early summer sun and decided to mount a counteroffensive by launching a polar vortex from the tower vents. Hell, they probably used one of TK's amateur weather models to calculate the impact.

"You must've felt strongly . . . to speak up like that," he finally said. "How did you know the bus was the right thing?"

"A little bit of logic, I suppose. And a strong gut feeling."

She considered sharing the story of her family influence—her father's Lovejoy logic and her mother's Willum intuition. Over the years, she had turned the tale into a cocktail party anecdote. An amusing way to explain how she'd embraced the rational side of her father's family, despite her need to marry away the deplorably fuzzy Lovejoy name. "Some people wed for love," she'd say, "but I married to obtain a name that better suited me." Partygoers with martinis and gimlets in their hands always laughed.

But TK didn't need the full backstory.

Anna nudged TK's arm. "You have to trust your instincts. Be brave enough to put yourself out there."

TK wandered back to his cube. "Guess so."

Anna took a sip of coffee and scrolled through more Chatterbox pages, surprised to see a new entry under Customer Service Ideas—the only entry there, in fact. Posted by Amadeus.

"Delivery drivers should meet w/sales reps to discuss service & upsell opps."

She remembered the first time the white-haired guy offered the suggestion at FB-One. *Still valid. Simple. Practical.* If she could push it through Operations, she'd show Will she'd gone beyond monitoring the conversations—to actively helping the Promisekeepers.

Anna clicked over to the company directory, looking for someone with Field Ops in their title. "Maggie Sanderson—you'll do for now." She dialed the extension. Maggie picked up, and Anna promised to only take a moment before explaining the suggestion.

"Oh dear," Maggie sighed. "It's pretty complicated. The Flourbox bonus program is based, in part, on being on-time. So we can't mess with their delivery hours. And meetings before or after their normal schedules would result in hundreds of thousands of dollars in overtime across the country."

Anna played with the curly cord of her antiquated desk phone. "I'm aware of the bonus metrics, but can't we change the delivery schedule to allow for an occasional meeting? Without impacting anyone's income?"

"Oh, dear," Maggie sighed again. "The whole system is like a chain reaction, with each part of the process dependent on the one that came before it—from staging to loading to drive times . . . all the way through to the guaranteed day and time customers receive their deliveries. It would take months to reengineer all that. Maybe years."

Anna politely ended the call and braced herself for the on-ramp to HR's highway to hell. Someone deep in that cauldron of tortured souls had to know how to adjust the Promisekeeper bonus plans. After getting bounced between three flighty generalists, she spoke with a director on the Rewards team.

"Actually, the Flourbox incentive plan would be only one of the hurdles," he explained in a raspy voice. "Our salespeople get commissioned for obtaining new customers—not talking about old ones. Sonny isn't going to be hip to any meeting that steals time from chasing leads. We'd have to alter the bonus structure for Delivery crews *and* the Sales commission model." He chuckled, which caused him to hack out a wet cough for a few seconds. "That would require an act of God. Or more impossible yet, Lyle Kirkland."

"Good to know. Thanks." Anna hung up and took a drink from her now lukewarm coffee.

So . . . all roads lead back to the Elf King.

She started to head up the aisle but paused when her phone vibrated with a group text—from a number she didn't recognize.

"Lottery Alert on 15. Operation jackpot. Commence recon ASAP!"

Anna frowned at TK. "Hey, did you get this weird text? About the lottery?"

TK snatched the phone from his desk and looked at the message. "Oh, wow! Meatballs! You want to go down there?"

Anna had no idea what TK meant, but his childlike enthusiasm made her giggle. "What?"

"It's Les's code." TK stepped out of his cube to look at Anna's phone. He pointed to her tiny screen. "See? Lottery Alert—that means someone in the tower is holding a potluck lunch, in this case on the fifteenth floor. Operation jackpot means a crockpot of barbecue meatballs—because, you know, nothing's better than that."

Anna took a step backward and looked TK up and down. "I'm sorry, but I have to ask. Are you people crazy?"

"Not at all." He reached over and snatched a color-coded spreadsheet from the wall inside Coffee's cube. "There's almost always free food somewhere in the tower, and nobody's better at finding it than Les. It took a while to figure out his codes, so we created this handy-dandy cheat sheet." He turned the laminated document toward Anna. "Code Crocker always refers to baked goods. Because, well, Betty Crocker. Could be birthday cake, banana bread, whatever. Tuxedo Junction is leftovers from a catered executive lunch. Can be tricky to get into the boardroom with Lois circling, but so worth it—gourmet sandwiches, pasta salads, chocolate truffles. You get the picture."

Anna glanced at the other codes and descriptions and then pushed the document onto TK's chest, giving him a playful push backward. "You better get going then. After all, nothing's better than meatballs, right?"

"Right!" TK spun and power walked toward the elevators.

Anna shook her head and turned her focus back to the Amadeus idea. A solid business case could get this approved by Kirkland. And in creating one, she would demonstrate her ability to fill his damn chief of staff role.

She hurried into the open elevator and used her phone to decline and reschedule her slate of afternoon meetings. Entering the busy cafeteria, Anna plucked a premade chicken-strawberry salad from the express lane and rushed back upstairs to work on the proposal. Holly hunched in her cube eating a homemade sandwich with TK standing nearby—sucking sauce from his fingers. Coffee sat at his desk clicking through a dense PowerPoint deck, a plastic bowl of barbecue meatballs cooling nearby.

"Well, you gosh-darn cockamamie piece of shipwreck!" Holly's high-pitched wail caused the others to peer over their cube walls. "Stupid, mother-loving security requirements!"

Coffee gave Anna a knowing look before turning to Holly. "Lemme guess: stuck in the password cycle of doom?"

Holly stood up from behind her oversized monitor and raised her arms in exasperation. "I've used every piece of memorable information I ever acquired—grandchildren, nephews, former neighbors, US presidents, and indigenous plant species. I'm tapped out."

"Make something up," Anna suggested, as TK nodded in support.

"I'll never remember it." Holly frowned at TK, who seemed oblivious to a red smear of sauce on his jawline. She snatched a towelette from her desk dispenser and marched over to scour the residue from his face. Holding his chin in her hand, Holly turned his face to inspect both sides for further traces of barbecue before returning to her seat.

"Well, whatever you do, keep it simple," Coffee advised. "A couple years ago I started using Chinese provinces. Big mistake."

"Oh, the heck with it," she said to no one in particular. "I guess I'll go with Russ Meyer films."

Anna watched Holly for a moment. Her bighearted friend hadn't seemed herself lately. Maybe the company's increasing craziness—Optelligence, the re-org, and now the cost-cutting—weighed on her. At least she had TK to fuss over, to take her mind off things.

Right now, though, the Amadeus idea called. Anna sat back down and finished calculating the math. An impressive figure. So much so, she decided to ask Coffee to double-check her work.

Coffee ambled over with the meatball bowl in his hands. He leaned in to read the document on Anna's screen, as she warily eyed the saucy meat orbs—hoping they didn't end up on her favorite A-line skirt. *The Saucy Meat Orbs. Not a bad band name.*

"Really? That's pretty aggressive." Coffee pointed to the eight-figure number.

Anna nodded. "I calculated one new sale for each client—based on average revenue per sales transaction."

He set the sticky bowl on her desk—precariously close to her keyboard—and licked a few of his thick fingers. "Well, that ARST number skews a little high because a copier is several grand, even though we do more volume in less-expensive products like paper and toner. That's where you'd get most of your sales lift—in supplies—so I'd reduce the revenue projection. And maybe you should include only the Minneapolis area. There's still big sales potential—but we wouldn't roll this nationally right out of the gate."

"Smart." Anna grabbed her calculator. But she planned to include the national numbers, too. A prospective buyer for the Copier business would want to see potential impact across the chain.

She added the metro area projection, put a footnote on the revenue number, and emailed the perfectly succinct, lucrative proposal to Kirkland and Dee Dee.

Will hustled past and darted into his cube. She hadn't seen him in person or on email all day—and wanted to tell him the news.

"We got our first real suggestion on the Chatterbox." Anna stood to get his attention. "Remember Amadeus and the meeting he wants with drivers and Sales reps?"

Will nodded as he grabbed a folder from the hanging rack on his desk. "That's great. It's a start, right? One of us should jump out there and thank him for posting it. We can highlight the idea in the next CEO update."

Anna gave him a wide smile. "Actually, we might have progress to report by then. I put together a business case and sent it to Kirkland."

Will stood up straight and spun around. "What? Why?"

Her smile faded at his alarmed expression. "To move the idea along. It'll look even better for us and the Promisekeepers if we show action."

"But an idea like that is more complicated than you think."

"I know. Delivery bonuses, Sales commissions—I did my homework. We're only talking one or two hours a month."

"But what about the executive bonus plan? It's a roll-up of those two plans."

Anna frowned. "Say one more sentence about that."

Will shook his head as he checked his watch. "A change to the Delivery and Sales plans would affect every exec's compensation, including Kirkland's. And I'd be very careful about fishing around in that guy's wallet."

He took a step closer to her cube and lowered his voice. "This idea would take a hell of a lot of work—and the meetings might be temporary, with everything going on. I'm not sure Kirkland or anyone else would see value in moving mountains for it to work." He sighed. "Look, I'm glad you're on board with the Chatterbox, but if we're going to work together on this stuff, we have to work together on this stuff."

Anna swore under her breath as he walked away. *Damn it, Reed. You jumped the gun.*

She reached for her desk phone, certain she could convince Dee Dee to delete the email before anyone saw it. But her cell phone vibrated first.

Kirkland.

She steadied her nerves and snatched it from her desk. "Hello, Lyle."

"Saw the brief you sent."

Anna swore to herself again. She had trained Dee Dee to print all Internal Comm requests and place them directly in Kirkland's tiny hands at the first possible opening. The approach not only got Anna's materials in front of the exec as expeditiously as possible, but the very act of an assistant hand delivering a document created an air of urgency. The trick worked well at previous jobs. But her gut told her this time it would backfire.

"What do you think?"

"It's deeply flawed. It doesn't align with any of our critical focus areas. The ARST calculation is at least twenty-five percent too high. Too many operational, compensational, and technological changes required to make it happen. By my count, fourteen distinct and critical processes would need to be altered. We would be downright foolish to embark on this."

"The business case might not be completely buttoned up," Anna protested, "but I thought the concept was worth exploring. An incremental lift in current contracts—"

"It's a distraction and not where I want you spending your time. Particularly in light of the delayering effort, which will drive work your way."

Anna froze, wondering if he'd said what she thought she heard. "I'm sorry—what effort?"

"You'll learn more at the appropriate time."

"Of course." She looked to the ceiling. "Thank you."

Anna clicked to end the call. Delayering. Executive code for layoffs. Typically utilized when companies planned to thin their middle manager ranks—often after an economic downturn or industry shakeup. But BSI's troubles? Self-inflicted.

It's like this company is beating itself to death with a Stupid Stick.

CHAPTER 22

Thursday morning came too early for Will. Running late due to a malfunctioning alarm clock, he now couldn't find the notebook he'd placed on the desk a second ago, his phone was ringing—again—while Coffee rubbernecked over the cube wall.

"Are we huddling this morning . . . or?"

"Oh shit. Yeah. I mean yes," Will grumbled. *Whose idea were these damn daily huddles, anyway?*

He grabbed his phone and jumped into the aisle to join his waiting team. "Hey, I'm late for a meeting, but let's do a quick round-the-horn."

He scanned his crew, standing in a loose semicircle. They looked like hell—overworked and exhausted. A pang of guilt edged into his gut. He'd been preoccupied with company issues and not helping his team manage the growing demands on their time.

"Listen, gang, we've been putting in a lot of hours." He slowed his delivery. Whatever Judd wanted to meet about could wait. "It's been crazier than usual around here. Thanks for holding it together."

He gestured to Holly with his phone. "Holly . . . great job keeping the Talent work moving. I looked at the recruiting materials last night. Nicely done."

"Thanks." Holly blushed. "Pete wrote the background info for the new Sales positions." She reached over and nudged Coffee's arm. "Thanks for the help."

Will nodded toward TK, who looked out of sorts in a wrinkled chambray shirt. "This guy was up all night stress-testing the Chatterbox after IT moved it to the new server." Will gave his employee a fist bump. "Nice work. Got a call from Big Al on the way in. Said it's running 'slicker than snot on a glass doorknob.'"

TK grinned and rubbed one eye. "You and Anna are the ones putting yourselves out there."

Coffee nodded. "You're the Fred and Daphne of the Chatterbox—helping Promisekeepers unravel the mystery of the Ambivalent Tower Dwellers."

"It's been good." *Frustrating, time-consuming, and as bumpy as hell . . . but good.* Will spied his missing notebook on top of his file cabinet and slipped it into his laptop bag. "We're finally getting some meaningful ideas and discussion."

Coffee smirked. "I thought you two were competing for Rainmaker of the Year or something—but it's hardly a fair fight. The warehouse guys have taken quite a shine to Ms. Reed."

"The bar is pretty low." Anna rolled her eyes. "Half of them have never talked to a girl before."

"Actually, Promisekeepers are trained not to converse with women—it's a productivity killer," Will kidded. "Mostly because we're so bad at it."

He glanced at Anna, wondering if she grasped the joke's subtext. Their last few interactions felt strained, and he assumed a good part of the blame. She didn't make things easy on him, but as her manager, he needed to make things work. He'd hoped her Flourbox visit would act as a turning point, but they still hadn't found any kind of groove.

Will checked his watch. "Anyway, thanks—your work's making an impact. And I'm sorry, but I've got to run. Shoot me a note if there's anything else."

"Before you go . . ." Holly stepped forward, blocking Will's path.

"There's another round of HR efficiencies coming. Important stuff."

"I heard they're selling the company jet." Coffee blew away the steam from the top of his mug. "The CEOs have to start flying commercial. I'd love to watch Ron try to cram his oversized boardroom booty into seat 32B."

"Oversized boardroom booty." TK yawned. "Band name?"

"More like an album title," Anna suggested.

"Or the world's least appealing porno," Coffee added.

Holly shot him a disgusted look and turned back to Will. "They're targeting benefits. And not just company store perks like Exfoliation Fridays. Big things like the 401(k) match and tuition reimbursement."

"Dammit," Coffee muttered. "That stuff hits Promisekeepers the hardest."

Will's chest tightened. The unfortunate news kept coming. "Wow . . . that's bad. Do you need help, Holly, with the announcements?"

"I'll probably need help handling Sommersby—he's involved with all that stuff, you know. But if you're busy, Anna can probably lend a hand."

"Great. I'll check in with you later." Will started down the aisle again, Anna at his heels.

"I know you're running off. But I wanted to offer my help with the efficiency communication. I have experience."

Will nodded, checking his watch again. "Yeah, Holly just said she'd bring you in."

Anna's heel caught a seam in the carpet, and she lurched a little as they slipped around three people holding an impromptu hallway meeting. "This isn't about Sommersby. It's . . . the efficiencies."

Will sighed. "What are you talking about?"

Anna's eyes darted between him and the people in the hall. She grabbed Will's arm and pulled him into the office assigned to Salvador Chan. The guy had ever deemed BSI important enough to visit. Will had forgotten Chan existed. Again.

Anna clicked the door shut. "I'm talking about the layoffs. These things become huge comm projects—too big for one person to handle alone."

Will's head spun, and he placed a hand on the wall to steady himself. "Layoffs?" he managed to sputter.

Anna's palm flew to her forehead. "Oh shit! I thought you knew. All your closed-door meetings with HR . . ." She swallowed hard. "Shit."

He looked at his watch again without even seeing the shiny bezel or ticking hand. BSI's onesy-twosy, cost-cutting efforts must not be enough. With Rayzor gone to OFW, the Copier business had no prospective buyers and a product line with a massive crater in it. Anna had nailed it—the CEOs needed big pools of money to cut.

"Will." Judging by the concern on her face, she had tried to call him back to the moment more than once. "I'm sorry. I thought you knew. I'm sure this is really difficult for you."

Will's mind continued to race. *When? How? How many people?* Completely distracted, he barely noticed Anna's hand on his forearm.

"What else do you know?" The thick gold band of her wedding ring felt cool against his skin. He gently pulled his arm away.

"Nothing. Kirkland let it slip by accident. I thought maybe you . . ."

Will shook his head and thought about Judd waiting for him in the Laura Ingalls Wilder room. *Maybe this is why he wanted to meet.* "Sure. Thanks. I've got to go."

"I need your help," Judd blurted as Will walked in, closing the door behind him. "For the first time in BSI's history, we're planning workforce reductions."

Will made sure to feign surprise and then settled into a chair as Judd laid out the details.

"It's pretty bad—about ten percent across the board." Judd

slumped in his unfinished wooden chair, looking defeated. "They're keeping the working team small. Cuts are coming fast."

Will rubbed his face with his hands, unsure what to do or ask. Part of him wanted to kick his replica pioneer chair away from the ungodly expensive, custom-made antique table—and leave this Little Flailing Tower on the Prairie in his dust. He'd get his old Flourbox job back, happily riding in a truck and carrying a clipboard. If they weren't selling off the trucks and clipboards.

Judd continued filling in the details. ". . . There are two ways to handle layoffs. The best is a *M*A*S*H* approach. Surgical. Carve out redundancies and eliminate unneeded work—and the people associated with it."

Like people working on the Chatterbox instead of Optelligence. He remembered Anna's comment in the Ciccarelli room.

"But the CEOs chose the peanut-butter method—spread the pain evenly across all departments. Fast and efficient, but not particularly strategic."

"What about those one thousand new Optelligence roles?" Will felt a spark of hope. "We wouldn't have to lay off employees if we cut those new openings."

Judd shook his head. "Already in the plan. All open positions have been frozen."

"Damn." Will looked up to the ceiling, processing. "Who's leading the charge on this? Oh, no—Synerpoint?"

"Even worse. They've brought in KPK. Another big-time consultancy, specializing in reductions in force."

"I haven't seen any new green badges around."

"And you won't. KPK does their work virtually, except for a few partner types who rocket straight up to twenty-two to meet with Ron and Jerry. This firm has layoffs down to a science. A bloodless efficiency, one might say."

"Of course," Will muttered. "Killers always hide their faces, right? Their approach is a twenty-first-century version of an executioner's mask." He tapped his index finger on the table a few times. "If our finances are in the hole, how can we afford another consulting contract?"

"There's no up-front cost. KPK gets a percentage of the labor savings."

Will rubbed his throbbing temples. "Ah. The deeper the cuts, the bigger their payday. Perfect."

"You're going to hate this, Will." Judd leaned forward. "As much as I do. But KPK is handling the communication. It's in their contract—they produce all manager scripts, employee notices, news releases."

"Are you kidding me?" Will's stomach churned at the thought of a faceless off-shore agency churning out templated drivel to tell his colleagues and friends they're losing their jobs.

"And the content is about what you'd imagine. Stilted, impersonal, and generic. They don't know our culture or history—and they sure as hell don't know our employees." Judd sighed again. "Since I'm on the project team, all the comm is coming through me. Can you help edit the materials from behind the scenes?"

"Of course."

"Only a small number of people are officially under the tent."

"Don't worry. Nobody needs to know. I don't want you to get in trouble. I get it's not personal."

"Okay, good." Judd lowered his voice, even though no one else sat in the conference room. "But, Will, get prepared for what's coming. When I say it's ten percent across all teams—I mean all teams. Even Internal Communications." He reached over and patted his colleague's arm. "You're going to have to lay off one person."

Will bent forward in his chair, nearly bumping his head on the table after this second sucker-punch of the morning.

Holy fuck. Now it's personal.

CHAPTER 23

Will hustled through the near-empty skyway, laptop bag bouncing off his hip. He didn't have to navigate the usual herd of corporate zombies at this early hour, allowing him to make good time on his way to a follow-up seven a.m. meeting with Judd.

The companywide layoff plans had continued to steamroll ahead over the last several days, and Judd now needed more help with KPK's materials. Will welcomed the diversion. Being busy kept him from dwelling on his own team's fate.

He cruised through the quiet BSI lobby, stepped into a waiting elevator and pressed "11." He headed for the Judy Garland room, a munchkin-sized nook on the only stretch of yellow carpet in the building. Judd had joked he liked to meet in Garland, given his status as a "friend of Dorothy." Will had to Google the reference.

With KPK's wretched, robotic attempt at FAQs in front of them, he and Judd discussed how to provide helpful language about BSI's inaugural layoffs, adding context that didn't make employees want to jump off a bridge.

"HR and Legal have agreed to use 'reduction in force,' or 'RIF' for short," Judd explained. "No 'layoffs,' no 'downsizing.' Certainly not 'rightsizing.' That's dumb—sounds like a diet. Anyone saying we're 'ventilating the organization' will be shot on sight. Also on the never-never list: 'termination,' 'firing,' and 'position elimination.' And don't even dream about calling it 'mandatory retirement.' Employees of a certain age would sue our socks off." Judd lifted an oxford in the air for emphasis.

Will scribbled notes on the pad next to his laptop. "So 'imminent ax-swinging'—that's out, too?"

Judd smirked. "Hey now. Dark humor in horrific situations is kind of *my* thing."

"Sorry. Didn't mean to step on your argyle-covered toes." Will clicked over to the most recent FAQ doc on-screen. "I've got a couple things on version nineteen. Employees will wonder why we used KPK instead of Synerpoint. Let's hit that head-on."

Judd nodded. "Truth is, our relationship with Synerpoint is practically incestuous. They're so deeply imbedded that we didn't trust them to keep their mouths shut about slicing the payroll. Plus—and you didn't hear this from me—I suspect we might be revisiting the cost and scope of Synerpoint's current contract." He leaned back in his chair. "Can you turn that into something that'll pass muster with the lawyers?"

"Due to the confidential and sensitive nature of these changes," Will spoke and typed at the same time, "BSI retained the services of KPK, an external firm with expertise in this specific area. Going forward, all consulting contracts and agency fees will undergo a thorough review to ensure the services rendered align with BSI's priorities."

Judd smiled and took a sip of iced coffee. "Brilliant. Do you think we need to explain who KPK is?"

Will pretended to type an answer, his fingers dancing above the keyboard as he spoke. "KPK has revealed themselves to be the dregs of the consulting industry—faceless, soulless humanoids who have been puppeteering the RIF work from an undisclosed location, dictating tactics and demanding obedience as if they were seated at the hand of God."

Judd laughed out loud. "Damn, you're good. But let's save that particular piece of content for the post-RIF, drowning-of-sorrows at the Drunken Monk."

"Agreed. But to create a more cohesive synergy with external comms, let's be straightforward about how we arrived at the ten-percent headcount target." Will cringed. *Jesus, I sound like such a corporate douche. Stupid consultants—stripping the humanity out of everything they touch. Including me.* "I mean, Bennie will need that info, too—for the press."

Judd finished another sip of cold caffeine. "My guess is Ron and Jerry had a large dollar figure in mind. And ten percent across the board is easier than dealing with the executive infighting. Can't you hear it? 'How come so-and-so had to cut only eight percent when I had to cut twelve?'" He chuckled. "It'd be like that WKRP episode when the DJs get drunk on-air to show the dangers of drinking and driving. Venus Flytrap gets completely bombed, and he's like . . ." Judd lolled his head side to side and slurred his words for the payoff quote: "'Cop's got a hat. I want a hat.'"

Will managed a smile and mulled how he'd spin that weak rationale. He hated being two clicks removed from the project's nerve center. Judd had been gamely smuggling out documents and relaying information, but Will found it difficult to convert secondhand news into persuasive copy.

"Listen, Will, you're helping take care of all employees through this—thanks for that. But have you taken time to think about your own team? One head, right?"

"Not yet." Will stared at his laptop screen. He'd been avoiding those thoughts. Focusing on the greater good kept his mind off his team's looming loss.

Judd leaned in. "I know it's difficult. And I don't have any easy answers. But don't leave this to the last minute. Take some time, get it right. And not to be too melodramatic, but decisions like this can define a leader—especially a new one—and you don't want to be a Columbia. Or a Jigsaw."

"A what?" Will looked up.

"A Columbia—like the space shuttle. A guy who screws up one pivotal thing and brings the entire crew down in a ball of flames." Judd winced at the explanation. "A Jigsaw leader preys on the fears of his employees, pitting them against each other to see who wants to survive the most."

Will didn't find the analogy helpful. "*Nice.*" He sighed. "They teach you that in HR sensitivity school?"

"Sorry. What I'm trying to say is . . . if you haven't identified that person yet, you could probably use some guidance on the decision criteria."

Will looked at his friend for a moment, amazed at Judd's ability to avoid any reference to actual people in this discussion. *Silly me. I thought I had to fire a human being. Turns out all I need to do is slice the payroll. Cut a head. Isolate the decision criteria.*

"Remember, this isn't personal." Judd jiggled the ice in his cup. "We're not letting people go because we don't like them. We have to drastically reduce costs, or this company could be in serious trouble. We're eliminating hundreds of jobs in order to save thousands. That's not a line, it's the truth."

Will crossed his arms. "Yes, we have to get our costs in line. But I'm never going to agree this isn't personal. This is going to be intensely personal for a lot of people."

"True. But look at it from a business perspective. You need to assess the talent on your team and keep your highest performers—the people who can adapt and thrive in a chaotic environment. Think about it. Many of our people and processes will disappear. It'll be crazy for a while."

Will nodded. Crazy? Not even close. *It's going to be a suck-fest.*

"As someone who's been through this before, at other companies, let me give you another piece of advice." Judd folded his hands on the table. "When you're in the room on layoff day, do *not* stray from the leader's guide. Say exactly what is in your script, not a word more, and not a word less."

Will frowned. "That seems like an awfully cold experience. I'd think we'd want to be a little more—I don't know—human."

"Here's the thing. It's a highly emotional environment. And the goal isn't to provide a good experience—because no matter what, losing your job stinks. The goal is to inform the person, which the script does, while also protecting the company. If you apologize or try to explain why one job gets cut and another doesn't, you put BSI at legal risk. Every manager has to provide the exact same justification and message to every employee. Period."

Judd cleared his throat. "In short, if you go off the script, you lose control of the situation. And these situations need to be tightly controlled."

"A tightly controlled situation," Will grumbled. "Nice." He looked at his watch. *Ten minutes until I have to be upstairs.*

"You know me pretty well, Will. I'm not a coldhearted bastard. The first time I had to let someone go, I worked for a company where the policy was to have HR do it—the manager wasn't even in the room. I had to fire Violet from Accounts Payable, who'd been there twenty-seven years. Only two years from retirement. I was young as hell and emotionally distraught at the idea of firing anyone, much less this sweet, old lady."

Judd spun his coffee cup on the table. The ice ratted again inside the clear plastic. "She walked in the door, and I couldn't bring myself to read the script. I started to break down. I told her I was sorry, that she didn't deserve to be treated like this. That she should be allowed to retire with dignity from this company she had faithfully served for so long. By the time I finished, I was openly weeping—a mess."

"Jeez, what happened?" Will could feel Judd's pain—like they both now sat in that room with the woman.

"She yelled at me." Judd broke into a raspy voice to mimic Violet's delivery. "'What the hell are *you* crying about!? I'm the one who should be crying. But I'm not because I'm thrilled to be walking out of this miserable company. And with a severance package, to boot!'" He chuckled before continuing. "She started to storm out of

the room but stopped at the door and said—I'll never forget this—
'You better toughen up, Cupcake, or you're never gonna last in this
business.'"

Will burst out laughing. "I'm sorry, Judd, but . . . wow."

Judd smiled. "I know, right? Great lesson. And something you
should keep in mind. Expect the unexpected. You're going to have
a conversation with every member of your team, whether they stay
or go, and someone will be the curveball. The person who reacts in
a way you wouldn't have predicted. One more reason it's critical to
follow the process."

Will's phone chimed with a calendar reminder, and he started
to mentally balance the end of this meeting with what was coming
next.

"You know." Judd leaned back in his chair. "This whole thing re-
minds me of that episode of *BJ and the Bear*. The one with the trouble by the creek . . ."

Will sighed. "Swear to God, man, if you compare me to the monkey in that stupid tweed hat, I'm going to have to kick your ass."

Judd smiled. "Fair enough. Just be logical, and stick to the script.
And when you make your decision let me know who it is, and I'll
make sure the severance packet gets created."

Will nodded. But his thoughts already drifted to his next appointment—on the twenty-second floor.

Will stood outside the boardroom, his back against the wall, waiting to be called inside. Lois had instructed him to wait there—at
that very spot on the carpet, next to the rolled-up yoga mat and size
fourteen studio slippers—before she departed for the mailroom.
Rigid as she could be about such details, at least she'd been flexible
enough to grant his request for a short-notice confab with the CEOs.

He looked at the PowerPoint presentations in his hand and re-
hearsed again what he'd tell them. *It's a supplement to KPK's comm*

plan—which had no messages from the top of the house. Employees need context from you. Reassurance we'll get through this together.

His sweaty hands dampening the papers, Will set the presentations on a visitor's chair. He dried his palms on his Dockers before sitting down.

Surely, the CEOs would see the flaws in the KPK plan. Jerry and Ron would understand the value in addressing their employees with a thoughtful, calming message. They'd be grateful Will came to them with a proactive plan. They'd remain blissfully unaware he wasn't under NDA or part of the project team—therefore seeing no need to behead him on the spot and order Judd's skull on a stick.

Will exhaled, listening to the dull murmur of voices on the other side of the door. He wondered what they were talking about. Wondered when he'd be allowed inside. Wondered how the hell he'd gotten to this point—standing outside the boardroom, about to take the biggest risk of his career.

"We're done." Ron swung open the boardroom door. "Ready?"

Will nodded, stood up straight and followed Ron into the room, where tension hung permanently in the air.

"We've got ten minutes before we have to jump back into Synerpoint negotiations." Jerry's voice sounded hoarse. "What's this about?"

Will sat down and slid copies of his comm plan in front of the CEOs. "I know you're busy. Thank you for making time to review this." He leaned forward. "I've looked at the KPK communications plan for the RIF. This is a plan to supplement that strategy—to make it more robust. It includes companywide communication to all employees—during the day of the RIFs as well as after—to keep them productive and focused on the future."

Will paused, waiting for a response. His heart thumped inside his chest. This was his first attempt to cash in a chip with the CEOs. His first time bringing them a plan they hadn't directed him to create. But he'd grown tired of playing Clean Up in Aisle Six—mopping up one mess after another on the trail of communication missteps the

CEOs left in their wake. So Will needed to step up and get them to do the right thing. *The infiltrator can't stay undercover forever.*

"Good, good." Jerry skimmed through the deck.

"I won't drain all the details." Will flipped to page two. "You'll probably want to focus on the key messages."

He let them read as his mind turned to next steps. Once the CEOs signed off, he'd inform Judd of the new and improved plan and convince his friend to present it to KPK—who would rubber-stamp it, thanks to the CEOs' preapproval. The only worry? The potential for Judd's head to explode when he found out about Will's high-stakes subterfuge.

"In the key messages—where you describe next steps for impacted teams." Ron pointed a thick finger at the page. "Change all of these 'BSI' and 'the company' references to 'we' and 'our.'"

Will nodded. "Nice catch, Ron. Yes, it's more personal that way."

Jerry nodded, too. "Good. What else?"

Will again flipped the page in his presentation. "If you look at page three, I want to make sure you're good with the tactics I'm proposing on the actual day of the RIFs."

He waited while they both found the page. "I'd like you to address all employees in the morning, on video, prior to the individual discussions. You'll frame up the day with the current business performance and the difficult but necessary decisions we're making. Then, you send a wrap-up email at close of business, candidly talking about how emotional the day was and thanking everyone."

Jerry rubbed his chin and frowned. "Absolutely not."

"No to the use of video?"

"No messaging from us on that day. Period."

Will's gut cramped again. "It's critical that you own the message and offer strength and hope to employees."

"We offer strength and hope by dealing with the Street and making tough decisions to keep this company running," Ron snapped. "We can't be the face of the first goddamn layoffs in company history and then turn around and be the vision of the future. Use your head, Evans."

An angry rebuttal flashed through his mind, but Will maintained calm eye contact. "I'd like you to reconsider, Ron. This is the right thing to do." He turned to Jerry. "It'll show sensitivity for impacted employees. It'll instill confidence in the employees who stay. And it mitigates the possibility that a disgruntled individual contacts the media and bad-mouths BSI. We can't afford more bad press."

"Employees don't need us to coddle them." Ron gave a dismissive wave. "They understand it's not personal. It's business."

"I agree." Jerry twisted the ring on his pinky finger. "We should respect the process and allow managers to relay the information. I'm sure most employees expect something like this is coming anyway. They'll probably be relieved when it becomes official."

Will gripped the edge of the table. *Have they seriously convinced themselves employees will be thankful for mass layoffs?* Apparently, "we" and "our" worked on paper, but in the darkest hours, every loyal, hardworking employee had to fend for himself. While Jerry and Ron holed up in their penthouse and let managers take the bullets for their mistakes. *Fucking cowards.*

Will stood and picked up his things. "Ships run aground not because captains lose sight of the shore but because they lose touch with their crews."

"Where the hell did you pick up that drivel?" Ron muttered.

"*Anchoring Your Business.*" Will spun and walked toward the door. "You know, one of those inane business books you made us read last year."

CHAPTER 24

Will found Bennie outside the "Kinley gig," as she put it. The CEOs loved holding charity events at the Walker Art Center, and the Kinley Foundation happily showed up to accept another oversized cardboard check.

Bennie waved as Will came up the sidewalk, and she steered him across the street to the Minneapolis Sculpture Garden—a peaceful oasis tucked beneath the intersection of two freeways at the western edge of downtown.

"Lunch is on me—well, Kinley." Bennie pushed a wadded up linen napkin into his hands. She'd smuggled him a sandwich from the event. "Goat cheese and roast beast on croissant, with some weird, leafy shit. Very frickin' fancy."

"How was Ron's speech?" Will mumbled through a bite.

"With the size of the big-ass check we cut them this year? Those Armani-wearing champagne sippers wouldn't have cared what he said."

They walked up the path as the bright summer sun filtered through the trees, spotlighting the various sculptures.

"The timing of this event is just stupid." Will ripped a flaky corner off the croissant. "Jerry and Ron are just trying to drum up some positive coverage before we get torched for the lay—" Will caught himself.

"Layoffs." Bennie finished for him. "I know. That's what I wanted to talk about."

"Good. Glad you're looped in."

"Yeah, just got NDA'ed yesterday. Told those shit-stains I needed to be the first fucking camper under the tent, not the last. Christ on a cracker. I'm already up to my ass-handles in negative coverage." She tugged at Will's elbow, veering him left on the path. "But this KPK outfit is scary, right? Some automaton in a tailored suit and green badge shows up at my desk. Takes a lock of my hair and makes me sign in my own blood. Jesus."

Will nodded as he chewed. "I know—and we thought Synerpoint was bad. Have you seen their headcount targets?"

"Yeah. HR and Finance are getting drilled like a prom queen."

Bennie pointed to a sculpture on the left side of the path—sixteen feet of twisted green steel, a temporary installation from a Helsinki artist. "Fifth Dimension of Belief," she read off the plaque. "Huh."

They dodged a few running children who had broken free from a nearby field trip.

"KPK showed me the FAQ doc," Bennie said. "Wasn't bad. Did ya see it?" She shook her head. "Of course you did. You probably wrote the damn thing."

He had, of course, with Judd's help. A strange experience, putting all of BSI's troubles on paper. Documenting the dysfunction. Trying to rationalize the company's self-inflicted wounds and explain away the need to fire more than a thousand loyal employees. Will could hardly believe BSI had reached this point. And he detested being part of it—having to sacrifice one of his perfectly good teammates to the Optelligence gods.

"I have to cut one person." He hated saying it out loud; the inevitability didn't seem real if he kept it in his head.

"Oh shit, Evans," Bennie gasped. "I got a pass because Jill's not coming back from maternity leave and I cut her position. What are you going to do?"

"Don't know yet."

Bennie scratched the back of her head, bobbing her loose knot of dark hair. "It's a tough decision, but remember, it's just business. Don't make it personal."

Will stopped again, crumbling the empty napkin in his hand. "I am so goddamn *sick* of people saying that."

A man with a little girl on his shoulders glared as he passed them. Will stepped to the side of the path and lowered his voice. "We need to stop pretending it's not personal. Losing your job, losing a teammate, being scared of losing your job, telling someone they've lost their job . . . it's all personal." Will took a deep breath, relieved to open the valve on his brain and let some anxiety out. "Listen, I understand we need to reduce costs. I do. But are layoffs the right way to do it? We're still pouring money into Technology and Innovation—all drowning in red ink. And Copiers is tanking without Rayzor. So how do we get an entirely new business model off the ground *and* fix the old one . . . with fewer people? It doesn't make sense."

A small dog ran toward them, straining at the end of a leash. Bennie crouched down and let the pug nuzzle her face as the dog's owner tried to tug the puppy away. "Lucy, stop. I'm sorry."

"It's fine." Bennie laughed. "I love these dogs! Super small with big attitudes."

Will managed a smirk. "The canine version of you."

"Except they poop like mad, and I'm always bound up like a dominatrix."

Bennie struggled to her feet—wiping lick marks off her cheek with the back of her hand—as the woman and dog moved on.

Bennie turned back to Will. "I know it sucks, dude. But we don't control these decisions, and we sure as hell can't change 'em."

"Don't I know it." Will bent down to retrieve a stone from the path, jiggled the rough surface against his palm, and then whipped it across the grassy expanse. "And now I have to make a decision on who to let go."

"Well, break it down. Decide what skills you need going forward and what you don't. Then look at the team—rack 'em and stack 'em against the new world order, and keep yer keepers."

Will nodded. He'd been doing a similar exercise in his brain. But Bennie made the decision sound simple.

She smacked him on the shoulder again. "Check it out."

The immense Spoonbridge and Cherry sculpture loomed in front of them.

"Now this is good art." She grinned, gesturing with a grand sweep of her arm. "Spoon. Cherry. I totally get it. Not some twisted pile of Tinker Toys like the Six Twisted Turns in My Colon, or whatever the hell that was."

Will pointed to an empty park bench nearby. "Let's sit." He scanned the area for a plaque. He'd hate to accidentally plop down on the latest masterpiece from Artsy McMarble or Hipster O'Granite.

"Let's do this, dude." Bennie leaned back on the bench, her feet swinging well above the ground. "Gimme your team scouting report."

Will looked down at the grass and folded the cloth napkin across his knee. "Okay. TK's a good learner. Still a little green and lacks confidence, but he's like a Swiss Army knife. Coffee's got great experience, and he's cool under pressure—so laid back, though, I'm afraid he'll miss important deadlines or details."

Will reached for his buzzing cell but realized Bennie's new smartphone had jumped to life. She ignored it.

"Holly, on the other hand, is very detailed and conscientious—but so empathetic and nice, people like Sommersby steamroll her. And Anna . . ." Will looked up at the sky as Bennie swung her clunky shoes. "She's smart and experienced. But sometimes, pushy as hell."

"Pushy?" Bennie cackled. "When has that been a problem, sugar-smack? I'm the loudest, pushiest chick you know. Next to me, Anna is Motherfucking Theresa."

Will snorted, and they both laughed for a minute. It felt good.

"Pushy or not, hon." Bennie wiped her eyes with the back of her hand. "You have to keep your strongest players."

Will nodded, not wanting to press the issue with Bennie; she and Anna had grown close. In reality, Will had a running list of pros and cons on every teammate. As with each of them, he had to weigh Anna's qualities—the good, the bad, and the ugly. Like her self-serving ambition. And her track record of jumping ship every couple years. Who's to say she wasn't already commandeering a lifeboat?

"You need to think about who'll do best. What with Optelligence being our main gig. In case you haven't heard, we're the goddamn market leader in that shit."

"We're the market leader, all right," Will sighed. "In corporate futility."

"I know it's tough. But, in the end, just make the best decision you can."

"You know what, Ben?" Will turned to her on the bench. "I could create a logical reason to cut any one of them. Follow the corporate manual, check off the criteria, and do the recommended assessments. But here's the thing. That's just an HR paper chase. A way to cover our asses in case some employee decides to lawyer up. The reality is . . ." He dropped his gaze to the ground. "In two days I have to tap someone on the shoulder and tell them they're not wanted anymore. But, hey, don't worry," he mocked, turning back toward Bennie. "It's not personal."

Bennie gave him a long look. Her phone vibrated again, and she fished the cell out of her pocket. "Jenny Q. Christmas! Who—oh, it's Lois." She punched Will on the shoulder. "Sorry. Gotta go."

Will started to stand, but Bennie reached down, snatched his napkin, and poked it into her pocket. "Take another five, Evans. Soak in the sun, pet a goddamn Chihuahua or something. It'll do you good." She clicked to answer the call and then covered the mouthpiece with her hand. "Just remember, Evans, everyone on your team respects you. They'll know you were painted into a corner—forced to make a tough call to help the company."

"Yeah," Will said. "Too bad it's a company I barely recognize anymore."

CHAPTER 25

"Be confident in your decision. Good luck today."

Will supposed Judd's text should have made him feel better. But sitting in the good booth the morning of layoff day, he didn't feel anything. Except empty.

He watched BSI's early risers shuffle in and pick up their coffees, muffins, and plastic containers of reasonably fresh fruit. He wondered which of them would leave early today, shocked and angry. He marveled that KPK and HR had managed to keep this historic event concealed from the masses. *Apparently, NDAs with explicit firing threats really quell the ol' rumor mill.*

A man stopped at Will's booth. "Charles Thomas?"

Will shook his head. "No, sorry. But good luck." *Seriously. Good luck today, Green Shirt Guy.*

A few minutes past seven thirty a.m., Will took the stairs to Jessica Lange—his assigned room on the same floor as his team's cubes. Careful orchestration to prevent a repeat of the Lemur Day elevator mayhem. He placed a water bottle on the main table. A box of tissues went on the small table in the corner. Close enough to grab if necessary, but not obvious enough to signal someone might end up in tears. He set the steno pad in front of him and his computer on his lap.

He cued up a predrafted email, sending it to his team at precisely 8:00 a.m. The brief message informed them that significant changes would happen today—and he'd ring their desk phones to meet with him, one by one. KPK had mandated this crappy, cryptic approach. He waited a few agonizing moments before dialing the first number on his list.

"Hey, it's Will."

"Hey."

"Listen, sorry about the mystery this morning. Can you join me in the Jessica Lange room right now? It's on the other side of the floor."

"Um, you mean, just me? Or . . ."

"Yes, just you, for now. I'll be talking to everyone individually."

"Sure, see you in a minute."

Will hung up and rearranged his materials on the table: steno pad to his left, script directly in front, departing employee's information packet on his right. He took a few deep breaths, controlling any emotions that might try to escape. *All right, Evans. You can do this.*

The door opened a crack, accompanied by a light tap on the frame.

"Hey, boss," TK said.

"Hey. Come in. Close the door and grab a seat."

TK sat down, rubbing his sweaty palms on his thighs. He forced a wary smile and looked across the table with raised eyebrows. *Like a puppy hoping for affection, but expecting discipline.* A surge of empathy and anxiety shot through Will. He hated that TK had to be the sacrificial lamb on BSI's chopping block. Hated that he had made this decision. And hated BSI for making him do it.

"Let me explain why you're here." Will stole a peek at the script. "As you know, the company invested materially in growth initiatives this year, and those investments haven't delivered returns as planned. In addition, our largest partner, Rayzor, took their business to a competitor. Therefore, expenses are up and revenues are down, which means we need to quickly and significantly reduce costs."

TK's weak smile faded from his colorless face.

"A large part of our expense structure is in payroll," Will continued. "And we need to find efficiencies. So, we are conducting a reduction in force—at corporate and in the field, across both of our business lines and the support teams. This is the first time in BSI's history that we've had a reduction in force, and we don't take this action lightly."

The script instructed Will to check for understanding. TK's gaping mouth and wide eyes made it clear he knew what came next. "I'm losing my job?" His lips quivered.

Will kept his eyes steady. "Unfortunately, yes, your position is being eliminated. I'm sorry." He paused, realizing he had messed up by apologizing. *Dammit!*

He glanced down to find his place in his script. But when he looked back up at his friend, the words wouldn't come out. Tears welled in TK's eyes, and he sniffled as he tried to wipe them away with his bare forearm. Will fought a rising lump in his throat.

"I'm sorry," TK said, followed by an awkward snorting sound— part laugh, part cry. Tears streamed down his cheeks now, and he couldn't clear them away fast enough. His voice cracked. "This is so stupid."

Will remembered the tissues, and he held out the box. TK grabbed a few and wiped his entire ruddy face. He balled the paper into his fist and tried to smile, but the corners of his mouth trembled. The front of his beige polo had four wet circles near the collar—runaway tears that had rolled off his jaw.

"This is so stupid," TK repeated.

"I know this is hard to hear." Will recited a message he knew existed in the script. Somewhere.

He had lost his place again and felt like a fool as his eyes darted between TK and the document on the table. He turned the page and then turned it back, desperately searching for a re-entry point. But every paragraph looked like the same words arranged in a different order. After nearly a minute of excruciating silence, he found the section labeled "*Severance Pay and Continuation of Health Benefits.*" Will cleared his throat. "The company is providing all impacted employees with severance pay. In your case, you'll receive six weeks of additional pay on your last check, which I'll give you in a few minutes."

"Wait," TK sniffed. "My last check? I have to leave today? W-what about all my stuff?" The hurt on his face evolved into irritation.

"You have until noon to pack up your personal belongings." Will did his best to maintain eye contact. "Listen, I know this isn't easy for you; it's hard for me, too. I want you to know how much I've personally appreciated your partnership."

"Is that part of your script?" TK pointed at the document. "Tell the employee we valued his work . . . try to make it feel personal?"

Will's voice wavered. "That's not some template bullshit, TK. Your friendship means a lot to me. I . . . I don't know what else to say. I wish things could be different. I really do." He cleared his throat and reached for a tissue to wipe his eyes. *No wonder Judd said to stick to the script. Dammit!*

Crumpling the tissue in his fist, Will plowed ahead. He opened the white envelope bearing TK's formal name—William Howard Kohler—and took out the acknowledgment form and a checklist.

Will slid the documents across the table. "In addition to your paycheck, this packet has critical information you'll need—health insurance, retirement accounts, outplacement assistance. Use this checklist to keep track of everything, and please sign the other form, acknowledging you received the packet."

TK scribbled his name and set down the pen. He didn't speak for a moment.

"Jeez, what do I do now? Pack up my stuff and go?"

Will cringed. "I have to ask you not to return to your desk for an hour. I need to talk to each person on the team before you do."

"Oh. Who else is getting laid off?"

Will looked down. "About twelve hundred people across the company. One from our team."

"Huh." TK's lip quivered again. "Well, I guess I'll go to the cafeteria and hang out with the other rejects. I need to call Kelsey anyway. Jeez, how am I going to break this to her?"

Will wanted to offer some kind of solace. Better words. A hand on TK's shoulder. Or a hug. Instead, he stood to signal the end of the meeting, waiting self-consciously as TK rose.

"Don't forget your packet."

"Of course. My packet," TK shot back. "I wouldn't want to forget THAT." He picked up the envelope and shuffled out the door.

Will slumped back in his chair and eyed the trash basket, thinking he might throw up. He felt awful for letting TK down. Will had plucked the kid out of the intern pool with grand plans to develop him into a top-flight communicator. But Will had gotten so wrapped up in other things—CEO support, Optelligence, the new team, the Chatterbox—he'd left the kid to fend for himself. *And then I kick him to the curb like a piece of trash.*

Once again near the brink of tears, Will flipped to the "Non-Impacted Employee" section of his script to regain focus. He stared blankly at the image of Jessica Lange and Dustin Hoffman on the opposite wall and called his next employee.

As expected, Coffee—a battle-tested layoff veteran with the severance scars to prove it—took the information in quiet stride. He offered to help TK update his résumé—a skill Coffee had perfected over the years.

Holly arrived next. She stepped into the room with a frown, her ever-present pen and notebook in her hands. "Oh, Will, how are you holding up? It's pretty clear what's happening today."

"I'm fine. Thanks for asking." Will hoped his face didn't betray how lousy he felt. "If you don't mind, I'll jump right in."

Holly nodded, peering over the glasses perched on her nose.

"As you know, the company invested materially in growth initiatives this year . . ." Will recited for the third time, hardly hearing his own voice. He tried to shake TK from his thoughts. "Your job is not being eliminated today, Holly. And I'm counting on you to help the company and our team move forward."

Holly furrowed her brow. "Thank you, Will. Of course. Was our team impacted?"

"We had to reduce one position, and it was TK's. I just—"

"What?! You son of a BITCH," Holly shrieked. "You chose TK?"

Will's mouth dropped open.

"How in God's blessed name are TK and Kelsey supposed to pay for a wedding when he's unemployed? How are they supposed to *live?*" Holly's lips pursed in a mixture of anger and disgust. "Shame on you, Will Evans!"

Her face turned from white-hot anger to a crimson, teary mess. She clawed the glasses off her face, and they swung from the cord around her neck. Sobbing and her chest heaving, she buried her face in her hands. Will tentatively offered the tissues, and she snatched the box away.

"I can't believe you'd do this." She glared at him. "I thought you were a good leader." She crumpled a few tissues and wiped her eyes.

"Holly, I know this is hard. I made the best decision I could based on the criteria I was given."

"Oh, don't bullshit me, Will." Holly gasped for breath. "I've been around a long time. I know how these things go. Managers always have the final say. You could have chosen any of us. You should have fired me before TK. Tom and I could survive. TK and Kelsey aren't going to make it on a teacher's salary. You know that."

She started to cry again. Will reached across the table and put a gentle hand on her arm, which she yanked away.

"Is that it?" she sobbed. "Do you have any other wisdom to impart—any other lives to destroy—before I go? I need to find TK. I'm sure he's shattered."

"He's in the cafeteria." Will wished he had something more to say—something sincere, strong, and comforting. But his mind fell blank. KPK's script—devoid of anything thoughtful or genuine— offered no options. And Judd's warning about someone being the curveball didn't help now, after the fact.

"Fine." Holly stood and threw her balled-up tissue toward the trash container, but it fell onto the floor. She swore under her breath, scooped it off the carpet, and stalked out.

Will rubbed his face with both hands. This morning had sucked—even worse than his worst-case scenario game predicted. The dull stomachache he'd been nursing for the last few days burned hotter than ever.

And now I have Anna. Why the hell did I leave her for last?

Anna found the Jessica Lange room and walked in. "Hey."

"Thanks for coming. Take a seat."

She closed the door and sat, crossing her high heels under her chair. Will skipped the small talk, launching headlong into the script.

"As you know, the company invested materially in growth initiatives this year . . ."

Anna studied him as he read. His eyes were red—maybe from lack of sleep, maybe from emotion. Probably both.

"We don't take this action lightly . . ."

Anna half-listened as Will continued with the preamble. She'd watched her teammates leave their cubes before her, each getting the call—one by one. Layoff protocol usually dictated managers meet with expendables before survivors, but that probably meant little at BSI. The market leader in ass-backward processes. *As Bennie would say: Spare me the foreplay, hon. Just tell me if I'm getting fucked.*

"Your job is not being eliminated today."

Anna's eyes widened. She turned her head to mask her surprise. She'd been sure he'd give her the boot. So sure, in fact, she'd updated her résumé, called her headhunter, and discreetly packed up parts of her cube. Desk photos, books, and even the crystal bus—all the little pieces of herself she'd only started to reveal.

"TK's role was eliminated, and we've given him a severance package. Today is his last day at BSI." Will stopped talking and looked down at the table.

Anna could see the pain on his face, and she felt for him. Will had never been through layoffs before, and he'd cut TK, his protégé. His compadre. And poor TK—young and naïve—probably never saw the ax coming. *I'm sure they're both devastated.*

She set her hands on the edge of the table and started to push her chair back.

Will raised his eyes to refocus on her. "What are you . . . you're leaving?"

She hesitated—trying to decipher the edge in his voice. "I thought we were done. Seems like maybe you could use some time . . . alone."

He closed the script. "The least you could do is tell me what you're thinking. Everyone else unloaded on me, and you've never been shy with your opinions before. So spill it."

His mouth quivered. His emotions ran dangerously close to the surface.

Anna tried to strike a neutralizing tone. "I'm not sure what you mean. My opinion on what?"

"All of this." He waved an arm toward the door. "TK. The layoffs. How I'm always making the wrong decisions."

Anna frowned. Was he baiting her into an argument? Suppressing his true feelings by putting up a tough front? If so, she could see through it. *Hell, I've perfected the concept.*

"Listen, Will. I don't think—"

"C'mon, out with it. I had to lay off one employee. Who should it have been?"

She studied Will for a moment. "Well . . . I think you should have fired . . . me." She hesitated. "And I was sure you were going to."

Will frowned, his skepticism apparent.

"Think about it." She could feel herself getting defensive, and she tried to keep her tone even and professional. "You don't let me help with anything important, like the CEOs. Or take care of anything on my own, like Sommersby. And you don't like it when I offer my opinions. Why even keep me around? I'm a pain for you."

"Oh, I get it," he mocked. "I'm holding you back, and it's hurting both of us." He looked down at the table and muttered something Anna couldn't hear.

Anna crossed her arms. She wanted to be empathetic, but he kept provoking her. "Besides, I didn't think you'd be logical about it. You're all about culture and relationships, and that's obviously the way you want your team to be. But that's not me. I don't fit into that box."

"It's not a box." Will shook his head. "More like a family—like the Promisekeepers."

"Teams can't be families, Will. That kind of idealism gets in the way of doing the work and prevents leaders from making tough decisions."

"Not true. You can make decisions and still treat people like family."

"Tell that to TK," Anna blurted. She pressed her eyes closed. *Shit! Too far. Way too far.*

Will recoiled and slammed his hand on the table. "Don't you *dare.*"

Anna bolted upright in her chair. She had sliced into an exposed nerve and needed to repair the damage. Stat. "I'm sorry, Will. I really am. But if you treat employees like family, things like this hurt them—and you—even more. This is work. It shouldn't be so personal."

"Says the corporate mercenary who jumps jobs every three years to advance her precious career." His face grew redder with every word he spat. "Avoiding any real relationships is convenient for people like you, but a fucking mess for everybody picking up the pieces in your wake."

The comment stung, and Anna felt a lump rise in her throat. "People like me."

"Yeah, like you. And Peyton and Kirkland. We're a means to an end for you. A path to the next promotion or title. So go ahead—

turn this company into a consultancy. Let Optelligence strip all the heart and loyalty and pride out of this place. You'll fit in that box just fine. Hell, you'll enjoy it."

"You don't—" Anna paused to steady her voice. "You don't know anything about me. You're making assumptions. Like everyone else in this company."

"I know enough. I know you don't care what happens to this company or the people in it."

"I don't care? I don't *care?*" Anna leaned forward, arms on the table, her frustration tumbling out. "If I don't care, why am I still here? Tell me. Why am I still here? Trying to help you when you keep blowing me off? Taking all the shit this company has thrown at me? From the minute I set foot in this place." Her pulse raced, but she pressed on.

"You have no idea what it's like to be misjudged and underestimated every time you walk into a meeting." The words kept coming. "To have to prove you've earned this job, over and over again. And to know—on top of all that—every time you speak out, you'll be branded a bitch."

Will started to speak, but Anna raised her voice over him. "Oh, but you have to. Because if you don't show you're the smartest person in the room—in every goddamn meeting—you'll be tagged as the whore who slept with the boss to get a seat at the table. So forgive me for not trying hard enough to be a perfect culture-fit, Will. I've been too fucking busy trying to be everything else."

Will shook his head. "You're so obsessed with achieving—"

"No!" Anna seethed. "I'm not Kirkland. And I'm no Rainmaker, despite what you think. I made a lot of choices to get to this point. Smart, deliberate choices." She pointed with a trembling hand. "But I'm no Peyton, either. I won't jump into bed with Kirkland—no matter how much easier it would be to gain his favor . . . or his chief of staff job."

Her vision blurring with tears, Anna leaned away. "I don't expect you to throw me a ticker-tape parade for choosing the harder path, but I do expect some goddamn respect for being good at my job."

Anna blinked a few times to keep the waterworks at bay. She couldn't believe she'd spilled her guts like that. She didn't want Will's pity. Didn't want him to see her as weak. But he could be so naïve sometimes—clueless about what his precious BSI felt like for other people. *Hell, what it feels like in any company, anywhere, when you're not coddled and carried up the ranks in the safety of your own little cocoon.*

Someone needed to spell it out for him.

Will's stare softened. "If I didn't think you were good at your job, TK would be sitting here right now instead of you." He cupped his weary face in his hands and leaned back. "You know, it's never been about your work. It's how you go about it—getting in people's faces, kicking down doors. It's like you want to control everything."

Anna opened her mouth to respond, but she had no defenses left. Tears rolled down her face, and she couldn't catch her breath. She lowered her head and wiped her nose with the back of an unsteady hand.

"I'm sorry." Will fidgeted in his chair. "I didn't know that would . . . I'm sorry."

"I'm not in control of anything anymore," Anna admitted through tears. "I'm not even married. My husband left me ten months ago . . ." She broke down in sobs. The humiliation of bawling in front of Will made her wish she could crawl under the table. She looked down at the floor, her voice a whisper. "I can't bring myself to sign the divorce papers because this isn't how it's supposed to work. I'm supposed to be in control. I'm the one who leaves."

Anna had never felt so pitiful and exposed. Beyond raw. Skinned alive.

Will didn't say anything. She heard his chair squeak as he moved, and the box of tissues slid into view on the edge of the table. He grabbed one for himself.

They sat in silence for a few minutes, avoiding eye contact. Anna took a series of deliberate breaths to recuperate from her pathetic, uncharacteristic—but admittedly cathartic—display of emotion. She grabbed more tissue before Will took the box back.

"You still wear your ring," he finally said. Of all of the things she expected he might say to clear the air, this didn't crack the top fifty.

Anna looked down at the diamond band, twisting it around her finger with her thumb.

"But when I take it off, it feels like . . . open season." She winced. "All these invasive questions and comments—guys can be aggressive. And it's not just that . . ." The words caught in her throat, and she hesitated, not wanting to cry again.

She also wore the ring for a more personal reason—because without it, her bare hand felt like a badge of dishonor. A constant reminder of how she couldn't keep Erik happy. How easily he'd walked away from her. *How badly I failed.*

She went for a less emotional explanation. "I wear it because it's easier. One of the many defenses of a conniving bitch."

"Don't say that. You're not a bitch. When you put down those walls you've built up, you're actually quite amazing." A shyness crept into Will's voice. "You know, your laugh makes me want to come into the office every day just to hear it."

Anna wilted and her eyes filled with tears again.

"Oh, man . . ." Will frowned and offered the tissues to her again. "I don't know what to say anymore. I'm sorry. I think I was taking out my frustrations about this fucking company on you, because . . . I don't know why. Because I'm an idiot. I'm sorry."

She dabbed the fresh moisture from her face. "You're not an idiot . . . you were being honest. And what you just said about my laugh is the sweetest thing anyone's ever said to me."

Will blushed as Anna pitched her wadded-up tissue into the trashcan. She cleared her throat. "Can I ask you something? I know I'm not supposed to . . . badge of honor and all that . . . but I still don't get the nickname thing. Why did Big Al give me one?"

Will smiled. "He saw that deep down you aren't really a Rainmaker, like you said. So he made you an honorary Promisekeeper."

Anna nodded. "And Pearl?"

"Took me a while to figure it out, too. Al's nicknames are deeper than most people realize. But then I got it. It's because of how pearls are formed—starting with a grain of sand. An irritant inside a shell."

Anna snorted a laugh, and she covered her nose with another tissue. "An irritant. *Nice.*"

"No, wait. It triggers a defense mechanism, and over time becomes this beaut—" He blushed again. "Something rare and valuable."

Anna wiped a lingering tear from the corner of her eye. "That's pretty smart, Evans."

Will smiled, then turned serious. "Can I tell you something? Something you might not like as much?"

"Sure."

"You mentioned a chief of staff position." He cringed. "That title is kind of a joke around here. It's not a real job—just a castle-building technique some execs use. To try to look important. They dangle it as incentive and then get people to jump through hoops to get the job. But it's a road to nowhere—an empty title and pile of tactical busywork. Most CoS's in this company are admins."

"Son of a bitch." Anna shook her head. "Kirkland's been playing me this whole time."

"Sorry to be the one to break it to you."

She shook her head. "I should've seen through it." She wiggled her ring finger. "If anyone should be able to spot a smokescreen, it's me."

Anna let out a deep sigh. The cramped, stuffy room felt different now. Better. Lighter.

"So what now?" she asked. "What do we do next?"

"Everything we can to help BSI get through this. So the employees who are left never have to experience another day like today."

His eyes were puffy, his hair a mess, his nose red. BSI had done little in the last few quarters to deserve anyone's optimism—but Will Evans refused to give up hope. Anna felt bad she had ever faulted him for it.

She smiled again and reached over to squeeze his arm. "BSI is lucky to have you, you know that? You and your stubborn, selfless idealism. Don't ever let people like me take that away from you."

"Not a chance. And don't use that phrase—'people like me.' You're not like Kirkland and Peyton—motivated by power and greed. I don't even know how you deal with those vultures."

"It's easy," Anna said. "Misplaced confidence . . . and kick-ass shoes."

Will packed up his layoff kit and looked at his phone for the first time in hours: seven missed calls, four voicemails, and eleven texts. He ignored all but the last text—from Coffee: *"Checked on TK. He's okay. Driving him home."*

Will sighed with relief. *We take care of our own.*

His emotional reservoir empty, Will needed to get out of the tower and clear his head. He stepped out of his tiny conference room as if emerging from a storm cellar—to a neighborhood ravaged by a tornado. Dozens of ex-BSIers stood in their cubes, packing career remnants into cardboard boxes. Others meandered shell-shocked from cube to cube, looking for survivors. A small group had gathered in the Cabin, whispering rumored names. A woman with a tear-streaked face stepped onto the elevator with Will.

They rode in silence until the doors opened to the crowded lobby. Freshly fired employees paced and talked on their phones, boxes at their feet. Commuters sat in guest chairs, waiting for hastily planned rides home. A line formed at an ad hoc Security desk, where the newly unemployed had been instructed to turn in badges, parking passes, and laptops on their way out. Someone yelled and waved his company-issued phone at the hapless guard.

Two news crews rolled cameras in the skyway, using BSI's lobby as a backdrop. Their blow-dried reporters stood in the foreground, pontificating over each other, describing how the troubled, local company had eliminated a hefty percentage of workers and open jobs.

Will walked near the lobby windows to avoid being captured in a live shot. Dazed ex-colleagues streamed out of the tower. Sara Connelly, who had overseen the call center for nine years, cried into her phone. He nodded to Chris Pearce, a marketing VP the company had recruited from General Mills. Andy Barry—who had posted the highest team scores on the annual employee engagement survey—threw open the lobby door. Kaitlyn Berens, one of the sharpest, kindest admins at BSI, brushed past.

Will merged into the river of outflowing talent—*all these good people*—and wandered into the skyway. He thought about the survivors, the people left behind to pick up the pieces. With BSI crumbling so fast, how would they even know which pieces to pick up?

His mind drifted back to Anna. He couldn't shake the image of her—sobbing, disillusioned, defeated.

She deserves better.

Will felt his phone vibrate in his pocket with a new missed call. He looked at the screen: TK.

We all do.

Dee Dee Ruggles
4 mins · Facebook

When life throws a curveball ☹, Jesus hands you a hot bat. To all my BSI peeps...may the Lord be in your batter's box today!!!!!!!!!! ☺ ☺

147 Likes   36 Comments

👍 Like   💬 Comment

CHAPTER 26

Anna walked through the quiet tower, making her way to the ninth floor. Mass layoffs always created emotional hangovers in the days that followed. So she slipped in early, hoping to avoid the inevitable graveside small talk in the elevators and hallways. While others tearfully memorialized their losses, she intended to fire up the Chatterbox—to see which of her Promisekeepers had made the cut. Layoffs had a steep impact on blue-collar workers. They didn't have access to headhunters, networking lunches, and generous severance packages. Once the paychecks stopped coming, they were on their own.

Anna perked up when she spotted Holly hovering in Coffee's cube while he pecked away at his keyboard.

"What's up, guys?"

"We're compiling the hit list." Coffee didn't look away from the screen.

Anna stepped behind him and examined the spreadsheet—color-coded by department, with employee names under every heading and a running tally at the end of each column.

"Is this the master layoff list?"

"Nah, built it mah-self," Coffee drawled. "This ain't my first rodeo, dawlin."

"Well, look at that." Anna pointed to Salvador Chan's name.

"Poor guy." Coffee's eyes remained fixed on the screen. "Hope he doesn't miss any yacht payments."

"Oh, Mr. Chan will be fine." Holly rolled her eyes. Her blotchy face revealed she'd already shed a few tears this morning. "He's guaranteed two full years of salary and bonuses—paid in a lump sum. He might need the boat to store all that cash."

Anna pointed to the HR tab. "Sommersby make the list?"

Coffee shook his head. "Sorry. The guy's a tick—hard to find, hard to kill."

"And sucks the life out of you." Anna watched him click to reveal the full list of HR Department casualties.

Holly gasped, then nudged Anna. "Tina Anderson! You know Tina."

Anna shook her head. "I don't."

"Yes, you do. Change management specialist. Reported to Kari Fischer. She always wore those rhinestone jeans with white stitching . . . you know, the kind that make my tushy look big . . ."

Anna flashed back to her first day. The meeting with Judd and Kari. *Skull Scarf. The Look.* "Oh, her. Didn't remember her name . . ."

"I suppose if anyone's equipped to handle the psychological impact of getting laid off, it's her." Holly held her palms upward. "She's a certified Synerpoint Change Curve instructor, you know."

Coffee snorted. "She should brush up on the curriculum because I heard she flipped out getting the news—started screaming and swearing at Kari. Greg from Security had to carry her out. Literally. Over his shoulder like a sack of kicking potatoes."

Anna frowned. Skull Scarf may have been a judgmental Work-Around, but she didn't deserve to be publicly humiliated on top of getting fired. And the poor security guy couldn't have enjoyed playing the hard-assed, company bouncer, either. *Layoffs suck for everyone.*

Anna changed the subject. "How did you compile this many names already?"

"Admins." Coffee tilted his head to look at Anna. "They keep their department email lists updated, so they're always in the know."

"Smart. Admins always know where the bodies are buried." Anna stepped into the aisle and dropped her bag on her desk. "So to speak."

"And, not to be morose, but it's easier to tally up the contents of a mass grave—instead of a constant trickle over time," Coffee said. "When I worked at WicTonix, they thought—instead of one big event—it'd garner less media attention to 'disappear' a few employees every week. Always on Tuesdays. Everyone tried to avoid meeting with their managers that day of the week. It became a thing. Termination Tuesdays."

"Followed by what?" Anna wheeled around in the aisle. "Whack-a-Mole Wednesdays? Anyone popping up from her cube gets bashed by the manager mallet?"

"And that's not the worst I've seen." Coffee rocked back in his chair and crossed his arms. "At Mid-Fab, I worked for the CFO. One day he hands me a layoff list—a third of our employees. Told me to find their titles and hire dates."

"Why didn't HR do it?" Holly sat on the edge of Coffee's desk, settling in for story time.

"Most of them were getting chopped. So I get the data, hand him the list, and he says 'good, now add your name at the bottom.'"

"That's awful." Holly gave his shoulder a gentle push.

Coffee brushed it off. "Meh. Led me to Laphroaig single-malt, so it wasn't all for naught."

"Wait a minute." Holly pointed to a name on the screen. "I just saw Ashley Hartman."

Coffee shook his head. "Phantom sightings are common after a massive workforce reduction. It's a mild form of PTSD—survivor's guilt."

"It wasn't a phantom sighting," Holly protested. "It was Ashley Hartman. In the cafeteria. Eating an egg-white omelet."

"In the case of this particular apparition, the omelet likely represents your mixed feeli—"

"Holy hell, I'm glad to see you guys." Les galloped up the aisle. He paused to give Anna the micro up-down, before continuing. "I knew cuts were coming, but didn't know where. Glad you escaped the reaper." The group fell silent, and Les's eyes darted among them. He took a slow step back and hung his head at the sight of TK's cleaned-out cubicle. "Oh, crap."

"Yeah." Coffee nodded toward the empty space. "We're a man down."

Holly started to cry again—she extracted a balled-up tissue from her shirtsleeve and dabbed her eyes. "We're not talking about this, okay? Not at work. Save it for the Monk."

"Sorry, guys." Les scratched the top of his head. "No sad stuff, then. Let's focus on the mysterious, instead. Like the State of the Business meeting. You hear about it? Week after next?"

"I just got word." The group turned to see Will standing in the aisle, laptop bag hanging from his shoulder. His voice lacked its usual energy. "The execs and some key support functions are attending. Apparently it's to reexamine company strategy for the rest of the year. Not surprising, given the cuts."

Anna watched Holly avoid eye contact with Will. Coffee looked back to his screen. If they hadn't viewed Will as a boss before, they did now. After all, he'd just fired one of their friends. The team dynamic already felt different. Probably would for quite a while.

"Speaking of our fearless leaders." Les leaned on the cube wall. "Where the hell were Jerry and Ron yesterday? First layoffs in BSI history, and they don't call . . . they don't write? Huge miss not to hear from the big kahunas."

Will set his laptop on his desk. "Trust me, it wasn't for lack of trying."

"But not even an email? Everyone was talk—"

"Say one more sentence about the State of the Business meeting. What's on the agenda?" Anna attempted to distract Les. Will didn't need Les's asshole badgering. Not today.

"Not sure." Les wiped one lens from his glasses on the front of his shirt. "They put a placeholder on our calendars. We're supposed to be getting more materials."

"We've been asked to help compile those materials," Will addressed his team. "Not sure what that means yet, but keep your schedules flexible. And if you haven't heard already, Chan was let go. I'm trying to find out where we fit in the new structure."

"Looks like you report to Will Evans now," Les teased.

"Yeah," Will sighed, "too bad I can't stand that guy." He raised his chin in a subtle gesture to Anna. "Hey, can I grab you for a minute?"

"Only one minute?" Les whistled low. "Ms. Reed, if you weren't already betrothed, I would endeavor to grab you for a wonderfully long and satisfying amount of time."

"Wonderfully long and satisfying." Anna brushed past him. "So, that's . . . two minutes?"

Les laughed as she followed Will up the aisle, to the office their former CMO never occupied. Anna sank into the cushy chair behind the desk.

Will closed the door, took a seat by the wall, and rested his elbows on his knees. "How are you doing today? Like I texted you last night, you didn't have to come in . . . if you need some time."

Anna smiled. *You're sweet, Evans.* "Thanks—but I'm fine. It's Holly I'm worried about."

Will nodded and looked down at the carpet. "I know. We had a tough conversation yesterday—she took the TK news hard." He sat up in his chair and extended his legs. "Should've seen it coming. Holly treats him like a son."

"I'll take her for coffee and see how she's doing," Anna offered. "Let her know you said she can go home if it gets to be too much."

"Thanks." Will looked toward the wall—a twenty-foot stare in a ten-foot room.

Anna wondered how much he'd slept last night—and if he should go home instead of Holly. But his stubborn sense of responsibility never would allow that. *Just like mine.* "So, are you okay?"

"Not really. Yesterday was"—his voice cracked—"the worst day of my career."

"I know." She cleared her throat, getting rid of the sudden lump rising there. "But like you said, we need to get BSI through this." *Game plan, Reed. Keep looking forward.*

She scooched her feet on the carpet, inching her chair around the end of the desk, closer to him. "Let's start by getting a sense of where we all stand. Coffee seems fine. I'll take care of Holly. What about Big Al and his crew?"

"Exchanged a few texts with Al last night. Pretty cryptic."

"I'll scour the Chatterbox. See what I can find out." Anna drummed her fingers on the desk. "Got a few friends out there I wanted to check on anyway."

Will nodded with a hint of a smile. "Great, thanks." He tapped his phone to silence an incoming call. "Have you heard anything about the Synerpoint contract renegotiation? Where we stand?"

"No, why?"

"Something's up." Will straightened up in his chair. "When Legal Bob reviewed the FAQs earlier this week, he freaked out at the Synerpoint reference. More than a typical overreaction."

Anna nodded. Corporate attorneys notoriously blew gaskets over the most innocuous word choices. In Anna's previous job, the general counsel admonished her for writing a benign internal news story describing an over-forty employee as "vibrant." An adjective virtually begging for a million-dollar ageism suit, according to the livid lawyer.

"Well, it only makes sense BSI and Synerpoint would renegotiate the pillars of Optelligence." Anna thought out loud. "With Chan gone, Innovation is gone, too."

Will nodded. "And Kirkland's baby—Technology—is hanging on by its gums. Talent's new positions were frozen as part of the layoffs. So maybe we're trying to take Synerpoint's price down by kicking the Optelligence can down the road a few months."

"Maybe." Anna rubbed a hand under her chin. "But I heard Kirkland wasn't thrilled with how long it'd take to recruit a thousand new employees, anyway. People with deep consulting experience are hard to find. There's only a handful of large firms with attractive prospects. After that, the talent pool gets pretty shallow, pretty fast." She slowed her delivery as the picture became clearer in her mind. "I heard he might leapfrog the rules and stuff the seats all at once. But it was just a rumor, so I dismissed it."

"What rumor?"

"That he was going to bid on a partial lot of Synerpoint employees. Land a thousand new bodies with a snap of his fingers."

"Wait . . . say, like, three more sentences about that."

"He wants to pull a badge-flip." She'd seen it on a smaller scale at the architecture firm where she had worked. "BSI would have to buy out the noncompetes for Synerpoint employees. Then throw in fair market price for their salaries, probably with raises for top performers, to limit attrition. Pony up a ten-to-fifteen-percent kicker to Synerpoint to smooth over relations and offset the loss of talent . . ."

Will shook his head. "Sounds crazy expensive."

"It's the Soldier of Fortune staffing model." Anna rubbed the polished, mahogany arms on Chan's chair. "And it doesn't come cheap. But it's fast. Hundreds of Synerminions walk out of the tower on Friday—and come back to work Monday as property of BSI. Green badges get swapped for purple, en masse. Classic badge-flip."

"Man, that's one for the handbook," Will muttered. "See also: Buying Employees in Bulk."

Anna didn't grasp the reference. She swiveled her chair back and forth with her toe. "So, maybe Synerpoint is balking at the deal, or we can't scrape up money for all those bodies anymore. Either way, negotiations must be getting tricky."

Her phone buzzed in the pocket of her jacket.

"Tricky or not, we've got to figure it out—to make sure we've got a story that holds water." Will stood, watching her check her caller ID. "Go ahead and take that. I've got to go jump on this State of the Business thing."

"SOB." Anna smirked. "Perfect acronym for the state of this company's business."

Will chuckled as he closed the door behind him.

"Alissa! Hi," Anna said into her phone.

"How's my future Chief Communications Officer doing?" the headhunter chirped in return.

"Hanging in there. Hey, listen . . . things have changed since I shot you that note last week. I thought I'd be impacted by the layoffs, but I wasn't."

"Uh-huh, uh-huh," Alissa said. "But it doesn't even matter, because the most amazing comm role just came across my desk—I would've called you anyway. It's a new position—and they want the person to help shape the role. They need a slugger on this, Anna. Solid writing, lots of energy, training, and interview experience. 'New media for a new world,' they said."

"Who's it for?"

"The Twins."

"The Minnesota Twins?"

Alissa laughed. "No, Mary Kate and Ashley. Yes—the Minnesota Twins!"

"Shut. Up." Blood rushed to Anna's head. Over the course of her career, she'd interviewed with dozens of companies, answering questions ranging from rudimentary to absurd. But every single prospective hiring manager asked one question, regardless of the role, organization or industry: What's your dream job?

Anna always offered a well-rehearsed, charming, and truthful answer: "My dream would be to work for a company that challenges me to learn and grow—where I'm able to provide value every day." Then, with an extra dose of charm, "But if someone offered me a chance to combine my love of writing with my desire to be at a ballpark all day, how could I turn that down?" Interviewers with ballpoint pens in their hands always smiled and nodded.

"The salary is negotiable depending on experience," Alissa continued. "There's a potential signing bonus for high-caliber candidates, plus all the perks. Office at the ballpark. Travel with the team. But that's not even the best part."

"Good Lord. What's the best part?"

"They're not posting it publicly. My agency signed an exclusive contract to fill it. I'm the only recruiter in the lower forty-eight who knows about it, and you're the first person I called."

Anna's mind flipped through flashcard images of life in this new job. Standing in her office, overlooking the Target Field third-base line. Boarding the team charter for a West-Coast road trip. Catching Joe Mauer for a photo op in the infield after a hard-earned victory.

"Anna, you're not hesitating on this are you?" Alissa cajoled her back to reality. "You're the biggest baseball fan I know. Who would be more perfect for this job than you? Meet me for lunch. I'll give you the skinny."

Anna took a breath and tamped down her excitement. "Sure. I'd love to hear more."

"Hate to say it, my dear, but BSI's in free-fall mode. We need to get you out before they hit rock bottom."

"I think we've already hit it." Anna leaned back in the cushy, leather chair. "At this point, I can't imagine what else could go wrong."

FOR IMMEDIATE RELEASE

Synerpoint Consulting, LLC
3300 Madison Ave, Ste. 400
New York, NY 10016

**Synerpoint Offers Operations Management Excellence
with Optitude® Software and Services Practice**

NEW YORK, N.Y. — Synerpoint today launched a new practice to help organizations create world-class operational aptitude to increase the productivity and effectiveness of their businesses. The Optitude® software and services practice is a scalable, portable technology platform that offers clients high-value, highly integrated management of inventory, payroll, compliance and financial systems.

Drawing on the expertise and innovation of more than 13,000 consulting experts, 103 system patents and $750 million invested in software and services capabilities over the last four years, Optitude® helps companies address the growing complexities of managing their business operations.

"Synerpoint is proud to bring Optitude® — a robust, holistic and unique set of offerings — to the marketplace," said Peyton B. Rayburn, Synerpoint Vice President and Managing Partner. "These new services and technologies put business data, analytics and operational visibility into the hands of those tasked with defending their organizations from inefficiency and delivering superior horizontal capability performance."

###

CHAPTER 27

"What kind of shit-shark maneuver did they pull, Evans?" Bennie bellowed, tripping into Will's cube. "Where did this fuckstorm come from?"

Will sprang from his chair, holding the desk phone to his ear with one hand, making a frantic throat-cutting motion with the other. "Yes, got it. I'll have a draft within the hour." He hung up and spun around to Bennie. "Jesus, Ben. Try to keep it PG-13 when I'm on with the CEOs, okay?"

"Sorry, succotash. Trying to get to the bottom of this goddamn Synerpoint fiasco. Looks like I'm not the only one." Bennie motioned behind Will, where the other members of his team prairie-dogged above the cube walls.

"All right, here's what I know," Will said to the group. "Just got off a call with Jerry, Ron, Kirkland, and Legal Bob. We'll get an internal message out ASAP. The official word is that contract renegotiations with Synerpoint—as part of our cost reduction efforts—broke down yesterday."

"Then what?" Bennie threw her hands in the air. "We bend over and take it up the poop chute again? Like with Rayzor?" Will shot her a dirty look. "Sorry, hon." She patted his shoulder. "Please . . . continue."

"We are exploring all possible legal options and intend to vigorously defend our intellectual property rights as it relates to Optelligence." Will mentally drafted the memo as he spoke. "In the meantime, we're placing a hold on all Optelligence-related activities. The senior leadership team is holding a State of the Business review next week, after which time more information will be made available."

Eyes grew wide across the team, and they mumbled to each other.

"So, Synerpoint beat us to market with their version of Optelligence." Coffee sighed. "Like the spoiled brat who doesn't like the other kid's rules. So he picks up his ball and goes home."

"Optitude is trademarked," Anna noted. "Which shows they've been getting ready for this—preparing a backup plan in case the partnership with us fell apart."

"Can Synerpoint make a go of this without us?" Holly folded her hands atop her cube wall. "They'll have to find their own clients now instead of accessing ours."

"We'll get those answers in due time." Will slid a laptop bag strap over his shoulder. "But right now, I have to get rolling on this announcement. How's everyone doing on their SOB assignments?"

Details of the State of the Business meeting remained sketchy, but execs had been working like hell to assemble reports and create presentations—justifying their budgets and offering new growth ideas. Will's team took charge of translating the wince-worthy jargon and cleaning up cluttered visuals.

"All good," Coffee reported. "I've got the Copier and Office Supplies overview. Sonny highlights the Chatterbox as a tool for ideas and engagement. It's pretty awesome."

"And I've got the deck Sommersby sent for Roswell." Holly pointed to Anna with a smile. "You want to trade, so you can battle with Sommersby again? Or do you want Kirkland?"

"Not even after three martinis, in a state of deep self-loathing."

Bennie and Holly guffawed, something Will hadn't heard in days. He hoped it signaled a "new normal" for his team—a willingness to laugh in the face of yet another jolt of bad news. God knows they needed it, given the constant stream of negative media articles about the company.

The Twin Cities' two newspapers had been waging a coverage war for several weeks, each trying to scoop the other with fresh intel about BSI's imminent demise. This morning, the Pioneer Press splashed the latest round of speculation across its front page: "BSI Hiding Deeper Financial Woes from Investors." Even before Synerpoint's news release hit the wire.

The negative coverage had hit Holly—with her deep love of the company and its employees—especially hard. She'd approached Will a few days earlier, asking if he'd the seen the reader comments piling up on the Strib's website. Nameless, faceless trolls jeering and calling for BSI's collapse. "Who are these people?" Holly had lamented. "Don't they know how many jobs we provide? All the good we do in the community? We're their friends and neighbors, and they want us to die?"

Will understood. For the first time in his career, he'd taken steps to hide the fact he worked at BSI when outside the office—even removing his company badge before walking through the skyway. He'd recently made the mistake of wearing a BSI polo to a coffee shop and had barely gotten out alive after being inundated with nosy questions and uninvited comments from espresso-sipping strangers. Best to ignore the haters, those with nothing better to do than pile-on. "People may love an underdog," he'd told Holly. "But what they really love is kicking a big dog when he's down."

Will left his team to their SOB work and headed to the cafeteria. He parked himself in the good booth, trying to determine how to spin this new chapter in Synerpoint's evil-empire saga, knowing he couldn't publish the sordid details on why negotiations had broken down.

Turns out Synerpoint had refused to budge on its fee for a thousand badge-flipped employees. Kirkland offered to pay the steep price only if Synerpoint canceled the remainder of its contract. Peyton and team countered by tripling the cost of the badge-flip, to compensate for losing the long-term revenue stream.

With negotiations teetering, Kirkland went for the kill. Seems Peyton's plush suite atop the W Hotel—where the devious exec spent a fair amount of his nights—violated BSI policy. Kirkland called out her "exorbitant and unprincipled expenditures" and threatened to sue for breach of contract. Never mind that he'd been the one raiding the mini bar and gorging on room-service lobster claws.

Stung by the double-cross, Peyton chose the nuclear option—ending negotiations, canceling the contract, and sprinting to market with Optitude before BSI's execs knew what hit them.

Will flipped open his laptop and cranked out a far less-detailed version of the internal announcement. The conversation with his team had helped him articulate the key points, and within a matter of minutes he had emailed a strong first draft to Lois.

With a little time to kill, he toggled over to the Chatterbox and noted the 127 new posts since his last visit—a blend of vitriol aimed at Synerpoint and ideas on how to overcome the company's troubles. *Promisekeepers still keeping up the good fight.*

He zeroed in on a post from Doug, a driver from FB-076. Doug had written about a real estate firm delivery, with a customer in tears. The copier broke, and the agent had a closing in thirty minutes. Doug cleared the extensive paper jam—and to save her a little time, unpacked her office supplies, too. He fell behind in his scheduled deliveries but said everything ended well—posting a picture of the monster basket of cookies she sent as a thank you.

She must've been hot, Will smiled, *or Doug wouldn't have risked getting reprimanded.*

Clicking through other comments, he landed on the still-raging conversation around Amadeus's idea for meetings between Delivery drivers and Sales reps. Some called for an end to the "less talk, more stops" mantra—a reminder for crews to squeeze in as many deliveries as possible.

An impassioned FB-023 employee made a case for BSI to acquire a West Coast office furniture retailer. Someone else argued to reduce the CEOs' pay to one dollar. Most of the cost-saving suggestions wouldn't make a material impact. But at least the Promisekeepers kept looking for ways to help.

Will's phone buzzed, and he pressed it between his ear and shoulder.

"Mr. Evans," Les said. "Is your team still compiling the SOB materials? Happenstance wants me to include a perspective on how analysts view us."

"Yep." Will continued scrolling. "Send it my way. I'll get it in the binder."

"Coolio. It'll be short and sweet. Half of them think we suck. The other half is sure of it."

Will smiled. "Brief is good. These binders are going to weigh a ton."

"So what else are you seeing in the presentations? Anything enlightening?"

"Some good plans."

"We need better than good." Les dropped his voice to a whisper. "The doomsday scenario in today's paper might've been a shot in the dark, but it's eerily accurate. Unless we find a Rayzor replacement with a model that copies, collates, TEPILs your day, and gives you a happy ending . . . we could run out of money and time."

Will looked away from his screen. "We'll turn it around."

"You keep that glass half-full, Will." Les laughed. "And speaking of full glasses, you up for the Monk tonight? If I exercise my vested options, I can afford to buy you exactly one skanky tequila shot."

"What?" Will snorted. "*You're* going to buy *me* a drink?"

"Sure, why not? I've got a few extra rubles in my pocket after stumbling into that Mario Mayday on twelve this afternoon."

Will nodded. He'd seen the text. Leftover pizza from a sales meeting. "Thanks for the offer, but I'll already be there. Meeting a friend."

"Ooooh, anyone I know? Is she—"

"It's Big Al," Will said as his phone beeped with an incoming call. He checked the screen and pressed the phone back to his ear. "Sorry,

I should probably take this."

He clicked to release Les and stared at Beth's name on the screen. She kept trying to reach him, and he needed to know why. *Closure? To get back together? That lamp she always liked so much?*

"Hello?"

"Hey, you." Beth's tone sounded soft and comforting.

Will's heart pounded a little faster. It seemed like forever since he'd heard her voice and her pet greeting for him. His mind flashed back to the apartment they'd shared and how he'd find her curled up on the sofa when he arrived home late from work. He missed that feeling of companionship. Coming home to someone waiting for him.

"I've been trying to reach you," she cooed.

His stomach fluttered. "I know . . . I saw you called. Sorry. Things have been a little crazy."

"Well, it's good to hear your voice. I've missed it." She fell silent for a few seconds. "And you."

"It's good to hear from you, too." Will realized his left hand shook. He transferred the phone to his right. "How have you been?"

"I've been good." A hint of melancholy crept into her delivery. "You know . . . been doing a lot of thinking . . . about things . . . about us."

Will didn't know what to say. "Yeah?"

"Yeah. I'm sorry about the way things ended."

"I'm sorry, too." His chest thumped now and echoed in his ears. He looked out the two-story window. *This is it. Has to be. She realizes her mistake and wants me back.* He fought the urge to close the deal, right then, right there. To invite her over tonight and work it all out.

But he had to be careful. It had hurt like hell when she dumped him. And the public embarrassment—changing her Facebook relationship status to single before leaving the parking lot—delivered an extra-special kick in the gut. She needed to show that she'd changed. That she understood the pain she'd caused. *Stay strong, Evans.*

"So . . . I saw your sister a while back," Beth said after a brief pause. "She told me about your promotion. Very exciting."

The left turn took Will by surprise. "Oh . . . yeah. Thanks."

"And then I saw the layoffs in the news. I was worried about you."

"It's okay. I made it through." Will wondered where this would go.

"Listen," Beth cooed again. "I'd love to see you. Maybe we could grab a drink. Vodka with no fruit?" She giggled. "You could tell me all about the new job. And then we could . . . you know, catch up."

Will recognized the manipulation behind her smooth tone. Beth loved to dangle sex as a reward when she wanted something from him.

"There's not much to say." He downplayed it, curious if she'd push for more. "It's just a job."

"Oh, you're being modest. It's a new title, right? One step away from VP? And more money, too, I'll bet. You're probably house-hunting on Lake Minnetonka as we speak."

Will's excitement deteriorated with every word she uttered. Oh, she wanted him back, all right—pending the verification of his up-graded financial status. He dropped his chin to his chest. *I should have seen this coming.*

"Listen, Anna, I'm in the middle of an important announcement. Maybe another time . . ."

The line went quiet. "Who's Anna?"

"What?"

"You called me Anna. Who's Anna?"

Will's mouth hung open for a second and then broke into a smile. *Anna is not Beth.* He looked out the window, allowing the phone to fall silent.

Why hadn't he realized this before? They both pushed him—it's why Anna made him wary from the start, why he questioned her motivations. But Beth and Anna weren't the same. Beth had always been self-serving. Anna just wanted to do the right thing.

"Will? Were you . . ." Beth began, with what sounded like faux pain in her voice. "Oh, never mind. I'm sure you saw other people."

In an instant, she grew chipper again. "So when can we get together? Tonight? Ooh, Friday night . . . we could sleep in and then get breakfast at Fat Nat's. You always loved that place."

Will set his jaw and looked straight ahead. "I don't think that's a good idea, Beth."

"What, the breakfast? Or . . ."

"Us. Me and you. It's not a good idea. I've moved on. Things are different now."

"Oh. I didn't know. But, Will. You can't just—"

"Thanks for reaching out, but I really need to go. Good-bye, Beth." He tossed the phone onto the table with a smile. He felt lighter. Hopeful. Happy.

Things are definitely different now.

CHAPTER 28

That evening, Will found Big Al waiting in front of the Walker-Patterson building. Al rarely strayed this far from his Northeast digs, but he had been delivering layoff paperwork to the BSI tower—a perfect excuse to get together in Will's territory.

They rode the elevator to the Drunken Monk and strolled inside. The Foo Fighters' "Learn to Fly" reverberated overhead as Al slipped off his jacket and took in the bar with a discerning eye.

"Downtown's pretentious take on a blue-collar watering hole. With fourteen-dollar microbrews and pseudointellectual garage bands." Al pointed to the easel sign announcing the debut of punk band Three Pea Standoff.

Inky sized up the pair as they approached the hostess stand, studying Al's tattered Carhartts and the T-shirt straining over his broad shoulders.

"So, No Fruit." Inky led them to a booth. "I didn't know it was Take-Your-Loading-Dock-Guy-to-Work Day." She placed a menu on the table between them and addressed Big Al. "So cute—the corporate shills pull you out of your cave to mingle with the cool kids. Here for the lunch-bucket special?"

Will's face reddened, but Al didn't flinch.

"Miller High Life. And a Juicy Lucy, but only if it's under a sawbuck and bigger than your nose ring. Hold the onions . . . and the emo attitude."

She placed her hand on the table, showing the freshly tattooed letters CBGB across her knuckles. "Listen, you may be the biggest cock on your roost. But this is my henhouse, big guy."

Al nodded. "And I'm sure you scare the hell out of these downtown desk jockeys. But you don't rattle me, kiddo. We're poured from the same mason jar."

Will slid down in his seat, convinced Inky would leap onto Al's shoulders like a feral monkey and claw at his eyes with her chewed-up fingernails. Instead, she hit him with a shockingly genuine smile. "Touché, my man. High Life and a Juicy Lucy it is."

"Side of fries." Al grinned in return.

Will started to speak, but Inky walked away. "Vodka Sprite," he called. She folded one arm behind her back and flipped him off with her B-knuckled finger.

"Hey, I heard about Pink Pantser." Will looked across the booth to his former boss. "I'm sorry."

"The cuts hurt." Al rubbed the back of his neck. "Had to release Redbone, Tito, HT, and Nashville, too."

"That sucks. But they're smart people. They'll land on their feet." Coffee had said the same thing about TK. Will hoped it was true. For all of them.

"I see most of the execs spared themselves," Al noted. "Figures. They come face to face with their own incompetence, and their answer is to cut ten percent of the employees who do this company's honest-to-God heavy lifting for a couple clicks above minimum wage. Peter Principle horseshit." He paused while Inky delivered their drinks. "How are the tower survivors holding up?"

"Not great. Everyone lost friends. And you've seen the press lately. Our credit rating got downgraded. And now the Synerpoint battle. Can't blame people for being skeptical. Doesn't help there's nothing but radio silence coming from the twenty-second floor."

"Is that where Jerry and Ron were hiding on layoff day?" Al spun his beer bottle in a calloused hand. "Can't believe they didn't say one goddamn word to the troops. Not even to the managers who carried out their cuts. It was . . . demoralizing."

Will swallowed hard. "I tried to get them on video or email—letting everyone know we'd get through it. They wouldn't go for it."

Al cocked his head. "Big miss. But I hear you and Pearl have been doing your best to keep my Promisekeepers up to speed."

Inky came back with a burger and heaping pile of fries. "That was fast," Al said.

"We make 'em early and keep 'em smoldering under the heat lamps." Inky cracked her knuckles and walked away.

Will slid the ketchup across the table. "Yeah, thanks. We're doing our best on the Chatterbox, but we don't have a lot of solid info to share."

Al picked up a crinkled French fry and poked a hole in the top of his burger—releasing a gust of steam while keeping the inner molten cheese intact.

"Veteran move." Will shot him a wry smile.

"What about you, Frodo? Where's your head at?"

Will took a gulp of vodka. "I'm all right. Holding up."

"You looking?"

"I don't . . . you mean, for another job?"

Al nodded, and Will poked at the ice in his drink before answering. The question caught him off-guard.

"No, I'm like you—I bleed purple. In the long run, we won't be the same company, but we'll be all right. The two of us are probably the exceptions, though. I'll bet the market is flooded with BSI résumés right now."

"Probably." Al took a swig of beer. "When companies start to circle the drain, the best employees are the first to scramble for higher ground. That's why I asked if you were looking."

"You think BSI is circling the drain?" Will's chest tightened.

"Well, Optelligence is dead, and Copiers is on life support. Mighty hard to keep the vital organs going when there's no income pumping through the veins."

Will wanted to ask Al whether he had started looking, too, but he didn't want to know the answer. Too weird—the thought of Big Al wearing some other company's colors.

"If you don't want another twelve-buck bottle, all taps are on happy hour," Will said instead, pointing to the beer list.

"Cool." Big Al set down his burger and blotted the grease and cheese from his hands with a paper napkin. He browsed the list as Will looked for a way to turn the conversation toward brighter territory.

"I guess we're close to getting MX nailed down as the Rayzor replacement. The CEOs and Sonny are in Japan this week for the final handshake. Still confidential."

Al pulled a pair of reading glasses from his pocket, to better see the beer list. "I hope it happens fast," he said. "There's a hell of a lot to do . . . ship inventory, train reps on the products, marketing collateral. And even then—replacing Rayzor only gets the core business back to solvent. It doesn't address the fundamental problem that got us into this mess in the first place. We need to show we can grow again."

Will tried to offer an answer. "You hear about the State of the Business meeting?"

Al nodded. "It was in the Synerpoint announcement."

"Right. Well, all the execs are creating plans to present. A few of the recommendations look promising—some solid margin-enhancing ideas."

"Margin isn't the problem." Al lowered the beer menu. "We need to grow the top line—sales, revenue . . . call it what you want. That's what the Street wants to see, and that's why they've been ripping us apart. Our business is shrinking, and we haven't delivered any returns on Optelligence. And now it might not ever happen."

Will reached across and stole a fry off Al's plate. "Don't be so sure. I haven't seen what Jerry and Ron have cooked up—they'll probably have new plans to unveil, too."

"You think Jerry and Ron know how to get us growing again?" Al stared over the top of his black-rimmed glasses at Will. "They're in Asia right now, trying to convince some greenhorn manufacturer we're not the broken-down shit-wagon analysts say we are. The CEOs are just trying to keep us afloat. And then what? When's the last time either of them came up with anything new that mattered? Something a consultant didn't feed them?"

For a guy who had convinced Will and hundreds of other part-timers to make BSI their home and career, Al sounded like one of the pessimists from outside.

"Doesn't sound like you have much hope left for this place." Will's stomach turned, not only from the grease-soaked fry he'd devoured.

Al tossed the beer list back onto the table. "Look, Ron and Jerry are two of the smartest, most resourceful guys I've ever met. They started this company with nothing but a maxed-out Visa card and a clammy handshake. I don't always like the way they do things, but I'm not ready to bet against them, either." He paused to take a long drag from his bottle.

"We got so goddamn big, so fast, Will. When we went public, I'm not sure anybody realized we signed a lifetime contract to run on a treadmill that never stops. And the treadmill keeps accelerating—so slowly at first, nobody realizes it. But you gotta keep growing—top and bottom line—every quarter, year-over-year, to please the Wall Street beast. It comes easy at first, and you assume growth like that is your birthright. But every good business plan reaches the end of its runway."

Will thought about the go-go days they had enjoyed in his first years with the company. BSI couldn't expand the Flourbox model fast enough. Every new market became a boomtown, and every quarter's performance outpaced the last. The result—a decade of double-digit comps and a multiplying share price envied across the industry.

"Then your performance starts to level off." Al used his hand to trace a flat line in the air. "And panic begins to creep in. Because you know if you can't keep growing, they'll shove you off the treadmill. Onto the scrapheap of failed companies whose only crime was not running at an unrealistic pace forever."

He wiped more cheese from his fingers before continuing.

"That's when every Tom, Dick, and D-bag comes circling—consultants, market researchers, B-school profs. They tell you to reinvent yourself. Forget the principles that made you successful. And then what happens? You cozy up to crooks like Synerpoint, and they stomp you in the crotch and take your lunch money."

Al took another bite of burger and another few swallows of beer, talking as he chewed. "I think over time Ron and Jerry lost faith in themselves. Then they stopped trusting their own leaders to figure shit out. Pretty soon, if you weren't wearing a visitor's badge, they couldn't hear you."

Inky came back with a fresh drink for Will and more napkins for Al, who ordered a Grain Belt Nordeast.

Will hesitated and then pointed to his drink. "Um, there's a lime in here."

Inky rolled her eyes, fished out the floating wedge with two bony fingers, and tossed the wet fruit onto the table. Will decided it best to accept the cocktail, lest she stab the swizzle stick into his eardrum.

Al wiped his mouth, pushed away his plate, and wiped crumbs from the table. Will studied his mentor—now in his late fifties—under the amber bar lights. The reading glasses magnified the wrinkles around Al's eyes and the sagging skin under them. Coarse strands of gray intertwined with his dark hair. He'd spent the most important years of his working life at FB-One, making his way into a position of authority and respect. Everything he had—friends, retirement accounts, and self-worth—had become inextricably woven into the fibers of BSI. He was probably too old and most certainly too unwilling to start over, even if someone would hire a man so set in his ways. A man so near the end of his own runway.

Al's not looking for another job. He has nowhere else to go.

Will blinked hard a few times. It hurt—seeing Al like this. Vulnerable. Mortal.

"So, what now?"

Al leaned back in the booth, his broad frame dwarfed by the puffy seat back. "You wondered if I had any hope left for this place. I do. I have hope in you—to help figure this out."

Will let out an uneasy laugh. "Yeah, like I have the answers. That's pretty far above my pay grade."

"Good ideas can come from anywhere," Al shrugged. "You know that. It's what you told my guys about the Chatterbox."

Will didn't like being pushed—*again*. It made him nervous. "Listen, I'm a middle manager. Not even 'middle.' More like two rungs from the bottom. Nothing I touch feeds the Wall Street beast."

Al's eyes narrowed as he stared across the booth—the look he used when wasn't getting what he wanted from a crewmember. "Knock it off." He waved a hand at Will. "I didn't give you a shot in this company so you could plop your ass on the middle rung and hope for a miracle. You have that vantage point for a reason. The Rainmakers are either paralyzed with fear or barking up the wrong tree. The Promisekeepers may have some answers—but they're not connected or confident enough to push anything through. And here you sit with access to both sides—a direct line into the C-suite and the 'Boxes. You can bridge the gap. You have to."

A swell of anxiety raised the hair on Will's arms. Big Al couldn't possibly be putting the weight of the entire company on his back. *I already see a chiropractor from lugging my laptop bag around.*

"Listen, I've tried cashing in chips with Jerry and Ron, but it hasn't done a damn bit of good. And if the ideas aren't good enough . . ."

"Goddammit, Frodo, *make* them good enough." Al lowered his voice and leaned in. "Don't overcomplicate it. Tell me—what's out there right now? On the Chatterbox?"

Will shook his head. He almost regretted ever creating the damn thing. "There's nothing that can . . . it's just little stuff. Like one of the drivers unpacking office supplies for a customer."

Al raised his thick eyebrows. "Can we scale it? What do you think a customer would pay for that?"

Will threw up his hands. "A basket of cookies, okay? That's it. That's what the customer paid. So I hope the beast likes chocolate-chip."

Al offered up a weary smile. "C'mon, Will. You need to think bigger. You know people who could help. Sonny. Anna. That Investor Relations loudmouth who never irons his shirts."

The house lights dimmed and a Zeppelin B-side roared overhead. The Monk's daily transition from happy-hour hot spot to nighttime live-music venue. Will wondered whether the darkness might allow him to slip out before Al assigned any more herculean tasks.

"Will." Al rested his elbows on the table. "You can't sit on your hands and hope for the best. We're running out of time. We could go under."

Will rubbed his forearms with his hands, trying to subdue his rising panic. High-profile assignments carried the very real risk of high-profile failures. He preferred hanging in the wings, making someone else look good. The thought of forcing himself off the sidelines and into this game—under the bright lights, with no margin for error—scared him.

But he dreaded one thing even more: disappointing Big Al.

"All right. I can do some digging on the Chatterbox ideas," Will conceded. "But don't get your hopes up. Anna tried to get Amadeus's idea approved a while back, and even that simple thing—meetings between Sales and Delivery guys—got shot down by Kirkland."

Al smiled and raised his eyebrows again. "Every man's got his motivation, right? If you need the Lilliputian Prince, figure out what it takes to get him on board."

Will nodded, wrapping his head around what he needed to do. With the execs scrambling for new sources of revenue, Kirkland would have to be more open this time around. And Will knew precisely what it would take to convince him.

Misplaced confidence and kick-ass shoes.

CHAPTER 29

Anna marched across the sixteenth floor on a mission—her flowered platform heels scuffing the carpet with every purposeful step. She and Will had been working day and night to cobble the best Chatterbox ideas into an actual business plan. Anna loved putting the pieces together. Underlying story and analysis? Check. Supporting data? Getting there. Executive buy-in? Next on the list.

"I heard you coming." Dee Dee smiled as Anna reached her cube. "You walk with such authority."

Anna rolled out her best polite tone of voice. "Sorry to bother you, but like I said in my note—I really need some time with Lyle."

"Let me check."

Dee Dee clicked and scrolled as Anna scanned the cube, looking for something to spark a personal conversation.

"Oh, cute." She gritted her teeth, hoping it resembled a smile. "A cat wearing a tiny top hat."

Dee Dee didn't look up. "That's Mr. Bootsy Bigglesworth. He loves getting dressed up for church." She frowned at her monitor. "I'm sorry . . . Lyle's booked solid. I'd move things if I could, but he's in a lot of vendor meetings."

Anna sat on the corner of the admin's desk and stole a glance at Kirkland's on-screen calendar—a color-blocked cluster of triple-booked time. "Vendor meetings? Isn't that Sonny's purview?"

"With Sonny in Japan, Lyle has to entertain the Cleary group tonight." Dee Dee stood up. "I'm sorry, I printed a confidential memo . . ."

"No problem; go get it. I don't mind."

Dee Dee hurried up the aisle as Anna slid off the desk and hunched in front of the screen. According to the notes in tonight's appointment, Kirkland was hosting a dozen Cleary VIPs. Steak and martinis at The Capital Grille and then a Tim McGraw concert. She made a mental note of the Target Center clubroom number, Kirkland's corporate credit card info, and the volume of Tex-Mex appetizers requested from the suite catering service. *Great—now I'll have seventy-five taquitos stuck in my head for the next five years.*

Anna met Dee Dee in the aisle and smiled again at the bouncy redhead. "Thanks for trying. I'll let you get back to work. You're too busy with things to have to worry about little ol' me."

"All right, bye—and I'm sorry." Dee Dee adjusted one of the cat pictures on her desk. "I had no idea being Lyle's new chief of staff would keep me hopping so much."

Anna rolled her eyes and stalked away. So the title went to Dee Dee. Not exactly a shock. *Though given Kirkland's fondness for pussy, I'm surprised Bigglesworth didn't get the job.*

Anna stepped onto the elevator and pushed the street-level button as Will's name appeared on her buzzing phone.

"Hey, how did it go with Customer Insights?"

"Great," he said on the other end of the line. "They had data to validate the enhanced service idea. They even suggested a name: Delivery Plus. Rolls off the tongue much better than 'Doug's Real Estate Cookie Basket Idea,' right? I'll update the deck."

Reaching street level, Anna threw open the tower door and hurried to get through the flashing light at the intersection, taking care not to catch her fabulous heel in the sewer grate. "Great. Everything's lining up, then."

"Sure is. Just a got note from Sonny, too. He said he'll sponsor the plan at the SOB meeting if the numbers add up. He wants me to send him the latest. The guy's on top of it today—it's like six a.m. in Japan." Will paused to take a breath. "Did you get on Kirkland's calendar?"

"Not exactly. He's at Target Center tonight. I'm on my way now."

"Wait . . . what?"

"I'm going to close the deal tonight," Anna explained. "His team needs time to put new compensation plans together—and we need to kiss the ring. Make sure Kirkland feels like he owns the idea. With five days until the SOB meeting, we've got to get this done."

"But . . . the deck's not ready."

Anna dodged two women wearing straw cowboy hats and maxi-dresses. Why the hell did Will sound so skeptical? "I don't need a deck. I know how to get his attention."

"That's what I'm worried about."

Anna paused, causing the two couples behind her to stop short and bump into each other. She mouthed "sorry" to them and stepped off the sidewalk and into a restaurant entryway.

"I don't understand. Trust me—I can do this."

"I know you can. You're devious as hell—in all the right the ways. It's just . . ."

Anna smiled. "What?"

"I trust you, but I don't trust Kirkland," Will continued. "He's probably three martinis into the night, and he's off-site—an HR-free zone. I'm worried you're walking into a lion's den."

The concern in his voice caught Anna off-guard. No one had cared enough to express concern for her well being in a long time. Not even the last few years with Erik—after he'd used her independence as an excuse to stop expressing much of anything. Her eyes welled up. She blinked and cleared her throat to recover.

"You're sweet, Will, but I'm no defenseless lamb." She straightened up and merged back into the busy walkway. "And everyone's counting on us—Big Al, the Promisekeepers, the team . . . everyone. The stakes couldn't be higher. I'm going to get Kirkland on board—

one way or another."

Will groaned. "What the hell are you planning to do?"

"The less you know, the better." She bypassed the milling-about crowd to enter the arena and paused before stepping inside. "Any other new details I should know, aside from calling it Delivery Plus?"

"No. Just . . . Anna, be smart."

"Always."

Anna slipped inside, dialed Bennie and hopped onto the escalator. "Hey, I need you to call me in thirty minutes. Rescue mission. I'll need a fast 'out.' No questions asked."

"Ooh, what's with the intrigue?" Bennie cooed. "Are you trafficking human organs or something?"

"Ben—"

"Wait, I got it! You're not Anna Reed . . . you're Natasha Vodkabeetch—sexy, undercover KGB agent, headed for clandestine tryst at Russian embassy. Yah?" Bennie's attempt at disguising her East Coast speech patterns with an Eastern Bloc accent made her comments almost indiscernible.

"What part of 'no questions asked' don't you understand?" Anna laughed. "And Minneapolis doesn't have a Russian embassy. Just give me an escape call."

"So mysterious . . ." Bennie fell silent for a moment before chirping, "Okeydokey."

Anna slipped the phone into her purse and tossed her e-ticket into a trash bin. The last-minute purchase of a nosebleed seat gained her entry to the arena—but it wouldn't get her past suite security. She pushed open the glass doors and walked through like a boss.

Target Center showed its age, but the dimly lit suite level still exuded an air of exclusivity. Music from the arena floor echoed through propped-open clubroom doors.

"Can I direct you to your suite?" The security guard—young and wearing a teal polo shirt—fell into step beside Anna.

"I'm fine." She flashed a smile at him. "I'm with Mr. Kirkland and the Business Solutions group. Thank you, though."

"I'm sorry, but I have to check your ticket."

"Oh, of course." Anna stopped and dug through her purse, feigning dismay. "Oh no, I'm such an idiot . . . I left my ticket in the suite. I'm sorry."

Ted, as his nametag said, rested an electronic tablet on his arm and tapped the screen. "No problem . . . I can pull up Mr. Kirkland's suite number and give him a call."

"Oh no!" Anna laid a hand on Ted's doughy arm. "Please don't do that. I'm his assistant. And I'm already in trouble with him for messing up his travel—it's a whole thing. If I bother him now, when he's entertaining clients, I could lose my job."

He looked into her eyes—filled now with a dose of genuine panic.

"I'm sorry, but I can't lose my job either. And I can't let you in without a ticket or having the suite owner vouch for you."

"But I reserved it." Anna smiled again. "It might be under his name, but technically, I'm the owner, right? Do you have my name—Dee Dee Ruggles—on the reservation? Using our Business Solutions corporate card?"

Ted scratched the back of his head and squinted at his screen. "Can you show me the credit card you used? I can confirm it against the number I have here."

Anna pictured Kirkland's calendar in her mind, zeroed in on the electronic receipt Dee Dee had added to the notes, and rattled off the sixteen-digit card number.

Ted nodded. "Wow, that's it, all right. Amazing memory you have there."

"Thanks for your patience, Ted."

"Enjoy your evening, Ms. Ruggles."

Anna passed him and entered the suite-level corridor, grinning like a madwoman. She wanted to pump her fist in the air—like a rom-com's plucky heroine. But she'd only gotten in the door, and she didn't have a trite-but-heartwarming script to tell her what to do next. She couldn't extrapolate life wisdom from '70s-era sitcoms like Judd.

Anna's phone vibrated in the outside pocket of her purse, and she dug it out as she walked. A text from her headhunter, Alissa.

"Twins confirm: interview rocked!!"

Anna halted and leaned her back against the wall. She'd pushed the Twins job out of her mind while helping Will develop Delivery Plus—the kind of high-risk, high-profile work she'd wanted from BSI all along. But Alissa's text reminded Anna she had been working two angles simultaneously. She stared down the long hall for a moment before thumbing a response.

"Awesome. Keep things moving."

Dropping the phone into her purse, Anna wheeled back into action. She read the suite numbers as she passed each door, feeling a bit out of place amid the rich and powerful. Like Melanie Griffith's character in *Working Girl*. Anna wracked her brain to remember what Tess McGill did after crashing the Trask wedding.

Aha. She danced with the dealmaker.

She didn't have to work hard to find him. Lyle Kirkland sat alone at the small, well-appointed public bar outside the suites. Probably avoiding small talk with the Cleary execs.

Anna took a few steps back—around the corner and out of his peripheral vision—to prepare herself. She straightened her form-fitting skirt and fluffed her hair. Suppressing her disgust—mostly with herself—she strode toward the bar.

"Lyle! Nice to see you."

Kirkland looked up with a confused expression—unable to place her outside the office context. She noted a flicker of anticipation in his eyes followed by a hint of disappointment. *Now you recognize me.*

"I'm here with a friend." The line tumbled from Anna's mouth without any forethought. "Are you here for BSI?"

Kirkland studied his drink again. "The Cleary group is in town."

Anna nodded. "Interesting."

He wrapped his hands around a lowball glass, and she studied the small pieces of hand-hammered silver augmenting his French cuffs.

"They're made from piston rod bearings," he said. "Reclaimed from a vintage Mercedes." Without so much as a glance in her direction, he'd noticed where her attention had focused.

"They're beautiful." Anna leaned an elbow on the bar. "One of a kind, I imagine. Especially being from such limited source material."

"Engines don't have true piston rods like that anymore."

"It's all crossheads now." She hoped like hell he wouldn't ask her to say one more sentence about that. She had no idea how or why her brain had acquired and retained the term.

Kirkland raised an eyebrow before nodding to the bartender. "What can Michael get you?"

Anna sighed. "I should be getting back, but I suppose I can't refuse one drink, right?"

She leaned over the bar, ostensibly to examine the top-shelf bottles. She caught a covert whiff of the booze in Kirkland's glass. He stole a sideways glance at the cleavage spilling into the V of her blouse.

Scotch. Of course. I hate scotch.

"Do you have anything other than Johnny Walker Red?" She pointed to a label she recognized.

"Pour her a Glenlivet twenty-year," Kirkland encouraged. "It's sweet yet smoky."

"On the rocks, lemon twist, splash of Seven." Anna hoped to dull the taste.

Kirkland frowned as the bartender added the pollutants to her glass. She slid onto the barstool next to him and waited for her drink. When she crossed her legs, her short black skirt rode higher, and she smoothed the fabric down, tracing the line of her thighs with her fingers. Kirkland made no attempt to hide his attention.

"So how do you know about vintage Mercedes engines, if you don't mind *me* asking?"

Anna flashed the same charismatic smile she offered Ted. With no good answer for the question, she stole one.

"The boys back home I grew up with—they bought cars cheap and fixed them up. I paid attention." She felt confident he wouldn't recognize the movie reference. "So, the Cleary group is in the suite, yet you're sitting out here. Why is that . . . if you don't mind me asking?"

He smirked. "Cleary is based in San Antonio. They rather enjoy the banjos and caterwauling. I, however, do not. And we already talked business over dinner."

"Ah, I see. I assume Cleary is skittish because of the Rayzor replacement. You're here to make them feel secure. About our partnership."

"And instill confidence about BSI's future." Kirkland raised the glass to his thin lips.

Anna took a tiny sip of her scotch and tried to appear pleased as the liquid scalded her throat.

"I'm curious how you addressed that with Cleary." She reached forward to rub a nonexistent itch on her bare calf. His gaze followed her hand. "With Salvador Chan's departure and the loss of Innovation . . . I'm finding it difficult to frame up Optelligence."

Kirkland raised his empty glass and gestured in Michael's direction. "Are you making an observation or asking for my perspective?"

Anna disregarded his condescending tone. "I'm struggling with what to tell employees in our communication channels. I'm asking for your help."

He smiled—smugly, Anna observed—and started to wax philosophical on the global economic malaise and the methods by which successful capitalists thrive.

She looked into his Raisinet eyes as he lectured. Company legend claimed he started as a charming intern with impressive business school credentials and an insatiable drive. Most likely, he'd have risen through the ranks solely through intelligence and ambition. But he propelled himself near the top of BSI's leadership hierarchy by playing the angles and manipulating people. Coercing them, pitting them against each other, crushing them when necessary. An

279

approach he'd raised to an art form.

"The Technology plan is still valid, given the ROIC of the value proposition, size of the market, and strength of our customer relationships. For employees, I suggest you highlight the future profit potential, calling it the first phase of Optelligence—to be followed by other strategies when the market is more receptive." Kirkland tugged at one of his shirt cuffs. "The key is to never acknowledge uncertainty or defeat. Any missteps should be repositioned as natural, educational byproducts of a constantly evolving, dynamic marketplace."

"That's smart." *And complete bullshit.* "But I was under the impression that your Technology strategy was also at risk. Due to budgets and Synerpoint going to market with their Optitude platform?"

"Synerpoint is irrelevant. With today's open architecture standards and the proliferation of technology in all aspects of business operations, there is plenty of marketplace opportunity for BSI. We're moving forward with a bias for action. My Technology strategy is BSI's ace in the hole."

Anna swirled the scotch in her glass and recrossed her legs. Most people believed Kirkland had a singular, primary motivation: sex. And one could hardly blame them, given his hard-earned reputation—not to mention the way he currently ogled her thighs. But sex, to Kirkland, came second to his game playing. A personally beneficial consequence of his mission to get what he truly craved: all-encompassing power. An addictive quest for control. Anna sometimes felt it, too.

"So you must be planning to present your updated rollout plan for Technology in the State of the Business meeting." She hooked her heel on her barstool rung and angled her body toward him. "I'm sure Ron and Jerry are anxious to have their concerns alleviated."

Kirkland raised his eyes to meet hers. "To what concerns are you referring?"

"Speed to market. Cost overruns. Minimal revenue potential." She subtly emphasized her last point. "Take your pick."

A flash of anger appeared in his eyes. Anna held up her hands in defense.

"Their words, not mine." She reached for her drink.

"Ron and Jerry told you this," he said, his skepticism apparent.

"No, no." Anna placed a hand on her chest. "They don't consult me on these things, of course. But I've been working on the State of the Business proposals, and the CEOs are clear what they're looking for—fast, lasting revenue and cash flow improvements." She tilted her head, doing her best to appear nonchalant while setting the hook. "And that's what I'm seeing in some materials from other leaders."

Kirkland grabbed his glass and twisted his head away from her and the bar, irritated. Anna hoped his mind swam with the implications of continuing to champion the remnants of the Optelligence boondoggle.

She allowed the silence to linger and then delicately nudged the conversation forward. "We're in such a strange environment right now. The local papers have turned into supermarket tabloids. The Street's left us for dead. The whole Rayzor thing. And all this legacy talk . . ."

Kirkland took a long swallow of scotch and set his glass on the bar—a little too forcefully. "Legacy talk."

"You know, the legacy Ron and Jerry will leave behind—eventually—making sure the business is in good shape. And good hands. I guess it explains why they're running out of patience with strategies that don't deliver. They certainly didn't give Chan much time with Innovation. It's hard to believe he was considered a succession candidate."

Anna watched the bartender refill Kirkland's drink. She shook her head politely when Michael held the bottle over her glass.

"Chan was not a succession candidate," Kirkland growled. "And Ron and Jerry aren't going anywhere. If they had a succession plan, I'd know about it."

I'm walking a fine line here. She wanted to summon his ambition, not his ire. "I'm sorry, succession is probably the wrong term. It's, you know, the t-talent pipeline." She added the stutter for effect. "Not just for CEO, but for other C-level jobs. Like all companies do. Identify a pool of execs that can take on more responsibility, now and in the future. Chan was obviously in that pool, given his title and his association with the board. I'm sure there are others in line."

"Of course there are."

"Present company included." She fluttered her long eyelashes, careful not to lay it on too thick.

One side of his mouth raised in a wry grin, and he took another long drink. Anna wondered how many glasses Michael had filled while Kirkland avoided the suite. She hoped he remained lucid enough to follow her story.

"But with things not—you know—panning out on the Optelligence side of the business . . ." *Your side*, Anna added in her head. "And Copiers on the forefront again, it's interesting how Sonny has inserted himself into that succession conversation."

Kirkland laughed out loud. A spontaneous, patronizing reaction.

"Sonny Larsson is *not* C-suite material. He lacks broad operational experience and strategic vision. Hell of a salesman, but he doesn't belong anywhere near the top of the house—unless Ron and Jerry are looking to buy a copier." He laughed again.

Anna sipped her drink, plotting how to proceed. *With caution.* Kirkland systematically dismantled his competitors, exploiting their weaknesses and preying on any motivations they were careless enough to reveal. She didn't want him to destroy Sonny. She needed them to work together.

Kirkland continued. "And Sonny doesn't have the ambition."

"Maybe not. But he *is* in Japan with the CEOs right now. And he's working on that killer idea for the State of the Business meeting."

The executive swallowed and stared at Anna again. "Say one more sentence about that."

Gotcha.

"It's in the deck he's working on for the meeting. Came directly from a Flourbox—Ron and Jerry will love the grassroots nature." She leaned forward as if sharing a secret. "It's a value-add service contract with Delivery drivers trained to provide regular, basic copier maintenance. And white-glove services like maintaining and restocking office supplies for companies with large-scale operations."

"Interesting."

Anna smiled. "Low investment with high-return annual contracts. Targeting existing customers. Some will likely pay up front, others over time. If it works, it's a direct infusion of cash coupled with a recurring revenue stream—and it can all be booked the minute the agreement is signed. Win-win-win."

"What are the financials?"

"Conservative estimates put it at $50 million for the balance of this year. Double that in year two. Market research backs it up."

Kirkland now leaned forward, uncomfortably close to Anna. She held her ground.

"Sonny can't deliver that plan." She could smell the scotch on his humid breath. "It would require a nationwide operational directive in the short term . . . and a new incentive structure for Sales and Delivery teams in the long term."

Anna kept her eyes locked with his. "I don't disagree. Sonny may have the framework. But he needs your vision and operational authority. He needs your co-sponsorship on this."

Kirkland nodded, consumed with his thoughts. For a moment, Anna worried he might be plotting to steal the idea for himself. But he knew Lois would send the SOB meeting materials as a pre-read to all attendees so the egotistical gnome couldn't claim it as his own. His only play—glom onto Sonny for a share of the glory.

She looked at the floor, where the phone in her purse began ringing.

"I'm sure that's my friend. I need to get back. I can send you the business case on this—it's called Delivery Plus."

Anna started to rise, but the exec put a hand on her arm. The touch of his fingers on her sleeve, wrapped around her forearm, made her cringe inside. She sat down again, looking at his silver wedding band that matched his cufflinks.

"This was a good conversation," he said.

"You sound surprised."

"I am, frankly." A corner of Kirkland's mouth curled upward. "When you joined BSI, I was told you were a rock star. Yet I haven't seen it. Now, that doesn't mean it's not true. But as more time goes by and I don't see the level of skill and knowledge I expected, I start to believe you're not that talented."

Anna kept the smile on her face, even though the words hurt— right down to the core of her accomplished, confident self. Which is exactly what he wanted. He exploited other people's motivations to control them. And she had served hers up on a platter. Every conversation where she had revealed her career ambitions, harping on the chief of staff promotion—she exposed a soft underbelly. Practically begging him to insert the knife.

Kirkland kept his eyes—and his hand—on her. *You think you can break me. Well, fuck off, you narcissistic sociopath.*

Anna steadied her voice. "I'm sorry you feel that way."

"And I'm sorry you've been such a big disappointment to me."

She tried to distance herself from the escalating emotional impact of his words and focus on why he chose to run this game on her now—after she had delivered him the strong, inside track on a winning strategy.

It's because I'm too strong, she realized. *And too inside.*

Kirkland surrounded himself with the supportive, naïve, and weak. He viewed intelligent, willful people as threats. Those who couldn't be disarmed got jettisoned or destroyed. He built no real relationships with people—he played them all. Dee Dee's loyalty? Bought with a pat on the head and an empty title. Peyton's allegiance? Obtained by making her feel young and desirable. Underlings across the company worked arduous hours on nebulous projects—spurred on by some combination of Kirkland hints, threats, or promises.

His current move? Attempting to neutralize Anna. Bring her to her knees. A position he especially favored for pretty blondes.

Anna showed him her best fuck-you smile and deftly removed his hand from her arm.

"I have to go, Lyle."

She slipped off the stool, grabbed her purse, and started down the corridor before the son of a bitch could see the tears in her eyes.

To: Anna Reed
From: William Evans
Subject: Hey...

I don't even know how to begin saying thanks for all your help on this crazy plan. No idea what happens next, but I just have to say you've been amazing.

To: William Evans
From: Anna Reed
Subject: Re: Hey...

Thanks for that. I'm glad you trusted me to help. It's not a big deal, really.

To: Anna Reed
From: William Evans
Subject: Re: Hey...

Are you kidding?? We've logged like 90 hours already this week. Worked all day Sat & Sun. Last night we must have printed 50 versions of that customer data section til we got it right—we were in the office til 4 a.m. Which, by the way, is my first time spending the night with a co-worker. ☺

To: William Evans
From: Anna Reed
Subject: Re: Hey...

Mine, too. I had no idea there'd be so much paperwork.

To: Anna Reed
From: William Evans
Subject: Re: Hey...

Haha! I just spit coffee all over myself. I'm going to change and I'll see you in a few.

CHAPTER 30

Will stood in the aisle outside his cube, frazzled. The SOB meeting started in forty minutes, but his mind scattered among seventeen different places. And not one of them explained why he had stood up and where he intended to go. *To the copier? No, I already printed off my speaking notes.*

He spun back to his cube and then turned up the aisle again, nearly crashing into Sommersby, who hurried toward him.

"Greetings, my friend." Sommersby smoothed back a hair that had sprung out of his low-slung ponytail. "I've got a change to our State of the Business prez."

"You've got . . . what?" Will tugged up the sleeve of his sport coat to double-check his watch. "Roswell's presentation? The binders went out yesterday."

"I understand. But Roswell agrees it'd be stronger if we changed the allegorical theme we're trying to pull through." Sommersby pinched his thumbs and forefingers together and then drew his hands apart, making an invisible line in the air. "It's important we tweak the graphics. And the headers."

Allegorical what? Is he kidding? Will glared. "You make the changes, and Roswell can bring updated pages for everyone."

"Hm, no, that's not going to work."

"What's not going to work?" Anna appeared in the aisle, BSI-logoed mug of coffee in-hand. Will had seen her just a few hours earlier, as they were wrapping up another sixteen-hour workday. Mentally wiped from the long hours, he couldn't believe how fresh and radiant she looked in her patterned dress and heels. *Downright stunning, actually.*

Sommersby took a step back as Anna approached. "Um, edits . . . For Roswell's . . . presentation today." Clearly, Anna intimidated him. Will hid a grin.

"Are you kidding?" Her hair swung when she shook her head. "It's way too late."

"Then make just the text edits." Sommersby turned back to Will. "A few keystrokes, click print, and put it in everyone's binder before the meeting. Simple."

"I assume you're familiar with the term 'pre-read'?" Anna emphasized the word as if talking to a child. "That means attendees have already read it. Thus rendering your changes irrelevant."

"Come on," Sommersby pleaded to Will. "Do me this little solid. I promised Roswell."

"You shouldn't promise things you can't deliver." Will scanned his cube for . . . *something.*

"Then you leave me no choice." Sommersby darted his gaze between Anna and Will. "I'm going to escalate this to the highest leader in your department."

"Go right ahead." Anna laughed and slipped around him to get into her cube. "Excuse me, Mr. Evans?" she said in an exaggerated, formal tone. "There's someone here who'd like to escalate something to you. Shall I send him in?"

She shot Will a mischievous smile. He smiled back, feeling a rush of warmth and attraction. He hoped to be alone with her again soon. In the middle of the night. Outside of work next time. And not debating the value of the Y-axis on some stupid PowerPoint chart.

Sommersby looked toward Chan's office door, where someone had finally peeled off the nameplate. He waved his hands in the air.

"This is ridiculous! All I'm asking is for you to do your job. Be a professional, Frodo."

Frodo. Something in Will's brain snapped. He marched out of his cube, standing toe-to-toe with the hipster, who took a tentative step backward.

"Don't you tell me what my job is." Will pointed his forefinger at Sommersby's chest. "You have no goddamn idea. Anna and I have worked 24/7 on a multimillion-dollar proposal to turn this company around. I can assure you nobody gives a *flying fuck* about your allegorical theme. Not Roswell. Not the CFO. Not Ron and Jerry. So get out of my face. The grown-ups will take it from here."

"You know what, Evans?" Sommersby huffed. "I always knew—"

"Not now, Richard." Will turned his attention back to the papers on his desk. "Daddy's working."

Sommersby wheeled around to Anna. "Did you hear that? That's a clear violation of our Double Check for Respect policy. I'm filing a complaint!"

Anna put a hand on his shoulder to prod him up the aisle. "I think you should. You can TEPIL your time as 737: Douchebag Interference with Mission Critical Activities."

"Arg!" Sommersby stomped his trendy boots toward the elevators.

Anna peered over Will's cube wall. "That went well."

Will laughed. "Best meeting *I* ever had with him, that's for damn sure."

"So . . . how do you feel? Have everything you need?"

Will pressed his eyes shut to refocus on the SOB meeting. "I think so. I have extra copies of our deck. And Lois already put my copy of Hail Mary in the room." Les had affectionately given the fifty-pound binder a name—and it stuck.

"And Sonny's feeling good?" Anna asked.

"Yep, texted me last night after getting in from Japan. He's on board." Will picked up his stack of materials and half the papers slid to the floor. "Dammit . . ."

Anna picked up his notes while Will retrieved the loose decks. He reached for the document, but she skimmed the contents, a blend of sympathy and amusement on her face. *"Aw."* Her voice lilted as if watching a Facebook video of a lion cub pouncing on a flower.

"What?"

"Your first bullet point. It says, 'Introduce yourself.' And then you actually wrote your name. Will Evans."

He snatched the notes from her hand and slid them back into the folder. "So?"

"It's adorable."

"It's not adorable," he groused. "It's called preparation. This is a big deal, Anna. If I have to chime in at this meeting, I don't want to forget anything important."

Will watched her stifle a laugh and then relented with a smirk. "Not even my name, I guess."

She nudged his arm. "Come on. I'll take you to the elevators. You'll be great. You know this plan backward and forward."

Will nodded, still nervous. He appreciated her confidence, but this meeting had so many unknowns—so many issues that could go wrong—he found it difficult to imagine everything going right. Yet, for Delivery Plus to be successful, that's exactly what he needed. A perfect confluence of factors rarely on display at BSI, mostly related to executive behaviors. Like collaborating instead of backstabbing. Breaking through BSI's entrenched bureaucracy. Emphasizing the greater good and setting aside their usual pissing matches.

"Thanks." He fell into step beside her. "But I still don't trust your boy Kirkland. I wish Sonny had the authority to push it through on his own. We don't even know if Kirkland created a new incentive plan. He missed the binder deadline, and he's been AWOL the last few days."

"No worries. I have complete faith in Kirkland's relentless drive for supremacy."

"Well, I have one worry: that he'll leave Sonny twisting in the wind. If Delivery Plus isn't met with a standing ovation, I could see the SVP of CYA acting like it's the first he's ever heard of it."

"Let's focus on what we can control. If the execs put you on the spot, what will they ask?"

Will nodded. "I suppose they might ask about the origins of the plan. Where the idea came from."

"And your answer?"

"It started with Doug and the real-estate office story. We combined it with the Amadeus suggestion about regular meetings between Sales and Delivery teams. Both of those came straight off the Chatterbox."

"That's great." She steered them toward the elevator bay. "One suggestion: if you mention Doug and Amadeus, use their full names and cite their FB locations. It sounds more professional and shows how connected you are with employees across the company."

"Oh, that's smart."

He pulled a pen and his speaking notes from the folder and pressed the document up against the wall—jotting a reminder in the margin. When he turned back again, he nearly bumped noses with Anna, who reached her hands behind his neck. Startled, he took a step back, bumping his head on the wall.

"What are you—?"

"Hold still. Your collar's all jacked up."

Her face came so close to Will's he could almost feel the warmth of her skin. He inhaled the lavender scent of her hair and held his breath as she smoothed his collar. She took a step backward, brushed and tugged at his lapels, and then patted his upper arms with both hands.

"There." She admired her handiwork. "You clean up pretty well for a Promisekeeper."

He smiled.

"What else?" she asked.

Will furrowed his brow. "Um . . . about . . . ?"

"What else might the execs ask you?"

"Oh, um . . . they might ask if employees would support an idea that changes their bonus plans."

"... And?"

"The Chatterbox is a good snapshot of what Promisekeepers want. They want to take care of their customers. And they want BSI to pull out of this tailspin. The bonus changes won't be a problem."

"That's great. I'll text you some stats—visits, views, posts. In case someone questions whether we've cast the net widely enough."

"Good. That sounds good." Will looked first at the materials in his hand and then at the elevators. "I'd better head up."

"Yep, it's time." Anna smiled. "Knock 'em dead, Frodo."

Will dropped his chin to his chest. *That stupid nickname.* He leveled his eyes on her. "Seriously? You, too? You know I can't stand that name. It's degrading."

Anna placed a gentle hand on his arm. "Will, didn't you read *The Lord of the Rings*?"

"No need." He pressed the elevator button. "I knew what it meant. Al was trying to knock me down a few pegs—name the 'pretty-boy college kid' after an ugly troll. Or hobbit, or whatever." He didn't really care. He had bigger things to worry about.

"Will." Anna's voice turned soft. "Frodo was the hero. He was the brave one who stepped up to destroy the evil ring when everyone else was fighting over it. He was the only one with a pure heart . . . the only one who wouldn't be corrupted by its power." Anna placed her hands on his shoulders and looked him straight in the eyes. "Not to get all corny, Will, but I think that's why Big Al called you Frodo. You said yourself the nicknames are deeper than people realize. He saw something in you from the beginning. He saw what was in your heart."

Will returned Anna's gaze, drinking in her stunning blue eyes. Her kindness and confidence in him almost made him forget how tired he'd become from the long hours and endless preparations. Tired from the pressure of the high-stakes gambit they had orchestrated. Tired of the game he and Anna played, pretending they didn't feel any attraction toward each other. Tired of wondering how it would feel to kiss her.

His heart pounded, drowning out the elevator bell behind him. Will leaned toward her, drawing closer, anticipating the touch of her soft lips against his. Anna rocked up on the balls of her feet and pulled on his shoulders, bringing his mouth closer to hers . . . before twisting away at the last second. She sprang backward, casting a panicked glance toward the muffled voices from the arriving elevator. His target gone, Will stumbled forward, hooking Anna's retreating heel with his pant leg, sending her sprawling backward onto the floor.

Two men emerged from the elevator and looked at Anna lying prone on her back as Will clumsily danced over her, trying to regain his balance without trampling her limbs.

"What the . . . are you okay?" one of them asked.

"Yes, yes, I'm fine." Anna laughed heartily.

"A little too much Bailey's in her coffee this morning." Will stood up straight and raised his hands. "Been a tough week, but we're good now. Nothing to see here."

The men shook their heads and moved on as Will reached with his free hand and helped Anna to her feet. She avoided his eyes but gave his hand an extended squeeze before letting it drop.

"As I was saying." She bounced back into a surprisingly normal and professional demeanor and then pressed the elevator button. "You should get going."

"Yes, yes I should." Will stepped into the empty elevator. "We're good, right? This is going to work?"

"You'll be great," she affirmed as the doors slid shut between them.

Anna veered into the Cabin break room and squeezed her eyes shut for a moment, unsure if her heartbeat hammered because of the near-miss kiss—or almost being caught in the act. Never a good idea to make out with the boss. And doing it on company property? Reputational and occupational suicide. And definitely not part of her Career Trajectory.

She opened her eyes and looked out the window—a stream of buses and morning commuters inched along the street, nine stories below. She resisted the temptation to thump her muddled head against the glass.

No rational person would give into a romantic workplace entanglement—the stuff of careless, impetuous greenhorns. Like young Anna, when she first met charming Erik—director in charge of Federated Financial's London expansion. That started out fun and innocent, too. *And look where that got me.*

No, a cool-headed, rational person would stop a nice guy like Will from getting in the ring with a woman like her. Save him the trouble—given he probably didn't have the fortitude for it, anyway. Erik had explained it best when he admitted to banging other women throughout their last two years of marriage: being with Anna— complicated, controlling, and blindly ambitious—had grown too damn exhausting for him. And she wasn't worth the effort.

Anna's phone vibrated with a text. She cringed. *Jesus, Evans— we'll deal with the kiss later. Concentrate on the SOB meeting.*

She looked at the screen. Alissa.

"Offer coming nxt wk! Gotta ask 1 more time . . . U sure?"

Anna leaned against the window ledge and stared at the text. *Am I sure?* She'd thought she'd made the right decision about the Twins job, but something about Alissa's question gnawed at her.

Anna never hesitated at new opportunities. The predictable cycle of her career transitions—find a fresh start, walk away and leave the mess—had always felt right. A series of rational, mapped-out decisions propelling her onward and upward. *Why am I questioning it now?*

After all, this bureaucratic, chaotic company had done nothing but throw obstacles in her path from the start. But it had been strangely fun and rewarding, too.

Anna filled her lungs with a big breath. The stale Cabin air smelled like burnt popcorn.

She wished she could think more clearly. But that goddamn spontaneous, screw-the-consequences side of her brain—the part of her that almost ravaged Will in the hall a minute ago—would *not* shut up.

And the rock-solid, pragmatic side wasn't doing its job, either. She needed that part of her brain to take over now, like it always did. Telling her to be smart. To make the right move.

Anna paced the floor. She thought about Will. She'd told him to save himself, but he refused to bail on the Promisekeepers. A gutsy move—gutsier than she'd expected. But it still might blow up in his face. *And then what? Where does he end up then?*

Anna always knew where she'd end up. Senior VP by forty-two. To make it happen, she'd need to more aggressively seize promotions—spending more time securing a seat at the exec table, and less at the happy hour booth. *Right?* Then Chief Communications Officer by fifty. That would require extraordinary focus; forget the personal life. Not that she had one now, anyway. *Right?* Then a run for office. Sure, the marriage thing created a blight on her record, but her publicist could spin Erik as a youthful indiscretion. And—in the end—it would all be worth it. *Right?*

She turned back to the window. Both sides of her brain snapped into alignment, telling her the same thing. *You were right all along: there's nothing wrong with saving yourself.*

Anna nodded to confirm her resolve and tapped a text back to Alissa.

"If Twins are sure, I'm sure. Make it happen!"

CHAPTER 31

Will sensed chaos and desperation the moment he stepped onto the twenty-second floor. A stressed-out Lois scurried between CEO offices, delivering documents and snapping orders at Ambrosia. A handful of dour execs stood in the reception area, speaking in hushed tones.

"Saved you a seat," Bennie whispered as Will entered the boardroom. She sat in a row of temporary folding chairs lining the perimeter. A massive Hail Mary binder reserved Will's chair. Les joined Will and Bennie in the cheap seats, along with a cluster of fidgety middle managers and notetakers. The faint sound of arguing could be heard from inside Ron's office.

Will stared at his notes as he sat, fighting to quiet the Greek chorus in his head.

What did I just do? Well, you almost kissed an intelligent, gorgeous woman . . . and good news, Evans—she seemed kinda into it. He smiled—and then it faded. *Or you tried to plant a sloppy kiss on a reluctant employee and then almost stomped her to death like a lumbering circus elephant. Idiot—what's wrong with you?*

Bennie snapped her fingers in front of Will's face. "Earth to Moon Monkey. You there?"

Will nodded and forced his mind back into the moment. He surveyed the room as the executive team filtered in.

"Delivery Plus looks great, Evans." Les nudged him from the next chair. "Nice job pulling the story together. It's the most plausible—"

"Where the hell is everybody?" Jerry stormed out of his office. He looked at his watch and then toward his cofounder's door. "Ron! Let's get started. We have a lot of ground to cover."

Ron and Kirkland entered from the far side of the room, anyone left standing scurried to their seats, and BSI's entire executive team convened in one place—maybe for the first time ever.

Jerry and Ron sat at opposite ends of the table. Kirkland, Happenstance, Sonny, and Legal Bob lined one side. Roswell and the IT exec, Larabee, sat across from them, along with Boone, the perpetually tanned, slick-haired head of Sales and Marketing.

Will recognized Boone only from pictures. A new addition to the executive ranks, he'd previously led BSI's Southwest regional reps and began overseeing the companywide Sales teams when Sonny got promoted to lead the overall business line. The CEOs tacked on the latter half of Boone's title—Marketing—when they needed someone ambitious and pliable to plug the hole left by Chan. And Boone fit the bill. Human spackle.

The execs situated their binders on the table, pecked to silence their phones, and generally avoided eye contact.

Lois and Ambrosia took seats near the door, their laptops and notebooks ready for what may come. Will stole a glance at the junior assistant. She looked insignificant and out of place in this high-stakes meeting. A shy, young professional earning her first real paycheck after college. Probably terrified she wouldn't be able to pay the rent if she lost this job. *Big Al was right. This is personal. For everybody.*

Ron called the meeting to order. "You know the situation. We're six weeks before quarter-end. Current trends indicate we'll miss our nut by forty to forty-five million. Our new vendor, MX, doesn't come on board until Q4. The recent—"

"Forty-three point two as of close of business yesterday." Happenstance squinted at his dog-eared binder.

Ron glowered at his CFO and then continued. "Headcount reductions have trimmed payroll expense, of course, but those reductions are being offset by our declining revenue. And severance obligations, along with our significant share repurchases over the last three years, have exhausted our cash reserves."

"The overbudget Optelligence investments also contributed to our cash depletion." Happenstance tapped a pencil on the table. A few others at the table cringed. "The collective ROI from these strategies is nonexis—"

"Save it for the papers," Ron snarled. "I don't want to hear that garbage in my own damn boardroom." Happenstance meekly put his nose back in the binder where it belonged.

Ron released an audible sigh. "Our bankers are concerned about cash flow and have started making noises about reining in our line of credit, which would cripple us."

Jerry spoke from the other end of the table, and all heads simultaneously turned toward his voice. "Bob, what's the latest on Synerpoint?"

Legal Bob cleared his throat. "They are alleging breach of contract—arguing the lack of good-faith negotiations on our end entitles them to all the IP created under the Optelligence umbrella."

Kirkland frowned. "We should be suing *them* for breach of contract. They walked away."

"This suit isn't about intellectual property or damages." Legal Bob shook his head. "It's a business strategy, pure and simple. Tie our hands with a protracted legal battle while they build a lead in the marketplace. By the time the suit is resolved—regardless of outcome—they assume we'll be out of business, or they'll be so far down the road with Optitude, it won't matter. It's rather brilliant, actually."

Jerry's face reddened and his eyes bulged, as if his head might pop off and roll across the table. "You know what would have been brilliant, Bob? If you had seen this coming and done something to stop it!" He looked skyward. "God as my witness, the next words out of your mouth better be about a counterstrategy."

Legal Bob shifted in his chair. "Yes, yes . . . I was . . . ah . . ." He cleared his throat again. "We've filed for an expedited hearing where we'll push for a cashless settlement. Federal magistrates have little patience for these he-said-she-said cases from the business community. Thus, our position is that we should compete in the marketplace, rather than the courts. Let Synerpoint keep the small amount of IP they developed with us if they agree to drop the litigation. Then we can fight it out on the street corner, as it were."

Jerry looked to his partner, who nodded in agreement. "Get it done," Ron said. "And keep us posted every step along the way."

"Next item." Jerry looked up one side of the table, then down the other. "The board is holding an emergency meeting next week. The assumption is we won't hit this quarter, and won't have the cash to survive another. They want to review all options and determine a course of action for that worst-case scenario. We need to show we have a plan. A way to close the $45 million gap in the next six weeks. Put a floor under our share price and buy more time."

"You can see the rationale for the board's position." Kirkland tossed out a casual wave of his hand. "Shareholders are livid. Look at the losses we've taken in this room alone."

A collective groan rose from around the table.

"Nobody in this room's lost a penny!" Sonny glared at Kirkland. "We get stock options as an incentive to create value for investors. We've been careless with budgets and shortsighted in our plans. We haven't done our jobs."

Kirkland raised an eyebrow again. "That's a rudimentary perspective."

"Tell that to our shareholders," Sonny countered.

Will rubbed the back of his neck as he observed the testy exchange. *Are these two even capable of co-sponsoring Delivery Plus without tearing each other apart?*

Roswell chimed in with her take on BSI's executive compensation philosophy, but Legal Bob cut her off with a rambling soliloquy on the Sarbanes-Oxley Act of 2002. Other execs joined the debate as those in the folding chairs watched the meeting deteriorate.

The scene reminded Will of *Gorillas in the Mist*. He and his colleagues on the perimeter were Dian Fossey and her scientists, observing these larger-than-life creatures in their natural habitat. Like the primates in the movie, this group had a defined social hierarchy, enforced by two menacing silverbacks at either end of the table. But Fossey had discovered dignified, familial relationships among the African mountain gorillas. Their Minneapolis cousins had obviously missed the memo—this pack appeared narcissistic and hostile.

Will eyeballed the small ficus tree near his chair. If one of the beasts charged, he would make like Sigourney Weaver and chew some vegetation to show he came in peace.

Jerry pounded a fist on the table to regain control. Everyone jumped.

"Enough!" he roared. "Let me be absolutely clear. There's a growing faction on our board that believes we should liquidate. Start with the copier business. Sell off the inventory, customer lists, fleet, and real estate separately. Everything, from the Flourboxes to the tower, to the goddamn chairs you're sitting on. Close the doors and auction off our assets."

Jerry now had the rapt attention of the table-dwellers.

"Next week, one of our directors will likely introduce a motion to dissolve BSI. As co-chairs, Ron and I will argue against it. But if they have enough votes lined up coming in—and if we don't have a viable plan—we'll be unable to stop it."

The room fell silent. Bennie gulped. Ambrosia stared at the open notebook in her lap—her pen motionless over the page. Will's stomach churned.

"We could file Chapter Eleven." Kirkland tugged on his shirtsleeve cuffs. "Keep our creditors at bay while we reorganize into a more nimble, streamlined organization."

"The first thing a bankruptcy judge would do is remove this entire management team," Ron shot back, "and appoint a new CEO. Jerry and I will not stand by and watch some outsider take a chainsaw to everything we built."

"We have thousands of people relying on us . . . and dozens of alternative solutions right here." Sonny tapped Hail Mary. "We should be exploring these options."

"We do not have dozens of solutions." Ron picked up the hefty binder in front of him and dropped it with a thud onto the table—the rush of air sent papers scattering. "What we have is a binder full of creative ways to restate our problems, coupled with small, slow-moving ideas that don't come anywhere close to solving them."

A pregnant pause hung over the room. Will had expected the group to review all of the binder materials and choose the best ideas. Cobble together a plan to get BSI back on track. Most of the execs probably thought the same. But Ron and Jerry wanted a silver bullet.

The execs sized up one another, wondering who might have the guts or stupidity to push an idea forward. *C'mon, Sonny, this is our shot. You can't wait on Kirkland—you have to stick your neck out first. Say something, you big ape.*

Boone, the new Sales and Marketing exec, ran a hand over his slicked-back hair. "All due respect, I'm not sure it's realistic to raise $45 million in six weeks. My guys are out there drumming up whatever business they can, but bankruptcy rumors are scaring off new prospects."

"Not realistic?" Jerry's red-hot glare threatened to burn a hole in Boone's skull. "When I ran Sales, I personally moved $45 million in machines in a single year. Selling one brand! And you're telling me a few hundred reps across the country can't collectively find a way to squeeze that much from all the brands we still carry? Bullshit! You're not driving them hard enough."

Boone's forehead beaded with sweat, and Will wondered for a nanosecond whether the slickster's bottle-tan would run.

"We still have every legal right to pursue a scaled-down version of the Technology strategy." Legal Bob removed his reading glasses, placing the bow at the edge of his mouth. "The Synerpoint suit doesn't preclude us from building a similar system to sell to existing customers. As long as we materially differentiate it from the Optelligence and Optitude brands. And we've already got an eager customer in St. Louis. How quickly can we get it built and implemented?"

Kirkland stared at the corporate lawyer until the tension became uncomfortable. "We are making progress." He paused and then turned his attention to Larabee, the IT exec. "But incompatibility with our legacy IT infrastructure has slowed us down—a critical dependency that was only recently brought to my attention."

"This is what happens when technology projects are managed outside the purview of IT." A vein bulged in Larabee's thick neck, a perfect complement to the tire tracks Kirkland had just left on his back. "It's not possible for my team to—"

"There we go again," Jerry boomed. "Not possible. Not realistic. Is there anyone in this room capable of talking about what *is* possible? Because we seem to be really, fucking clear about what we can't do."

Sonny leaned forward. "Our best shot isn't with new customers or new technologies . . . it's with our existing customers." He opened his binder about two-thirds of the way into the stack of reports. "I'd like to call your attention to Delivery Plus—a new service offering for current customers."

Yes! Will held his breath as the other execs started rifling through their materials.

"As you can see, this idea requires little investment and offers high revenue potential. The services would be offered on a contractual basis, which provides three significant advantages." Sonny raised a finger on his right hand for each item. "An immediate cash infusion from customers who pay in full. Ongoing revenue streams from customers who pay monthly. And the ability to book the full value of the contract right away, regardless of how they pay."

Happenstance poked up a tentative hand. Will stretched to see the pages in the CFO's open binder—marked up and littered with sticky notes. "How did you develop the pricing structure? I'm not convinced customers would be willing to pay for the top-tier service. If that's the case, your revenue estimates would be dubious, at best."

"Supporting data is on the following pages." Sonny crossed his arms. "We believe this is a conservative SWAG."

"It struck me as aggressive." Happenstance tapped his pencil on the table again.

"It does appear too optimistic," Ron agreed, to the CFO's apparent delight.

Boone rubbed his chin as he skimmed the materials. "How do we even know customers want this? I haven't heard anything from my reps."

"We identified the need through our Flourbox teams." Sonny shot Will a knowing look. "Customer Insights validated the premise and projected the revenue for each tier. I'm confident we can hit these numbers—and our quarter."

"Even if the numbers are verified." Jerry flipped through the pages. "I don't see enough detail on *how* you'd do it. Promotional materials, employee training . . ."

Will teetered on the edge of his seat. Sonny periodically looked toward Kirkland, who gave nothing in return—sitting on his hands until he knew which way the wind was blowing. And it was starting to blow back on Sonny.

"Promotion is a cinch—simple brochures the Sales teams can use to pitch the plans." Sonny became more forceful in his delivery. "And training is a slam dunk. Delivery crews want this. Their customers are asking for it. Hell, some teams are doing it already. We only need to adjust some processes and policies—and get out of their way."

"Those processes and policies are in place for a reason." Ron continued sifting through his binder. "You don't change decades of world-class efficiencies on a whim." He looked up at Sonny. "Still, it's an interesting premise . . ."

"I agree. It's interesting." Legal Bob seized the opportunity to offer a perfectly safe, tepid opinion that couldn't possibly come back to bite him.

Will's gaze darted between Sonny and Kirkland—the only two non-CEOs who could tilt the odds of success. None of the others had enough skin in the game or fire in their guts to offer a meaningful point of view.

Jerry turned the pages forward and then back again. "I don't see anything in here about incentive plans."

"Right." Ron leaned back, and his chair squeaked under the strain. "For Delivery teams to take this on, we'd have to change their efficiency metrics and related bonuses. That's a big miss."

The room honed in on Sonny, waiting for a response. Everyone except Kirkland, who lounged in his chair, a picture of everyday blasé. The pounding in Will's chest now echoed in his ears.

What the fuck is he doing? Will screamed in his mind, before his shoulders dropped with a sickening thought. *What if—in the ultimate display of power—Kirkland decides to let this company die? Just because he can?*

"We took the bonus plans into consideration." Sonny focused on Kirkland, drawing all eyes with him.

Kirkland relished the attention and the awkward silence that followed. "Yes," he finally said. "Success of Delivery Plus hinges on shifting the paradigm of operational excellence from efficiency to customer satisfaction."

Will looked at Bennie, then Les, then back at the table. *Kirkland just validated Delivery Plus . . . I think. Right?*

"I've formulated a new incentive model." Kirkland passed around presentations from a stack next to his binder. "We would sunset the existing quarterly bonuses in favor of monthly payouts based on customer satisfaction scores. Page five. We would also introduce a new annual incentive plan for all employees—predicated on BSI meeting predetermined revenue goals. Pages eight through ten."

Will exhaled and sat back in his chair. *Okay, okay. He did. He validated it. He's in, like Anna promised.* He resisted the urge to text her an update. And an expression of gratitude. And a thumbs-up selfie of him and the ficus.

The room filled with the sounds of rustling papers as the execs scanned Kirkland's materials. No one deemed the border residents worthy of copies—they strained to see over executive shoulders, whispering among themselves.

"The new incentives will inspire employees nationwide to serve customers better than ever." Sonny emphasized his point with a soft karate chop. "That goes for both Sales and Delivery teams—who have to work together to boost regional customer sat scores to get their joint reward."

Kirkland picked up the summary. "This plan would provide Flourbox employees larger and more frequent payout opportunities, and the annual incentive focuses every employee on a common goal. Near-term, this provides adequate motivation for the masses to support a wholesale change in operations."

Ron's eyebrows raised as he studied the deck. "This is tremendous work, Lyle. Very strong. But what about changing the current efficiency-based processes?"

Kirkland waved his hand again. "Negligible. There are fourteen processes that would need to evolve. I'll drive it—consider it done."

"I have to say." Jerry cocked his head while stroking his tie. "I'm impressed. This is the kind of transformational, out-of-the-box thinking we need at a time like this. But I have some reservations . . ."

"I do as well." Roswell wiggled a finger in the air. "We should consider how changes to our compensation model might affect our overall rewards philosophy. These programs are anchored to BSI's strategy. Changing even one element has a ripple effect throughout the portfolio. It changes what we stand for."

"That's precisely the point, Anita." Kirkland laid his palms on the tabletop. "Change is in the offing."

"These are not your changes to make, Lyle." Roswell's cheeks became bright pink. "I should have been consulted." She crossed her arms in a huff—the abrupt motion pushing up her blousy shirt-sleeves.

Bennie jabbed Will with her elbow and darted her eyes toward the HR exec. Dense, colorful artwork splashed across Roswell's fore-arms—even more glorious than the rumors. Knights in full armor. A castle in flames. A skull skewered with a sword. Will craned his neck to get a better look, but Roswell shot her hands downward—and the spectacular ink disappeared again into her cream-colored sleeves.

Boone leaned across the table. "This plan also modifies the way my reps operate and get paid—and it's the first I've heard of it. Jerry, you know better than anyone—mess with a salesman's commission, and you're practically begging him to leave." He slapped the table with an open hand. "We're already bleeding reps."

"As I said earlier . . ." A thin, superior smile creased Kirkland's mouth. "It's time to disrupt old paradigms. We need to focus on extending and deepening our customer relationships."

"You don't run Sales. I do!" Boone slapped the table again and then pointed at Kirkland with a shaky hand. "And my guys aren't babysitters, looking to sell some kind of . . . ticky-tack service plans. They're big-game hunters. We implement this plan, and half of them walk out the door. Probably to OfficeWorld."

Kirkland shrugged. "Sometimes turnover is healthy."

Boone swore under his breath, pushed his chair back and turned away from the group. Happenstance and Legal Bob exchanged a subtle glance as if deciding which man would throw himself into the fray next.

Legal Bob cleared his throat. "There are also some legal complex-ities to consider, as it relates to the contract."

"It's a service agreement, Bob." Kirkland raised his eyebrows and dropped his chin. "Akin to hiring a maid. If your crack staff can't handle it, I'm sure outside counsel can help us."

Happenstance raised his hand again. "We also have to consider the incremental expense impact of the incentive plans—ensure they don't offset the potential revenue gains."

Kirkland nodded. "Page twelve."

"I'd like my team to review it."

"Of course."

Will's palms began to sweat, and he rubbed them together. One-on-one backstabbing happened all the time between execs. But he hadn't anticipated a coordinated attempt to undermine Kirkland. This executive team seemed willing to destroy a viable plan—and BSI along with it—rather than cede any more control and glory to the Dwarf Lord.

"The timeline is absolutely unrealistic." Larabee glared at Kirkland. "Once again you have completely underestimated the technical considerations. There are separate systems and databases for the bonus calculations, payroll, commission, and TEPIL time-tracking. If you'd consulted me, I'd have told you that. This will require thousands of hours of coding and testing before I'd be comfortable supporting it."

"We could implement manual processes until the technology is ready." Kirkland examined his manicure. "As we did for Project Krypton."

"I'd like to see further validation of this so-called customer need." Boone had inched his chair back to the table, his reddened face returning to its cooler shade of fake-tan orange. "I don't believe there's a 'there' there."

Kirkland raised an eyebrow. "Even though your team did the market research?"

Boone's expression revealed a man who had forgotten that Marketing now reported to him.

"There are massive change implications here," Roswell sniffed. "Behavioral and cultural."

Happenstance piled on. "I'm still not comfortable with the top-tier pricing band and the expense implications of the bonus plan."

"Duly noted." Kirkland brushed a piece of nonexistent lint off his sleeve. "For the second time."

Happenstance tapped his pencil on the tabletop—the only sound in the boardroom. Jerry licked his finger and flipped several pages forward in Hail Mary, while his cofounder jotted notes with a chewed-up, plastic Synerpoint pen. A few moments ticked by. The other execs fidgeted in their chairs.

Ron removed his glasses, placed his elbows on the table, and folded his hands together. "All things considered, I believe this plan raises too many questions and requires a longer timeframe than we have."

Will buried his face in his hands. *No!*

"Unfortunately, I agree." Jerry flipped his binder shut. "You're talking about blue-collar employees—skilled in moving heavy equipment—offering concierge-type services. Not to mention the changes to the Sales model. Change like this doesn't happen overnight."

No, no, no! Will squeezed his fists so hard his knuckles turned white.

"It's a good plan—Sonny, Lyle." Ron looked from one man to the other. "But something like this requires careful planning and execution. And that takes time."

Jerry nodded. "It feels too much like a Hail Mary drawn up in the dirt."

Will's head spun. He couldn't believe how this had fallen apart, here, now, when they were so close. And for what? So these weak-willed execs could exact their revenge on Kirkland? At the expense of every other employee in the company? So Jerry and Ron could step away with their summer homes and snooker tables, too comfortable to get their hands dirty in saving the company they founded?

"We're too big now." Ron shook his head. "Not as nimble as the old days. We can't turn on a dime anymore."

"Like hell we can't!" Horrified, Will realized he had jumped to his feet, the sound of his inner thoughts somehow having escaped into the room. Everyone stared at him. Bennie tugged on the bottom of his sport coat, coaxing him back toward his chair.

"I'm sorry. I really am." Will took a small step forward. "I don't mean to be disrespectful. But I know Delivery Plus inside-out, and I know what our employees are capable of, and I'm telling you we absolutely *can* mobilize the company ar—"

Jerry frowned. "Will, this isn't the time—"

"Around this plan!" Will finished. He didn't care about shouting down the CEO. He didn't care if they fired him. He had the floor, goddammit. "I need you to *listen* to me."

He talked faster now, his hands in fists at his sides. "Like Sonny said, this plan came from Flourbox employees. They know our customers—and they know there's a market for this service. They've seen it. And they can do it. They're waiting for you to let them. Begging you to let them."

"Will, I think we all appreciate your passion." Roswell sounded like a nineteenth-century schoolmarm. "But if you understood some of the concerns we raised . . ."

"Fuck your concerns," Will spat over gasps from the other attendees. He'd crossed a line, but he didn't care. *I'm done being an executive chew toy.* "Technology, rewards, who got consulted on what, blah, blah, blah. It's all bullshit. This company is dying, and you're too busy trying to justify why you should let it happen instead of doing everything you can to save it!"

He shifted on his feet, afraid his knees would lock and he'd fall over. He could feel the weight of everyone staring at him. Still. Sonny sat motionless, mouth agape. Kirkland had an amused expression on his face, as if enjoying this unexpected commercial interruption.

"Jerry, Ron." Will lowered his voice, "There's no guarantee Delivery Plus will work. But why would you opt for liquidation before giving your employees a chance to turn things around? You always say our people are the secret sauce that makes this company great. Give them a chance to prove you right."

Will dreaded what might happen if he ceded the spotlight, but he stopped talking. He thought about sitting down but decided to hold his ground.

"I can vouch for the commitment of our employees." The conviction in Sonny's voice drew the meeting participants' attention. "Ron, Jerry . . . let's play this out for a minute."

"All right." Jerry pushed his chair away from the table so that he had room to cross his legs. "Let's say we pull together the incentive plans and processes. We somehow align the necessary marketing, training, and technology. Assume the board sees potential in this plan. Even if those disparate pieces come together—the amount of employee behavioral change is astronomical. How do you expect to rally an increasingly skeptical employee base in such a short amount of time? The usual trinkets and posters aren't going to—"

"You're right." Will stepped toward the front of the room, where he could better make eye contact with both CEOs. "That crap doesn't work. Never has. But here's what will. You and Ron taking the message directly to our employees with the utmost humility you can muster. Asking them to pull together to save the company. No more Rainmakers versus Promisekeepers, no more jargon or empty promises. You'll talk to them like real people. And you'll do it standing on the floor of FB-One—where you started this goddamn company—asking for the help of every employee who's still proud to work here and wants to see this company survive. And you'll make it personal. Because it is. For all of us."

Will hesitated, allowing his words to sink in. *That's a damn good closing line.*

He slipped back to his seat, thankful for the stability and safety of the folding chair. Bennie elbowed Will in the arm and shook a fist at him. Commending his courage? Or threatening to punch him in the head for being so reckless? He couldn't tell.

Kirkland leaned forward, his hands on the edge of the table, addressing both CEOs as he turned his head. "Ron, Jerry . . . allow us the opportunity to drive this solution. To reestablish this company's stature. To regain your faith in our leadership. And to enhance your legacy. This plan is not without risks, but you did not build BSI on safe bets."

Will's heart continued to pound as he waited for the CEOs' response.

Jerry leaned back in his chair and looked across the expansive length of the table to his BSI cofounder. "It's a huge risk."

"The contracts, processes, and revenue-booking estimates would need to be airtight." Ron pointed his pen toward the two rows of execs seated in front of him. "Airtight."

Kirkland nodded. "They will be. We will reverify all details and prepare for implementation." He scrutinized his colleagues around the table. "Collectively."

Jerry tapped his index finger on Hail Mary. "I want to see the next level of detail on every facet of this thing—pricing, customer outreach, marketing, training . . . everything. I want the 'how' hammered out in micro-fucking-scopic detail." He looked at his watch. "I want all of you back here in thirty minutes, along with anything and anyone you need to begin taking action. Immediately."

The execs stood and the meeting dissolved into a din of urgent debates, shuffled papers, and phone conversations. The perimeter participants began slipping out, one by one. Will leaned his forearms on his thighs and closed his eyes. *Did that really just happen?*

Rising to leave, he caught Sonny's eye from across the table. His old friend shot him a wink and a grin. "Great job," Sonny mouthed.

Will smiled in return and followed Bennie and Les into the reception area.

"Will." Ambrosia stood near her desk, still holding the notepad. She'd never spoken to him before and appeared unsure about it even now. "I wanted to tell you . . ." She cast a gaze downward before looking back up at him. "That was very brave."

"Thanks, Ambrosia. I appreciate it."

"Yes—very courageous, William." Lois swiveled around in her chair. "Though we could have done without the potty mouth."

"Thank you for the feedback, Lois." Will smirked. "I'll try to do better next time."

Turning to walk out, Will paused at the Flourbox map and scanned the network of purple pins dotting the country. He smoothed down one corner of the map, where it had peeled away from the corkboard.

Okay, Promisekeepers . . . let's break it down and bring it home.

CHAPTER 32

If the crooked, plastic clock on FB-One's wall had possessed a working minute hand, it would have showed seventy minutes before the figurative curtains rose on Delivery Plus. Will stood near the warehouse entrance, overseeing the frenzy as Big Al's crew cleared additional space for the kickoff.

Most of BSI's previous all-company meetings ended up as thinly disguised, executive brag-offs. A parade of leaders extolling the virtues of their pet projects, while BSIers sat dutifully in the audience playing FarmVille on their phones.

But, as Will had told the execs in the SOB meeting, the Delivery Plus kickoff needed to be different. Real. So the Comm team had dispensed with many of the usual live-event frills and obsessed instead over details that mattered.

This kickoff featured only one presenter with a deceptively simple message: BSI had a solution to its problems—but little time left. To save the company, employees across the company needed to band together to sell the hell out of Delivery Plus.

Starting in about an hour.

Will couldn't decide if his stomach roiled with hunger from skipping breakfast or all-encompassing anxiety. He checked his watch and stepped onto the makeshift warehouse stage. "Video signal back to tower—test two."

"Yeah, I see your skinny ass," Bennie reported from the tower cafeteria.

Anna stepped onto the stage and popped her head between Will and the camera.

"Holy Amazon blonde!" Bennie's voice reverberated through FB-One from speakers mounted atop temporary, aluminum poles. "You look twenty feet tall on the screen here!"

Anna waved at the lens.

"No time to put on makeup this morning?" Bennie cackled.

Anna flipped off the camera, and the PR director shrieked with laughter.

"Groovy—you got us." Coffee sat at the production table, tucked between two rows of warehouse copier shelves. "Back in ten for a full tech run."

Anna stomped her heels to test the strength of the stage—a dozen wooden shipping pallets with plywood nailed on top.

Will stepped back to avoid having his foot punctured by a stiletto. "Hey, the CEOs will be here any minute. You want to sit in on Jerry's prep?"

She shook her head. "Thanks, but no. Jerry needs to go yard on this. The fewer voices in his ear, the better. He trusts you."

"Fair enough. Can you handle Ron instead? Keep him occupied and get him to show some love to the crew?"

Anna smiled. "That's a tall order. Ron's not one to dole out hugs and kisses."

Hugs and kisses. The phrase hung in the air. They hadn't said a word about their aborted make-out/limb-trampling episode. Will looked around to ensure no one lurked within earshot.

"Hey, um . . . we should probably talk. About that little situation we had before the SOB meeting. I don't want things to be—you know—awkward." He lowered his chin but made sure to maintain eye contact.

She laughed and gave him that look—like when she saw how he'd written his own name on the SOB speaking notes. "Oh, Evans. We blew past Awkward City four exits ago."

Will laughed.

"Besides, not sure if you've noticed." She toggled her index finger between the two of them. "But neither of us is great at this 'talk about our feelings' stuff."

"You can say that again. It either ends up in tears or with someone knocked flat on her back."

"Hey, just to be clear . . ." Anna poked the index finger into his chest. "That takedown was a fluke. You distracted me."

"All part of my master strategy."

They smiled at each other, the voices of the FB-One crew echoing in the background.

Anna opened her mouth to speak but stopped when the side warehouse door flew open. Jerry strode inside, smiling and waving at the warehouse crew while Ron ambled in behind him.

"Mr. Evans!" Jerry spotted Will from across the floor. "Where's my greenroom?"

Will jumped from the low riser and then turned to give Anna a hand stepping down to the floor. "Nice to see you, gentlemen." He swept his arm toward the warehouse doorway. "We'll be using the conference room outside Al's office."

Anna took the opportunity to point out the plywood stage as they made their way to the prep session. "You'll see we've created a modest setup."

"It's good." Jerry nudged the stage with the toe of his shiny dress shoe. "I like the 'nothing fancy' feel. When Ron and I started out, my first office chair came from a dumpster—had a big hole in the seat."

"You don't say." Will smiled.

Jerry's well-worn tale played a legendary role in BSI's oral history, a reminder of the company's hardscrabble beginnings. Will glanced at Jerry as they walked, noting the perfect dimple in his silk tie and the impeccable cut of his suit.

Nothing fancy, indeed.

Sonny crossed their paths near the office area. He greeted each CEO with a hearty handshake, pumping their arms as if trying to coax water from an abandoned well.

"Everything on track?" Ron asked.

"All the local Sales reps are linked up with their FB-One drivers for the day." Sonny slid a hand over his rotund stomach, retucking the purple dress shirt into his gray slacks. "After the event, they'll hit the road to start pitching Delivery Plus. Together." He chuckled. "Making it rain and keeping promises in one fell swoop."

"Same plan for the rest of the country?" Ron crossed his arms.

"Yep, and after this initial surge, the official training program kicks in. Then all reps are scheduled for monthly ride-alongs. To make sure relationships are maintained."

"Terrific." Jerry draped an arm across Sonny's shoulders. "You know, we couldn't have done this without you. You've come through for all of us."

"Thank you." Sonny's eyes lit up. "Grateful to be a part of it. Good luck today."

Will and Anna led the CEOs into the meeting room.

"The FB-One crew is excited to be hosting the event." Will turned toward Ron. "While Jerry and I prep, Anna will take you around the 'Box. You can greet the team. Shake a few hands."

Ron—in a paisley tie and a wrinkle-free shirt that looked anything but—shook his head. "I'll stay here." Laying his left hand flat against the yellowed wall to steady himself, Ron raised his right arm and held out one leg in a surprisingly lithe yoga pose Will couldn't identify. *Injured Whooping Crane? Half-Inverted Lurching Malcontent?*

"Coffee, anyone?" Anna walked to the sputtering coffee pot in the corner.

"Yes, with a shot of organic soy milk." Jerry wiggled a few chairs until he found one that seemed sturdy enough to support him.

"Sorry, they're fresh out." Anna poked through the handful of powdered creamer packets on the table—some already torn open and half used. She grabbed two Styrofoam cups. "Ron, let's take some with us."

"I need to be in this prep session." He grunted and released the pose.

Jerry scoffed. "Like hell you do. You need to go with . . ." He paused and gestured to Anna, whose name he'd apparently forgotten again, ". . . this incredibly capable and intelligent communications expert. Get the crew's energy up. Prime the pump."

Anna filled the two cups with scalding coffee and handed one to Ron. "Let's go find Al."

Will shot her a grateful smile as she nudged the CEO from the room. Handling the curmudgeon wouldn't be easy. But Ron's loafers hadn't touched these cracked Flourbox floors in years, and he needed to reconnect with these people. Now, with everything at stake.

The door creaked shut and Will plopped into a dusty chair, checking his watch. Fifty-three minutes until showtime. He started to speak, but Jerry sprang out of his seat, holding up a finger while thumbing a speed-dial number with his other hand.

"Lois, I need you to check something for me . . ." Jerry paced the room as Will crossed his arms.

Is he stalling?

Jerry's prep sessions always became a game of cat and mouse, with Will trying to focus on messaging and delivery while the CEO countered with specific lighting or music requests. But today they needed to stay on point. In less than an hour, Jerry had to deliver the most important speech of his career. And he chose to piss away their precious time by checking on his upcoming travel schedule?

"Jerry." Will stood up and gave the exec a hard look. "We need to prep. Now."

The CEO held up the finger again, still speaking into the phone. "Got it. Good. Yes. That'll do." He hung up and tossed the device on the table. "OK, where were we?"

"It's almost showtime." Will slipped into a chair and motioned for the exec to do the same. "And I can tell there's something on your mind. If you don't tell me, I can't help."

Jerry leaned back in the ancient chair, which groaned with the motion. "This is the most important employee address I've ever delivered. And I'm doing it off-the-cuff. With no prompter, no slides . . . I'm going to look unprepared."

"You're going to look authentic. As we discussed, that's the tone we need to strike."

Will had already given the CEO guidance on the tenor of his remarks. Serious, but not defeatist. Humble, but not weak. Urgent, but not desperate. Jerry needed to thread the eye of a tiny needle on this one. "Just deliver it from the heart," Will had counseled.

"We should show the deck Sonny used in the State of the Business meeting. That's what sold us on it." Jerry fiddled with the clip on his $500 tie. "Use the same materials to sell it to employees."

Will shook his head. "That deck was for a different audience and purpose—to engage two CEOs in a business discussion on the financial merits of the plan. For employees, we need to be much more motivational. Don't sell it to them—inspire them."

"A few weeks ago we were preparing to jettison these employees along with the copier business." Jerry clasped his chair's armrests. "And now I'm supposed to inspire them?"

"They don't know that, and there's no need to mention it now. They see you and Ron as rock stars—the guys who built this company and made BSI what it is today. Trust me, they're eager to hear from you."

"Then let's make sure they hear something good!" The plea caught Will by surprise. He'd never heard fear in Jerry's voice before. "I need prompter notes to keep me on target, Will. You know that. You want me to be humble. But you and I both know that doesn't come naturally for me. I didn't get where I am by being humble."

Will nodded and struck a reassuring tone. "I get that. But you need to think less about where you are now—and think about putting yourself in the shoes of this FB-One crew."

Jerry waved a dismissive hand. "It's been a long time since I was one of them, Will."

"But you remember what it was like . . . working here in the beginning, don't you?"

"Sure." The CEO smoothed his tie—the perfect shade of BSI purple. "I think I know what you're saying. Connect them to the history of the company. Like when my first office chair had a big hole in it. I found it—"

"With all due respect, Jerry." Will patted a hand on the peeling tabletop. "No one gives a shit about that hole in your chair." Will found himself much more comfortable giving the CEOs direct feedback following his SOB outburst. Turns out, shouting obscenities at the entire executive team had a freeing effect.

"That's the only story you tell from the early days." Will scooted his chair closer to Jerry, removing the expanse of crusty table between them. "You've told it so often that it's lost any meaning—for you and employees." He rested his forearms on his knees. "You need to remember what it *felt* like. When you went home scared to death your company would fail and you'd lose your house."

Jerry nodded and looked toward the ceiling. "Early on, that was most nights."

Will pointed to the door. "Well, that's most nights for the employees out there." He paused to let the comment sink in. "But they also have that same confidence I imagine you and Ron did. They're proud of BSI—they want to show the naysayers are wrong about us. They want a fighting chance to prove themselves and lead this company forward."

Jerry frowned and silenced his ringing phone. "That's great, Will, and I know it's what we agreed to in the boardroom. But I think sometimes you forget—we aren't J&R Office Supply anymore. We have hundreds of locations, thousands of employees, and all the systems and hierarchies to go along with it. And when that infrastructure starts to go up in flames . . . well, you can't put out a fire like that with a damn bucket brigade."

Will began to worry he had overestimated Jerry's willingness to dig deep enough. To appeal to BSIers on a genuinely human level.

The CEO toyed with his tie clip again. "You know what I think, Will? This Delivery Plus plan impacts too many of our behaviors, systems, and processes. Optelligence was a big change, too, but we had months of planning in place—everything lined up to prepare for the shift." Jerry stood and paced near the door. "I don't know if we can pull this off in such a short timeframe, without everything falling apart. And there's nothing my remarks can do about that. One speech can't deliver such massive organizational change."

Will shifted sideways in his seat, and draped an arm over the chair's backrest. "You know what I think, Jerry? Change is over-rated. Companies study change, they invest in it, they train it, they obsess over how to do it. But what they don't understand is . . . when people and companies change, it's not always for the better. Because when you focus only on what you're trying to become, you lose sight of what made you successful in the first place."

Will checked his watch again. Forty-one minutes. "I wasn't there when you started J&R. But I know this: we need to get back to what made this company great and who we really are. And more than anyone, I think you know who BSI really is." He stood and leaned a hand on the edge of the table, looking Jerry in the eye. "Go out there and remind us."

Jerry stared at the floor for a moment, the ticking clock the only sound in the room. "Thanks, Will. I'd like to use the rest of this time to gather my thoughts."

Will nodded. "I'll be back to mic you up in fifteen." He slipped out and closed the door behind him.

CHAPTER 33

"Okay, everyone . . . in fifteen." Coffee's voice crackled through the headset. Anna strained to hear him over the heavy guitars of Pop Evil's "Unstoppable."

"Looking good," Bennie reported from her perch back in the BSI tower. "The cafeteria's filling up faster than Lois's shit list."

Anna surveyed the FB-One space, also chock-full of employees. In addition to Al's crew and their Sales rep counterparts, Will had recruited a live studio audience of regional staffers, handpicked members of his extended tribe and CEO ass-kissers—oh-so-eager to be invited anywhere the cofounders were performing.

Legal Bob, Happenstance, and Boone stood near an overhead door off to the side, like worried wallflowers at the Sadie Hawkins dance. Roswell bobbed and clapped to the music—entirely out of rhythm. Judd and Les chatted with a handful of Promisekeepers while Kari Fisher stood nearby with a broad grin, thrilled just to be invited. *So thrilled.* Ambrosia and Dee Dee flanked Kirkland—as if to shield him from being exposed to any dust, dirt, or human interaction.

Al and Ron worked the far side of the room. A young man leaned closer to Ron to say something, then extended his arm and held his phone high—nabbing a CEO selfie.

"Do you see that guy?" Holly pointed to a crewmember near the speaker tower. "He looks exactly like Bruce, my first husband."

Anna frowned. "Wait . . . what? You were married before Tom?"

Holly nodded, a trace of a dreamy happiness flitting across her face. "In college—only lasted six weeks. You can't build a marriage on haikus, LSD, and crazy sex, you know."

Coffee's voice hissed through the headset again. "Ten minutes before showtime, folks."

Anna stared at Holly. "Wha—?"

"Ten minutes, dear."

Anna pointed a finger at her colleague. "We're definitely putting a pin in this conversation for later."

She looked at her watch again. Nine minutes before showtime. For some reason, though, her brain reverted to a seventeen-minute countdown. *Why is 9:08 sticking in my brain?*

Anna bolted upright, becoming lightheaded as the horrifying realization hit her.

Trudy.

She jumped up, forgetting all about the A/V equipment tether. The earphones jerked her head back down, removing several strands of her hair. Stripping off the headset and throwing it onto her chair, she darted out from behind the table, stumbling when her heel caught one of the cables.

"Hey, what's—"

Ignoring Coffee, Anna plowed headlong into the crowd, searching for someone she recognized. She avoided Will, chatting with Jerry—she couldn't risk alerting them to a problem. Big Al, still glad-handing Ron, couldn't help, either. The shipping guy —*DEMO? DURBO? DEVO!*—leaned against an office supply rack. Anna darted toward him. He stepped backward to avoid getting bowled over.

"Take me to Trudy!"

With a shrug, he turned and started to walk. Anna prodded him with a firm hand against his back, causing him to stumble as he moved away from the crowd.

"What's the deal?" DEVO slowed and opened the unmarked door by the receiving desk.

"We've got to shut this thing off before it kicks in and ruins Jerry's speech."

"Um, that's not really my gig. Maybe call an electrician? Or those people at that table with all the equipment. They might know about, um, electrical stuff and . . . stuff."

Anna pushed him inside the small room. "No time. And those people at the table don't know shit about electrical stuff and stuff. We're going to figure this out. Fast."

DEVO clicked on the caged light bulb over their heads, illuminating Trudy—a dusty, green behemoth with a mess of silver ducts sprouting from all sides. Like a robotic octopus in a '50s horror film. She hummed softly. Ready to screech to life at the appointed time.

"Find a switch."

"Uh, okay." DEVO didn't have a shred of urgency in his voice, which fueled Anna's rising panic.

She squeezed into the narrow space between Trudy and the wall, feeling her way along the side. Cobwebs clung to her hair. She spit out something that felt like a spider but probably—*oh, dear God, hopefully*—was only a dust bunny.

"I don't think there's a switch." DEVO clanged into something on the other side of the furnace. "Hey, there's a thing, though. You know. Circuit box."

"Trudy's electric? I figured this thing ran on coal." She checked her watch. Six minutes 'til showtime.

"I thought we established electricity would be involved." DEVO poked his head around the ductwork. "You know . . . with the electrician and the people at the table and whatnot."

"What?" Anna clawed at a spider web strand above her left eye. "Where's the box?"

"Here." He pulled her by the elbow toward his side of the massive furnace. "They rewired her when they added AC. Replaced the old fuses and ran the wiring here." He ran his hands over the box until

his finger found a notch on the side. "Shoot . . . need a screwdriver
. . ."

Anna pushed him aside with a shoulder, pulled off her shoe, and
stabbed the tip of her stiletto heel into the notch. DEVO helped
her pull on the shoe with every one of his 145 pounds. The cover groaned against their combined force—and then popped open,
sending them both stumbling back into a clatter of ductwork.

Anna looked at the expensive shoe in her hand, now minus its
heel. DEVO wiggled the black spike free from the box cover. He
carefully placed the heel in Anna's hand, as if handling it gently
would somehow ensure its survival.

Anna stared at the rows of circuit breakers in front of them. "Shit,
shit, shit." No labels.

"We could flip the main kill."

"No, then we lose everything . . . lights, webcast, mics . . ."

Four minutes. Anna held her broken shoe in one hand and
propped herself against the wall with the other. DEVO grabbed the
bundle of wires hanging beneath the box and stripped off the plastic
sheath holding them together. He pulled up a thick line, coated with
a woven layer of grimy black thread. "This must be her. It's old."

"Are you sure?"

"Nope." DEVO fished a jackknife from his pocket.

Anna grabbed his arm. "Jesus, you'll electrocute yourself!"

"Call me DEVO," he corrected. "And it wouldn't be the first time."

Anna winced as he sawed through the ancient wire, waiting for
his body to hit the floor in a shower of sparks. Trudy's hum grew
louder as the old girl ramped up for her morning roar.

Three minutes.

Anna stepped back, hoping the inevitable jolt of current would be
unable to jump the gap between them. DEVO grimaced and continued sawing.

In an instant, the blade popped through the wire. Anna flinched
and then heard the beautiful silence that followed. The humming
had stopped. She waited for a moment, sure the lights would click

off and they'd hear a cry of alarm from the warehouse. But the muffled music and group conversation continued.

Yes!

She stood tall on her one good shoe, grabbed DEVO's skinny face with her hands, and pressed her mouth to his in a spontaneous, forceful kiss—the one she should've planted on Will outside the elevators. "You are the bravest, smartest man *ever.*"

DEVO looked down and shoved his hands into the pockets of his faded jeans. "So . . . um, same time tomorrow?"

Will stood behind the production table, his mind rattling through the event's final to-do list. From the corner of his eye, he saw a bedraggled Anna hobbling down a row of office supplies. She dropped into her chair, replaced her headset, and tossed a broken heel onto the table. Holly frowned and gingerly pulled debris from Anna's hair.

Will scowled. "What the—?"

Anna deflected his concern with a wave of her hand as Coffee's voice came through the intercom. "Two minutes . . . final walk-in music."

Mötley Crüe's "Kickstart My Heart" boomed through the speakers. The audience shuffled into position, closer to the stage. Three guys found a higher vantage point on a raised forklift, and several others sat on storage racks, feet dangling in the air. Big Al stood against a shrink-wrapped copier at the back, arms folded across his chest, eyes scanning the proceedings.

"All locations are signed into the webcast," Coffee announced. "Camera ready to go live in sixty . . ."

Will's leg jiggled under the table. He had no idea what Jerry planned to say. If he'd be able to rally thousands of scared, skeptical employees and make them believe they could help pull this massive company from the abyss.

"Twenty seconds, folks." Coffee's disembodied voice rang through the headset again. "Fade the music on my call."

Will nodded at Jerry, signaling the CEO to take the stage. He'd ditched the jacket and tie—on Will's advice—and now adjusted his rolled-up shirt sleeves. The subtle wardrobe change came from a classic PR playbook: when dropping an elected official into the aftermath of a crisis, make sure he looks ready to work side by side among the people.

Jerry talked over the music, ten seconds too early. "Good morning. Good morning." He tapped his clip-on mic.

"Cut the music, camera live, bring up his mic!" Anna ordered, holding the call button on her headset.

The music stopped abruptly, and Jerry's next greeting echoed through the speakers.

"Good morning," the Flourboxers uttered in semicoordinated reply.

Jerry smiled and laced his hands together. "Welcome to all of our locations joining virtually today. I'm Jerry Pruitt, and along with Ron Blankenship, we are the cofounders and co-CEOs of BSI. I'll be doing the speaking today because—with all the cost-cutting going on—we could only afford one microphone."

The FB-One crowd chuckled. Will used the pause to whisper into his headset, confirming camera and audio quality both in the tower and online.

"We have to laugh at ourselves sometimes, even though we have some serious things to talk about." Jerry placed his hands on his hips. "Let's start, though, by thanking the crew at FB-One here in Northeast Minneapolis for hosting us today. I'm sure you noticed I'm not standing in the usual spot . . . in the Magic Castle."

A few BSIers snickered while Jerry held up a hand in mock protest.

"Oh yes, I know what you call HQ. I also know some of you think that we've sold our souls to consultants—and that I'm more concerned with my golf score than our share price. Both have dropped considerably this year, by the way."

Nervous laughter filtered through the warehouse, and Will looked skyward. *If there's a Patron Saint of Silk Ties and Office Supplies up there, please keep Jerry humble and focused today.*

Jerry took a deep breath and paced the stage as he spoke. The camera operator, on a small platform amid the audience, followed Jerry with the lens.

"But don't believe the rumors, folks. Ron and I are all in when it comes to this company. Now I know these last few months have been difficult. I know your job, your paycheck, and your benefits are very important to you and your families. It's personal. For all of us. We understand that. Please know that we have done and continue to do everything we can to keep BSI alive and well for you. And that's nothing to joke about."

Jerry paused at center stage. A break for dramatic effect? Or a moment to plan his next point? Will couldn't tell.

"Webcast blipped out for a second—must be the satellite feed," Coffee whispered. "Back up now."

"Everyone's spreading the blame for our sliding results." Jerry resumed his slow stroll across the stage. "They say it's Rayzor's fault for leaving us. Or Wall Street, with their unrealistic expectations. Or Synerpoint for running off with our good ideas. But you know what? They don't run this company. We do."

He gestured to Ron offstage, who nodded and crossed his arms. The camera wheeled to capture the second CEO before focusing back on Jerry.

"Ron and I placed some strategic bets that haven't panned out as we expected. We made some mistakes. I apologize for that."

Spontaneous applause followed, and Jerry waited for the noise to subside. Anna nudged Will and motioned to her laptop, where BSIers filled the Chatterbox with comments as they viewed the webcast.

"Holy cow, a CEO apologized!" one employee posted. Others chimed in with surprise and gratitude for Jerry's honesty.

The applause died down, and the CEO started speaking again, louder.

"However, one thing we've learned through the years is that mistakes and problems can be fixed. Our primary problem today is related to revenue and the cash flow that comes along with it. To be honest, it's a fairly big problem that requires a pretty big solution. But here's one piece of the fix—we've signed a replacement for Rayzor."

The FB-One crowd cheered again while Jerry nodded.

"MX is a revolutionary manufacturer and tremendous new partner from Japan. We couldn't be more thrilled to be working together, and we're going to kick some serious butt with them at our side." He smiled through more applause. "But the machines won't hit our 'Boxes until the middle of next quarter. So we've got a big gap to fill until then. But we knew exactly where to go because we already had answers coming in from all corners of the company. From you."

Jerry turned sideways and pulled a small stack of index cards from the back pocket of his suit pants. "You'll have to excuse me for using a cheat sheet on this, but my memory is not what it used to be. And I want to get this right." He glanced at one of the cards and then peered into the camera lens. "Milio Pereze, are you watching from FB-037? Thank you for going onto the Chatterbox and offering your idea for more efficient product returns. Smart stuff, Milio. We're looking into it."

Jerry went on to tout ideas from Amadeus and Atticus—each written on its own card—artfully avoiding any firm commitments while giving props to the contributors.

Will smiled. He hadn't expected Jerry to cite any specific ideas beyond Delivery Plus. But apparently the CEO had read Will's dossier of all the Chatterbox input to date.

Jerry slid the cards back into his pocket. "This is the tip of the iceberg, folks. So many great ideas to serve our customers better and run this company more efficiently. But let's get back to the big problem that needs a big solution. Revenue and cash flow. Where is

Doug? Doug is visiting from FB-076."

The CEO scanned the audience and pointed to the stocky, bald man near the forklift.

"Doug, you've been working at BSI for all of six months, is that right?" Jerry turned back toward the camera. "Well, one day, Doug made a delivery to a client who was having a particularly hectic day. So he did something simple but powerful. He unjammed their copier and unboxed their supply order, probably creating a loyal customer for life."

Jerry slid a hand down the front of his shirt. Subconsciously searching for a tie to stroke. "Doug, that's not only the kind of personal service we should be delivering every day—it's the genesis of what I'm here to talk about today." He increased the volume and intensity of his delivery. "The launch of a new homegrown—Flourbox-approved—revenue-generating solution that's going to put BSI back in the black!"

A few Promisekeepers whooped from the back of the room, and employees around Doug slapped him on the back. Coffee called through the headset for the camera operator to capture the impromptu scene.

"Today, we are rolling this idea nationwide—to every 'Box and Sales team—with the support of our corporate departments. I'm talking about annual contracts for a personalized level of service. A world-class solution only a world-class company can provide. This is a game changer, team. And it's called Delivery Plus!"

The crowd roared its approval.

"Now, you're going to get more details today from your local management teams . . ."

Will tuned out the CEO for a moment to compile a midspeech report card in his head. He gave Jerry a "B" for tone and energy and an "A-" for the heartfelt apology. All in all, a solid start.

The CEO lowered his voice and slowed his cadence. ". . . I have to be honest, folks. We're under the gun. We've got to bring in $45 million with these plans in the next month."

A murmur rose through the audience while Will and Anna looked back to their screens. The Chatterbox lit up with comments again. "I know that seems like an extraordinary feat. So let's do a little math." Jerry smacked a fist into his other palm for each of the numbers he threw out. "Each of our fifteen regions needs to sell $750,000 in plans per week for the next four weeks. Given the breadth of our customer base and the strength of those relationships, it's doable, folks. This is a great service, and our customers are clamoring for it. And there's no doubt in my mind we can do this—even as most everyone else is counting us out."

He shook his head. "In difficult times, all the naysayers come out, don't they? Believe me, Ron and I see what they're saying about us— the reporters and analysts and bloggers giving their half-assed investment opinions. And we know what you're hearing from friends and family. They all think—hell, they *assume*—we're going out of business."

The warehouse fell silent. Jerry let the pause become uncomfortable and then raised his chin and again made eye contact with members of the crowd. "You know, I was just talking to one of our department leaders a few minutes ago as we were preparing for this talk. And he said something really compelling . . . something that got me thinking."

Anna smiled at Will, who raised his eyebrows. *I'll be damned.*

"He told me sometimes companies change so much that they lose sight of what made them successful in the first place. And let me tell you, I didn't appreciate hearing that." He chuckled as the Promisekeepers and assorted corporate types exchanged glances. "But there's a measure of truth to it. He also said we can be successful again if we focus on what made this company great from the beginning. Rediscover who we really are. Which begs the question, of course—who are we?"

Jerry walked to the edge of the platform, taking care to address the camera and the live audience. "Those bloggers and naysayers, they think they know who we are. To them, BSI is just a falling stock

price. A failing business model. A company at the end of its runway."
Jerry clenched a fist over his heart. "But that's not who we are in
here. We've always been something more. You know that. Ron and
I know that, too."

He stomped on the stage, and everyone at the production table
winced, hoping his foot wouldn't punch through the plywood.

"As you may know, I'm standing in the very spot where this
company began. Seriously, the exact spot." He pointed at his feet.
"Where Ron and I stood and decided this was where we'd start J&R
Office Supply. Right here."

Jerry gestured to Ron, left of the stage. "Remember what it felt
like, Ron? That moment we decided 'let's do this'? It was the most
exciting and terrifying moment of my life. I had a new baby at home,
twelve bucks in my pocket and a rusted-out Cutlass with 167,000
miles parked out back. We bet everything we had on this business,
which wasn't much at the time."

Jerry paced toward center stage. "Now, don't get me wrong. I'm
incredibly fortunate to have the role I have now and to enjoy the success we've built together. But back then, even when I had nothing—
especially when I had nothing . . ." He stopped and looked toward
the ceiling. "Man, I truly loved that job. It was the best time of my
life." His voice shook as he finished the thought.

Jerry cupped a hand over his clip-on mic and cleared the quiver
from his throat.

"I loved it because everyone working here loved their jobs and
each other, and we'd do anything to help our company succeed. Sha-
ron, our receptionist, learned to take sales calls during busy times.
I was head of Sales, but I'd cover for our one and only Delivery guy
when he was sick. We all manned the State Fair booth and handed
out T-shirts. Holy shit, that was a fun job."

Jerry chuckled. "Sorry for the language, folks." He reached for
the missing necktie again. "But it was great. It was a family, and
we could count on each other. Whatever the business needed, we
jumped in and did it together."

Will pried his attention away from the stage to gauge the crowd's reaction. People smiled and nodded their heads. Joe the Hammer gave Big Al a friendly punch to the shoulder. DEVO stared at Anna. Jerry nodded toward his cofounder. "Ron and I have always been competitive. A healthy tension is good for business because it pushes you to succeed in ways you never thought possible. But we've always been willing and able to put that competitive nature aside."

Jerry smiled, his eyes moving from face to face in the audience. "I know you all are fiercely competitive, too. I also know there's a history between the Rainmakers and Promisekeepers—some trash-talking. And some genuine hard feelings. Separate expectations and incentive plans haven't helped." He raised a finger in the air. "But I'm here to tell you . . . that's behind us. Starting today, for the first time in BSI's history, all employees will share the same bonus metrics, making sure everyone is rowing in the same direction, striving for the same outcomes."

A few Promisekeepers applauded as Jerry continued. "The future of this company literally depends on us setting aside our differences and our titles and remembering who we are and what we can do. And we will do what we always do when things get tough—jump in and *win* this together."

He paced the edge of the stage. "For the next month, we have one shared priority. What is it?"

"Delivery Plus," the audience replied.

"What is it?"

"Delivery Plus!"

"That's right." Jerry pushed his rolled-up shirt sleeves higher on his arms. "And there's only one scorecard—it's the value of all plans we sell as a company. And I have no doubt in the world that we'll reach that goal. Because we *know* who we are."

A few people started to clap again, but Jerry kept speaking, gaining volume.

"We are Milio Pereze from FB-037!" More applause. "We are Atticus and Doug and Amadeus!" Jerry picked up steam, pointing into the camera and around the warehouse as he called out the names. "We are Big Al Jansen . . . and Lois Emery . . . and Sonny Larsson, who's sold more copiers than anyone in BSI history!" Someone in the back let out a loud whistle. "We are Will Evans and Ron Blankenship and me and you and every employee who has made this company great through the years!"

The applause swelled, as BSIers pumped their fists in the air and shouted. Jerry boomed over the uproar.

"We know *exactly* who we are: it's who we've always been." He took another breath and finished at top volume. "We are Business Solutions, Incorporated! And you never—*never*—count out the *purple!*"

FB-One erupted in deafening cheers, and Ron stepped onto the stage to join Jerry. The CEOs clasped hands and raised them above their heads and then joined the applause to acknowledge the employees.

Will's team stood and watched the scene from behind the production table. Holly scrounged in her pockets for tissue, while Coffee pretended to have something in his eye.

Anna leaned over to Will and put a hand on his back. "That was perfect," she whispered, a tear rolling down her cheek.

He smiled at her and then looked out across the pool of Promisekeepers and Rainmakers cheering and celebrating. Big Al high-fived and bro-hugged his crew members as they started to pair off with their Sales reps, heading toward the loading docks. Jerry gave them a thumbs-up from the stage.

Will wiped his eyes with the back of his wrist and turned to Anna. "I can't believe it. He did it."

"No." She smiled and squeezed his arm. "We did it."

Fund Analysis > **Analyst Report Archive**

BSI: A Troubled Champ Comes Out Swinging

Hoffman, Wallin & Friesen

Discuss
See what other
investors are saying
about BSI

SUMMARY: **Business Solutions Inc.'s** third-quarter earnings surprised most industry observers. Street consensus forecasted an earnings decline of ($.05) per share/$250M loss, which could have been a death knell for the reeling company. The actual performance—nearly $.02 per share/$102 million of positive earnings growth—and more focused go-forward strategies, however, require a fresh analysis of the company.

The quarter's upside was driven largely by the new **Delivery Plus** plans—a low-investment, high-margin service offering that is incrementally profitable with current customers.

BSI's troubles have been well-documented, and one quarter of strong performance isn't a panacea for all its self-inflicted wounds. Still, the Street (this firm included) may have overlooked some compelling fundamentals that emerged in Q3.

Notably, the company has a large portfolio of satisfied, loyal customers; an established distribution network; and a deep, experienced management team whose resolve and resourcefulness have been underestimated.

The move to promote **Lyle Kirkland**—company veteran and Delivery Plus mastermind—to Chief Operating Officer is positive. It not only reflects BSI's renewed focus on operational excellence, but a newfound willingness to think about CEO succession. The promotion of another company veteran, **Fredrick "Sonny" Larsson**, to the new position of SVP of North America, signals what we hope is BSI's willingness to explore global growth—leveraging their copier and office supply expertise in markets outside U.S. borders.

While BSI still has to prove it can sustain growth over time, its attractive P/E ratio; its exclusive U.S. partnership with the innovative manufacturer MX beginning in Q4; and strong management team could create a compelling investment opportunity. Thus we are changing our rating from SELL to HOLD.

CHAPTER 34

Anna stepped into her workspace as Coffee—sporting a wide-brimmed hat—cajoled Will into joining the team at the Monk. He hung his arms over their boss's cube wall. "Come on . . . we're way overdue for a celebration."

Coffee had a point. Delivery Plus crushed its revenue projections, BSI made the quarter, and even the most fickle reporters and analysts jostled for position on the turnaround bandwagon. With some overdue business at hand—and some celebrating of her own to do—Anna figured she'd join them later.

Retrieving the Gerhardstein-Montgomery documents from her bag, she scanned them one last time before sliding them into the mailer she'd just brought from the copy room. *It's official.*

"Hey, haven't seen you all day." Coffee stepped closer to her cube.

"Hey, to you." Anna tilted her head at his wardrobe choice. "What's with the fedora? You planning to bootleg some whiskey over the weekend?" The cream-colored hat featured a purple trim-ribbon, with "Optelligence" silkscreened on one side and an equilateral triangle on the other.

"Pretty slick, huh?" Coffee doffed the hat and let it roll down his arm. "Three bucks on closeout at the company store. They're blowing out all the old Optelligence swag to make room for Delivery Plus items—backpacks, baby bibs, the usual."

"Yeah, pretty slick." Anna laughed.

"And what about you? You're in jeans."

"I am." Anna looked down at her outfit of high-heeled boots and a light autumn sweater. Not exactly couch-potato couture. But Fridays had become Casual Day in the tower—an idea pitched by a corporate Chatterbox user. Anna felt surprisingly good leaving her dry-clean-only wardrobe on hangers for a day. "First time for everything, right?"

Coffee nodded and flipped the fedora back onto his head. "You know, studies show companies who create an official Casual Day have fewer employees showing up in shower-shoes, mesh tops, and other fashion travesties the rest of the week. When I worked at—"

"You guys! You guys!" Holly ran up the aisle, waving her phone in the air. Anna turned to see the source of the commotion.

"It's TK!" Holly beamed. "I haven't talked to him in weeks, but he got a new job. I'm so excited!"

"Hey, that's terrific." Coffee leaned his elbow on Anna's cube wall. "I hope it's with the Weather Channel or something."

"No, get this." Holly panted, recovering from her sprint. "He's the new communications director for the Minnesota Twins! Can you believe it?"

Anna smiled to feign surprise.

"What?" Coffee laughed. "They were hiring? Damn! Talk about a great gig."

"Dream job if you're a hardball fanatic like TK." Will stepped into the aisle and joined the group. "Man, I'm so happy for him."

"He's got an office at the ballpark and gets to travel with the team sometimes." Holly placed her hand over her heart. "It's so perfect for him! Sometimes things happen for a reason, you know?"

"Good thing Reed didn't know about the job," Coffee teased, nodding toward Anna. "She'd be out of here so fast, we'd still be choking on the smoke coming off her ridiculously high heels."

Anna smiled. "What, and miss all this fun?"

She knew about TK, of course. And knew he'd be perfect for the job the moment she got the call. So Anna used Alissa as an intermediary and kept her own involvement a secret. TK needed to feel like he'd earned the job—displaying the abilities he too often hid underneath that oversized sport coat. She'd also kept her involvement hidden from Will and the team. No need to get their hopes up if the referral didn't work out. Besides, they would've done the same. *We take care of our own.*

Anna undocked her laptop and slid it into her bag as the team continued to chatter about TK's good fortune. Despite passing on the Twins job, she still considered leaving BSI. Finding a better fit somewhere. Another chance at bigger and better. Alissa could make it happen.

But when Anna added it all up—standing in the Cabin break room as Will made his way to the SOB meeting—she began to see the ultimate cost of her Career Trajectory. The tally of lost friends, failed marriages, and meaningful relationships. So she needed to break her comfortable, predictable cycle and stick it out at BSI. Get her life in a new kind of order and start to be herself, as messed up as that felt sometimes.

There's no shame in saving yourself.

Anna leaned on the corner of her desk and looked out the window. The low October sun peeked from behind a neighboring office tower.

"Let's see if TK can join us at the Mon—" A buzzing phone cut Will's comment short. Then another joined in.

"Not it." Coffee held his phone in the air.

"Not it," Holly concurred, her phone still in hand from TK's call.

Will fished his phone out of his back pocket. "Dang, it's Lois. I'm being summoned."

Anna grabbed her phone and looked at the text. "Me too. By Dee Dee."

"Good grief, I was just up there." Will looked at his watch. "What could've possibly blown up in the last . . . 23.6 minutes?"

Anna smiled again. An unscheduled meeting with the CEOs filled her with a delicious mixture of exhilaration and surprise. God only knew what plans the CEOs and their newly minted COO needed to hatch at five fifteen p.m. on a Friday. Whatever it might be, Anna knew she and Will could handle it. The execs knew it, too.

"Save us a seat at the Monk." Anna grabbed her bag. "We'll be there as soon as we can." She hurried up the aisle to catch Will, who made a beeline for the elevators.

"Hey, what's with the jeans?" Will nodded toward her outfit. "Some kind of new-fangled, designer denim imported from France?"

Anna shot him a look. "They're twenty-dollar jeans. From Old Navy."

"Ah." Will grinned and reached past her to poke the elevator button. "Have you been on twenty-two since the construction started? It's a freakin' mess."

Anna nodded. Kirkland intended to take up residence in the C-suite, and construction crews were tearing out the CEOs' walk-in cigar humidor to make room for his office.

"I realize Kirkland is COO now." Will leaned against the wall. "But I'm a little surprised Jerry and Ron would allow an interloper to join them in the penthouse."

"Oh my God," Anna gasped. "Penthouse Interloper. Best band name ever!"

They both laughed and watched the digital numbers change above the elevators. Most BSIers were on their way down and out for the weekend, making it damn near impossible to catch a car going up.

Will glanced at the FedEx mailer tucked into the crook of Anna's elbow. "What've you got there . . . charm school application?"

"More like a dropout form." Anna managed to hold onto her smile. "My divorce papers. Finally making it official."

She'd expected it would hurt to say the words out loud, but she felt something else instead. Butterflies? Excitement? A craving for Monk tater tots? Hard to say.

"Oh, I'm sorry." Will's eyes widened. "I wouldn't have joked . . ."

"It's okay."

"But are you?"

"I really am. It's a relief, actually. No more pretending to be something I'm not." She raised her left hand, showing the faint tan line on her ringless finger.

"Wow, the ring and everything, huh?" Will winced a little. "That couldn't have been easy."

"It wasn't easy. But it was time." Anna slipped the hand into her front pocket. "And my husba—I mean, my ex—deserved closure. A chance to get on with his life."

The elevator chimed, finally, and the doors opened.

"Ultimately, I think I started to realize . . ." Anna stepped inside first. "I had been holding myself back. And now I'm ready to move forward."

Will followed her in and pressed twenty-two as the doors closed. "Moving forward is good. We should definitely—" He cut himself off midsentence. "I didn't mean *we*. You know, like . . . 'we.' I just meant . . ."

Anna laughed.

"You are too funny." She nudged his arm. "I know what you meant. Moving forward is the right thing. And it's easier because . . . I know I'm not alone."

Will blushed and looked at the floor before raising his eyes to meet hers. "Of course, you're not. I'm right here."

Anna smiled. She considered slipping him a kiss right there but thought better of it. She still had rules. Like not starring as the office seductress on BSI's closed-circuit elevator cameras.

Get it together, Reed. You've got plenty of time.

They rode in silence for a moment, listening to the soft beep of each passing floor. For the first time in her life, Anna had little clue what came next—and it felt good. *No need to game plan.* She stole a sideways glance at Will. *Everything will work out. It always does.*

"I wonder what fresh drama awaits." Anna tilted her head upward, toward the C-suite. "Could be anything, right?"

"Right."

The doors opened on twenty-two, revealing midconstruction chaos—a sledgehammer banging, sawdust everywhere, cherrywood furniture draped in plastic sheeting. Will led Anna through the disorderly reception area, charting a path through the debris and tools cluttering the floor.

He paused outside the boardroom door. Voices echoed inside—barely audible above the din of the surrounding construction. Tapping a knuckle on the giant wooden door, Will cracked it open and poked his head inside. Lois motioned for them to enter.

The room bustled with activity. Jerry, Ron, and Kirkland leaned over one side of the long table, arguing as they pored through a stack of spreadsheets and charts. A cluster of BSI department heads huddled on the near side of the table, engaging in a separate debate, their backs to the door. Happenstance and Legal Bob sat to their right, holding a private conversation—something about currency exchange rates. Lois and Ambrosia scurried to refill coffee cups and dispose of table litter.

So much for making it to the Monk tonight.

Spotting Bennie at the left end of the table, Will headed that way. He ducked into a chair and pulled a second one out for Anna.

"Hey." Will kept his voice low. "What's going on, do you know?"

Bennie nodded and rolled her eyes skyward. "Strap my ass on a donkey pack, and call me Jezebel. We're goin' international."

"International. Already?" Will scanned the row of department heads, still talking among themselves. The VP of Real Estate, a few faces from Operations and Finance, and two of Boone's Marketing deputies, along with some guy he didn't recognize. "Where?"

Bennie shrugged, her voice just above a whisper. "Europe? Japan? Timbuk-fuck-yer-uncle-tu, for all I know. They're still figuring that part of it out."

Will turned toward Kirkland and the CEOs, where Jerry lectured the other two on his preferred overseas approach. "Greenfielding is the way to go." He banged a fist on the table. "Lead with our Flourbox model and plant the BSI flag around the world."

"It could take years before we reach scale and become profitable." Ron dropped a stack of papers on the tabletop. "We should explore a joint venture."

Kirkland responded, but Bennie leaned in front of Will to whisper at Anna. "The only good news? We just hired Victor the Viking over there to lead our global plundering strategy."

Will followed her gaze, to the guy he'd noticed earlier. Buff, square-jawed. Thick head of messy-by-design blond hair.

Anna's pen and notebook dropped to the floor.

"I gotta say . . ." Bennie cackled before settling back in her chair. "Wouldn't mind if that Nordic warrior pillaged my village."

Will bent over to retrieve Anna's things. She didn't move.

He straightened up, holding out her pen. "You okay?"

Anna wrapped her fingers around it without a word. Her face was ashen, devoid of emotion. Those usually expressive eyes dull.

What the . . .

Did she bang her knee on the table again? Spy the ghost of Salvador Chan?

"All right, people." Jerry tried to get the room's attention. "Let's bring it together."

Will touched Anna's arm. "Hey, you okay?"

Still nothing.

"First things first." Jerry paced near the windows as the voices in the room reduced to a murmur. "Today we stand on the cusp of a bold new growth initiative for BSI." He made a sweeping motion with his arm, drawing his audience's attention to the world outside the tinted tower glass. "International expansion."

Voices rose again as attendees affirmed Jerry's proclamation. "And as part of this strategy . . ." He motioned toward the new guy. "We've hired a VP of International Development." All heads in the room turned.

"Thank you, Jerry." New Guy smiled and gazed around the table, making eye contact with the attendees—holding his megawatt grin on Anna for a split second longer than the others. "And hello to all of you. My name is Erik Reed, and I'm thrilled to be here."

Will's focus snapped back to Anna as Erik rattled off highlights of his international consulting background.

Will leaned over, keeping his voice low. "He's not . . ."

"He's my ex." Anna's lips hardly moved.

"What?" Will felt his mouth fall open. He leaned backward, watching the blue-suited Norseman speak without hearing a word of it.

Anna closed her eyes and tipped her head backward. "I can't do this."

Will clenched his jaw, desperate to keep his voice to a whisper.

"Say one more sentence about that."

ACKNOWLEDGMENTS

JENNIFER WOULD LIKE TO THANK:

My family, who—from the minute I announced over Thanksgiving dinner that I quit my job and was going to finish this book—never once called me completely insane (at least not to my face). Helen, Sarah, Strathman, and Zenz, my sisters-from-other-misters, who were the first to teach me that your coworkers can indeed become family. My mom, who always made me believe I could do anything. Heartfelt apologies to my dad that I became a writer—I was his last shot at raising an accountant. And to all the friends who continue to encourage, support, and ask excited questions at our monthly happy hours. I'll never be able to thank you enough.

MIKE WOULD LIKE TO THANK:

Melissa, for her unwavering belief and support as I pursued a life-long dream—you have no idea how much it means to me. Riley and Sawyer, whose genuine enthusiasm for the book helped remind me that despite all the rejections and revisions, I had the great fortune of doing what I loved every day. My mom and dad, who instilled me with a strong work ethic from a very young age—a gift that has served me well my entire life and especially on this project. (But, for the record, I'll never split, chop, saw, or haul another piece of wood as long as I live.) Darren Voss, Lee Voss, Shelly Danowsky, and their families for their encouragement and support. Bonnie and Roman Malecha and their families (including Todd Sery), whose excitement about this book has rivaled my own. Brian J. Dunn and Bill Anderson for their steadfast support and friendship. And my many friends and extended family members—far too many to list here. Thank you for being a part of this.

JENNIFER AND MIKE WOULD LIKE TO THANK:

Everyone who helped take this story from wild idea to a tangible, published novel. We couldn't have done this without your support, tough love, and expertise. Our first editor, Caitlyn Alexander, whose input and encouragement made us and this story infinitely better. Editor Ally Bishop, who pushed us to go to more fun, quirky, edgy places. The smart, supportive experts at Wise Ink—especially editor and strategist extraordinaire, Laura Zats, who taught us to respect the Oxford comma, and eagle-eyed proofreader Patrick Maloney. Emily Rodvold, who introduced us to the good people at Wise Ink. Cover designer Jessie Sayward Bright, who brought a BSI employee's whiteboard doodles to life. Our advance readers—Bill Anderson, Brian J. Dunn, Jilly Gagnon, Jayne J. Jones, Matt Kramer, and Susan Busch Nehring—for their insights and endorsements. Photographers Louisa Podlich, who made us meow so we'd smile naturally in our author pics; and Andy Chow, who made Minneapolis look like the amazing city it is on www.rockandvossbooks.com. The talented, funny, and supportive authors from our workshop at the Algonkian Pitch Conference in NYC. Stoli vodka, our alternative fuel source when we got sick and tired of rejections, edits, and/or each other. And lastly, all of our incredible coworkers, teammates, and friends, who—even on our worst days—made corporate life awesome and who inspired the best in this book.